T0116455

Stacking in Rivertown

A NOVEL

Barbara Bell

SIMON & SCHUSTER
New York   London   Toronto   Sydney   Singapore

Simon & Schuster
Rockefeller Center
1230 Avenue of the Americas
New York, NY 10020

This book is a work of fiction. Names, characters,
places, and incidents either are products of the
author's imagination or are used fictitiously. Any
resemblance to actual events or locales or person,
living or dead, is entirely coincidental.

Copyright © 2000 by Barbara Bell
All rights reserved,
including the right of reproduction
in whole of in part in any form.

Simon & Schuster and colophon are registered trademarks
of Simon & Schuster, Inc.

Designed by Kyoko Watanabe

Manufactured in the United States of America

10 9 8 7 6 5 4 3 2 1

Library of Congress Cataloging-In-Publication Data

Bell, Barbara, date.
      Stacking in Rivertown : a novel / Barbara Bell.
            p.   cm.
      1. Ex prostitutes—Fiction.   2. Sadomasochism—Fiction.
      3. Young Women—Fiction.   I. Title.
      PS3552.E4855   S73   2000
      813'.6—dc21   00-036544

ISBN: 0-7432-4254-8

For information regarding the special discounts for bulk purchases, please contact Simon &
Schuster Special Sales at 1-800-456-6798 or business@simonandschuster.com

Acknowledgments

Into the mine field.

Both Ingrid Sato and Barbara Shoup must be mentioned first as they provided me with means and direction, enabling me to place this manuscript into the hands of a wonderful agent, Alice Martell. Alice could have been a fire marshall as she has put out many conflagrations and deserves a medal.

My editor, Michael Korda, has been patient and quite supportive of me in this, my initiation to the world of publishing. Michael's belief in my abilities has gone a long way toward helping me compensate for my terminal lack of cheerfulness and optimism. Chuck Adams and countless others at Simon & Schuster have worked hard on behalf of myself and *Stacking in Rivertown*. Many thanks.

My two most dedicated readers, Carolyn and Toni, have kept me writing during the long wait. Stephanie first helped me set out this way. Sarah carries the scars to prove her long-suffering support of my delusional activities.

Many others have knowingly and unknowingly aided me in this endeavor.

My thanks to everyone.

for
margaret ann

Stacking in Rivertown

PART I

Suicide

1

The Shoebox

Ten Chits. That was what Mama called me ever since the day I came home bloody in the mouth from having kicked Gedders' ass.

"His hands don't go by me," was all I'd tell her, and she called me Ten Chits. I guess because ten was the highest she ever learned to count, and a chit was just a something to her.

Anything could be a chit. Mostly I was the chit. You're just a chit, she'd say. Sometimes, my big brother Vin was the chit. Or maybe she called that whip-tailed hound dog from down the street a chit when she had another bag of "groceries," having come up from town, and "that chit of a mongrel" growled at her, smelling the steak bones, I guess, with some of the meat still on, but dainty bites sawed away, or healthy man-sized cuts knifed out. She brought home baked potato skins hollowed and still wrapped in foil, and wilted green stuff too slimy to swallow.

The river there bent near in half right around our two-room, as Daddy called it, and a long patch of grass went right down to the bank. In the summer the water shrank down, leaving a mucky rock-strewn mess that Vin, me, and Mandy squished into barefoot.

"Bag of twigs coming down the road," was what Daddy said whenever he saw Mandy skipping down the lane. She looked all sticks and hands with a head, and lived in a trailer with her mama down near where the titi and the pop ash grew too thick to wiggle through.

Mandy, me, and Vin spent our time digging out crawdads and sneaking up on bullfrogs that sat fat on the edges of puddles left flat, full of waterboatmen and striders skimming.

Swarms of mosquitoes and gnats danced over in the afternoons, and the brown water gone lazy carried a film on top that curved and caught cottonwood seeds floating down. Damselflies screwed all the time, floating by tail to tail, and the lacewing and mayfly all broke out fine in their time.

But now I'm off my story and the chits. I've begun to think of the chits as pieces of evidence, like in a detective novel, to be numbered, catalogued, and put in order. I never counted them up that year, the year the chits fell so heavy, but maybe there were ten altogether. Most people collect evidence to solve puzzles outside their lives. I need it to solve my own life. I appear to have a problem with memory.

I know now that none of what happened was Jeremy's fault, even if he was a screwball. It's just that I wasn't meant for marriage, especially to someone like Jeremy, or living that kind of life. The life where you write your books in a studio in the afternoons after a morning jog and a trip to the spa. Eating dinner for two in a house meant for twenty. Or sleeping at night and getting up before his alarm goes off just to have him smile that inane smile when he comes in the kitchen, adjusting his tie, maybe whistling a horrible cheerful tune.

But I do blame him. It was his fault that I sold the novel. I completed it under Jeremy's constant insistence, his gentle pressure on "your talent," as he said to me. He was the one that prepared queries, synopses, and outlines, printed out and stuffed into envelopes sent off to small presses, large presses, literary journals, agents, anyone at all who might show an interest.

"We'll keep trying," he said after every rejection, his confidence a disease that weakened me, kept me worrying about the upholstery, a need for new carpeting or a more tasteful tile for the shower.

Jeremy liked my stories. That's what drew him to me. Jeremy was seemingly blind to my other "talents," as Ben would say. Where most men I'd met thought my mouth had a better use, for Jeremy it was the stories.

And he believed in this weird notion called synchronicity. What with both of us having surgery in the same hospital on the same day and both recovering in blue gowns with wheelchairs and matching IVs, for him it was love at first sight. The synchronicity thing cinched it.

My appendectomy had been sudden, the obsolete fingerlike organ having burst without so much as a bleep in the symptom department. I had collapsed, Ben said (now there's a chit; I hadn't remembered that before), at the reception for the Senator. Fell right down the stairs in the black strapless (he added for my benefit), and had beat myself up pretty bad by the time I hit the last step.

Jeremy probably fell in love with my bruises, too.

He was always bringing home strays from Wall Street. He offered them scraps wrapped in napkins and saved from one more in a long line of power lunches.

Dogs loved Jeremy. They could tell he only had eyes for them. I think it would have pleased him immensely to be born a dog. He loved to adore, to press close excitedly. He was easily trained and loyal to a fault. So finding me all bruised and sick, after a minor gallstone removal on his part, was like finding the ultimate stray, the she-dog of his dreams. Except for Ben, I had no friends, no family.

Jeremy was in dog heaven.

Ben worried him. He's admitted that. Just to have Ben in the room with you felt like hanging around a pissed grizzly.

But Ben only visited me once at the hospital, holding buttercups nearly mangled in his massive, squat hand. His other hand was fat in a big white bandage. He must have hurt it trying to stop me from falling, I decided, a fall that for the life of me I couldn't remember, down those stairs in the ballroom.

Ben brought with him a shoebox and a small suitcase filled with my clothes. He gave me his card. "Call me when you're ready," he said. And I said I would, but then Jeremy wheeled by, measured Ben's extraordinary height with his eyes, and got his first look at me dressed in bruises.

The woman of his dreams.

After his first eyeful, Jeremy spent every minute at my bedside, offering me water when I was thirsty and helping me up to take my five trembly steps to the john. He offered me grapes and slices of oranges his mother had brought to enhance his healing in place of hospital fare over which she clucked her tongue in dismay.

I wasn't much on talking then, so he'd chatter away like a miniature schnauzer, pausing now and then to coax a few words out of me.

Jeremy asked me to marry him after a week. It was neither here nor there to me, but he could pester like a scotch terrier. And I was in some kind of shock, a shock that hung on like a leech for five years. I think I was lulled to sleep in suburbia, waking up like Rip Van Winkle and wondering where I'd been, and how I ended up married to such a clean-cut all-American guy as Jeremy.

No one gave me away at the wedding, which his mother has never been able to let be. And Jeremy's confused to this day about my lack of friends and family, my absence of a past. He gave up interrogating me about it after a year or so, instead substituting any number of various and increasingly bizarre fairy tales about my past of his own devising. Most of these included some fantastical intervention by a dog as a crucial element in the story.

Maybe he should write a novel.

So I kept Jeremy mollified with stories about the river and the bend of the river, about Grady, wild-eyed and muttering like a rabid possum. Grady lived not a stone's throw from our two-room in a shack, eating just about anything he could trap, spear, or grab bare-handed. Grady was quick, if nothing else.

But Jeremy could never get enough of me telling about the rise downriver where the oldest and the richest families in town deposited their dead, laid out in shelves, Mandy said, like dolls, but flat on their backs in boxes.

Stacking in Rivertown, we called it. Rivertown was me and Mandy's name for the cemetery because it was like a little village all by itself with small white stone houses and here and there a carved angel with the face of a mother, or a stern man with a sword. Flags waved there on holidays, and flowers wilted down. The river below was wider like a lake, and dull, overhung with willow and poplar all tied up with spiders.

My stories are like that river, muddy, buzzed over by flies, and wilting down by midday. It was the stories about the river and then the novel that got me in trouble with the chits.

At first, the publisher was low-key about it, narrow distribution, limited printing. And the book was slow in the uptake. My agent was just telling Jeremy and me that it wasn't even going to pay for its printing, when something started happening. An undercurrent, like the ones Mandy was always yammering about that pull you down and before you know it you're drowned like Grady. They found him a mile and a half downstream. The rats had done some damage.

Anyway, it's a muddy novel, as I said about my writing. "Dark," the reviewers began calling it as it was brought to their attention by the perplexing appearance of the buying undercurrent.

"Sometimes these things just happen," my agent said, trying to help me feel better about it. She appeared cheerful. "Sometimes you throw the dice and you win."

I was thinking that the last thing I needed right then was to win.

The novel began to have a "cult following." I'm not sure how that's different from having a reading audience, but it still sells books. Women were eating it up.

People became interested. The novel was called a "phenomenon." My agent began to get calls wanting interviews. The publisher demanded book signings, speaking engagements at colleges. Readers were beginning to wonder who I was and ask questions about my past.

"I had an appendectomy," I told my agent as we were constructing a bio for the book jacket. "It burst."

"College?" she asked.

"I try not to think about that," I replied, breaking into a cold sweat.

"Of course you think about it," she said, her voice catching in my head like a set of trolling hooks.

"All I did was write a book. Lots of people do that."

"They want to know about you, who you are, where you came from."

"Seems silly," I said. In fact, the whole thing was scaring the piss out of me.

After I arrived home from that enlightening conversation with my agent, I sat at my desk thinking about the fucking novel and my not-quite-right lifestyle. Jeremy's Porsche barreled into the garage. We owned matching Porsches, his Republican blue, mine hellish red.

I prepared myself for what came next, assuming my tenuous wife pose, making over him after he bounded up the stairs in search of me. Before the hour was out, we sat down to dinner, me toying with my food as usual.

I don't even remember when I lost my appetite. It just dried up and disappeared one day, like my memory, I guess.

Later that evening as I was busy avoiding Jeremy, pretending to clean out the closet in my studio, I found the shoebox. Ben's shoebox. I picked it up, then stood frozen. I felt so strange, and was surprised when I realized that I was homesick. I hadn't seen or talked to Ben since that last day in the hospital.

But it was more than that. I felt a vibration, a push behind, a thing that chased. This wasn't a new feeling, but holding the box like that brought it on strong.

It was like my nightmares, the ones of the woman in green. I always woke up chilled, trying to scream. And the need to run, to get the hell out of there, swarmed my brain like blackfly.

"Come to bed now, honey," Jeremy called from the bedroom.

Obedient to a fault, I turned to go. But first I dropped the shoebox in the back of my file cabinet.

After I joined Jeremy in bed, granted the mandatory good-night kiss and squeeze of the hand, Jeremy dropped off like a trapjaw on a log. Biff, his cocker-mix stray, was dead asleep at his feet. Jeremy slept like a mastiff, curled tight and breathing heavy. So I did the same thing I'd done for a long time; I sneaked out of bed to write.

Night was when the stories got dark and rough, swishing and filled with undercurrents roving the bottom of the river. And tonight, for some reason, the ghosts came. They hounded. They crawled all over me. Maybe it was the shoebox and the vibrations. Maybe it was an incredible lack of food and sleep.

And for whatever combination of reasons—the buying undercurrent, my not-quite-right lifestyle, or maybe just synchronicity—it was at this point that I turned a corner. Not a real corner; a corner in my head.

I don't like to admit this, but I think that up until that moment I had some kind of amnesia. As a matter of fact, I didn't remember a lot of things for months. Oh sure, there were things I knew all along, things that I kept from Jeremy. But nothing was set end to end. It was like having some pieces of a broken vase. You hold them, remember the shape, but don't want to force a thing together that will never be what it was before. I gave up on that kind of thing a long time ago.

But in that moment, pressured by the shoebox and the nightmares, I turned a corner.

Mama said, "Turn a corner, turn a cup." And she'd turn over

a cup, screeching bloody murder if it got knocked down before a week wore out. It was just a way Mama had of seeing things, of trying to make sure about the "dangers." She was always talking about the dangers like they were alive and buzzing in the air over our heads. For some reason it wasn't the dangers that bothered me. It was Gedders' daddy up the lane.

He grew worms. We called his worm farm a wormtree, all those layers and layers with thousands of worms packed together in casings and stacked like the village we called Rivertown.

Gedders' daddy was just Snuff to everybody there. He fished for all sorts of grubs and crawly things along the banks, and carted boxes of them up into town stacked on the back of a bike, where I guess he sold them to places where they put them in a cooler next to the meat.

One time, me and Mandy were fishing tadpoles up out of a layback. She was talking redfly, blubberbee, weaving her words together like buttercup bracelets. Snuff came out of nowhere. He stood real quiet, staring from one of us to the other.

"Too scrawny," he said to Mandy, then looked at me. "But there's a little more meat."

I was already backing off when he jumped me. He was such an underfed, wiry thing I never thought he could have moved so fast, but he had me and I screamed.

He stunk like a dead possum, and I bit him on his teeth, because he had his mouth on me. I only chipped my right front lower. He lost two teeth. They just cracked off in my mouth like they were made of rotten wood or saltines. Mandy was hitting him over the back with a stick, and he was saying words I'd never heard before like he was hexing me. Mandy and me ran, me spitting out those teeth.

Ben had said the same to me. That was why he favored me. "You've got enough meat," he said, "but not too much. Not fat. Straps don't look good on fat. The scrawny girls can't fill a cuff, don't wear it tight. It's your muscles pushing up, pressing against. It fills a man's eyes."

This is a chit, remembering Ben like that out of nowhere and what he did to me.

Ben was an artist. Ben was a playwright. It was Ben and his dark Sicilian eyes that I remembered most as I turned my corner.

He could devise theater strong enough to make men's hearts fail. One time it really happened. The guy was some CEO up out of Philly. After he collapsed over me, his driver and Ben got him lifted up onto a cart that Ben used to move some of his equipment. They wrestled his dead body into the guy's limo, and away the driver zoomed. I read the obit later that week, but didn't recognize his picture. I wasn't able to see him that night.

Ben started out just a regular pimp in Manhattan. Before that he'd worked the park taking tricks, but gave it up when he started "the bleed." He was much better as a pimp, carefully choosing his batch of girls and guys.

By the time he tagged me, he was already making his way into pimp history.

Ben wormed his way up, attracting clients from the sleazy clubs, but getting a reputation. He didn't just sell vaginas and assholes. He sold the whole show. It was his calling. And he kept getting better. He was already well known around the Manhattan hot spots with the wealthier set when I showed up.

Ben got all his business by word of mouth, refining his clientele as he went along. He picked me up on a corner in SoHo. I hadn't eaten in four days. When I think about it now, I'm surprised he bothered. I was only sixteen and must have looked like shit.

Ben liked his players a little older. They worked the plays better. But no matter what their age, he never took the blank ones. That was the reason he kept me for so long. Ten years.

"With you, it's always fresh. You've got a gift. If you were in Hollywood, you'd knock them dead."

I never did tell him the truth, that I wasn't acting a lot of the time.

Most prostitutes last five years tops. It's the monotony and the disease. And if I'd been tagged by anybody but Ben, I would have had that same dull expression, that "I've screwed you a thousand times" look which shuts down a man's excitement. They can still fuck, but it doesn't grab, doesn't scratch its way in.

Ben's customers were, for the most part, regulars. One night with Ben and his kids, and they were hooked, coming back as often as they could afford it.

Ben was pricey. That's how he did it. He was also a genius for timing and choosing his players. We didn't get worn and dull, because we only worked one trick a night. Sometimes it was a long night as we raised the pitch of arousal like Hitchcock worked fear.

I craved it.

I loved the feel of the straps binding, the unknown cocks (a new one every night), the forced strippings. The whip I could have gone without, and the clips, but not all his clients wanted that. I was great at faking the beatings. I learned that from Daddy.

Daddy beat Vin and me so often that we got good at his rhythm, how he moved from the face to the stomach. We knew the timing of his kicks. We'd compare notes afterward, one with a nose bleeding, the other with lumps rising along the back or the side.

"He went from the face to the back this time," or, "Watch his eyes. Watch his eyes. The hands follow."

I got to be an expert at absorbing the blow, but not the brunt of it, falling back hard when it was expected, crumpling prematurely, and taking the kicks. He only meted out three or four of those. When you were on the floor, he just got disgusted and bored.

"Hit the floor," I told Vin. "Act like he broke your nose. Squall like a baby and drop. The kicks are candy."

That's how I got through the first couple months with Ben. When he gets you, they lock you in the basement and call you a newborn. And after they dragged me up into the lights after what they did to me down there, I worshipped Ben with the vehemence of a good honest hatred. Ben was the only man I ever loved.

I guess that's love in a nutshell.

Remembering Ben like this, experiencing an unusual bout of nostalgia, and having turned a corner, I got suddenly exhausted. It was two thirty. So I did what I'd been doing every night. I curled up on the floor of my closet to finish off the night, leaving the door cracked just enough for me to see. Jeremy slept like a log, so he never noticed. To tell the truth, Jeremy didn't notice much.

The closet seemed the safest place to sleep, since I knew that the man would come some night and that he'd be wearing gym shoes. I hoped he wouldn't think to look for me in the closet.

I dozed off for about an hour and drifted back to my nightmare, then woke up in a sweat. Gym shoes, I thought. Watch out for the gym shoes. Then I had a flash of something. It was almost a memory, but I couldn't catch it. And it scared me so much, I got to shaking all over.

I pushed open the closet door a little and lay looking at my tastefully appointed studio.

Out, I thought. I've got to get out.

Then I heard Jeremy's alarm go off. The alarm was a recording of dogs barking. I promised myself each morning that someday I was going to get a gun and shoot that damn alarm clock.

I ripped downstairs, hit the button on the coffee machine, and prepared my wife face again.

But that particular morning it cracked, it poured, it drained away, and I knew that I couldn't take my life one more minute, the nightmares, Jeremy's damn alarm clock, and the buying undercurrent pressing on me.

Jeremy didn't even notice my lack of a smile.

He looked down at Pussy, his chihuahua stray. "Honey, do you think she looks sick?" he asked me.

Personally, I thought that little rat dog looked sick from the day he brought her home.

He worried over her all through his breakfast, me just nibbling at my piece of crumpet. Then he jumped up and kissed me, racing the engine of his Porsche in the garage and squealing off to a day on Wall Street.

I sat at the table in a daze, trying to imagine a way out, a clean escape.

When I look back at it now, I think that moment was touch and go, because the only thought that made sense was that I wanted to die. I have to admit, I wasn't surprised. I just wondered why it took me so damn long to figure out that kind of thing. I could have saved myself a lot of trouble if I'd only thought it sooner.

And as soon as I had my thought about dying, I felt better. So I threw on a very short skirt and a pair of heels, revved up the Porsche, and hit the gun stores.

The better the novel sold, the less I ate and slept. The less I slept, the more antsy I got, going for drives in the morning after Jeremy left. I did a pawnshop junket, fascinated by the knives. That's when I saw my first Smith and Wesson with a long, sleek barrel.

"More accurate at a distance," the pawnshop guy assured me, brushing his hand over mine as he handed it to me.

I wasn't concerned about accuracy at a distance. I thought of the barrel in my mouth, pressing up against my tongue. I desired that gun. I fantasized. I thought of it like a lover, because of the thing that chased. The push behind was growing more insistent.

I soon became bored with the lack of firepower assortment in the pawnshops, so I visited gun stores, taking in the incredible array of weaponry needed to preserve democracy and a safe society. And ammo. I discovered a diversity of bullets that would have made any ecosystem proud.

That morning, I was in a buying frame of mind. No jogging. No trip to the spa or pumping iron. No wearing out of stationary bikes or NordicTracking myself toward tranquility. I had a suicide to attend.

My favorite gun store was Bob's Guns.

What an original name. Bob thought it up.

I tooled into the parking lot, walked inside, and waved at Bob. We'd become something like friends.

"Today I'm in a buying mood," I said.

"The Smith and Wesson?"

"You got it."

"With that nice long barrel," he added, looking me up and down like he'd figured out my other talents, the ones Ben was so crazy about.

I'd thought ahead and brought my tote bag. So into the bag with my lipstick and blush, I dropped a box of bullets and a Smith and Wesson with a long barrel. They lay neat and cozy beside the seven-inch switchblade I'd picked up at Johnny's Pawn. (Another original name.)

So much for a safe society.

It was high noon just like in the movies. I had a good seven hours to go and get the job done. I sang along with a CD of Hendrix on my way home, happy as a bee. Stacking in Rivertown, I belted out to "Hey Joe" while the garage door closed behind my Porsche. As I keyed in the alarm and opened the door into the house, the heat from the engine warmed the back of my thighs. It gave me another flash of memory. But it didn't make any sense. I saw a knife pointing at my stomach. Dizzy now, I shook my head to make the picture go away. And the push got sharper, driving into me.

I skirted through the kitchen, leapt the back stairs, then floated, trying to prepare. I wafted into my studio, all the while assailed by the fine colonial house, the white carpeting, the dandelion-free lawn, the maid, and Jeremy.

I walked to my desk and sat in the great swivel chair, shoving six shiny cartridges into the chambers of the desirable S&W for my fabulous suicide. The phone rang and the answering machine picked up with my fake happy voice regretting our absence, pleading for a message, promising a call.

It was my agent telling me of two book signings, one in Manhattan and one in Philly, both next week. In my mind, everything went dull gray.

It's this feeling of future that I get. I never had this future problem until I met Jeremy. There was something about him and his friends and their "tomorrow" this and "planning for the future" that. They harped about newer and bigger houses, brighter cars, new babies, preschool enrollment, private school costs, and projected college tuition. It socked my brain in, poking and pricking me like I'd got the ghosts in Ben's basement.

Ben I could take, even on a bad day. But not Jeremy. Not interviews. Not a house big enough for twenty.

I turned the S&W around in my hands so that it was pointed at my face. I stuck the muzzle back near my throat, aiming toward my brain.

What a metaphor, I thought, remembering all those cocks I sucked working for Ben. That's what reminded me of Violet.

Oh, lovely Violet. I thought of her then because Violet had "teeth." She could suck a cock right off a man and swallow every drop of his mystery.

We all said, oh yes, Violet. Now Violet has teeth. That was the term. The really good cocksuckers had teeth. Never made any sense to me.

When Ben used us together, I was always in some grand strapped-down position of welcome. Violet was made to suck cock. Clients were always asking for Violet. Not only did she suck cock, she did it like she was terrified, struggling with her hands cuffed back.

They loved that, those men with their fat bellies, with their silly little drooping sacks, their powder puff skin, and their twitchy arrogant eyes. They were nothing but meat to us. We'd see the picture of one in the paper and laugh, saying, remember his thighs? They flapped. They trembled. His belly's too high.

I still see their faces in magazines and newspapers every now and then. Some of them are presidents of corporations, or chairmen of boards of directors, or elected to some public office.

So, another chit that. Remembering Violet, I mean. And I thought of her wearing green and that she had teeth as I sucked in that gun barrel.

I waited. I counted one to five.

But something was wrong with me. I couldn't get myself to do it.

I checked the clock. Four o'clock was coming on fast. I'd wasted a good four hours of a potentially excellent death. I sucked in the muzzle again, trying to concentrate. Nothing doing.

I guess those years with Ben, working myself into a state just to keep my head above water, had created a habit. On nights with Ben whipping me while some bumbling CEO screwed from behind, I thought I might stop breathing. The gag choked. And the blindfold. I hate blindfolds.

I gained a penchant for struggling. I fought. I survived.

So no wonder I couldn't pull the trigger.

All that pushing got to be a habit, a routine supported by special sayings, rituals performed before my act to ward off disease and to keep me safe from the fruitcake clients wanting more than sex, wanting blood.

Ben never left us unwatched. As he got more sophisticated, the rooms had a one-way mirror somewhere and a secret door. If Ben wasn't in the room, he watched from behind the mirror, interfering if things got too nasty. Ben was the best daddy a kid could ask for.

He kept us locked in most of the time. When I first came, the only players Ben had were Kat, Toni, Matt, and myself. He didn't pick up Violet until later.

I loved our rooms. They were tall and airy, at the top of a warehouse he'd renovated. A wall of windows looked out over the East River. The water glittered on sunny days. I had a pair of binoculars that I used to watch the boats go in and out the river. Pigeons roosted on our window ledges. We had a small patio on the south roof where we could lie out in the sun. Ben thought the air did us good.

I began to remember how Toni always tried to cheer me up with little gifts he picked up here and there. Matt was quiet, like me, but he always let me curl up in his lap when we watched scary videos together. For some reason I could never put my finger on, he reminded me of Vin.

I thought of Kat for the first time in five years. Kat's body and face came the closest I've ever seen to what I would call perfect. No man ever just glanced in her direction. But it was her inner grace, a sense of timelessness, of all the days gone by, that captured you. Kat was the one that mothered me, coaxing me back to life after Ben's basement.

As I began remembering them, I almost started to cry. I missed them so much.

And we had Charles and Princess Di, two cats Matt found in a Dumpster one day. Eventually, we caught on that Charles was really a girl. It didn't matter to us. Di was disappointed. And there was Buster. Good old Buster. He must have weighed in over one hundred pounds and was part mastiff, part St. Bernard. Ben gave it away as a reward to be able to take Buster out to Central Park. Ben had Buster trained as an attack dog. For our protection, he said.

I have to keep my family safe, Ben said over and over. That's how we said it. We said we were family. On nights we had off, we'd make popcorn and watch videos. We celebrated holidays and made up birthdays, spending weeks agonizing over gifts for one another. Kat posted charts of the cleaning duties. We bought groceries and cooked, spending mealtime niggling back and forth. And we cared for each other like our lives depended on it.

I laid the gun on top of my keyboard.

Why me? Why did I have to get a cult following and an undercurrent? Why couldn't they have just ignored me?

So that was when I thought to take out the shoebox again. I lifted the top off it and found Ben's business card. Beneath that

were all my old IDs, all fake. I pulled them out, staring in amazement, the wheels turning in my head.

I couldn't even remember what my name was when I lived by
that river. But during my ten years with Ben, I was Elizabeth
Boone.

It reminded me (another chit) of Ben visiting me in that hospital, but I was in a different room from the one where I first saw
Jeremy. This was a lockdown ward where I got off the smack cold
turkey, soaking the bed with sweat and shaking like a baby. I was
restrained hand and foot, which didn't bother me at all. But Ben
kept waving the new IDs before my eyes.

"You're Clarisse Broder. Remember that. And when the police
ask, say you were Ekker's girl. Don't mention me."

I couldn't get it in my head why, and I asked him if I had appendicitis. At first he laughed, but when I kept asking about the
surgery, he got to looking pale. I'd never seen him like that.

"Yeah. Appendicitis," he said at last. And he took my hand
with that gentleness that he showed sometimes, and told me the
story about falling down the stairs. I remembered the ballroom
and the black strapless, but I didn't remember falling.

After I had the police as confused as Ben about the appendicitis, they stopped bothering me and wheeled me into a regular
ward.

Ben came that last time and handed me my things. Thinking
about it now, I'd almost say he looked sad. Then I met good old
Jeremy and got married.

In the shoebox beneath my old IDs was a savings account
book. It showed that Elizabeth Boone had some twenty thousand
dollars saved in First Mutual. That was a stunner. And beneath
that I found a batch of folded papers of stories I'd written years
back.

So it started. The beginning of my "year," as I call it, when I
began counting up chits and thinking about a different type of
suicide, the kind where you end up free, in a new life that you
yourself decide.

Holding the IDs in my hand and having my recurring problem with memory, I picked up my phone to call Ben. He was the only person I knew that could get me a batch of new IDs.

And it's funny how you forget the important things. How the bad stuff just falls right out of your head and you remember a whole ten years of your life with a man like Ben, thinking that everything that happened was only natural and not all that terrible when you get right down to it.

So at that moment, for some crazy reason, I was thinking that Ben was the one to help me.

It turned out to be the stupidest thing I've ever done.

2

Weekend Number One

Ben's message machine drones on. I almost hang up, but then say fast, "It's Beth, Ben. I'll call back."

I pack my pistol into my bag and make reservations at an Italian place Jeremy likes. Then I work on my new plan. It's like making up a story. First you get the general idea. Then you embroider, working the details. You search for the tragedy and irony. If you're lucky, you're surprised by unexpected twists and a satisfying ending.

Kat taught me Shakespeare when I was at Ben's. She'd been with Ben the longest, and was almost twenty-five when I first came. Ben didn't usually have players that old, but Kat was different. I guess she spent a year in college somewhere. That seemed weird. She kept a whole collection of Shakespeare on a shelf.

Sigh no more, I'd say to her.

We'd hang our heads and lie back on her bed. Sigh no more. I got a real appetite for Bill, or B.S., as we called him. We even acted out some of the plays. I practically knew *Romeo and Juliet* by heart. But for me, nothing could be better than *The Tempest*. All that forgiveness at the end, the blessedness.

I want to write a story like that.

Kat took care of the rest of us. After our plays, we'd bathe, worn out but flush with arousal and fear. She'd check us over, tending to any bruises or open cuts. We'd sleep past noon, then Kat would cook breakfast.

The evening hours could be the hardest as we waited for the plays to begin. Ben never told us what to expect. It added to the show as far as he was concerned.

The scare worked its way into me. That's when Kat would sit me down with a book. I thought it was dumb at first, but Kat was insistent. And once she got me hooked, I couldn't get enough.

Kat guided me. Whenever she returned from a shopping trip, she dropped another book in my lap. Later on, she'd get me sitting right next to her. We'd talk about what I was reading. Kat taught me more about everything than any teacher I ever had.

The morning after my failed suicide, I go jogging. About a mile down the road, a limo with black windows wheels up and stops a little ahead. The back window slides down as I come alongside. It's Ben.

He smiles that awful smile that he gets just before something bad, and I decide that maybe I don't want to see Ben after all. The driver jumps out and opens a door for me.

"Hop in," Ben says.

I look around, not a soul in sight. I sigh and slide in, sitting across from him.

"You took your time," Ben says as the limo pulls away from the curb. "You're what, thirty-one now? That's too old."

"I just need some IDs," I say. "I'll pay."

"We'll see," he says. "Strip for me."

This isn't what I had in mind at all, but I don't see that I have too many choices, so I take off my clothes.

When I'm done, he says, "Bring up your knees. Spread."

He checks me over.

"Crouch. Good. Now hands and knees." He feels my sides, runs his hands over my rump. "Head up." He pokes my thighs. "You're clean and fresh," he says. "Like new. Jeremy's been taking good care of you. You don't look a day over twenty-five."

"I just need IDs," I say again.

"Planning on going away?" He cups my breasts and works them over like a doctor feeling for lumps. "Still firm. Still good."

Ben reaches into his black bag and pulls out a blindfold, fixing it over my eyes. He knows how much I hate that.

"Crouch again." I crouch. Wait.

"It's your lucky day. I'm down a player right now. I could use you. Not every night. Weekends. What IDs you want?"

"The usual," I say. "Driver's license. Social Security card. Maybe a birth certificate."

"That's four weekends. Friday and Saturday, the biggest nights. You up to it?"

I begin to shake. "I'd rather just buy them."

The limo slows, and Ben throws a blanket over me. The driver leaps out, opening the side door. Somebody steps in. Ben takes off the blanket.

"So. What do you think?" he says. I feel hands on me. Ben's big hand grabs my hair and turns my face toward the person.

"Yes." A man's voice. "I think they'd like her."

"I think they'll be more than satisfied," Ben says. "Next Friday then?"

"That will be fine."

The blanket goes over me again. The door opens, and the man steps out. The limo takes off, and we cruise around in silence. Ben slides the blanket off, caresses my cheek, and runs his hand along my back.

"Sit up," he says. He removes the blindfold.

"Put on your clothes." Ben watches out the window as the neighborhoods roll by. Then he hands me a card. "Arrive at this hotel at eight o'clock sharp Friday evening. The key for your room will be under the name Elizabeth Boone. Carry a bag as though you're there for a night or two. I want that body of yours to sing when you cross the lobby. You're naive, innocent. So turn their heads, Beth."

I stare at the card. "Nothing in the face, Ben. It'll be too hard to explain to Jeremy."

He nods. "I still have your whip. I never got rid of it." He smiles that awful smile of his again. "If you don't show, we'll be around to pick you up. I wouldn't want that. I never liked hurting you, Beth." He touches my cheek. The limo stops, the driver comes around, opening the door. I step out.

That's what I get for not being able to pull that trigger.

Mandy turned a corner one day. We were at school in gym class, with us in our freaky gym outfits. And Mandy was laughing. She had the ball in her hands, getting ready to pitch it at me in dodgeball.

But Mandy clutched her side, made a little cry, and stood still.

The school nurse came to get her, leading her out, head down and still holding her side, with the nurse saying something about the period. All the girls tittered, but she turned on us with such a glare that we all shut up fast.

Mandy got sicker.

Sometimes it's this way, the rumor went around, started by who knows who. When they first start up, when it comes so young.

And I waited, but Mandy didn't come back to school. She didn't come over to dig crawdads and chase the snakes.

Mandy died five days later. Appendicitis, the principal announced at the school, shaking his head. If only she'd seen a doctor, the teachers said.

I got the idea that doctors had something to do with periods and somehow appendicitis came along with whatever a period was.

Appendicitis, and it just busted right open, just burst inside her, they kept repeating, wiping their eyes with handkerchiefs.

I suspected it was the dangers that got her.

I wore white gloves at her funeral, though I was told it wasn't right. But I knew Mandy loved white gloves. She used to talk about the white-gloved ladies who shopped on Dew Street. I didn't go in for them myself. But we had a stash of money saved.

We sold lemonade and crawdads, and sometimes frog legs. I had enough to buy the gloves.

After that, the dangers got hold of me. They were everywhere. For some reason Snuff kept showing up wherever I went, with Gedders in tow. I got good at keeping an eye out and not walking alone. But I couldn't keep it up forever. They caught me near Ansel's trailer and dragged me behind.

I bled then, thinking I was going to die like Mandy. But I didn't. Pretty soon after that I started my blood. I thought for a long time that it had to do with what happened behind that trailer.

Snuff and Gedders held me down on my back to do what they did. When I was first at Ben's, Kat, Toni, and Matt made me get up on my hands and knees doing me a different way. They started me slow, and I never liked it much, especially after all those weeks in the basement, crying.

And sitting at home after seeing Ben, I'm shaking just like I did then. I'm thinking that calling Ben was a big fat mistake.

And I forgot to explain about the whips.

Ben kept a whip for each of us with our name on the handle. They were all different. Kat's was thin, with a split in the end. Matt's was short with lots of strands, each ending in a knot. Ben never used a whip on Violet. With her, he used a cane.

My whip was thick. It was long and mean. BETH, it said in red paint on the hefty handle.

Because of your will, Ben said, your strength. It's what makes you so good in the straps.

Thinking about my whip, I fret. I'm not sure I can do it now. Maybe it's like falling off a horse. Maybe I'll jump right back on.

But it's more than that. From the moment I saw Ben's face again, the thing that's pushing from behind began pushing harder.

That week, I attend my two book signings in a daze. Jeremy sits beside me. He's so proud. My agent starts bugging me for a photo for the book jacket of the next printing the publisher's planning. I send her a picture of Jeremy's sister.

"This isn't you." My agent, the complainer.

"Nobody needs to know that," I say.

In the meantime, I get busy with my other details. I check on my savings account and find that now I have a whopping twenty-eight thousand dollars in it. I switch it into checking, using my old IDs to pose as Elizabeth Boone. By Thursday afternoon, I've purchased a 1993 Taurus for eight thousand dollars and rented a garage in upper Manhattan.

Friday morning, the dangers buzz me. I take a long bath, administering an array of lotions and creams. Then I dress and hit Manhattan by mid-afternoon, getting in some shopping. I find an incredible black silk dress that falls just above the knee. When I walk, it flows like water. I pick up new stockings, new heels, and a bra of green silk trimmed in black lace.

My hair appointment is at five. I have it cut shorter. If it's too long, it gets in the way. Then I have Ronny do my face. He's a minimalist when it comes to makeup, which suits me fine.

"You're humming today, Clarisse," he says. "You look like a model ready for a shoot."

Now Violet could have been a model if she'd had the right breaks. And like I said, she had teeth. The real problem with Violet was that she never got over the berserks. Being tied down can get to you if you're left like that too long with all sorts of things happening to you. We all got the berserks in the beginning, but after awhile, they go away.

Violet never got over them. That's why she usually just sucked cock. Not the multiple-orifice approach for Violet. She almost always berserked on that. Or a lot of straps. If she hadn't had teeth, Ben would have dumped her fast. She also kept that little-girl look. Violet carried it into her twenties.

Pulling off a weekend away from Jeremy is a little touch and go.

"My screwy agent called," I say. "She's lined up a lecture and a dinner for Friday and Saturday. I think I'm going to throttle her."

"I'll be there to help you, sweetie." I think of him curling up at my feet like a Labrador while I'm at the podium.

"No," I say like I'm talking to one of his strays. "I need peace and quiet."

"I want to go," he says, tucking his tail. Stay, I think. Lie down. Be a good doggie.

He pouts for two days, cultivating a hangdog look for my benefit.

I hate lying.

I guess you could say the last five years of my life were a great big fat lie. Except I didn't always remember it that way.

Violet lied. She'd get so mixed up she couldn't remember the truth. Her lying put Ben in a real bad frame of mind. There was something between those two. I thought of it like watching one person trying to outcheat the other at poker. It's not even the same game at some point.

So here I am into the first five days of my "year." Men are staring at me right and left as I'm strolling north along Fifth Avenue. I get a whiff of the old days as I turn west on Fifty-Ninth, walking beside the park.

Kat would take me shopping for clothes here, in the Village, and in SoHo. She taught me New York, the delis, the shops, how to snag a cab. She hauled me into MoMA, the Metropolitan, and taught me how to use the library.

I near the hotel, passing a line of waiting limos and cabs, hitting a wall of white panic. As I prepare for my entrance, I stop still, seeing a cab at the curb, empty and waiting. But then I remember what Ben said. I remember that whip. I shut my eyes and count one to five just like Kat taught me in the basement. I push myself forward.

I swear I can smell the mud in the water. I can hear the black-fly drone and the willow leaves shake. I feel the sway of that river. Stacking in Rivertown comes to my mind. It makes me smile. That shoots me right in the hotel doors like I'm floating downstream.

I feel plush. I flush out every square inch of my skin. As soon as I'm in the door, a bellboy jumps over and lifts the bag from my shoulder. Men turn to watch me. I walk like a writer, like I'm married to Jeremy, but powerful in need of a screw. Naive, Ben said. Innocent.

At the check-in desk, I flash the young man a smile and say I'm Elizabeth Boone. As he hands my room key to the bellboy, he informs me that my husband checked in an hour ago.

I cross the lobby like I own every man in the place, and catch sight of Ben leaning against a column and reading the *Times*. I search the strangers milling around him.

Which one? No. The man in the car said they. God. Multiple screws. Ben's going to teach me a lesson. He likes to make sure you know he's the boss. I figure he's going to go out of his way on that point this weekend.

Jump back on that horse, I keep telling myself as the elevator doors close behind me. At the top floor, the bellboy leads me to a set of double doors at the end of the hall. He opens them inward, revealing a large anteroom. I walk through into a grand and gracious sitting room with a bank of windows dead ahead. The windows draw me over, and I look across Manhattan at night, the dark smudge of Central Park smack in the middle, just below.

For that moment, I forget about everything. I think of the river at night, fireflies blinking a thousand deep in the tupelo and the sweetbush on the far shore. I can smell sweet bay nearby and woodsmoke from over at Grady's. The rumble of the city beneath reminds me of the crush of water that scrapes between the banks and over the bed of the river.

The bellboy makes a sound. Embarrassed, I turn, hand him his tip, and watch him flirt with his eyes once before he disappears behind the doors.

I take in the room. A colossal arrangement of cut flowers stands in a vase on a table in the center. Walking over to them, I check the card.

More instructions.

The card says to eat dinner alone in the hotel restaurant, then have the valet bring around my car. A black Jaguar. I imagine myself wheeling down Central Park South in a cool, sleek Jag.

Maybe this is going to be fun after all.

That's when I get out my stuff. After you've been in the business for awhile, you begin to get nervous. You watch the others disappear, fade away. You know it's just a matter of time before the dangers get you. And like I said, Ben started getting meaner.

Violet started our ritual. She stole a candle from St. Pat's and put it in a cup next to her bed. Before each play, she would light it and blow it out three times.

I began sitting with her, never going down to a play without doing the candle. After awhile, I got a cup. We'd light the candle three times, then I'd turn the cup over, thinking of the dangers buzzing everywhere.

So I take the candle and cup out of my bag, setting them both on the floor. I perform our ritual kneeling. It's the first time I'd ever done it alone, which almost starts me crying. I sit quiet then, trying to get up my nerve.

After a time, I leave the room, pulling the doors shut behind, feeling a bit floaty in the head. I take the elevator down and hit the restaurant. A table is reserved for Elizabeth Boone.

My waiter flirts to beat the band. He wants me to order a large spread. I'm sorry to disappoint him, keeping it light. A salad. No wine. Alcohol and Ben never mixed for me. I did acquire a poisonous taste for smack. Ben didn't mind. He was the one that got me started, handing it out for a reward like it was candy.

I'm forcing myself to eat when the concierge arrives, offering me a note on a small tray. I wait for him to leave before I open it.

It says: "Finish up quick and return to your room. We need to talk."

Something must have gone wrong. Maybe they didn't like me. I charge the meal to the room. The waiter helps me up, smiling hopefully. I blow him a kiss and grab my purse, then head for the elevators.

As I'm going up, I think I might lose that nice salad. One to five, I say to myself. Count one to five and then start again. Don't mind the lights. (I tell myself this because I'm seeing a few lights roving in the air.) One to five.

The elevator opens. My heels *tick, tick* over the marble entryway floor. I'd thought the play was going to be a grab. Now I'm not so sure. I walk into the anteroom, closing the doors behind me and dropping my purse on a boringly tasteful table. Then I stroll into the sitting room, expecting to see Ben.

Across the room, and sitting with drinks in hand like they're in their own home, are a man and woman wearing masks that look like something out of a costume ball. I stand, shocked. That goddamn Ben has tricked me again.

That's when they get me.

The first guy jerks back on my mouth so hard, I bite my lip. So I'm thinking, shit, shit, shit. So much for leaving the face clean.

He stuffs a wad of cloth deep into my mouth. I fight hard. Ben appears out of nowhere, similarly masked, and helps them hold me down on my back.

One of the boys, a blond Aryan type sporting a Lone Ranger mask, holds my mouth and starts fondling. That's when I get a nasty surprise. They begin taping me.

Tape is playing dirty for Ben.

I try to scream, shooting a nasty look at him.

"Shut up, bitch," the blond says as he's taping my mouth. He slaps me good and hard a couple times after he's done.

From the look in Ben's eyes, a mixture of anger and delight, I'm beginning to get the feeling this isn't play. He leans down and slaps me a good one. They tape my eyes, then turn me over, taping ankles, knees, and my wrists behind. I hear somebody laugh and I'm slapped on my ass, and then they all three stand back from me. I'm breathing hard and still kicking.

What do you think? Ben says. I hear the lovely couple walk over to me. Ben kicks me.

Turn on your side, he says.

I turn, curling my knees up. Ben grabs my hair and turns my face toward them.

Perfect, a woman says.

She'll do fine, a man says.

You could start on her here. It's Ben's voice.

I feel hands on my breasts. I struggle, trying to get away. I'm pushed over and held tight to the floor on my back.

A knife cuts my dress open from my neck down to my waist. My bra is cut in front and pulled back.

Someone's touching my head and my cheek. Hands move down to my nipples.

You're beautiful, the woman says. We're going to have a little fun with you tonight.

Let's get her out of here, the man says. It makes me nervous.

All right then, Ben says. Boys, go ahead and pack her up.

I hear them walk away and return, dropping something heavy near me. Turning me on my side, they tie my knees to my neck and my ankles to my wrists so that I'm folded up tight.

As I'm lying there in my helpless state, one guy kneels over me and says in my ear so that the lovely couple can't hear. "Ben wants you to know that you're a newborn again, Beth."

I almost lose it then. The basement comes into my head. I attempt to count one to five, but I try to scream anyway. He laughs a little, sounding too much like Ben. The two of them lift me up and settle me down in what I'm assuming is a luggage trunk, just big enough for me. The lid is slammed shut, latched, and locked.

Panic slams into me. I try to breathe steady. I try to count. Time passes. I hear voices, then the trunk is lifted onto a wheeled cart and off I go. I'm stopped after a rough ride during which my tailbone is jarred into the base of my brain. The trunk is lifted and set down. I hear something slam shut.

Shit. They've packed me into a van like a piece of cargo. For some reason, this finally breaks me. I start to cry, breathing heavier now from the heat and the lack of air. I begin to sweat.

I don't remember how long the drive is because I think I pass out for a bit, the lights flashing in front of my eyes to beat the band. I wake when the van doors are opened and slammed. I feel myself lifted out and set down. The lid is unlatched. Fresh air curls around my body and face. I could weep for it. They turn over the trunk and I tumble out, hitting the floor hard. Someone cuts the ropes holding me so tight together. I stretch out, moaning.

Then the two guys each grab an arm and drag me off, I'm assuming in front of the lovely couple so they can take in the whole show. Now they haul me through several halls and then down a flight of stairs. I start to cry again, start to fight.

I've gotten out of practice, I guess.

A door is opened and they dump me on a cold tile floor. Something about the room seems surgical, maybe the smell. I begin to wonder if the clients are just going to watch, or if they're going to be players too.

I hear the door open. They walk in. The door closes. A knife cuts the tape on my ankles and knees. It's ripped away. They stand me up. Somebody socks me hard in the stomach. Lucky for me, I'm ready. That's one of Ben's favorite moves. Hit them when they can't see. I buckle good and drop. They stand me up again and my gorgeous dress is cut off. I'm stripped.

The two guys hold me by the arms to display. The clients approach, stroke me, fondle. Then I'm slapped. Slapped again.

"Okay," the man says, and we're off on the play.

Ben works me hard. It seems like they do me for hours, Ben using a whip on me. Sometime near the end, I break. I start to scream, pushing against the straps. I can't stop. They'd removed the tape from my mouth a long time ago, for obvious reasons. Ben quick-jams a gag in before I start spewing trash out at him, which I have a knack of doing. The berserks get hold of me. Then I cry again.

I know Ben must be all smiles. What a good show I gave. Command performance. Not just any whore can do that.

I hear them talking.

Keep her, they say. We're in town until tomorrow. We'll pay. Tomorrow evening. Early. Maybe five.

Holding fees are high, he says.

We'll pay, they say again. Tomorrow at five. Can we watch you put her away?

Sure, says Ben. He scratches out a figure on a pad. I hear the man get out a wallet. Bills are exchanged. Ben calls on the intercom. They come in, undoing me from the contraption I'm in and cuffing my ankles and wrists together in back, just like in that damn basement. They drag me to another room, fitting me in a dog cage.

It was probably Buster's, I think. I'm crying hard now. I hear the door close. They all go away.

Every summer, Vin, Mandy, and me would try to build a raft. One of us, must have been Vin, read about Tom Sawyer in school. When we were little, we didn't have any idea what we were doing. We'd work on a raft for weeks, weaving charms as we built and making up stories that grew increasingly bizarre about the raft and where it would take us.

Vin was always adding little time-saving devices like the automatic fishing pole. He'd nail on some contorted-looking arm with a string and hook hanging off it. Mandy and me added stuff willy-nilly. Who knows why.

By the time we were done, our rafts looked like fantastic multi-limbed creatures in an agony of protuberances. No wonder they all sank. I figured that if we lost enough rafts at the same point on the river, sooner or later, at least we'd have a dock.

We mined our materials from the wreck of an old barn, long ago fallen in, that lay a ways upriver. Each year, we practiced our craft, learning through trial and error how you keep something afloat. It wasn't until Mandy's last summer that we got one to work. I'm still not sure why it floated when all the others sank. Maybe because of Mandy. Maybe she got lighter and lighter that last year.

I think of us gliding. Damselflies skirt the brown water. The heat makes us sleepy, and Vin lets the river carry us, using the pole to keep us off the banks.

It was like a dream you'd make up, because you knew it would never be true. But there it was, the three of us floating. The willows draped above. The cottonwoods flicked. We saw two herons on stalk legs and a doe with a fawn.

The raft floated past the rise and the cemetery where the stones caught the light.

This is the river then. It is passing by slow, leaving even Rivertown behind.

I'll never forget that feeling of watching it all go by, not guiding, not pushing. And listening to the lapping of the doe.

After Ben leaves with his clients, I wait for the boys to come and let me loose. I wait a long time, getting a bad feeling about the whole thing. I kick the side of the cage. I scream into the gag. All in all, I'm pretty ineffectual. I start thinking about what the guy said about me being a newborn again.

That's when it comes clear. Ben has decided to make me the star in his own personal play. Sure, there are the other plays, this weirdo couple for one. But Ben's getting his rocks off big. He's probably watching me on video right now. I kick the cage again for his benefit.

And what occurs to me next, which should have occurred to me sooner before I got myself into this mess, is that Ben might be playing for keeps again. This weekend could stretch out into God knows how many years.

But I'm old, I think. He doesn't use players this old.

I lie quiet, pissed off at myself for being such an imbecile.

We had an imbecile in our school. Well, I like to say we had a lot of imbeciles, but only one that we actually called an imbecile. He tended to drool and he liked to rock with one arm bent over his head. I felt sorry for him because he didn't look comfortable the way he sat in the back of the room with his legs clutched up under the chair. He preferred to do his rocking on the floor, but Miss Summers always made him get back into the chair. Maybe she thought he would learn better that way.

He never made any bother. He just rocked, sometimes drooling, with his other hand tight in a fist and jammed in his mouth.

Mandy didn't like him. She said he gave her the shivers. I sat close to him and just watched, not saying a thing, chin on my hand. I studied him like he was an African bird or something.

We'd read about Africa and its borderlines that week. Rwanda. Zaire. Funny-sounding names. I raised my hand.

"What about the birds, Miss Summers, ma'am?"

Miss Summers in her pretty cotton print dress looked stumped. "The birds?"

"They have good birds there, don't they, ma'am?"

Now she was getting that twitchy way like I'd said something stupid. A few kids giggled. I marked them. I'd beat the shit out of them later.

"Big birds with green and blue wings, ma'am?"

I was thinking about the magazine I found in one of the Dumpsters where Mama looked for her groceries. On the front it said: "Africa, Land of Wonders." I took it home, angling for extra credit.

"We're not talking about the birds," Miss Summers said. "We're talking about Zaire."

"The birds are more interesting, ma'am."

She sent me to the back to sit in the corner. So there I was next to the imbecile. I have no idea what his name was. Miss Summers forgot about me, so I stared at him.

He's a bird from Africa, I thought. Look at that nose and the way he curves over his wing. No wonder. Somebody made a mistake and he got dumped in the whole wrong country. Somebody should take him home.

I knew that I would take him there if I knew the way. It would be so good to go home.

That's when ice-cold water starts peeling off my skin. I must have fallen asleep. It's a high-pressure spray. I try to turn away in the cage, but another spray hits me from the other side. Now I'm freezing.

I hear them leave.

They come back every so often and spray me again. I never get any sleep.

After seven or eight doses of this, the two boys drag me out. They put me on my knees with my wrists still cuffed behind to my ankles, and then buckle a collar around my neck, hooking it somewhere above.

That's a nasty position. You lose all the feeling in your legs and arms, and it hurts like hell. They wind something else around my neck, leaving the grip dangling down my back. I know what it is. It has BETH written on the handle. Ben is playing me ripe. They spray me with water again and leave. I wait, shivering.

That's when the ghosts come like they'd never been gone. In the basement, when you get the ghosts, Ben knows that you're almost ready. And now the ghosts whisper all around me. I feel their breath against my face. As I watch their twisting shapes forming behind the tape on my eyes, I miss the fact that Ben has come into the room.

"You thought you'd take your time," he says. "I've got five years stored up for you."

His hand rests on my head, then slides down and lifts my chin. Ben's other hand reaches behind my head and loosens the gag.

"You're not going to make it home until Monday morning," he says. "I'll put the phone up to your ear and you tell that to Jeremy."

"Fuck, Ben," I say as soon as the gag is out.

He slaps me.

I hear him dialing. The phone is against my head.

"Hello."

Jeremy's so cheerful to answer the phone, as though it's always good news. I never answer the phone unless I have to.

"It's me, Jeremy. Something more has come up. I won't make it in until Monday sometime."

"Are you sick, sweetie? You sound sick."

No, just fucking scared shitless.

"Doing these talk things gets on my nerves," I say. "I'll be glad to get home." If I ever get home. That's a big if.

"You're so sensitive, honey. You need to get a thicker skin."

Thinking about Ben's whip around my neck, I say, "I'll work on it. See you Monday."

Ben takes the phone away. "Are you thirsty?"

I nod my head. He holds a bottle to my mouth and I drink. Gatorade. Ben swears by its beneficial properties. He always hands it out after the plays.

I hear the empty bottle hit the floor behind me. Then I feel him unwind the whip.

In my book, there's nothing worse than being whipped bound and blind. I know how to fake the punches, how to drop. I know how to play the men so they don't hurt me too much. But when you're bound, there's not a damn thing you can do about a whip but take every stitch. And Ben is a mean whipper. To him, it's all about business.

He whips me front and back. I lose count after sixteen. When he's done, he says, "You're back home, Beth. You're back with your family."

That's when I pass out.

The first time I saw Violet, she was in the basement on the mattress, bound, gagged, and blindfolded. He started us all that way. Kat was gone by then, and I was the only girl Ben had.

Toni, Matt, and I worked Violet good. We made over her. We kissed. We stroked. We said, count your breaths one to five. It looked to me that Ben had been especially rough with her.

I remember her lips, so talented eventually, but then, so guiltless, so chaste. I tasted them over and over.

Violet's breasts were small. She always looked to be about thirteen. While she was bound down there, I cleaned her, fondled her, and fed her. I held her and whispered strange songs to her that I made up about water moving and the river.

When the ghosts got me, they whispered. For Violet, they

screamed. I worried over her and found myself waiting for Ben to say, go down to Violet now. She's ready again.

She didn't speak a word for a month after we brought her up, and early on, she began to creep onto my mattress after the plays and curl up next to me.

Our sleeping arrangements were slim. We each had a mattress with sheets and blankets. And we all slept in the same room. Ben didn't mind if we screwed and moved around one to the other. He encouraged it. But he didn't like it if any two started pairing off. That was reason for a whipping. So I tried to keep Violet off me for her sake. She was a persistent little animal. That's what she was like then, a rabbit or a puppy. So I'd sing to her and she'd go to sleep.

This time, Ben didn't interfere. He used it on me, knowing I was getting attached to her. He'd even let me out to take Buster for a walk on my own sometimes. He knew I'd come back, that I wouldn't leave Violet alone with him.

In the plays, if Ben wanted to get me worked up good and pushing on the straps, all he had to do was to start whipping Violet.

Ben made her go in the box more than any of the rest of us, and he made her beg for her food. He'd sit in the big recliner with her plate on his lap. She'd have to plead for each bite.

I couldn't stand to watch it.

In that long weekend I was spending with Ben, I remembered more and more about Violet. I thought I heard her voice among the ghosts. But I couldn't remember what she looked like. I did remember her lips, her breasts, and how silent she was then.

When I wake up, I'm in warm water. My eyes are still taped, but my arms and legs are free. A boy is behind me in the tub, leaning me back against him, my head on his shoulder. They make over me, cleaning the welts, washing me.

You got the ghosts? A girl asks.

Yes, I say.

He said you would. He said they come back on you fast.

What day is it? I say.

Saturday.

Still Saturday? I thought I was dead. I thought I was gone past Saturday, past Monday, past all the days passing.

Shh, one of them says. Shh.

The welts burn.

You got a play coming, says the girl. They'll be here for you soon.

I can't, I say.

Shh. Shh.

They feed me then, a bowl of mashed potatoes. Ben remembered. It was all I could ever eat after a really hard play.

Now a gag is pushed in my mouth.

They lift me out of the tub and dry me, then tie my hands in front. They put a collar on and lead me out with a leash. I'm taken into a room where my favorite couple is waiting.

"Poor dear," the obnoxious woman says, running her hands over the welts. If I had a gun, I'd shoot her.

"We must move on," Ben says. "She has another appointment after you."

I'm convinced Ben is trying to murder me with sex.

They fit me into another contraption, this time with me hanging upside down. In the middle of the play, the goofy guy says to me, "Nasty little scar."

Funny, the things you notice at times like these.

Appendectomy, I'd say politely if my mouth were free.

I'm hearing more than the ghosts now. I'm hearing Kat. She's talking to someone about a knifing. A deep cut. I'm on a gurney, not strapped to it (a new experience), but I can't move.

The lovely couple wind down their activities on me.

Why don't you keep her, they say after they're done. We'd come once a week. It's not that far.

She's got a husband, says Ben. The police, you know.

Too bad. They sigh. Too bad.

They should both have lobotomies.

Ben ushers them out and leaves me upside down. The ghosts move in. The lights come and go. They spike.

That's the way I stay for a long time. When they come to get me out, I can't walk, so they drag me back to the dog cage.

Ben has never done me this hard.

He wakes me up at some point and takes my arm. He wraps a rubber tourniquet around, patting up a vein. I hear him flip a syringe. I feel the stick. The smack speeds into me.

I'm off in la-la land.

Rivertown was our own fairyland. It had grave markers of all shapes and sizes, and buildings with columns and odd creatures carved inside. In Rivertown, we had a whole world of characters, of angels and sad women holding folds of their clothing, of men on horses, a soldier clutching a flag. On either side of the entrance to one building there were two little gnomes, and some guy named Gilbert put in a statue of his dog.

Jeremy would have approved.

Yes, the wealthy of our fair town lavished money on their sorry deaths.

In an old, forgotten corner back near a grove of mimosa, we found a statue of a little girl. She was the only one smiling in the whole place. Beloved daughter, the plaque said.

Mandy and me called them our people, and got to dressing them up if we found an old cast-off jacket or dress in one of our Dumpster runs. Mandy stole Miss Summers' hat. We put it on the head of a very sad woman looking to the side.

Somebody was always coming and taking off our little additions to the cemetery. Dishonoring the dead, they said. Defacing the tombs.

The tooms, Mandy said.

On May Day, we stole the ribbon off the pole, winding it all over the people of our special town. Our people were pleased. They almost looked to be smiling, even the sad lady whose face was turned to the side. She had been even sadder since they took back her hat.

After that, sadness reigned. Mandy got appendicitis. About two years later, our two-room burned down. Mama forgot and left the hot plate on was my guess. Vin got me out. Mama never woke up.

Daddy was dead drunk out behind the live oak. Vin and me sat alone and watched the place go down to ashes. Nobody came. We found Daddy the next morning.

I'll never forget his face when he stood looking at that pile of ash. It pretty much broke him, and he kept drinking from then on. Vin and I slept by the river while it was still warm, then we moved to Rivertown. After that, I can't remember too well except that Vin left. If we did happen to run across one another someplace, it was like we were embarrassed. I got to sleeping under an overhang of one of the little houses between two columns.

I found myself bringing back extra groceries from the Dumpsters and leaving a bag at the feet of one of the gnomes. It looked like Mama, so short and fat. And I dressed the little girl. I kept her in hats. I hung buttercup bracelets around her neck.

My memories of the next few years are like the fog that hangs thick on the river below Rivertown during the winter rains. But I do recall hitching rides on highways and riding in big trucks. I got turned around sometimes, but always in my head I had a dream of a home. I was looking for a better life.

As I come back from the beauty of smack into ugliness, somebody is saying my name. I'm lying on my back on a cool floor, my head propped on a pillow. The tape is still on my eyes. My hands are still tied in front. The junk has my skin twitching like the gnats are doing me in.

Beth, Ben says. He strokes my cheek and opens my mouth, squirting in some Gatorade. I choke, swallow.

Enough Ben, I say. You win.

Poor Beth. He squirts in more Gatorade. I missed you so much. After you were gone, things weren't the same.

You knew where I was. You could have gotten me.

I waited for you. I knew you'd call. You can't live without me, Beth. I know you the best.

Yes, I say. Yes. What about Violet? When did she go?

A long time ago. Don't worry about Violet. She's happy now. Stacked in Rivertown, I think. High and low.

Ben kisses me. He feels my throat, my breasts.

The boys come and help me up. They shower me, then lead me through hallways and down stairs. They sit me in a car. The door shuts and the car starts moving.

Someone works the tape off my eyes. It appears to have fused with my skin. After it comes free, I can't see right away, but sense that it's Ben next to me. He cleans the goo off my face with some nasty-smelling liquid and unties my hands. We're in the limo again. On the seat across from me is my bag with my extra clothes.

"Get dressed," he says.

My hands shake. The shit he shot into my vein whipped my ass. I dress, the feel of the clothes making me crazy. I can see that we're winding through the maze of streets with houses way too big for the people who live in them.

"What day is it?" I ask.

"Monday. About nine in the morning."

He hands me a Social Security card. At the top is my new name, Katherine Benson. That's a cute touch.

"You'll get another piece next week," he says.

The car pulls up in front of my house.

"The limo will be waiting for you outside of Penn Station. Five o'clock Friday." He kisses me again, both hands on my throat. I can take a hint.

I don't know how I make it to the front door on two feet. Once inside, I collapse. I crawl to the kitchen and chug a quart of orange juice, taking three Valium. Then I drag myself up the stairs to my favorite closet, curling into a ball on the floor and dropping into dreamland.

3

Violet

Something wet is in my eye. I punch it, a bit of the berserks.

"Honey!" It's Jeremy protecting his new terrier-type mutt named Mitzi.

I roll onto my back. Jeremy's trying hard to look cheerful, but I can see it's a strain.

"What happened to your face?" He reaches to touch me, but I grab his wrists.

The skin around my eyes is raw. "It's a rash. I used to get it all the time when I was a kid. I find that if I lie down in a closet, it helps."

"And your lip?"

"I tripped. You know how these book things drive me nuts. I get clumsy, and then I get this rash, and I have to sleep in a closet."

"It's okay, honey. I understand. I know what you're going through, and I've taken care of everything."

I tense.

Jeremy kneels beside me. "I found you sleeping in this closet with your face looking that way. That made me a little worried. So I called Helen, you know, Jerry's wife, the psychiatrist? She said not to worry, just a nervous breakdown. Women have them all the time. So I set up an appointment for you. Tomorrow at ten."

I'm having jetlag or something. I just flew in from the dark continent of Ben to the little Balkan state of Jeremy.

"An appointment."

"At ten. She'll call me and let me know how it went so you don't have to worry about it. Why don't you come out of here?"

He grabs my shoulders to help me up. God, the welts burn. I convince him that I'm feeling sick on top of having a nervous breakdown, and I slip into bed. He goes off to heat up some soup.

While I'm alone, I start planning like there's no tomorrow. The stakes have skyrocketed. I can't believe I was so stupid as to call Ben.

Jeremy returns and worries over me, patting my head. I'm thinking I've got to get out of this place fast. And I'm sick to death of feeling like I'm one of Jeremy's mutts.

Of course, later on he's horny. Lucky for me, he likes to screw in the dark. I don't think I could explain the marks around my back and chest. As he's pumping me, I wish for once that I did have a gag, so I could scream my lungs out.

The next morning, after Jeremy has taken his happy face and departed, I log on to my computer. I'm worried that Jeremy might start rifling my things now that he thinks I'm going loony. So I bury the file I'm writing in the middle of an old disk.

I make two lists. The first list is called "In the Taurus." Underneath that I write: new clothes, new sunglasses, wig, CDs, money, new IDs. The other list is called "In the Porsche." Beneath that one I write: Clarisse Broder IDs and purse, switchblade, black hooded jacket, garage key for the Taurus.

Pleased with this, I type in the things that I have to get done this week, adding at the bottom to delete this file when I've completed my tasks. I don't want any posthumous discoveries.

I shower and paint on a heavy coating of makeup to cover my suspiciously rectangular rash. The phone rings. It's my agent so I pick up thinking that otherwise, I would have to call her back. I hate making phone calls more than I hate answering them.

"*Time* wants to do an interview," she says, her voice filled with triumph.

"God," I say.

"Thursday. And they're going to want to take pictures."

I must have been some terrible shit in my previous life to deserve this. "I've got a rash," I say. "On my face."

"Oh."

"The doctor said it would clear in three weeks. Couldn't we do it then?" I guess I don't hate lying so much after all.

"I'll have to call you back on that."

"Fine. You're a dear."

I fire up the Porsche and make a side trip while on my way to my great psychiatrist appointment. I go to see Bob. You know, of Bob's Guns.

While in there, I pick up a Smith and Wesson Ladysmith, the one with the wood grip (so appealing to women). I buy a body holster so that I can keep it next to me. Then because I'm in a shopping mood, I think what the hell, and spring for a twelve-gauge shotgun to boot. It's like Christmas in July. Picking out bullets reminds me of going through a Toys "R" Us.

I lean over the counter so Bob can see more than my cleavage.

"An Uzi," I say to him, certain that more firepower would be an aid in my present circumstances. "Full automatic," I add, having done my research.

Bob's eyes are fixed on my breasts. I let one of the straps of my dress slip a bit to the side.

"Sorry, babe," he says, his eyes wide but sad, and his hands clutched beneath the counter. "No can do. Major illegal weapon. You want to land me in jail?"

I slide around to the end of the counter and slip my dress strap farther down so he can see the real thing. I stare at his crotch. "But you know somebody, right? I'll pay. Cash."

He rubs his hand over my breast. I unzip his pants and reach in.

He starts breathing heavy. "There's a place in South Philly. I have their card."

I hear the door open and shut behind me. He looks over, his eyes half open. I stay where I am and keep it up as the other shopper browses in another part of the store. Bob is quick about it. I zip him up and pull my strap back in place.

He slips me a card.

"Don't tell anybody where you got this."

"Not a word."

I pack my new purchases into the Porsche and rip into the city to make my shrink appointment.

"Jeremy said you were hiding in the closet," she says.

"I wasn't hiding. I was sleeping."

"Why in the closet?"

"Seemed the best thing to do."

She scribbles something down on her pad.

"When did you first begin this behavior?"

I fidget, trying to think back.

"As a child?" she ventures.

God, you'd think they'd come up with something new every once in a while.

"I didn't have a childhood."

"Everybody has a childhood."

"I'm pretty sure I didn't."

She keeps probing here and there for some tidbit, some clue to my dementia. I'm beginning to think of her as a persistent poodle, which suddenly makes me wonder about Jeremy, who plays poker with his Harvard pals on Sunday afternoon. I get this sudden flash that maybe he's screwing Helen instead.

Go for it, Helen.

"So how did you meet Jeremy?"

"I had an appendectomy. We met in the hospital. I have a scar right here." I make a motion with my hand.

"Couldn't be," she says.

"That's what it was."

"It's on the wrong side. An appendectomy scar would be on your right side." She smiles at me, having won a point.

I ponder this information. "Maybe my appendix was on the wrong side. It wouldn't be the first time I was backwards in some way."

"I don't think so."

I reveal the scar to her, careful not to show any of the other nice marks.

"That's a jagged cut. Not surgical, unless your surgeon was drunk. Looks like a wound."

I'm really stumped. The rest of the interview is a waste.

She gives up and hands me a free packet of Prozac. "What did you do to your face?"

"I have a rash."

Helen makes an appointment for me in a week. On the way out, I ditch the Prozac.

While stewing about my famous scar and its being on the wrong side, I begin to whack things off my list. The first order of business is the bank. I use my Elizabeth Boone IDs to withdraw the whole pile of money from my account. Ben has a way of getting to things. And after last weekend, I have a suspicion that Ben isn't going to let me go anywhere if he can help it.

I have them put the lump sum in a bank check. Then I jump into my Porsche again and tool down to South Philly, averaging about ninety. I swing into the first bank I see and cash the check, having them put it in small bills. At the next bank, I keep five thousand out and dump the rest in a safety deposit box. I check the card Bob gave me and ask directions.

It's in one of the seediest neighborhoods I've been to for a long time. I walk in. Shopping in gun stores is like eating at McDonald's. You begin to feel at home. I take my time, asking lots of questions like some dumb chick. Then I reach in my purse and flash a big wad of bills.

"Uzi?" I say. "With all the extras."

The gun guy's an Asian man in his late sixties, I'd say. He has a heavy accent. "You cop?"

"Would a cop have a face looking like this?"

He frowns.

"It's my boyfriend." I begin to sniffle. "He threatened to kill me." I show him a couple welts.

He shakes his head, waves his hands, and starts talking to me in his native dialect. I think he's giving me a lecture.

"One week," he says. "You come back."

I bite my lip, wondering if it's a setup. But what would be worse, Ben or the cops?

"Okay," I say, turning to leave. Then I have a brilliant idea. As a matter of fact, given the present circumstances, I think it rates as one of the smartest things I've ever done.

"Fake IDs." I drop a fifty on the counter. "I need to blow town." He sits staring at me, his face unreadable.

Just as I'm thinking I should make a quick exit before he calls the cops, he writes out an address on a scrap of paper. I check the address and see that the place is just a block away. I thank him as I back out the door.

But I have to make another stop first. So I cruise the neighborhood until I find a beauty shop with bars over the windows and door. Inside, one whole wall has row upon row of fake heads with wigs. It looks like a night at the symphony.

Mandy and me found a wig and a toupee in a Dumpster behind the Beauty Box in town. It appeared as though some couple had to arrive in tandem to get their retreads. We tied the toupee to a string and hung it from a tree branch like it was a spider, and we used the wig at night when Vin, me, and Mandy did séances sitting by the river in the dark.

At night the river swells and grows in power, getting you to feel like you should just give up, lie down, and let it drag you off. It can throw up a thick fog or thin-layered mists. I'd lie awake in the two-room, hearing its low thunder, its wearing down the banks.

When I was little, sometimes I'd scare myself listening like that and take up crying. Mama would bend over me whispering, willow, willow wand, willow weep, willow song. She hummed like the night hummed. Mama stroked my head and cheek. Sleep, sleep. Wander the river and the river's long creep.

And the cool, she'd say, drawing it out long and low. And the cool, cool stream. The lily leaves floating.

I choose a blond wig. The hair falls shoulder length with a little bounce. The layered bangs tend to the side.

"That's some lip you got there, girlfriend," the store clerk says to me.

"He didn't like my hair."

I stick on my new hair and drive back to the address the gun guy gave me. It's a little copy and print shop run by some people of unknown Asian origin who look a lot like the man in the gun store. In the back room they have a camera. Half the money down and the other half when the IDs are ready.

"Two weeks, honey," she says to me.

"Two weeks? You're killing me."

"You want birth certificate? Two weeks."

As I'm breaking the speed limit right and left on my way back to Connecticut, I feel myself overhyped and bristling with weapons. I slide in a CD by Arvo Pärt. *Miserere.*

Miserere mei, I sing. Dies irae dies illie.

I learned music at Ben's. When we were working out with the weights and the machines, we'd turn up the volume and blast out everything from Metallica to Mozart. If any of us got out to do some shopping, the record store was always the first place on the agenda.

Kat was the one that turned me on to Arvo and Janice Joplin. A good mix, I think. About that time, Kat also handed me a copy of *To the Lighthouse* by Virginia Woolf. I learned revery. I learned sublime. From Virginia I learned of the brightness and the dark wedge. And after I read about the fin in the water, I was prepared for what followed.

Kat got so sick one day that Ben took her away. She never came back. Toni got AIDS. Then Violet came. Ben wouldn't let

Violet be, and his moods got bad. He kept the whips close at hand. His plays got more dangerous. The longer it went on, the more I clung to Violet, who, when all is said and done, was the stronger of us two.

I was willful and Ben whipped me regular for it, but Violet was smarter than me about these things. And she was determined to get out.

Oh, I loved her, I remember now (another chit) waking after a night of cuffs and whips to the smell of her hair and the warmth of her skin along my side. We became lovers. I waited for the moment when her eyes moved to me slow, like the way the river flowed, lazy in the heat, but forceful beneath. She hated Ben for whipping me. She hated the way he used me for his darkest shows.

He's in love with you, she'd say.

No, Violet. He rides me too hard.

She'd narrow her eyes.

You're not paying attention. I see his eyes when you walk by.

That's just Ben being Ben, I convinced myself.

We got to break out of here. Got to, Violet said.

I remember her voice. It had the ache of a sigh.

Just like I could learn the punches, she learned Ben's mind, his moods. She'd egg him into putting her in the box, just to see if she could. Just as he handed her pieces of food, she'd let go a look, a touch. She used me, parading my love of her in front of him daily, pushing him, sinking in barbs.

Those two were poison.

And watching Ben as I always did, as we all did for self-protection, I wondered how much he just played along with her, letting her dig herself in deeper.

Ben darkened. He growled. The plays got rough. I'd have to sit out some nights because my bruises were too bad. Clients didn't like the merchandise damaged before they got to it.

Another chit now. The night Ben went crazy like he had some form of the berserks.

We'd just finished a long play. I was still bound. Violet was
starting to undo my straps, and Jason was cleaning the floor.

Matt was bent over a table, strapped down. Ben let loose his
arms, but not his feet and neck. He held Matt's wrists tight.

"Everybody listen to what Matt has to say." He smiled that
bad smile and started pushing up on Matt's arms.

We froze.

Nothing, nothing, Matt said.

Tell them, Matty.

I'm sorry, Ben. Stop.

Ben kept pushing up. What for? Matt's arms were too high.

I cheated you, Ben. I did a trick in the park. I won't do it again.

He took a trick in the park. Ben laughed. He pushed up hard.
I heard a pop and a crack. Matt's arm was hanging loose, popped
out of the socket. And his screaming was bad enough to make
you shrink.

Ben jammed a gag in Matt's mouth. He lifted the other arm.
He was smiling big.

That was when Violet jumped Ben. He threw her off like he
was swatting a fly, and Violet smashed into the wall. Ben grabbed
her by the throat and lifted her off her feet. She hung up in the
air, struggling, her mouth and eyes wide. Ben pressed his thumbs
deeper. I yelled at him. He dropped her. Violet collapsed on the
floor, heaving, making a noise like her tongue was stuck in her
throat.

Don't touch him, yelled Ben, pointing at Matt. He left.

Jason slunk over and let me loose. We helped Violet up, grabbing onto each other, and backed slow out of that room.

My agent leaves a message. "*Time* wants the interview Thursday.
Pictures when your face clears."

I curse.

When Jeremy gets home, he wants to talk about Helen and
our appointment. Did it help? Was I sad? Were the drugs helping yet?

He's like a German shepherd panting at your thigh.

I finally tell him I want to go write. He's so proud of me, pulling myself out of my nervous breakdown.

While at my computer, I add to the "In the Taurus" list. I type in: Ladysmith. I peck out: shotgun and bullets.

The next morning, I start on my new program. At the spa I swim laps in the pool. After an hour, I lift weights. Then I do laps again and practice holding my breath.

I could always hold my breath the longest and by a long shot. Mandy was a lightweight in the breath-holding department.

We had a spot upriver where we tied a rope out over the water. It was a good ten-foot drop down.

The river curled in there, fattened out, and fell quiet. When you dropped off the rope, the water was hot on top, but before you knew it, you were down in something cold. I hated that cold underlayer, that shapeless ache below. I tried not to drop in too deep, but sometimes it reached up to get me.

We had a long week of rain from some hurricane that petered out before it hit the coast. The river was running full, lapping up near the two-room, and the next days beat on us hateful with the sun, so that all we could do was faint down in the shade of the willows in the afternoon. That's when we decided to swing the rope.

It's good I went first because of my breath thing. Down below, the river was tough. It wouldn't let go, dragging me on. The undercurrent. Once I broke surface, I had to ride it all the way to Fowler. I trudged out of the eddy, water-soaked and scared clean through.

Maybe it was just water in my ears. But when I was down there thrashing mindless and struggling to get back up, I'm sure I heard that river laugh. It reminded me of Daddy.

He laughed when he started hitting. And sometimes people laughed at Mama behind her back. She was about as wide as she was tall and always carrying her bags of garbage.

At night, I'd get Mama to sit down in our one stuffed chair, and I'd rub her neck, singing her the songs they taught us in school. She loved that.

I loved Mama, even though she was fat. After she burned up, I pretended that she was light, just a breath of air, that I could carry her around, that I could lift her up and set her in the tops of the willows where the leaves shone silver.

When Mama and Vin were gone and I was alone, I'd jump down in that river and hold my breath, sinking into that shapeless ache, staying as long as I could. I promised myself that I'd get used to it, that nothing would touch me ever again.

In my head, I start trying to compose my letter to Jeremy.

Dear Jeremy.

No.

Dearest.

Oh, God, how can you lie like a rug in a suicide letter?

It'll come to me.

After my workout Wednesday morning, I drive to the hospital where Jeremy and I had our synchronicity thing. I show my Clarisse Broder ID and ask to see the records of my stay five years ago.

It takes awhile.

The receptionist returns with a wad of papers newly printed out. I find what I'm looking for about five pages back. I read the diagnosis.

"Knife wound. Lower-left side."

This chit could eat you alive. I've grown attached to my appendectomy.

After that, I drive to the garage where I've parked the Taurus. I open the back and pack in the loaded shotgun and a box of shells. I keep checking to make sure that my scar is on the left side. Maybe I've been wrong about it all these years.

Thursday comes with me all messed in the head about the interview with *Time*. I don't know why I bother.

"You write a lot about your childhood."

"Not *my* childhood," I say.

"Off the record, how did you get that rash?"

And here I was thinking it was going away real nice. I become self-conscious. "It's something I ate."

"Tell me about *your* childhood."

I shift around. "Like what?"

"Where were you born?"

I think fast. "Ohio" is all I can come up with on the spur of the moment.

"Where in Ohio?"

I don't know a thing about Ohio, so I say, "I forget." My lying capabilities waned after the age of five.

"You forget?"

"Yeah," I say, on a roll. "Too traumatic. My therapist says I'm not supposed to talk about it. Just thinking about it gives me a rash."

"It's always that way with artists, isn't it?"

"What, the rash?"

"The sensitivity, the dark underbelly of life."

Honey, what I could tell you about the dark underbelly. Some of those dark underbellies are well-known public figures.

Ben and I were at the reception the night of my fake appendectomy because of the Senator. At Ben's, he asked for me special, always having me in manacles and bent over. Ben would make an appearance at public functions every now and then to give certain clients a scare, to hold a little sway. I guess that's why Ben never had any problems with the cops.

But the cop at the hospital, when I was still restrained and half out of my mind with a hunger for smack, that cop kept asking me about Ben.

"I'm Ekker's girl," I said over and over.

"Some people say you aren't," he said. "On the street, some people say you're Ben's girl."

"What difference does it make?" I said. "I had an appendectomy."

He frowned.

Detective Bates. That was his name.

"Did you know this girl?" He showed me a picture that made me want to throw up. I didn't look at her face. I didn't want to see it.

"No! I don't know her. Shit!" I fought the straps. "I had an appendectomy. I fell down the stairs."

He left me his card. "I'd be careful, if I were you," he said. "You're in water over your head."

As though I could do anything at all about the water I was in.

Detective Bates showed up a couple more times, wanting to show me the pictures, but I refused to look. He stopped coming.

Which is really weird because on Friday after I return home from doing my hours of laps and holding my breath, there he is standing on my doorstep. I park the Porsche and meet him at the front door.

He's not much taller than me and must be twice my weight, but he carries it funny for a man. He looks padded all over, like someone has taped pillows front, back, and sides, from shoulders to waist. He's got the round face of a choirboy with the angelic part having disintegrated in bits. I guess because of carrying around too many pictures like the ones he tried to show me at the hospital.

"Mrs. Boone," he says, holding out his hand. His clothes look like he balls them up in the bottom of his closet for a month or so until they're just right.

"Broder," I say. "It's Broder." He almost got me there. I don't take his hand. "You know, you could benefit from a night course on ironing."

He gets a smile somewhat like Ben's. "Funniest thing," he says. "I found an old mug shot. Looks a lot like you, with the name Elizabeth Boone." He shows it to me.

Oh yeah. I forgot to say I spent a couple of days in jail for shoplifting. Ben locked me in the box for that.

"So what do you want?" I say.

"Can I come in?"

I smile. Coffee, tea, or me? He follows me into our nicely appointed living room, taking a moment to stare up into the three-story entry, arched over by the winding stair and pouring with sunlight. I offer him a chair and wince as he sits in it. I hope he at least cleans his mangled clothes.

"Why don't you look at these pictures now," he says.

I don't say anything.

"You wouldn't want anybody to find out about your past, would you now, Mrs. Broder? Can I call you Beth?"

I stare straight through him.

He shows me the first photo. It's a woman in a Dumpster. A blanket has been pulled away from her body and she's lying on her back. There's a smile across her stomach and out of that, some of her guts are pouring out. Her neck has a line along it. The head is near cut off. Her face is covered with a red-stained towel.

I try not to flinch. I've had a good amount of practice at not flinching. But the picture gets to me.

He hands me the next. It's a close-up of her face.

A dead face doesn't look quite like a living face. You can see a resemblance, but the face is missing some element that binds it into one, making it alive.

"You know her," he says.

"No."

"Are you sure?"

He's in my face now. I throw the picture at him. "I told you no. Now get out of here."

He gathers his photographs and slides them in his case. "Tape can be nasty stuff," he says. "Makes the skin raw."

I turn away so that I don't try to strangle him.

"Be careful, Miss Boone. Very deep water."

I want to make a crack about how long I can hold my breath, but I feel too sick.

After he leaves, I close the front door and lean against it, sliding down. I cry like a baby. I keep seeing those small breasts.

Those lips so pure, so chaste. The dead face, beaten badly. The face that used to belong to Violet.

I'm wishing I had the Prozac now.

Upstairs, I fill our tub that's big enough for six and settle in for a long soak. I sink down, counting one to five, checking how many minutes until I come up for air. I curl on the bottom, pretending I'm dead and that everyone has forgotten me. Oh, for a memory wiped clean.

Miserere mei.

After my bath, I write a note to Jeremy:

> Left town. Needed some space. Be back in a couple of days. Your adoring wife,
>
> Clarisse

Jesus, the things I do.

I rifle my blouses and skirts in a closet that's as big as a living room. I choose a blouse made of cobalt silk and tuck it into a luscious blue print midlength skirt with a slit up the side. After I'm dressed, I sit in front of my mirror, blotting out what remains of my rash with makeup.

Now my head is starting to spin with the push, the need to get the hell away from here, and my memory of the pictures of Violet.

I ride the commuter to Penn Station, arriving a little before five. The limo is waiting. Just the sight of that car freaks me into high gear as I float, my body going along on automatic pilot.

The muscular hunk of a driver opens the door. I slide in. Ben's two girls are inside. The larger one apologizes and slips a hood over my head.

We drive for a bit. Then the other girl says to me, lie down across the seat on your back.

I comply, lying with my knees up.

Take hold of the armrest, she says, grasping my wrists and

raising them above my head. Then the girl leans over me, raising the hood enough to kiss me. The other begins fondling me.

Ben has this theory about men. He says that a man can smell a woman in heat, that it draws him, gets hold of his eyes, brain, and you know what else. That's why he always has the players "prepped" before they go into the plays.

So they work me up, one of them admiring my skirt, wanting to know where I bought it. How much? Could she try it on?

By the time we arrive, I'm well prepped and shaking. We go into a room. One of them removes the hood.

Lying out on a bed replete with straps is a leather corset, gorgeous calfhide boots that look to go over the knee, elbow-length leather gloves, and a whip.

"You're so lucky," the smaller one says as she begins to undress me. "I've always wanted to wear boots like these."

Ben taught me how to use a whip, taking me under his wing. He always complained that I didn't have a thirst.

You've got to love the tip of the whip, he said. You've got to want it to leave its best mark.

It never appealed to me. Kat now, she was ripe when she had a whip in her hand. But when she disappeared, Ben needed a woman who could handle one well. Clients were always clamoring for it. Mostly men. And with the mood I was in, I thought I might enjoy this play more than I did before.

The corset cups cradle the lower half of my breasts, leaving the nipples exposed and pushing the breast up, rounding it, making it full. The boots are enough to die for, supple and soft, with lacing at the top.

After I'm gloved, I pick up the whip and practice a few strikes against the wall.

There are some things you never forget.

The smaller of the girls says, "Ben says you're supposed to practice on me." Her eyes are round and wet. Dewy. Like a fawn.

Ben made me practice on Violet before. That's when I really started to hate him and began to listen to Violet's constant chatter about getting out. But the thought of being free in the world scared me. It reminded me of houses burned down, of mothers roasted alive, of being hungry for days. I suspected there were other things even worse to know.

So I practiced on Violet, and it pleased Ben. After I was done, he'd take me to one of the playrooms and make love to me. I never could figure it out. And as he worked his magic hands, lips, and penis on me, I worried about Violet, anxious to get back to her. Sometimes he'd keep me with him there the rest of the day, tying me down and feeding me, making over me.

He loves you, Violet would repeat after Ben brought me back upstairs. I just felt my head go blank as I laid her on her stomach and tended the welts I'd given her.

I stare at this young girl as she removes her top and crouches down for me. I wish that I would go blind. Then I pace around her in circles, working her over good, growing more hateful with each strike, remembering Detective Bates' pictures and Violet's beaten face.

Someone calls on the intercom and says that they're ready. They hood me and lead me to another room. The hood comes off. I'm in a small room with a one-way mirror. Ben is standing near, looking into the adjoining room. He pats my ass.

The door to the other room flies open, and in come Ben's two brutes pulling along a guy who keeps himself in good shape. His hands are tied in front. He's naked from the waist up and barefoot, with a hood on his head and manacles on his ankles. They hook his hands above, raising them until he's stretched out.

"Anesthesiologist," says Ben. "I guess he's doing this instead of playing golf. It's his first time, so give him his money's worth."

He squeezes my ass.

I wait, letting the young doctor hang for a bit. For some reason, the fact that he's an anesthesiologist really bugs me. He begins to squirm, so I curl my whip in my hand and enter the room.

I walk around him slow, dropping his pants down to his knees. "Little shit," I say. "You fucked up. Now you're going to get what you deserve." By the way, I want to say, could a person have an appendectomy on the left side?

Unrolling my whip, I find my distance and stance and go to work on him. And something about those pictures flares up in me. For the first time, I want this fucking man to feel the bite. I want him to suffer. Goddamn anesthesiologist.

I walk around, grab the top of the hood, and yank it off, standing back so he can see me in all my leather glory. His eyes go bright with lust. Sliding the whip around his neck, I stand nose to nose with him. His eyes are wan with desire. After a few more whacks he doesn't take long, erupting and making a mess as I'm getting in a final lick. I stand silent as he wilts down, trembles, and hangs harder on his hands.

Then I turn and glare into the mirror, throwing the whip down, knowing Ben's back there, watching. Smiling.

When Jeremy first brought me home from the hospital, I wouldn't go out of doors. He thought that a little strange, me being twenty-six and all, but he'd had so much practice with coaxing strays that he worked his dog talents on me.

Jeremy used words and phrases like "T-bonds" or "buying futures." That one always stumped me. How the hell can you buy a future? And I'm thinking that if the past weren't so great, why the hell would you bother?

Once Jeremy got me to leave the house, we went out to eat almost every night. I cut dainty bites from wet, rippling hunks of beef. I scooped out my potatoes. And I thought of all my leavings gathering into one place, all those red fatty hanks of leftover meat and green stuff too rotten to eat, all filling up Dumpsters in a row.

Paradise.

After Jeremy taught me to drive, there was no stopping me. And I learned to manage a house and how to cook. Kat had taught me some cooking basics at Ben's. But now I pushed on cantaloupes. I could choose a peach, thump an eggplant, and squeeze an artichoke. I had a talent for it.

I was picky about my shrimp, the white sauce for the crab, the beluga, the foie gras, the morel dressing for the veal.

That's what I'm thinking of now as I look back at that anesthesiologist's white, whipped ass. Veal. I pick up the hood from the floor and fit it over his head again.

"Come back and see me," I whisper in his ear. He quakes a little at the thought of it. Then I pick up my whip and head for the door.

No one's there. I sit in a chair and wait. Eventually, the boys come and take the anesthesiologist out.

I'm thinking about the people in Rivertown all frozen in place. I wonder about being frozen and if it's better to watch the tooms or be stacked in them.

The girl I whipped earlier comes in the room. In her hand is Ben's black bag.

"I'm sorry," she says.

You're sorry, I think. Why you?

She reaches in the bag and takes out a collar, then walks behind me, fitting it around my neck and buckling it on.

She's sorry?

Then she returns in front of me and removes my gloves and boots, kissing my fingers and feet.

The whole world's sorry. One great big fucking sorry.

Violet haunts. She swims the air.

"Turn around in the chair," the fawn says, her voice just as one might imagine coming from so gentle a creature as a young deer.

I turn and lean onto the chair back, exhausted by the dangers.

Once she's removed my corset, she rubs my shoulders and back like Violet would do after Ben had worked me for too long. She kisses down along my spine, again like Violet. Ben has prepared her for me.

"Another play already?" I say.

"Shh."

I wait, feeling myself respond to her as I would to Violet. She gently takes both my wrists, cuffing them together in back. Now a blindfold is placed over my eyes.

She stands me up, leading me back into the room where the smell of the good doctor permeates. I hear the motor run and feel her put the hook in the ring of my collar. She raises it enough to keep me standing straight.

Now she goes into high gear, caressing me, fondling, kissing. So much like Violet, worming her way through my tough outer layers, the ones that made me so hard to crack.

I want to love this dew-eyed fawn. I want my blindness. I want to be deaf.

I see how well he has her trained, how refined her gifts, and why Ben chose the fawn to do this to me. She goes up on her tiptoes and kisses me on my lips. Then she leaves me. I hear the ticking of her hoofed feet retreating.

Now I wait. I know that Ben will come next. It's his style. I've been prepped, ripe for his play on me.

The door opens and closes again. Someone circles me. A hand runs along my shoulders.

I've never seen you so beautiful as when you walked through that lobby last week, says Ben. You've gotten better.

He keeps circling, running one hand around my waist.

I want you to come back, Beth. I've missed you.

You can take me back any time you please. I can't stop you.

No. I want you to come to me. That other life isn't for you. This is where you belong.

I'm too old, Ben. I wouldn't last.

Not for the plays. For me.

I shiver, remembering what Violet said. He loves you. Then I think of the picture of the Dumpster, of the blanket drawn back.

Give me time, Ben. I'm not ready.

Oh, you're ready.

He grasps both my breasts from behind. I lie my head against his chest. He slides one hand down between my legs.

You were meant for me. I loved you the first time I saw you.

He continues with his hands, knowing me so well. My legs start to shake.

Ben moves around me like a whisper and he slides down and then up, guiding in his penis. Then his hands slip down my sides and back to my ass, one hand beneath each cheek. He lifts me up and begins to thrust.

I feel poverty. He is starved for me. If I had been Violet, I would have smiled, would have known my power over him, would have made him pay.

Instead, I am riveted by his need and by his power over me. He pulls me tight against him, my body so full of pleasure, I think I might shatter. Ben comes, holding me off the floor, quaking, which sends me over the edge. I come then, shuddering against his body.

He keeps me like that until I have wilted upon him, my cheek resting along his chest. Then he sets me down, kissing me over my face, his big hands on both sides of my chin.

I'm stymied and dull with pleasure as I hear him walk behind me to the other room. When he comes back, he stands silent for a long time.

What did you do with the money? he says.

What money?

Don't fuck with me, Beth. I don't want to hurt you. I never liked hurting you. But I will if I have to.

My eyes shoot back and forth, trying to clear my head.

I gave it to my brother, I say.

Your brother. Now he paces, slapping something in his hand. I know that sound. It's his length of rubber hose. He whacks me hard on the side.

Don't lie to me, Beth. I can smell a lie.

Whack.

He found me, Ben. From the book, the novel. Those stories were our stories, from when we were kids. He needed money.

Whack. Whack. Along my back and shoulders.

I'm not lying, Ben. I don't have the money.

Whack just beneath my breasts.

Now he stops. I can feel it coming, like when a wind hits the trees far off, then tosses the ones nearer, shooting dust in front. I can see it as clear as if my eyes were uncovered. I don't turn. I don't let it fall light. I want him to break my face.

His fist slams into my nose. I lose balance and begin to choke as the collar tightens on the hook. I get my feet back under me and ease off the pressure.

Kill me, I scream. Fucking kill me. Go on.

His big arms grab me like I'm nothing, and in one movement he jerks me off the hook, throwing me into the wall. I catch most of it on my shoulder, then slide to the floor. Before I know what's going on, he's shoved me into the hall and is dragging me by the collar, then getting me on my feet and pushing me in front. He shoves and drags me up a flight of stairs.

Lying on the landing, I kick out in the direction where I hear keys going into a lock. A door opens.

It was some fucking client of yours, wasn't it, Ben? Who was it? Who the fuck did it?

I force myself up on my knees. He shakes me. You're not making any sense.

Ben hits me in the face again and I take the floor hard, lying there woozy. He grabs my ankles and drags me through the door into a room with carpeting.

Violet, I say, tasting the blood running out my nose. Who cut her so bad? You know, don't you?

He's fiddling with something. You're a crazy bitch, he says. Maybe this will teach you not to lie to me.

I hear a padlock open. He pulls a door back, then he drags me over and sits me inside. It's a very snug fit. My knees are up to my chest, my feet against the back of my thighs.

The door slams shut. He clicks the padlock together. I piss all over the floor of the box, and I sit in it, thinking about Dumpsters and stacks of the dead.

4

Brooklyn Bridge

Ben had a simple setup that he called the rail. He had several rails spread throughout the warehouse. You were tied with your hands above your head, so that you leaned just a bit forward, the rail hitting at the hips. It was Ben's form of a whipping post.

There was only one box. Ben kept it in the middle of our living space upstairs. The box was narrow, just wide enough for shoulders and hips. To fit into it, the boys had to bend their heads down. I doubt Ben could have packed himself into the thing.

One side had hinges on the bottom and a hasp at the top with a padlock. He would leave the key on the top of the box as a reminder. We weren't allowed to touch it no matter how much the person locked inside screamed.

I sit in a puddle of piss, the muscles in my back and thighs cramping. Panic hits like a Mack truck. I try to stay calm. I try to breathe slow, but I'm losing ground.

Hours pass. At first I hear muffled voices and a TV. Then silence surrounds like a solid, pressing thing. Through my thighs and the bottoms of my feet, I sense the trains roving underground like flies buzzing the river. And the hum of the city is the river's thunder, pounding against banks saturated by rain.

The ghosts are near, but I fight them off, drowsing at times, losing track. My thighs have cramped for so long that I don't feel the pain anymore. A deadness has crept from my ass as far as my waist. My hands and arms went numb a long time ago.

I think that I piss again, but I can't tell for sure.

I keep telling myself to wait, to breathe, but I'm getting flashes of light so bright that they bite my eyes, turned in, filled with their own form of death.

Violet comes to me. She strokes my head. She kisses the lumps Ben left on me and wipes the blood off my lip. We kiss and kiss. I've forgotten how sweet, how like food and water she is to me, her beaten face strange and wonderful to my eyes.

You are lovely, I whisper. Lovely.

When you hear the person in the box whispering, you know pretty soon, they're going to be screaming.

Violet raises my face, kissing me long and with care. Sigh no more, she says. Then I see her falling away, disappearing.

Blackness rises up beneath and engulfs. I remember this blackness from before and am ready to go. Wipe memory clean, I plead. Wipe it away.

I don't know why I start screaming. I just do.

Silence drops again. I wait. Someone starts to cry.

Kat comes to me. I've been lying on a floor, drenched in blood. Her face is older than I remember, but she's still so beautiful. Others come and carry me out. Then I'm wrapped in a blanket and riding in the backseat of a car. I see a soaking wet spot at my side.

Faces look down at me. Hands lift me out of the car and onto a gurney. I'm not strapped down, but I can't move. My body is sticky all over.

Kat stays in place, but I am gliding away.

Rivertown comes, high on the rise. I see the live oak arching, the mimosa spreading out to cover. And my people wait, shining, the blue sky behind.

*   *   *

I feel them lifting me out of the box. They lie me on my side and let loose my hands. The blindfold and collar are removed.

"Jesus, she pissed in here."

"What do you expect? He left her in there too long."

They leave me and go about their business. I don't move. I don't even open my eyes.

The fawn kneels beside and kisses me on the cheek. "Beth," she says. "Wake up."

I ignore her. If I have to move or speak, I think I'll go mad.

She pulls me onto my back. "Beth." She runs her fingers through my hair. I open my eyes a slit. "I have food," she says. "And something to drink."

She helps me to lean back against a couch, then wraps my fingers around a bottle of water. I raise it to my mouth, missing at first. The fawn guides it to my lips.

After I eat a bowl of mashed potatoes, she hands me another bottle. "What day?" I say.

"Sunday," she says. "Early."

"God."

"You need a bath," she says. "Finish your water."

I suck down the second bottle like it's nothing.

"You've got a play coming later."

"God, no." My vocabulary appears to have gone to shit in the last who knows how many hours.

"Come on." She coaxes me like Jeremy. I crawl on my hands and knees, following her into the bathroom. When the tub is full, she helps me to settle in, then goes away.

My head is splitting from the punch to my nose, which is fattened and still leaking a drop at a time through the clots in each nostril. My face is tender from my lip to my forehead. I think again about buying futures. Seems a mistake to me.

Ben arrives. He's dressed in a black silk shirt, gray Armani suit pants, and Italian shoes.

"You might as well kill me," I say. "I can't take this."

He stoops beside the sunken tub. "It's almost over, Beth. Not much longer. One more play."

He leaves. I soak for a long time, sinking down and holding my breath, letting the minutes go by, pushing the limit on how long I can stay under.

When I'm done, I drag myself out and lie on the tile in the sun. I fall asleep.

I wake when the boys come in with a wide belt and manacles. They help me to stand, very friendly with me as they chain me up. They chatter away about some baseball game they've been watching on TV. The boys appear to have gotten over cleaning up my puddle of piss.

One fits the belt around my waist, covering my now famously erroneous scar. The other pulls a chain through the ring in the front of the belt so that it moves freely. They manacle my wrists and ankles, attaching them with locks to each end of the chain. Another in a long series of hoods is fit over my head and a collar is buckled in place. I hobble along as they lead me out.

In the room they take me to, they have me climb onto a cold metal table on hands and knees. Nice doggie, one says. Good girl, the other adds.

Oh, God. Not that.

They leave.

Before long the door opens and someone comes in. The door shuts.

What do you think? says Ben.

I feel hands stroking my back as though petting, then rubbing my ass. The hands check the tightness of the collar.

I don't like a hood, the man says. You know I like to admire their markings.

I stop breathing. I know that voice.

Not this one, says Ben. She's still in training. We have to keep the hood on. See? She was bad. We had to beat her.

I would have figured out who it was right off, if I had ever had a clue about it. But I wasn't thinking along those lines. I didn't know how good Ben was working me.

The man touches the marks where Ben beat me.

She's got good in her though, he says. I can see it.

That's all I need. Good old "the world is a happy place" Jeremy. Jesus. And I thought he was using Sunday afternoons to screw Helen.

My view of the world, the planet in general, the universe, and my very hazy idea of a weak and bumbling God, all of it crashes in with a lot of noise and dust. If you can't figure Jeremy, you can't figure anything.

I had already decided that I wasn't going to see the light of day again, that Ben was going to keep me this time. Jeremy's presence here cinched it for me. Good old synchronicity. Good old Mr. Bubbly. Arf, Arf.

I wonder how long Ben cultivated him. I imagine Ben and Jeremy sitting together in the Grill Room at the Four Seasons, Ben eventually getting Jeremy to confess his deepest fantasies. Rather embarrassing for your deepest fantasy to come out looking like this.

Ben. Ben. Ben. I hadn't thought about him for five years, and the whole time he was busy preparing himself for just this moment.

Gotcha!

Jeremy's petting me again, stroking me. If I had a tail, I'd wag.

God, if I'd only known. I could have saved him a lot of trouble. And money.

She's a beautiful dog, Ben. Do you have a leash?

Ben clips one on my collar and hands the end to Jeremy. This seems to really get Jeremy cranking. I can hear him walking around, taking me in. How, after five years, can he not recognize me? Oh well. So much for marriage. He tugs the leash a little.

Sit.

I try not to laugh.

Sit, he says again in a stern voice.

I sit.

Lie down.

God, what a fucking gas. I crouch. I'd pant if he could see my face.

I wish he'd hand me a bit of food. Maybe if I didn't have on the hood, he would. Maybe he comes to these little appointments at Ben's with his napkin-wrapped scraps to give as rewards.

Jeremy eventually gets down to business. He finishes fast. Jeremy always finishes fast. I expect him to ask me how it was.

Oh yes, Jeremy, yes, yes.

Good old Jeremy, paying a small fortune to screw his wife doggie-style. T-bonds make it possible. Of all the futures you might want to buy, this one seems to me a silly choice.

I'm starting to chuckle, a little of the berserks coming over me.

How's Clarisse? asks Ben.

Oh she's fine. A little stressed. Nervous breakdown. Women have them all the time. The Prozac should help.

Good, says Ben as he opens the door to show Jeremy out. I hear them chatting as they walk down the hall.

Shuffling through a Dumpster one day, I found part of a broken cup. Painted in the glaze was the tip of a tree limb hanging over a small house. So I spent the whole afternoon sifting through the trash until I thought I had the whole cup.

The next day at school, I lifted a tube of glue. I worked on that cup all evening.

I discovered dragons wrapping their tails around the side. The tree was in full blossom and underneath it a woman was walking, holding an umbrella. I worked and worked on it. After I was done, all I had was a cracked-up mess with glue dried on in blotches.

I had been going to give it to Miss Summers, but I knew she'd give me that look that made me feel stupid.

That's when I learned that if something's broke, no matter

how fine it is, you got to let it be. It's best to get rid of the pieces so they don't always remind you of things, stuffing your heart with mud and the smell of the laybacks. They have their own special stink. If you're worried about that kind of thing, it's best to edge around.

When Ben comes back, I'm lying on my back on the doggie table, my head splitting from my battered nose. He lifts me in his arms like I'm a baby and carries me into what turns out to be his rooms.

Ben removes my chains and unhoods me. I look around in amazement. I've never been in here before. He has a small kitchen, a bath, a living room, and a bedroom. It's downright common.

Ben hands me yet another bottle of Gatorade, which I consume, watching as he goes into the kitchen and boils pasta. After it's done, he mixes it with a white sauce, puts salad in bowls, opens wine, and serves me dinner. I walk to the bedroom, taking in his view over Manhattan. Then I wrap a blanket around me.

After I sit down to eat, Ben walks behind me and folds the blanket down from my shoulders, revealing my breasts. He sits opposite, keeping his eyes on me.

We're silent. Frankly, I don't know what to say. If I'd been with Jeremy and a pair of his friends and their wives, we would have prattled on inane and batty about lawns and weedkillers. We might have moaned like idiots about our maids. The guys would have gone off together, trying to cream each other with their latest stock market numbers.

What do you say to the guy who just a day or so ago screwed and beat you? And then locked you in a box, for God's sakes. For me, it has a nice family feel.

I push back my plate. "Have you got some aspirin? I feel like shit. I think I need to lie down."

Ben leads me to his bed without saying a word. He folds back the duvet and sheet. I lie down and he actually brings me some aspirin.

Now he undresses and joins me, turning me to him and kissing me, not asking, as though I belong to him. I guess I do. We make love like we're married, for God's sakes. I have to admit, Ben is an excellent screw, but I've had enough of him for a good long while. I've had enough semen for awhile, too.

I fall asleep in his arms, trying to keep the ghosts back, seeing the dangers whizzing inside my head.

When I wake, I hear him moving nearby. He's already dressed. My headache has spread down into my neck. My nose burns if I try to breathe, which appears to be a necessary function. I see my blue skirt and blouse folded over a chair, but Ben hands me some jeans and a T-shirt, socks and a pair of sneakers.

"Clean up and get dressed," he says.

I'm looking forward to the life we're going to have together. All the fun, the freedom, the broken ribs.

After I'm dressed, we eat a light breakfast.

"The Jeremy thing was a nice touch," I say, trying to chat.

He wipes his mouth with his napkin, showing just a hint of that smile. "The driver will drop you at home," he says. "Get what you need from the house and bring me the money that you cleared out of your account last Tuesday. Finish things with Jeremy. The driver will pick you up at five this evening. If you don't show, we'll find you." He has his smile on full now. "And you know what I'll do when they bring you back."

I try to hide my joy. Oh blessed moment. Agnus dei.

He takes me to the limo with his big arm wrapped around me. The driver opens the door. Before I get in, I turn to him.

"You owe me one thing, Ben. Who was it? Which fucking client of yours cut Violet?"

He turns me around and sits me in the car. Before he slams the door, he leans close and says, "You should know, Beth. You were there."

The limo stops in front of my house. It's Monday morning again. Another wasted weekend. Once inside, I watch the limo edge away from the curb and disappear around a corner.

This is it. My last chance. Today is the day.

I stumble up the stairs, still weak, and bumble into my studio. The answering machine is blinking. I think, what the hell, and punch the button. The first message is from my agent. She called me on Sunday. What gall. Doesn't she know it's the day of rest?

She tells me I have a book signing next week.

Not on your life.

The second is from Jeremy. "Honey, if you get home today, give me a call. We all miss you so much."

Little fucker.

I flip through my disks and take out the one with my most recent stories. I clean out the shoebox, slipping Ben's card in my pocket. It's so hard to let go.

I sweep the room with my eyes.

Good-bye. Go to hell.

Making for the refrigerator in the kitchen, I chug some orange juice.

The doorbell rings.

Dropping on all fours, I crawl into the living room. I spy out the window, seeing the angel-faced Detective Bates standing at my door holding his ugly briefcase.

He rings again. I wait. He dawdles on the way to his car, then gets in, cranking the engine. As the Chevy pulls away, I breathe a sigh of relief. But then he stops and backs into a side street, parking at a place where he has a clear view of my house.

Shit.

I go back upstairs and pull up my two lists on the computer, trying to memorize them. Then I run downstairs, grabbing my purse and a black windbreaker. I make for the garage.

Sitting in the Porsche, I search my purse, removing the switchblade and slipping it in a side pocket of the nice jeans Ben gave me. Then I open my billfold and take out the Elizabeth Boone IDs, stuffing them in a back pocket with Ben's card. Just for fun, I put my Clarisse Broder calling card in with them and the Katherine Benson Social Security card. I wouldn't want to make too clean a break. In the other back pocket, I put a few dollars and some change.

I punch the garage door button and rev the Porsche all in the same moment, shooting out. Tires squeal as I throw it into first and race off. In my rearview mirror, I see Detective Bates fumbling around. I laugh.

After making sure I've lost him, I hit the mall. I'm not mall-inclined in general, but today I need speed. I purchase a pair of black jeans and a black T-shirt. Then I go on a small buying spree, picking up some clothes and toiletries, including a bottle of extra-strength Tylenol and a pile of CDs.

Back in the Porsche, I ride the turnpike into Jersey, arriving in Philly just after noon. I park in front of my favorite print shop and slap on my wig.

"Not ready," the motherly Asian woman says when I approach the counter. I take off my sunglasses so she can see the bridge of my nose and my two black eyes.

"It's an emergency," I say.

She makes a little bow and disappears into the back. I hear a squabble of dialect punctuated, I imagine, by the waving of arms.

She returns. "Half hour. No birth certificate."

While I'm waiting, I jog to the gun store. The Uzi is the most beautiful metal object I've ever seen, and I'm flabbergasted by the amount of money the gun guy wants for it. I shell it out. I'm thinking about Ben.

For a little added firepower, I have him throw in a nine-millimeter semiautomatic pistol. Now I'm pumping.

Back at the print shop, my IDs are ready. Rebecca Cynthia Cross. Maybe my luck will change if I get away from the B names. Rebecca is a blonde. They're supposed to have more fun.

I pay the woman full price even though I don't get the birth certificate. She smiles and bows. I bow back, wishing life was just a series of easy bows.

Now I hit the bank and clean out the safety deposit box,

stuffing the cash in the gun bag (which has a smiley face on it, by the way). I pick up some lunch, forcing myself to eat.

Back in the Porsche, I see it's about two in the afternoon. My hands shake when I think of Ben and what will happen if he catches up with me. I tool back to New York, crossing into Manhattan through the Holland Tunnel. Then I get stopped dead in rush-hour traffic.

I check the clock. Five forty-five. Ben's in a stew by now. I can see the van roaring toward suburbia, filled with cuffs and hoods. I shiver.

After the traffic starts to move, I make for the Brooklyn Bridge, cruising in the slow lane. Once off the bridge, I park at the ferry and check the shoreline. Not so good. The seawalls are formidable. I peruse the little restaurant next to that. It has a dock and a small stair, but it makes me nervous. I enter the state park and stare up at the bridge from below.

Uh-oh. It's a hell of a long drop.

I return to my waiting Porsche and rip back into Manhattan, thinking about the pictures from Bates' briefcase, and Ben with his rubber hose. Then there's Jeremy and his dog routine. I'm not sure I care about anything.

Maybe life is just watching the tooms. Maybe that's who I am, a toom watcher. And they keep stacking while I'm watching, never moving, never crying.

I open the garage where my Taurus is parked and dump my purchases in the backseat, taking out the black jeans and T-shirt. I change clothes. Then I stuff my two S&W's under the front driver's seat. I stick the semiautomatic in the glove box and the Uzi beneath the front passenger seat with several boxes of bullets. I hide my bag of money in a compartment in the trunk.

One last thing. I get out my Rebecca Cross IDs, my Elizabeth Boone IDs, my Clarisse Broder calling card, the Katherine Benson card, Ben's business card, my disk of stories, and the handful of folded papers, stashing everything in the glove box over the pistol.

I might start having identity problems.

It's seven in the evening.

I wait.

I'm beginning to get comfortable when I remember that I left that stupid disk with the Taurus and Porsche lists in my computer, ready to be viewed by the next person opening the program.

I scream. I pound my head on the steering wheel, making my headache ripple out into my elbows.

Maybe no one will figure it out. Maybe . . .

I think of the ardent Detective Bates.

Ben comes to mind.

I fire up the Porsche and head back north, toward the suburbs.

Violet started making plans. One day in the park while she was walking Buster, she met some guy named Slim, of all things. Violet could suck a person in. It was her one true talent, showing itself in so many varied and ingenious ways.

The plan that she hatched was that Slim and a friend would contact Ben and reserve a night. They would ask for two girls. They'd bring guns and act like they were kidnapping us.

As easy as that, we'd be free. Then we'd give them our piles of money that Ben kept for us in the bank. Ben always told us it was like a retirement fund. He provided such nice employment benefits.

I had a bad feeling about the plan from the beginning. And I remember Violet the night before our plan was supposed to go. I remember us lighting our candle and turning our glass. I was sick afraid of Ben, like I am now, driving through the neighborhoods.

I park about three blocks behind the house. It's ten thirty-five. I cut through the lawns, dashing from bush to bush like they do in the cartoons. Making a beeline for the back corner of our yard, I crouch among the blue spruce and watch the house for a long time. Then I slink along the side of the garage, looking up and down the road in front. I don't see a thing.

I wish I had a cup to turn over.

Gliding to the garage door in back, I key in the alarm code and unlock the door. I slide in fast and hold still, waiting for my eyes to adjust to the dark. Now I key the alarm at the door to the house. I open that door and slip in, shutting it behind. I sit quietly between the kitchen cabinets on either side, waiting and listening, thinking I hear voices, but I'm not sure.

Crawling along the floor, I leave the kitchen and enter the hall. I'm almost to the winding stairs when I see a man standing inside the front door, holding the curtain back with one hand and staring out at the road. In his other hand is a gun. I curse my lack of firepower.

I back away.

Now I'm more cautious, hitting the back stairs, which are carpeted. I run up silently, getting that floaty feeling like I did before my weekends with Ben. While waiting and watching at the top of the stairs, I hear voices. I look down the hall, which bends to the left and heads toward the master bedroom. A light is coming from that direction, as are the voices.

Across the hall is my studio. I sneak over, crawl to my desk, and hit the eject button on the drive. I take out the disk to check. It's the right one. Then I get a hair, as they say. I don't know why I do these things. It's my own personal version of the berserks.

I take out a Post-it pad and write Jeremy the note I've been worrying over for days:

> Dearest Jeremy,
>   I can't take my life anymore. You've been good to me,
> but it's not enough. I'm going to end everything now.

I sign it and stick it on my computer screen, but I can't let it be. I pull it off and add,

> P.S.: I had a great time screwing with you yesterday. Sit. Lie
> down. Arf, arf.

I put it back on the screen and crawl to the door. That's when I hear the familiar thud. I've been hearing it ever since I can remember. You never forget the sound of a fist hitting flesh.

"I don't know!" I've never heard Jeremy yell before.

"It's easy, Jeremy." Ben's voice. "Just tell us where she is, and we'll stop. We'll let you go."

God, I never wanted this for Jeremy, even if he is a screwball. I creep to the corner of the hall and look toward the bedroom. Jeremy is taped to a chair and there's tape over his eyes. At first the only thing I can think is, uh-oh, Jeremy's going to get a nasty rash.

Ben winds up and hits him again. Blood spatters from his mouth. Now I worry about the white carpeting.

"I don't know," Jeremy wails. I can't take my eyes off Ben's shoes. Gym shoes.

I hear a woman's voice. "Ben, I think he really doesn't know."

I get a thrill and turn my head to hear better. God, I know that voice, but I can't place it.

Ben slugs Jeremy again. That's enough for me. I creep back, hitting the stairs so fast that I slide down the last half of them on my ass. I head for the kitchen. Almost too late, I see that the guy from the front door is standing and looking out the kitchen windows to the backyard. I freeze, edging back into the hallway, hearing the muffled beating happening upstairs.

The guy turns and walks back toward the living room. I slither forward, aiming for the door, when somebody grabs me around the waist. I twist and rise up on my knees ready to fight, but the muzzle of a gun is poking into my cheek. It's the guy who I thought had left the kitchen.

"Gotcha," he says real quiet, smiling at me. Then he yells, "Ben, she's down here."

What's amazing to me is that you don't think or anything. If you think about it, you lose your nerve.

I head-butt the guy right under his chin. Then I jump up, grab the iron skillet dangling from a hook above the butcher block and cream the stupid guy's head. It makes a dull thunk.

Hearing feet running upstairs, I drop the skillet and tear out of there. I slam open the door to the garage, racing out. Just before I make my break across the lawn, I trip the alarm.

It screams. It wails. It reminds me of a thing I know inside of me.

I skate on that scream, sprinting through the lawns like a 'gator's behind. Jumping in the Porsche, I fumble with the keys, slide them in, and fire it up. I jam it into gear, thinking of Jeremy, and steer toward our house without headlights. As I whip onto my road, I see a van has appeared and three figures are running out the front door toward it. One is holding his head.

I rev the engine, shriek the tires, and hit the headlights, roaring down the road. Ben and the others jump out of my way as I speed past, hoping to draw them along in my wake.

Out of nowhere, a car pulls out, blocking the road. I notice belatedly that it's a Chevy Caprice.

Slamming on the brakes, I fishtail and swerve onto Marge and David's lawn, cutting it up like sushi. I take out the next two lawns, too. Ripping onto the pavement again, I feel rather pleased. Weedkiller. T-bonds.

Good-bye. Nice to know you.

Now that which chases behind is real. The van follows, weaving and listing to the side at each turn. I think of the pictures again, of the Dumpster full of garbage. Somebody had tossed Violet in like she was trash. I remember that thin, long body and the soaking red towel that covered her face. It follows. It chases. It roars behind.

A police car appears, lights and siren whipping the air. I swerve, hit a side street, and shoot away toward my one big play.

Ben taught me well. I watched him work them for ten long years, seeing his last play created all for me. Tonight he'll see my play.

The river comes into me again. The water moving, the shush, the low thunder. I feel tears pouring for Violet because I've hit some place beyond, a place gone haywire. I'm bent on one thing. I slice apart the night.

The van and the Caprice follow me the whole way as I cut down through Manhattan, ignoring the stop lights. It's the only time I've driven through there that I didn't get stuck in traffic.

Behind our threesome, like a lengthening snake, we pick up several squad cars, wailing and whipping their lights. As I speed through, I put on the windbreaker one arm at a time, weaving as I almost take out a lamppost.

I hit the ramp for the Brooklyn Bridge doing about eighty, bottoming out at a dip. I weave, passing cars like they're stopped in time.

If nothing else, it's going to be quite an exit.

I near the Brooklyn shore, freaked now, not sure I can do it. Maybe I should just drive on by. I can lose Ben and Bates easy. I can disappear.

Then I remember the box. I think of all those whippings. I feel the whack of Ben's rubber hose.

I slam on the brakes, skidding and fishtailing, coming to a stupendous halt. Leaping out, I jump up on the sidewall, balancing with my hand on a fat cable. Cars are stopping and people are getting out.

"Stay back," I scream, now leaning over the water. I look down. Nothing but black that way, but I feel it in my chest and heart. The river wants me. It's been waiting. The van screeches to a stop behind the blockade of cars. I see Ben and another guy spill out.

"Beth," he yells and starts throwing people out of his way, making a beeline for me. The sirens shriek. I look down again, turn back, and see all those people once more, all frozen, all silent, just like in Rivertown.

"Sigh no more," I say.

I step off the bridge.

PART II

Afterlife

5

Kat

I see Violet in green grass by the river. She stands with her back to me. I watch her dress loosen, rippling in the breeze. She draws one arm free of her sleeve as the wind crosses the river and reaches the leaves of trees on the far shore. Cottonwoods tremble. Branches lit by sun go gold and green.

A cloud covers the sun, and Violet darkens, pulls her other arm free, and presses the dress to her chest with her forearm. Twisting at the waist, her back is revealed, her breasts from the side, and her dark eyes grown blacker raise, shift to the side, and settle on mine.

The skin at her temple beats. In her lips, chin, throat, and eyes, I read her death, our second shape from which we draw back, avert our eyes, and learn to pretend.

Her dress falls. She turns and steps forward fresh as spring, and enters the water as the cloud passes and the river goes bright, flushing her skin rosy, her hair amber and from the center, gleaming.

This is my love then, the surrounding air of a body submerged. An air that scatters, evaporates, and disappears.

She bends low, pushing forward, swimming alone. I watch as she follows the water beyond my sight. I lift and smell her dress, draping it as I go walking the bank down.

*   *   *

I straighten my body. Listing to the side, I panic, regain balance, and drop like a rock. Pressing both hands over my face, I pull in my elbows tight. The windbreaker whips in the roar. It can't be more than a few seconds. The drop seems forever.

I can't remember hitting the water or going under. But at times, just as I'm falling asleep, a fire runs from my toes to head. My brain goes like a pipe bomb.

When we enter the river, our bodies change form. Arms and legs are more like wings.

But in my dreams, I am limp in the East River, my body rising white, blue in lip and finger, my eyes locked open and gone to mush, my skin saturated and over-rinsed, now sloughing off. Barges and cranes describe shorelines like spider's nests. And behind, Manhattan's famous skyline, man's monuments to man, looks to me just like the stones at Rivertown.

I wake in the water, numb in the head, and I go wild, flapping my arms and legs like some African bird. I break surface and suck in air, stabbed clean through from side to side. Hearing shouts, I look up and see blurry lights, then gasp and drop back into the cold.

I've died. I've committed suicide, that wild ride, and lived to tell the tale.

Holding my breath as I've practiced for so long, I stretch forward, swimming underwater.

My laps pass by as I fight the tide, arms and legs numb. Sirens scream. Slithering onto the pilings, I jump the seawall and lie flat in the weeds, my chest heaving, shaking so hard it hurts me. Back over the bridge, a helicopter whaps the air, nosing its way downstream, its spotlight coursing the river.

I force myself up. It's at this point, because sensation is returning to my feet, that I notice I'm missing a shoe. I shoot across the grass and scramble up the chain link in a clatter, then drop to the other side. Falling down, I grind my palms into broken cement and glass. I scoot across the street in a crouch, wiggling like a hognose under an old wooden loading dock. As I lie on my stomach, I search for my switchblade and press it open.

From my vantage point, I can see most of the bridge arching its way to Manhattan. TV crews have arrived on site. I count my breathing one to five, but tonight, no ghosts but Violet's haunt me.

I remember her breath wetting my cheek as she slept next to me, and how she said so quiet you'd think it was in your head, I love you. Love you.

Hours pass. My chest is still quaking, but I have feeling back in my limbs. As I comb my hair with my fingers, dirt drops on my face. Crawling out, I stand and zip my jacket, pulling the hood over my head.

Shaking like an alcoholic and walking without a shoe, I become invisible to people on the streets. I slip underground, the shock setting in and the berserks in my head. The train brings me to upper Manhattan just as the sky is starting to go light. I stumble into the garage where the Taurus is waiting and lock the door.

Now I think I'm going to throw up. Now all I can do is lie across the backseat of the Taurus shaking again.

I wake myself up moaning. I think my body must be one big bruise. Like some kind of drunk, I get myself into the front seat and check the clock. It's about five. I change clothes in the manner of some kind of remedial nutcase. I slap on my new hair, then a pair of sunglasses. Why didn't I add "bottle of Gatorade" to my list?

Then I drive off as though I'm in a Ford, for God's sakes.

Imagine it. Me in a family car.

After being caught in rush-hour gridlock, I cross into Jersey, where I stop to pick up hamburgers and a copy of the *Times*. It's June 21. I died about one in the morning, near as I can figure. Maybe I should hold a wake.

I search the front page, finding it in the lower-left corner. Shit. Where'd they get that picture of me?

I think back to holidays with the cheerful Jeremy clan all scattered warmly around a seared and puffed-up turkey. It was Jeremy's sister and that damn camera of hers. She was always snapping away like she was poking you in the eye.

BRIDGE CLAIMS AUTHOR'S LIFE, the headline screams. Below it says, "Woman plummets, feared dead. No body recovered." I consider this for a moment, wondering what it would be like if they did recover a body. I'm thinking about the impact on me.

Later in the article, they mention Jeremy and how he was found taped to a chair and beaten. The police are investigating. They won't reveal the details. They have suspicions.

I think of the crumpled Detective Bates. He's a worry.

So I jettison myself out of fast-food heaven and tool along on Highway 80, putting miles between me and all my "friends and family." I head west through Jersey, listening to Joplin wail about her ball and chain.

She carries me into Pennsylvania, where I pick up a late dinner at Scranton. All the people I see have very white faces, a little puffy and stale.

No wonder people live in New York. The world out here is loaded with freaks. Maybe they're all cousins, I think. Maybe they're just sisters and brothers.

People used to say that about Violet and me. They'd ask if we were sisters. Maybe it's some guy that just got done screwing both of us.

"Hey, are you two sisters?"

What's the polite thing to say?

Some of Ben's clients asked for "the sisters." Maybe that gave them a special thrill.

Violet was lean, though, making her look tall. I was medium height, but solid and tight. We both had olive skin and deep-set eyes. Her hair was black and coarser, mine tending toward auburn after hours of sunning on the roof.

I buy a Scranton paper and take a room at a hotel. When I get to my room, which is, by the way, smelling of prison disinfectant

(I remember from my days incarcerated for shoplifting), I open the paper. There I am again, my face staring out of the front page.

God. This is making me nervous. I read the article, which says the same as the one in the *Times,* ending of course with that distasteful reminder. The police are investigating.

Walking to the bathroom, I look in the mirror, taking the wig off and slapping it back on, trying to see if it really works. And I'm worried about the Taurus. Now that the inimitable Detective Bates is investigating, as I'm sure he is, I think of the car and license registered under the name Elizabeth Boone.

Next morning, after choking down a glass of fermented orange juice and the white toast offering in the lobby, I ask directions at the desk. First, I hit the Goodwill, where I pick up some men's clothes that are too big for me. I find a Chicago Bulls baseball-style hat and a ripped pair of sneakers.

At some generic "mart" store, I buy a road atlas, a duffel bag, a couple blankets, an Ace bandage, a slick pair of sunglasses, and a zippered bag. At the beauty supply shop, I get a bleaching rinse, a pair of scissors, and a buzz clipper.

Returning to my room, I get busy.

I cut my hair in handfuls, dropping it in the wastebasket. Then I buzz it all over and bleach what's left. I wrap the Ace bandage around my breasts to flatten them, and I try on my new oversize clothes, the baseball cap turned around backward, and the new sunglasses. I strut and posture like I have a wanger between my legs.

Kat and I used to do it for fun. I think of Kat now like I haven't for years.

We'd dress like boys and tool around the Village, whistling at girls like we were stupid. One time we ventured into a men's john. We stood on either side of this short guy squirting into the urinal. Kat and I took turns commenting on his style, his method, and aim. I had a dildo in a harness that I whipped out and started slapping from side to side. The guy ran out of there, stuffing in his poker as he went.

I check in the mirror. Yep. I can pull it off. My identity, how-ever, is beginning to fade.

Switching back into my Rebecca Cross wig and clothes, I clean my stuff out of the car. I hook the body holster onto the back of my jeans, then check the clip and slide in the semiauto-matic. I practice drawing it a few times. Over that goes a flannel shirt. My extra IDs and my writing go in the zippered bag. I pack the guns in the duffel bag, then throw it in the car, checking out of the hotel.

At the Ford dealership, they make a nice bid on the Taurus, but they're sad that I don't want to buy a car. I'm sad, too. I'm thinking about my Porsche left running on the bridge.

After signing the title, I take the check, slinging my duffel bag over my shoulder. About a half mile down the road, I cash the check at a bank. Then I eat more hamburgers, feeling a little sick to be doing this so-called food two days in a row. In the bathroom, I change into a guy.

Out on the road, I stick out my thumb, slouching, acting like my musculature has possession of me. A trucker picks me up. He's heading south on eighty-one.

I toss in my bag and set off, chatting with Jack, the truck dri-ver, about manly things as we barrel along the highway toward God knows where. It reminds me of hitchhiking to New York fif-teen years ago.

I slept under bridges, ate out of Dumpsters, and shoplifted my way to the city. I got caught one time, but I'm a fast runner. I left the hefty security guy in my wake, his stomach bouncing like it was made of water.

Back then, I still carried the weight of Rivertown. I talked the talk of the river. I walked like I was made of iron, like I was Ged-ders, banging at life like a hammer.

Kat changed all that. I always wondered about her, where she came from, because she was so different from the rest of us that Ben picked up off the streets. Kat was like silk and the rest of us were wool.

I took to Kat like a puppy dog, always edging up next to her. She never pushed me away. She petted me, curled her arm around. When I first came out of the basement and couldn't talk, she read Dickinson and Shelley to me, slow and singsong.

> To make a prairie it takes a clover and one bee,
> One clover, and a bee,
> And revery.
> The revery alone will do,
> If bees are few.

And revery, and revery, she'd say like you were dreaming.

While I was in training, Ben taught me how to please a man. Kat taught me the pleasure of women. She would come into my bed at night and undress me, teaching me the lips, the tongue, the skin along the back, how to press a nipple, how to tug, how to tease it with the tongue. She taught me her clitoris, the proper way to stroke, how to enclose it with the lips, the use of fingers, and how to thrust.

Kat's face was square, with high cheekbones and amber eyes. Her hair, the color of sand, fell the length of her back. She let me braid it for the plays so that it lay like rope showing off her spine, the elegant lines of her body, her rounded thighs. She looked good in the cuffs, her head high, her full breasts much to be desired.

She taught me lace bras and camisoles. She taught me corsets and hosiery. She dressed me in silk and jewelry, teaching me to walk, to sit, how to lie waiting, how to curve the back, to flush the lips.

Just as I practiced on Violet with the whip, Kat practiced on me. Not that I think Ben ever made her. She chose me herself for her own pleasure. I thought of it as a way to be near her.

Kat would pack me in the box sometimes for no reason. So that you'll mind me, she said. It made me draw nearer, need her, look to her. I couldn't bear for her to leave without me for even a few hours.

Kat started throwing up blood one day. When Ben came in, she turned halfway toward him, then collapsed on the floor. I started crying, trying to get Kat to wake up.

Ben left the bathroom and came back a few minutes later with a blanket. He wrapped her in it and carried her out the door. I never saw her again.

He kept me near him then. He knew how it hurt me. It was always bad whenever we lost one of the family.

Sitting in the big rig, wheeling south toward Harrisburg, I think I can smell her clothes and her skin. I remember Kat's laughter, how it fell like rain.

The night I first hit New York, it was storming like crazy. A trucker with a load of caskets from Ohio, my made-up birthplace, picked me up in Jersey, riding me all the way into Manhattan. It was one in the morning. Seemed like a good time to be delivering caskets.

The next few days I found that vying for food in New York was a mean business. The last time I ate was out of a Dumpster at the truck stop where I hooked up with the casket courier.

That's when Ben spotted me. I hadn't washed for two weeks at least. I'd certainly never been bulky, and the trip to New York had taken a toll. I don't know what he saw in me as he cruised the streets.

He parked his car and walked to where I was sitting, getting weaker, wondering if I should try to find a shelter.

"Hey, kid," he said to me.

I pretended he wasn't talking to me.

"Hey," he said, his voice kind. "You look new." He took my chin gently and turned my face to him. Ben coaxed me into going to a pizza joint with him. I knew he was going to want something for it, but at that point, I didn't have many choices.

He bought me pizza and milk, I remember. And he gave me his card.

"Look," he said. "My wife and I live just down the street. We try to help out runaways and either get you back home or set up with a job here. It's better than living out on the streets."

When I was done, I waited for him to tell me what he wanted in return. He had them put the rest of the pizza in a bag for me. I hid it in my clothes.

"If you get tired of being out like this," he said. "Come over to our place." He got in his car then and drove off. The whole thing was different than what I expected.

God, he was smart. I wonder if any of the kids he primes never show up at his "apartment." I wonder if they know that they got away.

A cold wind set up that night, driving the rain down the streets. It kept up the next day. I tried a shelter, but it was full. As night came on again and looking to get even colder, a group of three boys, drunk on their asses, chased me near half a mile until I lost them.

That's when I thought of Ben and walked to his place. I pushed the buzzer and waited. A woman's voice answered.

"Ben gave me a card," I said. "He said I could crash here for awhile."

She buzzed me in.

I liked Kat as soon as I saw her.

"Need a drink? Some Coke?" She took a blanket off the couch and draped it over my shoulders. I felt warmth for the first time in days. She brought me a tall glass of Coke, which I sucked up fast. She smiled and took the glass from me, going back to the kitchen. I heard her make a phone call.

When she came back, she handed me a glass of orange juice. Then she showed me around the place, talking on and on about stuff I didn't care about.

Kat led me to the back bedroom. It had several mattresses on the floor with blankets folded on each.

"This is where you sleep while you're here," she said, watching me close.

I looked the room over, feeling funny.

"Sit down," she said and helped me to a mattress. I leaned

against the wall. "You haven't been eating enough. You're light-headed from the Coke."

The door to the apartment opened and shut. Ben came in. The room was getting fuzzy and spinning. My body felt heavy.

"She's young," Kat said.

Ben stooped and looked in my eyes. I started sliding sideways down the wall. He lay his large palm along my cheek.

"I think she might end up being good."

"When she's cleaned up, she'll be beautiful."

The last thing I remember is Ben asking, "How much did she drink?"

Kat was stroking my head, looking down at me. "All of it."

When my buddy Jack and I hit Cumberland, I have him drop me off. I become Rebecca again. Then I find a Ford dealership, picking up another Taurus, this time the station wagon.

After that, I buy a newspaper. Clarisse is nowhere to be found.

I think about Jeremy in the hospital for another stay. I wonder if his synchronicity problem will recur. Maybe some woman who's a lover of dogs will find him all bruised and battered. She'll tell him to sit. Stay. Roll over.

I spread out my guns in the car like before and study the atlas. I want to lie low someplace and let this thing blow over. Let Detective Bates decide that I'm scooting the bottom of the East River.

I head for Monongahela National Forest. It looks so green on the map. Anything that color must be good. I've never camped a day in my life, but I figure it can't be any harder than sleeping under bridges and eating out of Dumpsters.

On my way downstate, I stop and buy a case of Coke, lots of canned food, and a can opener. I also buy a spoon.

At the ABC I pick up two big bottles of Southern Comfort, thinking of Joplin. It's the push behind that's starting to rise again like it was only sleeping for a couple of days.

I find myself crying as I drive, not remembering when I

started or why. And pictures are coming to me, quick slices of action stripped of color and backdrop. I think of Mama and Mandy, just bones in the ground. I think of Kat's touch. And Violet. She's in a pauper's grave, a pine box. Another Jane Doe forgotten.

I cry myself into the mountains, finding that they are, indeed, a beautiful color of green. I pick a camping spot under pines that wave and sigh, opening my first bottle of whiskey and starting my long slide into forgetfulness.

I don't remember much about the next week except for puking. That begins to wane as I stop eating and just drink the whole day.

I have the campground all to myself except for a sweet retired couple that show up midweek. They're driving a piece of aluminum so big and long, they have to back up and go forward about ten times just to get it around a bend in the road. I've never seen such a thing, and I think maybe the whiskey has something to do with it.

In my drunken stupor, I amuse myself by changing back and forth throughout the day from Becker, my male identity, to Becca, as I refer to Rebecca now.

As Becker, I help Joe and Mildred set up a nifty screened tent thing around their picnic table. Later on, I visit as Becca.

"Your boyfriend is so nice," they say. "The two of you should come over for dinner. Do you like to play cards?"

I decline, telling them, as I stumble over nothing and sag against a tree, that we just got married and all we can do is screw.

Their faces go white, but not as white as those people in Scranton.

After a week in this state, I notice while reading the campground rules for the hundredth time, since it's the only thing to do, that each site may be occupied for seven days max. This information slowly worms its way into my alcohol-soaked brain.

So I move to the next campground, finding that it's bigger and that more people are camped there. A wide, rocky stream flows enthusiastically along one side. That's where everybody is camping. I choose a spot the farthest away.

Still dressed as Becca but without the wig, I settle in for the night. I unfold the short lawn chair I picked up at the camp store while en route to my new home. Then I plop my bottle down beside it.

As I happily scan the day's newspaper, the type of which appears to be getting more blurry, I notice a suspicious headline:

TWO TEENS DIE IN COPYCAT SUICIDE.

I read on.

Two female teens jumped in tandem from the Brooklyn Bridge last night, copying the recent suicide of author Clarisse Broder.

Since her suicide jump from the same bridge on June 21 Mrs. Broder is fast becoming an icon among teens and college students. Flowers are often found placed in the area from which she jumped, possibly fleeing an unknown male assailant. Sales of her novel have skyrocketed, selling out in many locations across the country.

It goes on to quote a police spokesman and give the same old endline. "Police are still investigating Mrs. Broder's suicide."

My God. What's the matter with those girls? Are they crazy? Are they out of their minds?

It's soon too dark to read. That's what I tell myself, since the writing is blurred. I'm not in the mood for the paper now anyway. I try to stand up, but can't. I can hardly get myself out of the screwy chair. Eventually, I fall to the side and crawl to the bushes to pee. As I'm doing my business, I hear a train crying and wailing in the distance. It reminds me of nights sleeping in the two-room.

After I'm done, I haul myself up like an imbecile, struggling with my pants. I give up and leave them down around my ankles, and I stagger to the car. Once there, I slump into the backseat like I do every night, with a blanket thrown over me, and on my chest beneath it, resting happy as you please, my Uzi.

Down in Fowler, the trains flew by at night. I used to lie awake listening to their sad weep. Daddy snored through it all like a sick dog. But I'd take his snoring any day. He could butcher a melody better than Grady cleaned his meat. It was all the drink, I guess, made his ears go slack and his voice slip around. But he used it to frighten people off.

There was a woman came to the house sometimes when I was little. She always acted friendly, handing out hugs and candy to me and Vin and saying things like, "How's my babies doing?"

She'd talk to Mama so nice at first, calling her Mama just like me and Vin did. It all just got me mixed up. Mama called her Betty and I recognized her from a picture that Mama kept in the bedroom. Mama and Betty were both in the picture, younger, and standing with some man I didn't know.

Every time Betty came, it was in a different car with a different man. They always dressed fancy like they just came from church.

"We don't like them," Vin would say to me.

"But she gave me redhots." I was easily bribed in those days.

"We hate their stupid fat cars. We hate how clean they are. We hate the white shoes on their feet." I always got the feeling he knew something about them that I didn't, but I couldn't pry a thing out of him.

And he was right of course, not just about the hate, but about the white shoes. To me, it seemed a waste.

How you going to dig the crawdads? What happens in the mudflats where the gnats swarm over you like sleep? You'd have to be cleaning those white shoes all the time. You'd have to stay way back from the river.

I tried not to think about that.

So Vin and me would work the sinkholes good with our feet

and zoom in close, aiming for their shoes. That made the woman and her different men not so sweet.

And that's when Daddy would start to sing. He'd belt out like a bullfrog all sick from eating bees. Me and Vin would cover our ears.

I think that was one of the reasons Mama put up with Daddy and his drink. Because Betty and her man would pack up and leave. Then Daddy and Mama would sit in the swing.

Chewing grass, me and Vin lay around nearby, thinking about the damage we did to their feet. Mama would smile and swing, happy about something I never did get.

If I asked Mama who they were, she'd shrug and say, "Don't you worry yourself over Betty and her men. Listen to the river. Listen to the wind in the trees. You can't do any better than that."

I wake, hearing the sound of voices nearby. Startled, I lose balance and fall onto the floor between the seats. My head screams. I need a drink, pronto. So I sneak a peek out my window.

Shit! Two children are stooped down near my chair. Then I notice that my whiskey bottle is on its side. This makes me sad. It was near to full when I left it to its own devices last night.

I open the car door and fall out. The two children—one a girl, about eight I'd say, and a boy, ten or eleven—stand up, staring at me. The trees spin as I try to decide if I should attempt to stand.

"You've got ants," the girl says.

"Lots of ants and in a long line," the boy adds.

I let that settle in around the whiskey in my brain. "I do?"

They wave me over. I stagger up and weave to the chair, seeing that yes indeed, I do have ants, rather the ants have the whiskey.

"Do you think ants get drunk?" I ask, trying to keep my flammable breath away from the two of them.

They both giggle at my comment. Then they begin telling me all sorts of things about ants, most of which goes right by me.

"Ben. Sarah. Don't bother this lady, man, lady." She finally makes up her mind when she sees my breasts beneath my T-shirt. I turn too fast, which sets my head into another spin, and I see a woman about my own age dressed in hiking boots, jeans, and a flannel shirt.

I notice I'm dressed half as Becker and half as Becca.

She takes one look at me, and I expect her to pull a face and chase her kids away. Instead she surprises me, which is nice, and she smiles, holding out her hand.

"I'm Jill."

I feel suddenly shy, but shake her hand. "Becca."

"I'm sorry about my kids," she says. "They're into this ant thing lately."

"It's okay. No problem."

I see her eyes fix on the whiskey bottle lying on its side. I feel my face go red. She smiles at me again before she shoos her kids off to the outhouse.

Later, I notice that they're in the campsite closest to me. Jill's husband is decked out in gear. He has on rubber boots up to the crotch, and he wears this cool vest with lots of pockets. Wading out into the stream, he waves a fancy fishing rod back and forth over his head.

We used to make our rods out of young willow saplings. Vin and me would search the banks to find line and hooks other fishermen had snagged up in trees. Occasionally, we caught catfish, which pleased Mama no end. One time I caught the head off a doll, dripping with water and muck. It scared the living daylights out of me.

That head haunted. It prowled. It was red-cheeked and missing one glassy eye. We used it in the center of our séances, Mandy with our wig on her head trying to rouse the dead.

I kept the doll's head in the crotch of a willow tree, checking daily to make sure it was still there. I didn't want it sneaking up on me. I figured there were places for these kinds of things. As long as they stayed put, a person could rest easy.

I slowed on the whiskey that day, fascinated by the activity

at that campsite. I'd never seen the workings of a real family before. Around dinnertime, as I was walking back from the john, I
passed Jill's husband. I got a good look at his vest, liking it even
more from close up.

"So what are you doing out there?" I say to him, later learning that his name is Rob. I make a back-and-forth movement with
my hand, imitating what he did with his fishing pole.

"It makes the trout rise," he says. "They think it's a fly."

The next morning, I stroll over to the stream and sit on a boul-
der. Rob's upstream, the sun behind him. He whips his fishing
rod back and forth. The line arcs and curves, gleaming in the sun.

It brings the trout up. The trout rise.

I wonder if that's a good idea, if a person should entice a thing
to come up, to know it from one end to the other.

About mid-afternoon, Jill appears at the edge of the stream,
asking me to dinner, saying I need to bring something to add to
the meal. I bring a can of ravioli. The kids think that's great. As
they go searching for the can opener in their box of kitchen gear,
Jill asks me where I'm from.

"Ohio," I say, stuck on my great lie. Thank God she doesn't
ask me brightly, where in Ohio?

"What about you?" I'm terrible at conversation. I pretty
much keep my remarks to wisecracks.

"New York," she says. I freeze.

She continues, stirring a pan of baked beans. "I thought you
might be from New York. You've got that feel." She looks at me.
"When I first saw you, I thought I knew you from somewhere.
But I've never been to Ohio."

"People are always saying that to me," I say fast. "They say it
all the time." If I'm going to be such a lousy liar, I should keep my
trap shut.

"You look like that woman that jumped off the bridge. What's
her name, Broder."

I think I might faint. "What? I look like I've drowned?" Actually, after so much whiskey, I probably do.

She thinks that's funny.

After dinner, we sit around the fire. One of the kids hears something and we turn our heads. There's a doe and two fawns not ten feet away, drinking from the stream.

Sarah whispers to Jill, "I wish I had my camera."

Jill says, "This is one of those pictures you keep in your head."

I think about that while I'm lying in the backseat of the Taurus, fingering the Uzi. I wonder what it would be like to have those kind of pictures filling my head.

Instead, the trout begin to rise. At first, I think of Violet in the Dumpster. But then I start remembering something I'd forgotten a long time ago. I remember what happened to me in Ben's basement.

I woke up in the basement lying on a cold concrete floor. They'd stripped me. The toilet was just a drain, and a dim light flickered overhead. The place stunk.

I remember freaking out, running back and forth from corner to corner, searching for an opening. But everything was bricked in. There was only a stair up and a door at the top.

At first, I sat and waited in a corner facing the stair. Nobody came. So I climbed the stairs and beat on the door. I screamed. I wore myself down.

Nobody.

I went back down the stairs and curled in a corner, so hungry I hurt all over. I remember hitting this point when I decided I was dying. Something changed in me then that's never changed back.

That's when he came.

Ben kicked me awake. I looked up at him, remembering Daddy, waiting for what I knew would come next.

"Get up," he said.

For the first time, I saw Ben's smile. He dragged me up on my feet and beat me, then raped me.

That's how it went for awhile. After the first two beatings, I learned him just like I learned Daddy. Otherwise, I don't think I'd have gotten through it.

After Ben was done, he'd put out a bowl of water and dump a can of dog food on the floor, not letting me use my hands to eat or drink. As days went by, he got me to eating out of his hand.

Between beatings and feedings, if I yelled and screamed, I had to wait longer for Ben to come with the food. It didn't take a genius. I shut up.

Soon after that, Ben arrived with his famous black bag. He smiled real big as he walked toward me.

The next morning, Jill asks me if I want to drive in to the camp store with her. We set off in my Taurus, talking about the scenery, how beautiful, etc. She spots an eagle floating high.

Then she asks, "Why do you carry a gun?"

I don't look at her. "Is it that obvious?"

"No. My pop was a cop, so I notice those things. And the whiskey. It'll kill you."

If she weren't so matter-of-fact, I would have ejected her from the car. "I won't let the kids see it again," I say. "I felt bad about that."

"I'm not worried about them."

She doesn't know about the teeming arsenal in her vicinity.

"I had a bad year," I say as an explanation. And I'm thinking, I really am drowned by the way. Then I add, "I think I'm having a bad lifetime."

She laughs. "I don't mean to tell you how to live your life. I don't know a thing about you. But I think you could do better. You seem to be a good person."

I want to laugh. God, if she only knew. But she catches me. I don't think I've been caught by kindness and honesty before. It makes the push behind get stronger. I begin to want a drink.

We hit the store then, and I'm trying to decide if I want to chance buying a paper when I catch sight of *Time*. I duck my head and shove on my sunglasses. There I am splattered all over the cover in red and black. I'm too shocked to read the headline, but grab one and buy it with my assortment of canned goods, Coke, and whiskey. I head out the door and hide in the car. Jill comes out later, and I zip off as fast as possible.

Back at my campsite, I take out the magazine. The story? "Suicide Author's Family Discovered. Haven't Seen Daughter For Years."

What a grab. What a kick in the guts.

I flip through. There are pictures of me as a teenager and a yearbook picture. There's me and a supposed sister standing outside a clean white suburban house. I keep staring. This can't be. Who are these people? The only person I recognize is the man who is my would-be stepfather curling his arm over my thin teen shoulders.

That's Snuff in the flesh. You know, "wormtree" Snuff. Snuff of the rotten broken-off teeth. Good old "screw her behind the trailer" Snuff.

I read the article, losing my mind with each paragraph. Some editor has carefully excised my remarks from that unsightly interview I had with the *Time* reporter, and placed them neatly into the story out of context from the original questions.

Allow me to summarize.

I was a bright child, an A student until out of nowhere at age fourteen, about the time Betty (my supposed mother) marries Dave, I started to decline.

Betty? The same Betty that used to come visit with redhots? I search the pictures, but there aren't any shots of my supposed mother.

The story goes on. I disappeared at age sixteen. I had just given birth to a baby (a baby?) and had given it up for adoption. (Betty and Dave don't believe in abortion. They want to make that very clear.) I left the hospital just before being discharged. They never saw their baby daughter again. They thought I was dead. Now, after all these years, sob, sob, they find me again only to discover that I'm a suicide.

Pitiful.

These people are headline-grabbers. They're fakes. Their names are Betty and Dave. They live in Dayton, Ohio. (That's a kicker.) Dave's an anesthesiologist.

For some reason, I really hate anesthesiologists.

I look up Dayton, Ohio, in the atlas. It doesn't look familiar on the map, and I don't see a good healthy river anywhere near the place.

The article says my birth name was Theresa Sue Lumley. (Lumley? My God. No one would want to remember a name like that.) The article says that Betty and Dave plan to meet with the grieving husband, Jeremy, to share stories and pictures.

I'm reading this dead sober. I check the photos again. I have to admit that it sure could be me. But people can do anything with computers these days. It's Dave that catches me. There's Snuff all right, written all over Dave's stolid face. My identity thing is suffering yet another massive blow. And I'm beginning to get a good feel for how my memory problem is much worse than I ever imagined.

I roll up the fucking magazine and pitch it at the Taurus, trying to decide whether or not I should set it on fire.

That evening, I eat with Rob, Jill, and the kids. Their allotted week is almost up. They tell me about another campground nearby where they're going to move in the morning and invite me to come along. I think I'm getting to be a project to them so I say I'll think about it.

That evening as I fall asleep, I hold the Uzi in one hand and the semiautomatic in the other.

6

Dayton

In the basement, Ben stood over me as I hunched on the floor, waiting for the first kick.

"You're in training now, Beth."

That was the first I'd heard my new name. Ben stooped and dropped his bag next to me, taking out two pairs of cuffs.

"Kneel," he said. I pushed myself up, weak and dizzy. Ben steadied me as he cuffed my wrists in back and then my ankles. He strapped them together.

Matt and Toni came down the stairs with an old mattress. Ben ran his fingers down the side of my face. "See? You've done so well that I'm giving you a present."

He kissed my cheek then. "Open your mouth," he whispered. Ben fitted in a gag. Grabbing my hair, he yanked back my head, almost pulling me over. He placed a round pad of gauze over each eye, then taped them. The boys picked me up and lay me on the mattress.

They went away.

I don't know how long I was left like that. The way Kat talked about it afterward, I must have been lying there for weeks.

They would come down in different groupings, Kat and Matt, or all three. I never knew when they'd come. And they'd make over me, kiss me, run their hands over my body so soft and gentle. They let my legs loose and walked me.

In my blindness, the room shrank, being nothing but my legs, my arms, the feel of the gag, the tape on my eyes. I ached for them to come.

When they arrived, one would screw me while another would take out the gag and feed me by hand. They touched, sucked, rocked, talked to me, so gentle, so kind. I cried like a baby, begging them not to leave, to protect me from Ben, to help me get out.

There's nowhere to go, Beth, one would say, patient and loving. There's only here for you now.

Oh how sweet, how strange their voices coming from the far side of my blindness as they washed my body and hair. And they tended my bruises and cuts that weren't healing.

Blindness took me over. I melted down. I collapsed. That basement became a single pee-soaked mattress upon which I floated. Their voices, their caresses, all of their cleaning became liquid, flowing around me like water.

I loved Kat's touch. Ben kept her around because of her timing, her skill with the babies. That's what I was then. A newborn.

She taught me to count my breaths, one to five, back to one again. For hours, days, weeks, bound in the same position, blind, gagged. I watched the lights flash.

Don't worry the lights, Beth, Kat whispered. Watch them come and go. They flash and spike, don't they?

I nodded, afraid of her voice, without body as it was, sweeping over me. Her hands were swirls of pleasure.

Count your breathing, she reminded. Let the lights spike, let them strike.

I counted. I waited. I made a horrible mess of that mattress.

Then the ghosts came.

She's got the ghosts, I heard them saying.

When you get the ghosts, you're near ready.

*   *   *

I wake in the morning to a downpour. Peeking out the side window, I see that Jill is under their kitchen tarp, cooking already. Sarah slumps on the picnic table.

After I hit the john, I sprint over to see Jill.

"You still leaving this morning?" I say.

"If the rain lets up."

I sit quiet, listening to the rain. I smell resin, rain, and woodsmoke. "I think I'm going on somewhere else."

She nods. "Back to Ohio?"

"I'm thinking that way."

She gets a funny smile and says, "I've got something for you." She opens her car door. "Sarah, the rain's let up. Why don't you go to the bathroom now?"

Sarah shrugs and leaves.

Jill hands me another copy of *Time*. I stare at it.

"So I guess maybe I need a nose job or something. The hair change isn't good enough?"

Jill sits beside me. "Most people wouldn't work it out. I notice little things. And besides, I don't believe a thing that I read." She waits as I fidget. "You've got a husband. A family. You could go back."

If she'd said that to me a few days ago, I would have wanted to choke her, but now I know there's something deeper, like she knows the cold and the ache down there, but it doesn't work her bad like it does me.

"It's worse than that, Jill. My past wants to eat me alive. They beat the shit out of my husband that night. You don't want to know what they did to me. God, do you think I would have jumped off that bridge if I didn't have to? And there's something else, not just the guy that's after me. It chases my dreams. All I know to do is run away."

"What about the police?"

I snort, thinking of Detective Bates. "No offense, Jill, but have you read the paper? 'Unknown male assailant.' They know who he is. He was there on the bridge that night, but they can't touch him. He's got them all by the nuts. Literally."

She's quiet now. I get up and tell her to say good-bye to Rob and the kids for me. She gives me their address and phone number.

"Take care of yourself," she says to me.

I nod and go back to my car, packing up my stuff, which consists of the lawn chair and a half-full bottle of whiskey. I stop at the john on my way out and change into Becker. As I get into my car, I see Jill watching me. She waves.

I drive off.

The night before the two-room burned down, I remember Mama sitting out on the porch in a rickety metal rocker that we found with somebody's garbage. Mama's ankles were so wide, she didn't look like she had any. Instead, they swelled out like she had matching goiters just above her feet.

The ring of fat around her neck sagged, and she sweated just below that, a triangle of wet at the collar of her cotton dress, stretched to the limit around her swollen body.

But that night, she sang. Mama knew old songs about blue-bottle flies and train whistles, about some girl who died, and about fiddles and dancing girls.

I think of it like pictures going into the sky and falling back different, full of moonlight, full of water shifting, rising off the river like ghosts and filling the air, the sky, coming into your face and lungs and making you the same inside and outside.

When I think of dying, I think of Mama. I want her there beside me, singing me out to where the river goes blue into the sea. I want to be so fine that nothing keeps its hold on me, just passes right through the same inside and out as I'm gliding down the delta with Mama and her fat neck and swollen ankles, perfect as you please. Her dress up in the sky like a willow branch sweet as rain and blowing.

*   *   *

On my way out, I stop at the store and buy some real food and another paper. I don't buy more whiskey.

I try to convince myself that I don't know where I'm going, that I'm heading west, putting more miles between me and the city. I end up in Ohio anyway, and take a campsite in Wayne National Forest. I'm getting to be a real camping freak.

That evening as I'm reading the paper, I see a picture of an old friend. It's the venerable Senator from New York. I stare at his picture, remembering that evening again.

Violet and I had done our ritual early since Ben was taking me to the reception. She kissed me hard before I left because Slim and his friend were in line for a play in a few hours. Our plan was in gear.

I remember riding in the limo with Ben and then waiting in the reception line. I remember the Senator's eyes, the look on his face, a mixture of nervousness and lust. Ben has me in a choker and with bracelets on both wrists. And I remember drinking just a few sips of champagne as Ben chatted with other notable clients I didn't recognize.

As I sit in my camping spot, I try to keep following my memory, but after that, I draw a blank. I move my brain back and forth as though I'm hoping the trout will rise. Nothing doing.

I unscrew the cap of what remains of my whiskey, but the smell of it turns my gut. So I drag the *Time* out of the car and look at the pictures again.

What about that river? What about the mud and the stacks of the dead? What about Gedders and Mandy? And I get that thing again, like the ghosts, but not. Of movement, of shape. Then one of Ben's favorite play rooms comes into my head. I begin to feel a little shaky, so I try not to think about it.

I fall asleep in my little lawn chair, but wake in the middle of the night when the rain takes up again. Then I climb into the car and hold my Uzi close, the only comfort I can get while the rain taps, wanting in.

*　　*　　*

Ben socks me. "What's your name?"

My hands are cuffed back and I'm down in the basement, blind. Kat is behind, holding me in place by my arms.

She leans close to my ear. "You remember. Say it."

"No," I say, and Ben socks me again.

"Tell me your name."

Kat won't let me drop to my knees. I'm crying now, bending over at the waist. Ben grabs my hair and jerks my head up. I prepare for a punch to the face.

"Beth," I say, having had enough.

Kat strokes my head, kisses my back. "Good, Beth. That's so good."

She and Ben help me stumble to the mattress. Kat feeds me, even though I don't want it, even though I think I'm going to be sick.

"Do you know where you're from, Beth?" Her voice stretches into darkness.

"Nowhere."

She kisses me. "That's right. That's good. A river of nowhere."

Of course I went to Dayton. I don't see how I could have stayed away. It's not until I'm sitting in the middle of town that I notice I don't know Dave's last name. The *Time* article said he was Betty's third husband. He wasn't cursed with a name like Lumley. I find a ripped-up phone book in a booth and flip through it, looking up anesthesiologists.

There it is, Dr. David Thompson. It gives his clinic phone. I call and ask the address, pressing for directions, which the receptionist is pleased to give.

Helpful people are such a joy.

I zip over and wait in the parking lot. Sure enough, out walks Snuff, looking mighty impressive in suit coat and tie. It's like something in my head explodes. I can't get anything to fit, and I start to wonder if I made my entire childhood up in my head. Except then I see his feet. White shoes. My feet itch to stomp them.

Betty must have a fetish.

I smell the worms on Dave's hands as he walks by, and I wonder about his two front teeth. I follow him to his house big enough for twenty, maybe twenty-five, and park on a side street like I learned from Detective Bates.

I'm beginning to get a whiff of the dangers. But this time the dangers aren't out in the air buzzing over my head. This time the dangers are buzzing in me.

I begin to make plans.

As I'm sitting in my car, pondering the details of my play, I notice a car edging along the street. I ignore it at first, but duck down after taking a closer look. It's a Chevy Caprice.

I take a peek. The car stops at Dave and Betty's. Out steps you-know-who with that briefcase. I feel my lip curl. I want to make Bates eat it. I want to change the name to griefcase.

I watch as they let him in the house.

It's getting late, so I find a bright, white shopping mecca. I buy a flashlight. I buy a big gym bag. I pick up a ski mask on clearance, and as a last thought, I buy a roll of duct tape. I don't know why.

At one in the morning, I drive back and park about a block away. Dressed as Becker in dark clothes, I sling the gym bag over my shoulder. The semiautomatic is hooked in place, so I mosey over.

For some reason that I can't explain, I have a feeling that I can get in through the basement window at the back of the house. I huddle down in the bushes and creep around, finding it just where I assumed it would be, and I push on it, feeling how the latch is weak. After rattling it back and forth, it plops open, looking like a black mouth wanting to swallow me.

I slide in feet first, dragging my gym bag behind me. Stepping onto a workbench that's underneath the window, I whip out the nifty mini-flashlight that I picked up while shopping. The beam is sharp and bright.

I wiggle it around the room. It's awful neat down here, which reminds me of Jeremy. I imagine him and Betty and Dave getting together and talking about their big houses. I think of them discussing weedkillers and the dandelion problem. It gives me the shivers thinking about them trading pictures and dredging up touching stories.

Sliding off the workbench, I walk out into the rest of the basement, starting up the stairs. Now that I've had practice breaking into my own house the night I died, I'm beginning to feel comfortable with this sort of thing.

I don't know what I'm looking for, just something to let me know about these people. I search the kitchen and the living room. I'm certain I've never set foot in this place.

And I really hate the couch.

I check the other rooms downstairs, then mount the stairs like I live there, slipping on the ski mask, just in case. I slide across the upstairs hall and search the first bedroom.

Everything in here is frilly and deadly pink. A dated poster of Donny Osmond as big as life scares the shit out of me. God. Donny Osmond? Obviously, this is the wrong lifetime.

I return to the hall, wandering into a bathroom. I swoop the flashlight over the toilet, bathtub, sink. I open the medicine cabinet. Inside, I find a pharmacopoeia.

I peruse the bottles and pocket a large bottle half full of Valium. I'm sad to see that the codeine is almost empty. I pocket it anyway.

Out in the hall again, I hit the next bedroom. This room is different. A kite hangs from the ceiling. Some stuffed animals are huddled together on the pillow of the bed like I've frightened them. I'm getting a bad feeling now. I think I smell Ben's basement. I see a picture on the dresser and pick it up.

It's of a girl who could be a young me swinging a bat. I take it and lie down on the bed, trying to get a feel for the room. My eyes start drooping as I gaze up at the kite, then over at some shelves.

I freeze. Then I shine my light there.

For God's sakes, there's the doll's head big as you please with one eye popped out. A toupee drapes over its horrifyingly pink head. Next to it is a cup. I jump off the bed and reach up, taking it down. It's a cup with a dragon on the side curling around. There's a woman with a parasol and tiny feet.

God, I feel bad now, like all of me is going to water or something. I sit in a chair nearby and lose my balance, falling backward. Clutching at the desk, I knock off a jar of pens and pencils.

I lie still on the floor. Voices murmur and a light goes on. I roll over and crouch behind the bed. Dave/Snuff pads down the hall, looking this way and that.

"Be careful, dear," Betty says. He stomps downstairs checking the house. Now I hear Betty's feet whisper along the floor. She pushes the door to this room open farther and flips on the light, seeing the chair that fell back. I watch her looking in the door, and it comes back to me all in a flash, the look on her face years ago when this was my bedroom.

She had opened this door in almost the same way. At first she looked concerned, then confused, then she went a cold, cruel white. She looked at me direct in the eyes, hate shining not at Dave, for God's sakes. She hated me.

She shut the door and left me alone with him, the anesthesiologist, pumping up and down on top of me.

A baby, I think. A fucking baby. Fucking Dave got me pregnant.

But this time, in the present, Betty sees me crouching and screams. I leap up and whip out my gun, pointing it at her. She freezes.

Yep. It's the same Betty that used to come with her goddamn redhots. She's older and thinner, but I bet she has a closetful of white shoes.

My head is reeling, and for the first time, it all makes sense about Betty visiting us by the river years ago and Mama and her not getting along. This bitch is my goddamn mother.

Sometimes I can be very dense.

Dave comes barreling up the stairs and stops dead when he sees me. I want to shoot them both. I want to pour gasoline over them and light a match. I want to be Ben for just one hour.

We stand there, all three of us frozen. Finally, good old "take charge of everything including your stepdaughter" Dave clears his throat.

"What do you want?" he says. "We'll give you money."

That's right, throw money at the situation. That should fix it. Betty and Dave should get together with Ben instead of Jeremy. They could swap stories about screwing me.

I then remember that I have on the ski mask. How smart of me.

"Back to your bedroom." I wave my gun at them.

They back off, edging toward the bedroom. I pick up my gym bag and follow. Once in the master bedroom, I wave them toward the bed, feeling Ben well up in me.

"You," I say to Dave. "Lie facedown on the bed."

Betty's crying now. I get out the duct tape and throw it at Betty. "Tape his wrists behind his back. Tape his ankles."

It takes her awhile as she whimpers. I check her work to make sure it's tight.

"Now you," I say. "Lie down beside him. Same way."

She does this, weeping like a train. I tape her the same way. In a moment of malice, I tape Dave's eyes, thinking of what it will do to his face.

"Lots of money," he says. "I can get you lots of money."

"Oh shut up, shithead."

Perusing the room, I see that on the dresser there are a whole bunch of pictures lined up in neat rows. Keeping my eye on the happy couple, I ease over and browse the pictures. Betty and Dave. Betty and Dave. My supposed sister. Then a picture of the supposed me. I pick it up and walk over to the bed, sticking it in Betty's face.

Did you love her? I ask.

She's still crying.

Of course I loved her. She was my baby.

But you left her, I say. You left her to Dave. You let him screw her. How often? Once a week? Twice a day?

No, she wails. No.

Dave, I say, strolling around the bed. What was she like? Was she a really good screw? Is that why you did her like that?

What do you know? he yells. You don't know shit.

I want to bust him over the head.

But I do, Dave, I say. I knew her. She told me all about you. That's why I came. To let you know that somebody knows what you did to her. I loved her something awful. It was you chased her into that river.

I put the muzzle up to his head. He goes still.

No, Betty cries. No.

I stay there. I wait. I'm so good at waiting.

Tell the truth, Dave. You screwed her, didn't you?

His lips tremble. I push the muzzle against his temple harder.

Yes, he says.

It was your baby she had, wasn't it?

Yes.

Are you going to talk to the press anymore, telling them lies?

No.

I wait, wanting to pull the trigger, wishing, wishing, wishing that I could.

Why can't I ever pull the trigger?

I go back to the dresser and see a picture that stops my heart. It's Mama. It's fat old Mama and me sitting in a swing. I look to be five or six.

I take the picture over to Betty. Who's this?

That's Mama, she says. And Terri.

Terri. Hearing her say it like that gives me a jolt. That was my name back then, before Ben beat it out of me.

She raised Terri, she says. Mama took care of Terri and James Vincent, my son from a different marriage. I got Terri back when she was twelve.

Mama, I think. A picture of Mama.

Why then? Why when she was twelve?

The house burned down. The kids got out. Mama died.

She burned up, I say. Roasted alive.

What's this to you? shouts Dave. Who are you?

I pick up the tape, jogging around the bed, and rip a piece off, slapping it over Dave's incestuous mouth.

I told you to shut up. You're lucky I don't slice off your prick.

I look at the picture again and want to start crying. Slipping it into the front of my jeans, I pace back to the dresser. I hold up my gym bag and push all the pictures into it.

What about your boy. James?

He ran off when I came to get him.

I start shaking. The whole event is beginning to clobber me.

You've got photo albums, don't you?

Yes, Betty says. Over there on the shelves.

I walk over and find three hefty volumes. I dump these into my bag.

I don't want to read about this in the paper, I say. I don't want to find out you've been fucking lying to the media again. I'll come back. I'll send friends that hate you even more than I do. (Now I'm sounding like a deranged five-year-old.)

Betty whimpers.

I back out of the room but stop in my old bedroom, picking up the cup, the doll's head, and the toupee. I race out of that house, thinking I should have poured it over with gas. I should have lit a match. I should have watched it go up in flames.

By four in the morning, I finally find my way back to the highway. Lucky for me (or unlucky, depending on your perspective), there's a twenty-four-hour liquor store at the interchange. I decide to break out of my rhythm and go for a bottle of tequila.

Then I hook on to I-75 and follow it north to I-70, stopping after about an hour of driving. I take a room at a hotel named, of all things, El Rancho. At this point, I've devoured a third of my tequila.

I lug my gym bag and duffel bag into my room, and a few

guns just in case I need them. I think I start going through the
pictures, though I'm not sure. By the time the tequila is near
gone, I swallow the bottle of Valium. I would have taken the
codeine too if I'd been able to manage it.

Kat and the boys stopped coming to me. The ghosts pressed in. I
twitched. I followed them with my eyes.

Now Ben came. He let my hands and legs go. He made love to
me. I was starved for touch and craved his presence, his watery
voice and body.

He began to teach me by feel. Touch this here. Stroke like
that. Now wait. Pay attention to the body. This with the tongue,
that with the fingers.

Ben kept me blind, still gagged most of the time unless he
wanted me to use my mouth. When he went away, it was a torture for me. But now, he left my arms and legs free, forbidding
me to touch the tape at my eyes or the gag. I lay obedient and
filled with such a pressure of constant arousal that my thighs
wept for his touch.

Then there was nothing. No one came.

I hummed all Mama's songs. I talked and talked, jerking from
the pinching ghost fingers.

At first I didn't know. I didn't understand that it wasn't the
ghosts that had gotten me to my feet. And they were pushing me,
but I couldn't walk very well.

Ben's voice came from behind me. "This is your last lesson,
Beth. So you don't ever forget."

They dragged me to the rail. They tied my hands to a pipe
over my head, the rail catching me at the waist.

That was the worst time ever. He whipped me loud. He
whipped me inside out. By the time he was done, Ben had
whipped me deaf.

After that whipping, they cut me down and left me lying like
a puddle on the floor. I didn't make a sound. I didn't move. I
didn't wait anymore.

They came to get me later on, having to carry me up the stairs. My eyes were so crusted over that Kat had to work at cleaning them for hours, making over me, saying, revery and revery. Bright lights and shapes scared me for near a year afterward.

But Kat and the boys were so sweet, so good to me.

I had graduated. I was seasoned. I was a child born from a sharp and sorry womb.

"Oh my God."

My eyes go half-open. I lift my head a bit and smell rather than see that my cheek is smack in the middle of a pile of vomit. My left nostril is half buried in it and burns like hell from sucking it in.

A guy bends down. His face looms before my eyes.

"She's still alive." He steps over me. I can see out into the corridor. Two maids, one an elderly black woman with horn-rimmed glasses and a watery eye, and the other fresh from south of the border, stare at me.

I hear the phone pick up. He dials. Waits.

"Yes. I need an ambulance."

I try to push up, but can't, so I roll over and say, "No."

He ignores me and keeps talking.

"No," I say again and pull myself onto my feet, using a chair for support. I stagger and fall toward him, slapping my hand down on the phone, disconnecting the call. Then I slump against the guy, wiping puke down his sleeve.

"Fuck," he says, and steps back, staring at me like I'm a piece of shit.

"You've got a half hour to get out of here," he says. "Or I'm calling the cops."

He stalks away and slams the door behind him. The two nice ladies disappear from view.

I fall onto the bed and use the sheet to clean off my face and blow my nose. I can't believe how bad I feel.

Crawling to the bathroom, I stumble into the tub, turn on the shower, and lie back, letting it drench both myself and my clothes. After I worm out of the shower, I brace against the sink to look in the mirror.

If Dave and Betty could only see me now. How gratified they'd feel. I wonder how long it took them to get free. I wonder how Dave's face is doing. I bet it looks better than mine.

I trudge back to the other room and find some dry clothes, thinking I should hit a Laundromat soon.

That's the problem, isn't it? If you're alive, you have to deal with all the niggly things. The keeping things clean, when all they want to do is get dirty. And the having to keep your guns handy.

That's a trick.

Somebody pounds on my door.

"Okay," I yell. I dress and stuff everything else into the duffel bag. Hoisting it onto my shoulder, I almost collapse. Then I drag the gym bag with its stolen merchandise along the floor, opening the door. The lovely man who's been so helpful is standing with his arms crossed and a nasty look on his face.

Cramming everything and myself into the car, I weave out of the parking lot, cross the street to his competitor, and take a room there. Then I stumble to a nearby service station. I buy a gallon of Gatorade.

When I wake up the next day, my head feels like a jackhammer on concrete. My stomach is shredded. I think somebody rearranged all my organs, squeezing them first so that they ache. I spring for another night.

Theresa Sue Lumley. Terri. I try saying it in different ways like I might have said it before. Then I take out the picture of Mama. I cry. To have a picture of her like this is the best thing in the world.

I flip through the photo albums. Most of the pictures are recent ones of Dave barbecuing, Betty in the kitchen, or the two of them on a cruise. They seem to cruise a lot. There's just a few of me, or the little girl parading as me. The pictures of my supposed sister abound, flowing like a veritable fountain.

I close the album. This trip into midwestern familyhood is making me even sicker. I pick up a framed picture of Dave in his golf clothes with his arms around the shoulders of two buddies. They're all smiling. I wonder if it's a special club of childfuckers. They're all happy about the fact that when they get home, they can throw one of their daughters on the bed and hump themselves even happier.

I pitch the picture at the wall.

I guess I showed him.

After sleeping again, I take out the pictures of me. I find another photo of Mama sitting in a kitchen. I grab that one too, sticking the stuff I don't want in the gym bag.

When I pick up the picture I threw against the wall, I find that the glass broke, and behind that picture are two small school photos. One is of me. The other is Vin. He must be about ten. I cry again.

Oh Vin, Vin, Vin. Or James, I guess. I stash these two pictures in my pocket.

Two days later, after gallons of Gatorade and a few packs of crackers, I force down two eggs and toast for breakfast, tossing the pictures of Dave and Betty in a Dumpster.

I rev up the Taurus and hit I-70, heading west.

7

Utopia

As I buzz along the interstate, I'm all wigged up in my Becca outfit, still sick and dismal about Betty and good old Dave. My head all of a sudden slips back to Ben and Violet and what I think of in my mind as "the night." I ride with Ben in the limo again. I wait in the reception line. I sip champagne.

Ben's talking very serious with a guy I've never seen before. He's about as big as Ben, but has long hair pulled back into a ponytail. I admire his ass as I stand, bored to death, in the center of a group of lobbyists.

It suddenly comes to me how the man that Ben was talking to wore gym shoes. Tux coat and pants, and black gym shoes.

Driving along the highway, I can't get Ben out of my head. I never would have thought him to be someone to fall in love. But then I remember his face when he ran out of the van that night on the bridge. I think maybe Violet was right, and that even in someone like Ben, the ache drives you forward, stuffing your lungs and your belly until you're drowned for sure and you fix yourself up to get stacked in Rivertown.

That's when I notice that the interstate I'm following is winding through some dark, industrial wasteland. According to the map, I'm heading full-tilt toward Chicago. Thinking back, I decide that I must have gotten turned ass-backward on that screwy junction in some place called Indianapolis. At first I'm a little pissed about the change in my hazy planning procedure, but when I see the Chicago skyline, I get homesick for Manhattan.

Getting downtown is a trick, since road construction is more like a disease in Chicago than a beneficial activity. Once I hit downtown, I find a room and eat at a nice, civilized restaurant. Afterward, I pick up a copy of the *Times* and a notebook. The stories are pushing again. The something behind is chasing.

Strolling into Grant Park, I sit on a bench and open the paper. I get my worst chit yet. The headline says: SERIAL KILLER IN MANHATTAN? But it's not the headline that gets me. It's the pictures. There are seven photos in all and one drawing. Four guys and four girls. Most of them are strangers to me, but one of them is definitely Matt. The article names him John Weathers from Tennessee. It's his yearbook picture.

I hear the sound of that pop again, from when Ben broke Matt's arm, and my head goes a little blank. I never saw Matt after we left him in that room. None of us did.

My dinner starts feeling like it might want to make a second showing. And there's this feeling that works itself into me. I can smell that play room. I hear Matt's screams clear as if he were next to me. My skin is electrified.

None of the other photos looks familiar. It's the drawing that gets me. She's named Jane Doe, as no positive identification has ever been made. I can see why they might not want to use Detective Bates' photos. The artist's rendition of Violet doesn't capture the moment of her lips brushing mine.

The article says, similar wounds. It says, all runaways and prostitutes. It says, no witnesses or clues. Except. And now the really big chit. Except a woman brought in the same night as the murder of Jane Doe, who had a wound believed to be made by the same knife. The woman's name is being withheld by the police for reasons of confidentiality.

I curl up on my park bench, feeling like somebody's sending jolts of current into my head. I get a picture in my mind of that same play room of Ben's. He liked it a lot. Violet is on the floor, her hands cuffed behind. It looks like she's sleeping, except for her body is all wrong. It shouldn't bend quite that way. I see a man leaning over her. He has a ponytail and is wearing a long overcoat. On his feet are black gym shoes.

I can't get to her. I can't scream. All I can think is that I must be strapped up some way.

I'm off the bench now and running. I stop myself at some point and walk fast, glancing behind like somebody might be after me.

It's too neat. Too true. All the chits falling in a row.

And where was Ben? He was usually watching, or else he had one of the big boys do it for him. And what happened to Slim and his friend? Why, instead of being free of Ben, did Violet end up dead?

I think of Detective Bates. He knew all along. God, he's patient, waiting five years to hit me again for information. And Ben, why didn't he want them to know I was his girl?

He didn't want it to hurt business.

Violet dead on the floor, and he's worried about business.

Nearby, a young couple stroll with a baby carriage. I see Violet's eyes on every side, pale, glassy. Muddy water passes over, dragging me down.

This is what I get for trying to learn fly-fishing.

I think of my fall from the bridge that night, of my longing to find something I lost a long time ago. I think of my new life, my messy, screwy new life. And Violet pursues.

We are captured not by the living, but by the dead.

Mandy and me knew that a long time ago.

In the winter, the river didn't change much except that the water got colder. Leaves dropped from the willows and the cottonwoods. In the swamps downstream, the snakes went away for a time. The peepers and the crickets went silent.

Vin and me would sleep near on top of each other to stay

warm some nights, with Mama snoring nearby like a dog choked with a bone.

In the spring, though, the river was like suicide. It rose fitful, crawling up near the porch like it wanted in. Then there'd be a sudden surge and you'd wake in the morning with the water surrounding on all sides and below.

The spring was when all sorts of things broke loose in the water, things that froze up north, I guess, and after the melt were being dragged downstream. We found pieces of boats and broken furniture. Big logs and branches swept down. Vin and me and Mandy would climb a willow and sit up over the water, watching to see what might come down.

We saw a bright red tablecloth. We saw barrels and barbed wire. We saw a mattress all muddy and torn. The next day we watched the bed frame slide down. We saw photos of women and men, and once we saw a dead goat, thinking at first it was a man with a big nose. We had a terrible fit at that, and Mandy just about fell in it scared her so bad.

I dream of being over the river and watching it pass. Everything goes by, floating off in a river like suicide, some happiness waiting just beyond the bend, until it makes the eddy near Fowler, where all the trash collects and sinks down in.

I spend the night in the bathroom of my hotel room curled up between the tub and the toilet, clutching a gun in each hand, listening for the gym shoes. As soon as it's light out, I change into Becker and duck out of the hotel, packing everything back in the Taurus. Then I weave through the streets, searching out a pay phone. I call information. The automated voice barks out a number in NYC. I dial and wait.

The precinct desk guy picks up, and I ask for Detective Bates. I hold, having to jam in quarters.

"Bates here." It's his rat's ass voice all right, like something trying to sneak up on you in the dark.

I can't speak. I think I might have to hang up.

"Detective Bates," I manage to say.

"Yes?"

"I have a tip. Some information about the article in the *Times* yesterday."

"Who is this?"

"It doesn't matter. It's about Jane Doe. The killer had a ponytail. He was tall. He was at a reception that night for one of New York's senators."

"Beth," he says.

I go silent.

"Betty and Dave were real shook up."

I chew my lip.

"How the hell did you survive that drop?"

I hang up. Asshole. How did he know?

I rev the Taurus, wishing it were a Porsche, and tear out of there as if Bates might be right around the corner watching me. I don't slow down until I find myself near someplace called Joliet.

That's when I begin to get back what little nerve I've retained through the past few days. I stop at an old metal diner like the kind you might see in some TV sitcom.

Sitting in a booth with my hands shaking, I open my atlas, thinking I better lie low again. The nearest national forest is Shawnee, down in south Illinois.

Before I leave, I pump my waitress for directions to a sports store. Then I sneak into the women's john and dress as Becca, leaving off the wig. I'm thinking of trashing that idea. I barrel into downtown Joliet, looking to pick up some gear.

Having a hard time making up my mind, I shop for over an hour. There are so many cool choices, so many color combinations to set off against each other. As I wait at the checkout counter with my pile of stuff, I peruse the message board next to me.

Farmhand wanted, it says. Male or female worker needed to help out on organic farm. Room, board, and stipend. There's a phone number. It grinds around in my brain as I wait and wait while the lady ahead of me keeps trying to find a charge card that will get accepted. I locate a phone on the wall near the door, so I wheel my stuff over, dialing the number.

"Hello." A man's voice.

"Hi. I'm calling about the farmhand needed."

"You're hired," he says.

I'm stumped. "You don't want to meet me first? I could be a paraplegic. I might be too ugly to look at day after day."

He doesn't laugh. Bad sign.

"If we don't get help soon, we're going to start losing some of our crops. You're the first person to call since we put the notice up three weeks ago."

"Why doesn't anybody else want it?" I say, nervous.

This time he laughs. "People don't like the labor or the heat. They like desks with soft chairs. They want air conditioning. They prefer to wear uncomfortable clothing like ties and high heels."

Now I laugh. "You don't have air conditioning? And by the way, I'm real attached to my heels."

"I'll work on the AC," he says. "I don't care what you wear on your feet."

He gives me directions and I end up at a tall, narrow old farmhouse with a large red barn, some outbuildings, five large oaks hanging over the house, and four very large, very noisy, mangy-looking dogs. I wait in my car. I see that beside the house is an old Volkswagen van that looks like it used to have paisley and flowers painted all over it.

Hippies, I think. Organic farm. Utopia.

A woman steps out of the house looking like the original earth mother. Behind her is a little boy, sticking to her like glue. She calls off the dogs and shakes my hand when I get out of the car.

"Joan," she says. Her eyes are soft at the edges, and the lines on her face, accentuated by so much sun, look to be from smiling a lot.

"Becca."

She pulls the little boy in front of her. "Tut."

I stare down. "Hi Tut."

He doesn't say a thing. Tut's clutching a small boombox, and he looks at me with gorgeous wide brown eyes deep as the river. His skin is milk chocolate and his hair is reddish-brown with a good amount of kink. He looks to be about six or seven.

She shows me a room off the side of the barn. It has a bed, dresser, a small kitchen with a sink, hot plate, and toaster oven. The john is tiny. A tall guy wouldn't be able to sit on the seat without having to pull his knees up.

"We could use you in the field now," she says.

Tut is sitting on my bed, fiddling with his boombox. He's so serious. I watch as he reaches in a pocket of Joan's skirt, takes out a CD very carefully, and slides it in. It's one of the younger female singers that are coming on right now.

I drop my duffel bag and face Joan. "I want to be paid in cash. No papers signed. And I like to wear a pistol."

She doesn't blink an eye. "It's a deal."

That's the beginning of something fine. John and Joan treat me like family. We get up before dawn and hit the rows as soon as we can see to pick. Then we traipse into the barn and wash it down.

They have regular customers that they pack up boxes for. But they also have several restaurants and health-food stores in Chicago and the suburbs that they supply twice weekly, filling up the back of the Volkswagen van, and hiking it up to the city. Whatever's left they sell at local fruit and vegetable stands.

I work myself dead every day, sleeping hard at night. By the end of three weeks, even though I still hurt from all the bending over and kneeling, I'm feeling strong again.

John is one of those tall, lanky guys that you're always worrying how his jeans might just drop right off. His hair is bleached from the sun, and his mustache and beard are part gone to gray. His eyes glitter. Before I worked there, I was already good at choosing vegetables and fruits. But John's vast knowledge of varieties helps me perfect my talent.

Most of the time, Tut stays with Joan, but the longer I'm there, the more I find him following me as I'm bent over picking beans or cutting broccoli.

It turns out that Tut is a foster child that John and Joan took on when both their kids left for college a couple years ago. This year their son Tom and daughter Susan are taking summer classes, which is why they hired me.

Of course they want to know about me, so I fabricate an abusive husband from whom I'm running, which is why the pistol and the need for secrecy. I guess in some ways I'm not lying all that much.

I have a copy of the *Times* sent to the farm every day. I feel a need to keep my eyes peeled. And I'm beginning to worry about Ben. If the round-bodied Detective Bates figured me out, Ben might have figured it, too. And he has contacts in the police.

One morning when I get up, I'm having more trouble than usual with my back. It turns out that Joan's too sick to make the Chicago deliveries. Since we'd hit a lull in weeding, John suggests that I do the route. He makes me a map with directions. I worry. Maps obviously aren't my strong point or I wouldn't have ended up near Joliet in the first place.

After we have the van so full the front wheels are almost off the ground, Joan surprises me by suggesting that Tut go along with me. I'm about to say no when I see his face light up. It's the first time I've seen him smile since I've been here.

So I throw my backpack into the van and Tut scrambles into the passenger seat. As the van weaves and lumbers its way to Chicago, Tut drops that same CD into his boombox again, and the two of us listen to it.

I didn't like it the first time I heard it, but now, as I begin to take in the words, I feel drawn down, like I'm in the river again and sinking below where the current is strong and cold, where the ache runs hard. But there's more in the music than that. I have a sense of a woman's face, of her eyes watching me, knowing Beth and Clarisse, seeing Terri.

"Who is this singing?" I ask Tut.

"Miriam Dubois," he says.

Before we hit Chicago, I pull in at a rest stop and change into Becker.

"This is our little secret," I say to Tut as I sit in my seat.

He smiles at me and giggles. Much to my surprise, I find myself smiling back. He looks in my eyes for the first time. And gazing at him, I feel some kind of lightness inside of me. I wonder how it would be to live a life without Ben in my head and Violet bleeding onto the floor. I wonder what it would feel like to be happy.

So we go about our business, unloading through the day, finishing up about dinnertime. I'm not in the mood to head home yet, so we stop at a mall in a suburb just south of Chicago, looking to pick up dinner.

We take our time, nosing out the stores. As we're hiking down a long expanse of marble glaring into our brains, surrounded on all sides by loads and loads of stuff, I hear Tut say real loud, "Is that your sister?"

I turn and look, seeing my Clarisse Broder face a hundred times repeated in the display windows of a bookstore. A sign yells in my face: "Available Now!"

I slouch. I pull around the brim of my hat. I punch my sunglasses tight against my face.

"Shut up, Tut," I say as people look at us. I shuffle over and study the picture. It's different than the one they had in the papers. I have no idea where Jeremy found this one. Tut and I mosey inside, where I pick up a copy. It's the new printing.

They added lots of pictures from Jeremy's sister's archives. There's us in front of a Christmas tree. There's Jeremy's mother and me trying to avoid touching each other. There's me staring at the turkey like it's a scary petrified meat.

When did she manage to take all these pictures? The sneak.

I also see a batch of Betty and Dave's earlier photos, including the one of Mama and me. I think I might start crying.

The last two pictures near the end take the cake. The first is a view down to the water from the Brooklyn Bridge. The other is of a pile of flowers left at the place where I jumped.

God, they're milking this. I want to call my agent and tell her she should be ashamed of herself.

On the back of the book jacket it says, tragic suicide. It says, dark novel, cult phenomenon. It doesn't say, undercurrent. It doesn't say, the dangers got her. There's so much it doesn't say that it makes me sick.

I buy a copy, contributing to Jeremy's investment strategies in futures. Searching for Tut, I find him plopped on the floor with a Dr. Seuss book spread on his knees, happy as a bee.

I think preschool. I think college tuition.

I buy him the book.

We get back to the farm late that night. Tut wants to sleep with me, so I let him curl up at my side. But I lie awake, worried again. Even here in Utopia, my past has a way of sneaking up on me. I decide that I'm going to have to leave soon, before my ugly little world reaches in and snatches Utopia away.

Every night after we brought Violet up from the basement, she curled against me just like Tut. I got to looking forward to her slipping in next to me. She helped the ache.

And later, when we were making love, when she was rubbing my back or tending welts or bruises on me, or when I held her in my arms, the ache became finer, weaker. But it never went away.

The last few months of that time are coming clearer to me now. I think of Violet moody. I think of her watching Ben with hate undisguised. I remember how the ache grew in me as Violet got pushy about getting out, as she worked me like she tried with Ben, withholding her love at times. That was a misery to me, so that I pushed Ben into whipping me just to get her affection.

And I remember orgasm after orgasm of nothing but despair. Violet made her plans. She drew me along by the power of my misery and love.

I remember kissing her good-bye that night as clear as though it happened just now. She had helped me dress in the black strapless gown, adjusting my slip and hose.

I can smell her breath, taste on my lips that which made her Violet and no other. I see her eyes, still roving and wet, still sly, and her skin smooth, flush, a world made round.

That was just a few hours before the Dumpster, before the blanket drawn back, before the sky wept Violet clean through, melting her off like salt, washing her down through the sewers.

The next week, I begin to go down. I want whiskey. My eyes start itching for smack. At the end of the week, they send me on the Chicago route again because Tom, their son, is flying in from Berkeley. Joan's too busy cooking up some heart-clogging farm dinner and John is balancing the books. Tut's not able to go with me this time since his social worker is visiting that afternoon.

Before I hit O'Hare, I find a record store where I look up Miriam Dubois, intending to buy Tut another CD of hers. When I finally find her, I check the picture. I stop.

She could be Violet's sister. In fact, the similarities are so strong she could almost be a twin, though she has lighter skin and hair. She holds her eyes different. Her lips are softened, as though waiting, and her chin less adamant. I gaze at her, unable to look away. I think of her music. How the ache runs through.

So I buy a CD for Tut and three for me. I'm thinking I'll get to know her, as though it might make those other pictures fade, the ones in Detective Bates' briefcase.

Later, as I'm waiting at the terminal, dressed as Becca, paranoid as hell, I see a tall man with a ponytail in a business suit. I freak and stare at his shoes. Thank God they're not gym shoes.

But it throws me backward, and I hate Ben so hard, I think I'm going to bust open. He didn't do anything to help Violet. He just let her die like a stuck pig.

"Hi."

I jump and reach for my gun.

"You must be Becca." A young guy looking a lot like Joan in the eyes and chin is looking me up and down. "Dad gave me a general description," his eyes rest on my breasts, "but he left out some important points." Now his eyes drift downward. "I think I should have come home sooner."

So within a few days, who shows up in my room at night but Tommy-boy.

I'm becoming such a part of the family, I think, as Tom undoes my shorts, as he lifts my shirt over my head.

I show him new positions and advise him on pleasuring a woman. I tie his hands to the bedposts and tease him for hours.

The young are so fun to teach.

After he departs for the night, I put on the CDs of Miriam Dubois, or M.D., as I've started referring to her in my mind. I gaze at her pictures, amazed at how she's so like Violet. I let her music draw me under. I know I'm getting goofy, but I think I fall in love with her like I'm a teenager. I dream of her eyes looking at me. If I still believed in hexing, I'd have made a doll to draw her to me. I keep telling myself it's just because of Violet, and how she died, and how much I miss her.

That's when things start to really go down. The *Times* arrives one day with you-know-who on the front page once more. Or should I say, two different incarnations of you-know-who.

There's the mug shot of Beth the shoplifter next to the cover picture of Clarisse Broder. The headline? ARE THESE THE SAME WOMAN? SECRET PAST REVEALED.

The *Times* has been getting a little slack lately, dipping into yellow journalism to boost sales.

And as I'm reading the story, I get a creepy feeling my favorite detective is baiting me. I'm sure he leaked this out, trying to scare the rabbit from its hole, which I'm determined is not going to happen. That is, until I read the last paragraph about Mrs. Broder's alleged death.

Alleged?

After all, it goes on to say, no body was ever recovered.

I think of Ben reading this article, and I try not to panic. No one can possibly know where I am. My trail is cold, except, I have to concede, for my little excursion into criminal behavior at Dave and Betty's. And then there was that incident at the hotel with all the puke.

I grind my teeth. I'm going to have to call that little shit of a detective again and get him off my case, maybe have him retract this alleged crap.

Later, I convince John to let me run the Chicago deliveries again, so they can spend more time with their horny son. It's good I'm leaving anyway, since Susan is due to show up that evening. Utopia's getting a little crowded for my taste these days.

I have a hard time about not letting Tut come with me, but I worry that Ben's on my trail. To distract him, I hand over the CD I bought for him the last trip. This makes him so excited, he forgets about me.

Once I'm in Chicago, I buy a phone card, ringing up New York.

"Bates here."

"Hi," I say.

"Beth," he says. "I've been expecting your call. Or are you going by Becky now?"

"You little shit," I say. "Are you trying to get me screwed up? Do you have any idea what Ben will do to me if he finds me? I thought the police were supposed to be nice to their witnesses."

"All I want is your cooperation," he says.

"Maybe you should look the word up so you know what it means."

"I need to see you and ask you questions."

"Nothing doing. Ask me your questions now. I'm listening."

"Beth, I'll find you if I have to put your face on wanted posters and milk cartons."

"God, why don't you go after someone like Ben this hard?"

"I'm working on that one," he says.

That scares the shit out of me. "You should talk to some of the kids he gets and sticks in that basement of his. They'd give you an earful."

"Why don't you tell me what he did to you in the basement, Beth?" His voice is soft. It's got something in it so much like sorrow, I think I might go crazy.

"Don't ask me that, Bates. You want to put me in the loony bin? I never think about that anymore. You can't. It'll make you do something bad."

"Like jump off a bridge?"

I'm crying now. I can't stop it. I slide down to a crouch in the phone booth.

"You can do this for Violet," he says. "She was your friend."

"You don't know shit," I say, but I'm still crying.

"Calm down, Beth. I'm sorry. I'm sorry for everything. I wish to hell he'd never gotten his hands on any of you." He stops, waiting for me to quiet down. "So tell me what you remember. I need more of a description. Where did it happen?"

"That's the thing," I say. "I only now started remembering it a little. I really thought I had a fucking appendectomy for five years. And near as I can tell, it happened at Ben's, which is strange. Ben always stops that kind of thing. He doesn't like to waste all his training."

"You were in the room?"

"Yes."

"So the guy kills Violet and starts on you, but you get away?"

"No. That's the weird thing. I couldn't move. I must have been strapped down some way, and maybe gagged. I can't remember that part."

"Why didn't he kill you?"

"I don't know. I don't remember being stabbed. All I remember is him bending over Violet. Her hands are cuffed back, and her neck is . . ." I begin to gag.

He waits as I compose myself. "You said he was at a reception earlier that evening?"

"Yes. I saw Ben talking to him. I don't remember his face other than that I thought he was handsome, about Ben's size. He had a nice ass. And long brown hair in a ponytail. Oh, and he wore black gym shoes even though he was in a tux."

He's quiet. "Do you think you'd recognize the guy again?"

"Maybe."

"Can I send you some pictures?"

"No. I'm not telling you where I am. Your police force has too many connections with Ben."

"Beth, why do you think he let you go for five years? Ben never does that. He doesn't just let go of his . . . players? Isn't that what he calls you?"

I rub my eyes and cover them. "He's in love with me, Bates. Lucky me. That's why I jumped off the damn bridge. He'd given me eight hours to get my things and come back to his great prison. I would have never gotten out again."

"Took a lot of guts."

"No. All it took was a memory of that basement and a whipping and a beating. That's what it took. I'm not going back to him. I'm not giving anybody any clue as to where I am. I'll do whatever it takes to stay away from Ben, even if I really have to kill myself."

He's quiet now. "We have hypnotists here that can help you remember things. There's probably some around where you are. It could help us to get the killer."

I chew a fingernail. "I'm scared to remember."

"I know. I can see why. But we're trying to catch this guy before he kills someone else. I don't care if they are prostitutes."

I find myself beginning to like him.

"How can I get in touch with you?" he asks.

"I read the *Times* every day. You can put a message in the classifieds."

"Okay. I'll put it in the personals. What name do you want it under?"

"Tut," I say.

"Tut," he repeats. "I'll sign it Beefy."

I laugh. "Beefy?"

"Yeah. You can probably guess why."

"How about 'crumpled' or 'in need of an iron'?"

"It's not my fault my wife left me."

"That's what they all say."

"You take care of yourself, Beth."

I think of my Uzi, my pistol, my shotgun. "I'm giving it my best shot, Bates."

I dream of Violet in the Dumpster. Her eyes are open like in the picture. I have kissed those eyes. They were warm. They were wet. Kissing them now and touching her again, I see how much she's changed, how far she's gone beyond my sight.

When I look at the pavement beneath her Dumpster, I see streams of red. Violet is bleeding again, I think. When will she ever be done?

Violet sleeping in the Dumpster. We would be wrong to wake her, to make her remember that night, wouldn't we? Shouldn't we let her sleep in peace?

Policemen lean forward and take pictures. They draw back the blanket to reveal nothing but all my love heaped over her skin. They see her ruined body, her imperfection, and imagine her to be different from them.

I'm overcome by the drape of her fingers, her hair dark and rich like night, and how deep she is sleeping. In this moment, her needs become clear to me. I gather the policemen together.

Let us all leave quietly.

8

Berkeley

I arrive at the farm late, having stopped to guzzle a few shots of Southern Comfort on the way back. Everyone's out on the porch, laughing. I stumble out of the van and trip up the steps, falling down flat.

I'm introduced to Susan, then I pass out on the porch, where they leave me all night. When I wake in the morning, I can hardly move. As I roll over and stretch, Sue comes out of the house with a cup of coffee for me. I stare at her lips, wondering what they would taste like. Tom walks out after her, and the three of us sit watching the sun come up.

That afternoon, Tom and I load extra produce into the van, and we putter into Joliet, hitting a couple vegetable stands. After we're done, we stop at the silver diner. We aren't there very long when I notice that a guy looks to be watching us.

"Let's blow this place," I say to Tom, throwing some change on the table and making for the door.

He shoots me a funny look, but follows me out. Once we're on the road, I keep my eye out behind. Tom's staring at me.

"There was a guy in there watching us," I say.

Tom's waiting, still staring at me.

"My husband might have hired somebody to kill me."

Tom hits the gas. We sputter down the road in our great escape vehicle.

I sit and brood about Bates, thinking it's time to move on again, but I have no idea where I'm going or what the hell I'm doing.

"You know, Becca," Tom says. "My girlfriend and I decided to live together this year, so I need to find someone who'll sublet my apartment from me." He shoots me a winning smile and adds, "But don't tell Mom and Dad."

I lean back against the seat. San Francisco. It has a nice ring.

"You'd love it out there," he says, "And I've got this great job at a classy restaurant on the bay. I might be able to get you a job there. Have you ever been a waitress?"

I consider the possibilities. Can't be any harder than being strapped down and whipped for a living. "Oh, sure," I say, remembering Jeremy and his morning coffee. "Women are born with waitress order pads in their hands."

He looks me up and down like he did at the airport terminal. "You've got all the qualifications you need."

I smile, looking out the window, wondering what great shops await me in San Francisco. "We can drive through in the Taurus," I say.

"Great," he says, staring at my breasts.

That night, after Tom and I are done, I stay up late listening to Miriam, but Violet intrudes.

I see now that it had to have been Ben that threw her in that Dumpster. Just another cleanup after a play. And as I go over and over it, the trout beginning to rise, I swear that I smell blood. It's all over me. I smell Ben, and behind that, I catch a hint of Kat's perfume.

My skin goes haywire like I've got bugs all over me. I scramble up and run out into the night, not stopping until my throat is raw. And after I've calmed, I climb up in the haymow and watch the night pass, my finger on the trigger of the Uzi. In a half-dream, I see Miriam's eyes. Way back inside her dark pupils, I watch the moving of the river. It's flowing rough and the undercurrent is wicked. But Miriam is smiling. I think she knows something that I don't. I wish she'd tell me, because of Violet and how she haunts and how she won't let me be.

Violet is whispering, wanting me to know everything.

I want silence and a simple appendectomy.

During breakfast that morning, I break the news of my departure to John and Joan. They start obsessing about the farmwork.

"I'm worried about my husband. He's very violent," I say, getting in some good practice on that particular lie. "Don't tell anyone about me, even if they say they're a cop. My husband's a cop." I should get an Emmy. "If anybody comes around asking questions, call Tom so he can tell me."

Tom and I pack the Taurus that evening, and we buzz out of town before sunup the next morning. It's somewhere in the middle of Utah two days later that Tom's groping around for something on the floor of the car. He comes up with the Uzi.

"My God, Becca," he says. "Just a little paranoid?"

Just a little.

"I also have a shotgun and three pistols," I say. "And boxes of ammo. Let's start a religious commune."

He thinks it's funny. So we stop, set up Coke bottles, and practice shooting different weapons at them. What a gas. The shotgun knocks me back so hard on the recoil that I get a bruise on my shoulder. We're terrible shots, which makes me determined to correct the situation once I get to Berkeley.

The next day, we tool into town late. I bed down with Tom since his girlfriend isn't back yet.

Free love.

In the morning, Tom and I make a pilgrimage into the city (as they call San Francisco out here, as though it's New York for God's sakes). I graze the shops of San Francisco with a wad of cash in the pocket of my rangy-looking jeans. It makes my head spin after so many weeks of grunging my way across the country. By the time I'm done, I've wasted a couple thousand dollars.

After we cross back to Berkeley, Tom shows me my new apartment. It's an efficiency on the fourth floor not far from the university, sporting three windows, one of which looks down on the street. The other two have great views of brick walls. The furnishings are reminiscent of the decor in the two-room so long ago. I feel right at home.

Then Tom calls up the restaurant, Tutti, a pricey purveyor of California cuisine. After he has Burt, the owner, on the line, he gives me a good plug as a hard worker. I know he's really thinking about either my tits or my ass.

It turns out that Burt is short a waitress and a kitchen manager at the moment, so he tells Tommy-boy to bring me over in the morning.

I'm up early the next day, worrying. I shower and prep, agonizing over my clipped, bleached hair.

"Lots of people wear it that way out here," Tom says when he arrives. "If you want to finish off the look, you should get your face pierced in about three or four places."

I'm beginning to like the West Coast already.

Dressed to the teeth again, like Ben always expected, I'm armed and dangerous, concealing my holster and gun beneath a silk cardigan. Tom drives me over to Tutti while I fret. I've never interviewed for a job in my life.

Burt is a solid man, looking me straight in the eye when I shake his hand. He takes his time checking me over. Burt's dressed in a well-tailored suit, but something about him tells me he'd be more comfortable in jeans and driving around in a banged-up truck. It's his eyes that catch me. He's seen things he wishes he could forget.

Once we're seated in his office, he asks me a few questions, not really listening to my answers as I lean a little forward to give him a view of the tops of my breasts cupped in just a touch of lace revealed. I cross my legs, hiking up my skirt.

He hires me on the spot, before I get a chance to make an asshole of myself, which is all for the better. He wants me to start that evening.

The first thing I notice as I begin my new occupation is how much the people get on my nerves. They're so indecisive about what to eat. And they make such bad choices. Wine coolers when you can order a vintage wine? And who would eat ranch dressing in a place like Tutti? I find out that Burt keeps a huge jar of it in his office, hidden from Larry, the chef, who would have smashed it on the floor.

I begin to wander through the kitchen, checking out the produce, the cuts of meat, the fish brought straight from the boat. Larry and I become fast friends. We toss the items of which we don't approve at Burt's office door.

The first night, I'm introduced to Josh, the maitre d', a tall, well-built man of gorgeous black skin. He bows and kisses my hand. Then he laughs, telling me that I'm lovely in his Haitian French.

As the days go by, I begin to refer to certain parties who are dining as "the dangers." Josh likes that. We compare notes on them. Tom, who's now working mainly as a wine steward, Josh, and I form huddles around Josh's desk, gossiping and deciding which women are the best dressed. All Tom cares about are tits and ass.

Josh and I peruse the accessories, with me occasionally making a comment like, "She could wear a gun beneath that," or, "A twelve-gauge would slip in there easy as pie." My best, "That's a purse big enough for an Uzi." Josh eyes me. Tom looks the other way and whistles.

After a couple of weeks pass and I settle into the job, I find myself beginning to argue with people about their choice of food. "You wouldn't like that," I say about the salmon. "It's only farm-raised today." Or, "No, no. Beef is never cooked to medium, you should eat the chicken."

Burt keeps nagging me. "Just nod when they order. Don't even open those lovely lips of yours, as they appear to be untrainable."

I try. I guess all those gags at Ben's never allowed me the opportunity to learn verbal control.

So Burt takes me aside after I've been there about a month. "I keep getting complaints about you, Becca. You've got to stop bossing the clientele."

I sigh. "Nice tie today, Burt." I stand close and adjust it for him. Burt's cheeks flush and he escapes, sitting behind his desk. It makes me like him a lot.

"If it were anyone else causing these problems, I'd have to let the person go, but I've come up with a better idea. My buyer is leaving next week, and I still haven't found a good kitchen manager. Since you seem to be so picky about the food, and since you're so good at being bossy, why don't you take on both positions? I'll take care of the wine."

I sit in his lap and kiss him, which makes his ears go hot pink. Thank God I'm going to get a little distance between the dangers and myself. Josh and Tom and I celebrate after hours that night with a bottle of *grand cru.*

That next week, Tom and I start shooting. I found a big gun store with a shooting range a few weeks back and began cultivating the owner, a nasty old lecher it turns out, named Orville of all things. Tom and I go and shoot while Orville slobbers like a pit bull. He feels me up in the booth as he pretends to teach me the finer points of marksmanship.

Both Tom and I get to be decent shots and more picky about our weapons. It turns out that Orville is happy to move guns around under the table. So I trade the Ladysmith and the semiautomatic for a Walther P99 double-action semiautomatic. Tom springs for an H&K USP compact, using the money he saved to fly home for Thanksgiving and Christmas. We talk about our guns as if they're our dates.

"She's aching for a good round," Tom says, his eyes dreamy.

"Walther's feeling punk today." I sigh. "He got loaded again last night."

Because of my double salary, I make enough money to garage

the Taurus, which helps to ease my paranoia about Ben finding me. But at Tutti, whenever a limo glides up to the entrance, I get woozy, certain that Ben will step out with that smile on his face. And the undercurrent begins to pull. The ache vibrates. I find myself listening to Miriam Dubois during almost all my free time. At times, I refer to her as Violet in my head.

Miriam haunts me. Her music runs through my skin like one of the ghosts pricking me. I yearn to find her. I want her to watch me with those eyes. I want to trap her into loving me.

But it's Violet that keeps returning, wanting to tell me everything I don't want to know. I run from her. I take to drinking some nights. In desperation and loneliness, I turn my attention to Josh.

I'm informed by Cinda, a really blond, really white waitress who could have been from Scranton, that Josh is gay. Cinda, by the way, has all the personal depth of a sheet of paper.

So what? I think. Why make a big deal about it?

I begin flirting with Josh, and after I'm introduced to his boyfriend, Greg, who's another hunk, I start flirting with him, too.

The three of us begin to go shopping for clothes together. They especially like to help me choose lingerie. I think they're secretly jealous.

Even though I'm flirting to beat the band, I'm not getting a rise (so to speak) out of either of them. I begin to make blatant passes, confused, having never been refused by a man before. As the days go by and I fail again and again, I find myself slipping backward, remembering Ben, how he was so good to me at times. I catch myself taking out his card and fingering it. He's just a phone call away. Some nights I turn Miriam off in a fit of anger, near to tears, the ache choking me, the ghosts coming into my head.

One night as we're closing, I reach between Josh's legs from behind, taking hold of him. He doesn't move. Ashamed, I remove my hand and walk away, thinking about the S&W I have near my bed. The one with the long barrel. I think of Violet. I think that maybe tonight I'll finally be able to pull the trigger.

Josh catches me around the waist from behind. I try to pull away, but he holds me there.

"Becca," he says, whispering. "Come over to my place now. Greg is there." He turns me around and holds me to him. "I won't give you sex, but I can give you this."

I find that tears are filling my eyes. I fight them and try to pull away, but he keeps me there. Then he holds me at arm's length and stares at me. I turn my face.

"Will you come?" he says.

I won't look at him.

Josh takes my hand and brings me to his place. By then, I'm seeing lights and hearing Miriam's voice in my head. Josh wants to talk to me, but I can't. I don't know what's happening to me. All my pieces, so badly held together, like that little blue cup, are coming undone.

"Come on," Josh says. "I'm putting you to bed."

I shake my head, but he coos to me in French, which reminds me of Mama. I wonder if he's repeating what his mother said to him when he was a boy and unable to sleep.

Josh and Greg each take one of my arms and lead me to the bedroom, lying me between them, with Josh still talking singsong in French. I have to work hard to keep from crying. That night, I wake every hour, watching the ghosts dance around the room.

After that, Josh invites me over to spend the night from time to time. He seems to have some second sense, able to tell when I'm near some edge I can't define.

Josh and Greg lie me between the two of them on those nights because they see how much it pleases me. I sometimes wake, thinking I'm back in the two-room, sleeping with Mama and Vin.

The days pass and November sets in, cool and wet. I let my hair grow out a little, having it bleached just on the tips. That's when Josh starts commenting about how I look like Clarisse, how I could win one of those look-alike contests and get to meet the star, only too bad, Clarisse Broder is dead. He thinks we should sponsor an afterlife Clarisse Broder book signing at the restaurant as a promotion, with me posing as her.

I play along, but ignore him when he starts making plans.

One morning when I'm dressing at Greg's, Josh walks in by accident. Startled, I turn, wearing only my bra and underwear. He's halfway out the door when he stops.

"Becca."

He's staring at my scar.

"Appendectomy," I say automatically.

Greg sticks in his head. "Wrong side," he says.

How does everybody know this but me?

I shrug my shoulders and drop my T-shirt over my head. But Josh walks up to me, lifting the shirt. I pull it down out of his hands and turn to face him. There's something in his eyes. I know what he's seen. The other marks, the ones Jeremy never saw because we were in the dark when we had sex, and Tom was too polite to ask. The whip marks, from that first God-awful whipping by Ben.

"I was in a motorcycle accident," I say, keeping my voice steady. "Slid along the pavement. I was wearing a leather jacket, but it shredded off me."

Josh shakes his head and walks out of the room. Neither of them bring it up again.

But I'm sliding, slipping back toward Violet and her secrets. At times I'm "disappearing," as Burt calls it. I might be in the kitchen checking the sauces when I start seeing or hearing things I can't make out.

Burt takes me into his office again.

"What's going on, Becca?"

"Nothing. I don't know what you mean."

"Look," he says, "I was in Nam. I know that look. I've seen it on my buddies. They've seen it on me. It took me years to get past the flashbacks. There's people that can help you with it."

So that's what's in his eyes.

I snort. "I wasn't in Nam, Burt. I was a little kid then." I'm not liking the way this is going, so my mouth takes over. "By the way, the rest of us call it Vietnam, or just 'that police action thing.'"

"Look," he says again. It's his favorite word. Maybe he picked it up in Nam. "I know you carry a gun. I saw it the first day. And I know the signs of bad shit in a person's face. I know you, Becca. Better than you know yourself maybe. After you see enough of your buddies die, you get a second sight."

I'm getting dizzy at this moment and feeling my stomach shift. One to five. Count the breaths. Go back again. "Don't push me, Burt. I just can't remember something that was really bad. And what I do remember, I'd rather forget."

He sits staring at me, and I look away. After awhile, I stand. "Is that all, Dad?"

"No, that's not all." He slams open a drawer and takes out a pad. Then he whips off a name and phone number. He hands it to me. "This woman can help you. She helped me a lot. When you start remembering, you shouldn't do it by yourself."

I take it, rolling my eyes when I turn away. Some weirdo therapist. They're a dime a dozen out here.

I go and sit at my miniature desk squeezed in the back hall by the kitchen, trembling. To distract myself, I open a copy of the *Times* I bought on the way in to work. On page three is an article about a body found, this one female and floating in the Hudson. The article hints at a connection to the suspected serial killer.

Flipping to the back, I go through the personals. Sure enough, I find a blurb for Tut from Beefy. Call me, it says.

I tell Burt that I've got to check on some produce. Catching a cab, I buzz over to Hayward as fast as I can. I find a phone booth.

"Bates," he says when he picks up his phone.

"Hi."

"Beth. It's good to talk to you. Read the paper today?"

"Yeah."

"We got another witness, not a good look, but someone who

narrowed the pictures down for us. We've got about fifty possibles. I would love it if you could look at them."

"I don't know," I say.

He waits. "Have you worked on the memories? Have you been to anybody?"

"No. I've been busy trying to have a normal life."

"This isn't going to go away, Beth. It will follow you around."

I think of Miriam's voice in my head all the time. And Violet. "I know."

"Will you look at the pictures?"

"Let me think about it. I'll give you a call tomorrow."

The weeds lining the banks sway. Water skimmers trip along the surface. Two vultures circle silent, and the catfish strike our hooks, loaded with crawlers, stripping them away. Mandy and me sit, watching where our lines go down into the water. A cloud of gnats discovers us. We lie down. I cover my eyes.

The day floats forward slow, almost stopped, almost arrested in motion. The sun hangs in the sky.

I want to prevent all that has passed since, keeping the seconds held back. I want to take the two of us to Rivertown and make us into stone, Mandy and me, each of us frozen and watching.

Instead, I have become a toom. Inside, all the bodies are stacked neatly in rows. More of the dead are brought to me each day. I swallow them. I won't give up their secrets.

The sweet air beneath the live oaks passes back and forth over me.

I call Jill that night.

"It's Becca," I say, hoping she hasn't forgotten me.

She seems genuinely pleased to hear from me.

"I need a favor," I say. "I don't think it would put you at risk, but I'm not sure. Maybe you could get your dad to do it for me. He's a police officer, right?"

"Retired," she said. "He'd love to do something dangerous. He's bored to death."

"There's a detective that wants me to look at some pictures to help nail a guy for a murder I witnessed." I sway a little, sick again. "I don't want him to know where I am. If the detective drops them somewhere and your dad picks them up, then you could mail them to me." I wait, holding my breath.

"That's no problem, Becca. When, what, and where?"

"I'll have to phone you again with the details."

We talk about their kids a bit. Before I hang up, she asks me, "How's Betty and Dave in Dayton?"

"A little shook up," I say. "And Dave got an awful rash on his face."

I call Bates back the next day.

"Here's the deal. Go to the third floor of the Public Library on Forty-second Street. Turn right at the entrance to the reference section and go all the way to the left corner. Place an envelope containing the pictures on one of the tables. Then leave. And no looking. And don't bring anybody with you or tell anyone what you're doing. Which reminds me, does anyone else there know that I'm alive and you've been talking to me?"

"No," he says. "When?"

"Tomorrow when the library opens. I'll get the pictures in a couple of days."

He thinks this over. "Okay, Beth. And work on those memories. They'll come out one way or another. It would be better if someone was helping you. As they say, you have to be present to win."

I hang up. I'm beginning to like Bates more and more.

That afternoon, as I'm going over the delivery lists, and Larry is screaming about the tuna, I take out the note Burt gave me. I make the phone call, setting up an appointment for the end of the week.

During my evening break, I call Jill again and firm up our plans. She tells me her father is in great spirits. That I've brought some joy back into his life.

"My pleasure," I say. "If only I could do that in my own life."

I close that night at Tutti like always. It's after three by the time I call a cab and have him drive me home. As I step out on the street, I hear the ghosts like they're all around me. I freak, drawing my gun and racing up the four flights. I check the apartment after I get in. I'm sweating.

Listening to Miriam, I change into shorts and a T-shirt, curling up with my notebook. I've started the stories full swing again. The river is in my head, and Mama and Mandy. I look over at Mama's picture where I put it on the dresser and wish I had a picture of Mandy, too. I wonder what ever happened to Vin.

About the time the sky is getting light, I lie down in my only closet, leaving the door open just a crack so that I can see the man when he comes. I know he'll be wearing gym shoes.

The pictures arrive at Tutti on Friday. Burt hands the envelope to me and I toss it in my desk. A couple hours later, I take a cab to my "appointment with death," as I've been referring to it in my mind. I tell myself it's just a joke, but for once, I'm not enjoying my own sense of humor.

As I'm sitting in the therapist's office, I decide that, as much as I hate it, I have to be honest.

"I witnessed a murder," I say. "The police want more details." I'm really screwed up, I want to add. I'm scared shitless, by the way.

Near the end of our session, she tells me that I might start feeling worse for awhile. She wants me to see a psychiatrist. I thank her, but say no.

Just a nervous breakdown. Women have them all the time.

When I go back in the kitchen, Josh is jumping all over the place.

"You got to see this," he says in his lovely accent. His skin is so dark it's glowing. I want to kiss him, but Cinda is nearby. I wouldn't want to blow her mind.

He whips out a *Globe* magazine.

"God, do you actually read those things, Josh?"

"Look at the headline."

It says: "Clarisse Broder Seen Alive and Well in Chicago." Under that I see a faked-up picture of me with the Sears Tower in the background.

I try to remain calm.

"Let's dress you up like Clarisse," he says. "We'll get you a wig. We could have some sightings here in Berkeley. You could stand out on the Golden Gate. Scare the shit out of everybody."

I throw the magazine at him. "You're acting like a five-year-old, Josh." I notice too late that my voice is a bit loud. Josh stares at me. I stalk out of the kitchen.

Josh gets over my little tirade and asks me over that evening, saying that he and Greg want to see what it's like to spend time with a walking ghost. I almost decline, but then I think about sleeping in my closet again.

I tell him I'll do my best to play the part.

During my break, I close myself in Burt's office and take out the pictures. I look at each one a long time. I spread them out and take them en masse.

None of them look familiar.

After we close, Josh and I catch a cab over to Greg's place. I slosh down a double shot of whiskey neat while Josh and Greg chatter about the "appearances" they want to set up. After another couple of doubles, I pass out on the couch, but Josh wakes me in the middle of the night, freaking me. He brings me to bed with them. I fall asleep dreaming about Bates' pictures floating before my eyes.

I'm in the limo with Ben. I've had a glass of champagne, and I'm thinking about the Senator.

"He'll be calling tomorrow is my guess," says Ben. "He's head over heels for you, Beth."

"He likes the manacles," I say.

Ben sits quiet then. I watch him. He keeps chewing his thumbnail, something I've never seen him do before. And he's rubbing his eyes.

I look out at the buildings passing by, thinking about Slim and his friend, worried. The dangers are close.

Ben slumps down and stares at me funny. I shrug it off. You can't figure Ben.

The limo pulls into the warehouse and stops. Ben takes my hand, helping me out of the car. He undoes the choker at my neck and removes the bracelets from my wrists, pocketing them. "Leave the gown on," he says. "Go back upstairs and wait." When I get up to our room, I see that Violet is gone. It makes me nervous. Maybe Slim didn't work it out right. Maybe Ben's going to separate Violet and me tonight.

An hour goes by.

Brett, one of Ben's new boys, comes in. He takes me around the waist and lies me on a couch, fondling me. Reaching under the gown, he preps me, not saying a thing. Then he leads me down to the play.

I wake up screaming, scaring Josh and Greg near to death. Josh wants me to lie down with him holding me, but I can't. So I get up, fix a pot of coffee, and fry up some bacon and eggs.

We hit the park and exercise, then change clothes and go shopping. Today, I find a pair of cowboy boots that will look great with the skirt I'm to wear this evening. We get back late, so I go home and dress, taking a cab to the north end of Berkeley, where I locate another pay phone.

"It's me," I say when Bates answers.

"Well?"

"I hate to say this, but none of the pictures trips a light."

He's quiet. "What about the memories?"

"I've started working on that. I've gotten some of it, but nothing on the guy yet. I'll let you know when anything comes up."

"Okay." He sounds depressed.

I hang up and head for Tutti. All evening I watch the food go out and come in. Artichokes half-eaten, asparagus with the tips gnawed off. I see them scrape the plates into the trash can, watch them drag the bags out. I can see it in my head all mixed together, swimming in the Dumpster.

It forms her body. It fleshes out her shape. Violet is out on the loading dock, naked, the blanket drawn back, her head nearly severed from her neck, her blood draining out onto the street.

By closing time, I'm a walking wreck. Josh asks me if I'm sick. I say yes. He checks me for a fever and worries over me. I tell him to go home, then I lock up. While I'm waiting for my cab, I look through the garbage. I sort through it with one of the big stirring spoons. I can't find her. Even though I keep saying her name, Violet won't answer me.

As I ride home, I think of Mama, how if she saw that Dumpster she'd be so happy.

Except for Violet, I think. When she found Violet, it would ruin everything.

9

Miriam

The next week is rough on me. It's hard to work seventy hours a week and sleep in a closet. I wake up every hour, making sure I still have the Uzi in my hands, and that the Walther is resting on its side over my head.

Tom's acting a little weird, so I ask him about his love life. He brushes me off. And Josh and Greg keep harping on the Clarisse Broder shit. My appetite begins to dry up, and because I'm so hyped all the time, I jog around campus like a demon.

So by the time I see my therapist again, I'm skating on some pretty thin ice. I keep seeing the faces of those men in the pictures that Bates sent me, or remembering Bates' other pictures. The ones of Violet.

As I'm tasting the sauces at Tutti later that evening, Josh peeks in the door to the kitchen, sees me, and sprints over.

"Celebrity bayside," he says.

I roll my eyes, not in the mood for this tonight.

"Anybody I know?" I'm notorious for not recognizing famous people.

"Miriam Dubois," he says.

I drop some béarnaise on the floor and jump back so that it won't splatter my skirt.

"You're making that up."

"No." Josh knows my weakness for M.D. "But there's a table-ful of 'dangers' right next to her. A real twosome," he adds.

I take Josh by the arm, walking him back to the door. "Whose table is she at?" I peek out.

"Cinda's," he says.

Just then Cinda slams in, almost creaming my face.

"Sorry," she says and starts checking her orders.

"Did she order a drink?" I say to Cinda.

She looks at me like I'm from another planet.

"Miriam Dubois," I remind her.

"Oh, yeah. Clos Pégase. Ninety-three. Tom's getting it."

"Give me your pad. I'm going to wait on her."

"You?" Her white face gleams even whiter in the kitchen fluorescents.

"Have you been to Scranton, Cinda?"

"Where?"

"Scranton, P.A." I think of all those puffy, stale faces.

"Oh yeah, yeah. No. But I have relatives there."

Bingo.

I take her pad, and I whip away before she can stop me, intercepting Tom with M.D.'s bottle of wine.

"Clos Pégase?" I take the bottle out of his hands. "I'll get this one."

He tries to get the bottle back, but I hide it behind my back.

"Let me," he whines.

"I'll have her autograph the tablecloth for you," I say as I speed off.

I weave my way bayside, imagining myself as plush, stretching into water. She's sitting with her back to the restaurant, staring over the bay, dressed in a pair of jeans that have seen better days and a sweater that clings to her thin frame. She's had her hair cut quite short, though not as short as mine.

I step beside her table and present the bottle. "Ninety-three," I say, thinking the ninety-two would have been better. I bite my tongue.

She nods and looks back to the bay as I open the bottle. I learned wine opening with a flourish when I was with Jeremy. Remembering old Arf, Arf makes me smile.

Now she's watching me. I pour her a taste. Wait. She nods for more.

"Are you ready to order?" I say, putting on my best waitress act.

"What happened to the other waitress?" she asks.

I shake my head. "Did you see how white she was?"

She hesitates. "Yes."

"She ate the sushi a little earlier. They're pumping her stomach out back. So I'd stay clear of the sushi tonight." I smile.

Her eyes, reflecting the moon off the bay, look to be a greenish-violet, but with a depth, like I'm looking down through water. They search my face. I return her gaze, allowing mine to come clear.

"Really?" she asks.

"About the sushi or about the waitress?"

She smiles a little then, but looks away. "Give me a few minutes," she says. "To order, I mean."

I trip over a chair as I leave. Josh and Tom have been watching my every move from Josh's private lectern near the entrance. I refuse to notice them and walk back to the kitchen. They follow, pumping me for information.

"I stuck my foot in my mouth," I say.

"What else is new?" Josh says. "What's she like?"

"You'd hate her. Very bossy. Bad attitude."

Tom looks up at the ceiling and leaves. Josh eyes me. "You're in love," he says.

I smile and shrug. "Silly of me," I say. "Tragic."

"Be careful." Josh goes back to his post.

After a bit, I return to her table.

"Do you do everything here?" she asks.

"Pardon?"

"Waitress. Wine steward."

"Good help is so hard," I say. "Have you made a decision?"

"What do you recommend?" she says.

I smile. How perfect. And she's so lucky to have me, the one who loves to make decisions for everyone. "Not the filet mignon. Larry, our schizo chef, has already thrown it on the floor in disgust twice today."

She laughs. "Are you a waitress or the entertainment?"

"I'm the manager. I used to be a waitress, but I scared too many people away. So they promoted me."

She turns to face me, her eyes locked on. "Is there anything that hasn't been on the floor yet?"

Me, I'm thinking, which might not be entirely true.

"The salmon in béarnaise. The asparagus is unbelievable today."

"What about the quail?"

"They came in yesterday," I say. "Too gamy. A little thin in the leg."

She smiles. "I'll take the quail."

I roll my eyes. "It's your tastebuds." I turn to leave.

"By the way," she says, "I love your boots."

"Thanks." I flash her my best charming look.

But as I turn away, I hear two voices behind me that seem familiar. I look at the table beside Miriam's, the one that Josh said held "the dangers."

I hear the woman say, "Perfect."

The man says, "It looks fine."

I see them and freeze, remembering where I heard those voices before. At Ben's. The "kidnap" couple. The "into gadgets and contraptions" couple. The "why don't you keep her so we can screw her once a week?" couple.

The woman looks up at me. It's too late. She recognizes me. So does her husband.

Josh is so right. The dangers are way too close.

I whirl back. Who knows what my face looks like, but I feel my dress being stripped away. I feel the slaps, the punch in the stomach. The berserks swarm me like flies.

And Miriam's watching. In that moment, I have a sense that the space between us has disappeared.

"You okay?" She strains to look behind me, checking out the nice couple.

One to five. Then back again. "Just my personality disorder thing," I say, trying to regain my smile. It's a sad attempt.

She sips her wine, keeping those violet eyes on me, now having taken on a sheen.

I spin back to the couple with whom I've shared so much intimacy. "I wouldn't touch that veal," I say. "We smuggled it out of the UK." I widen my eyes. "Mad cow." I stalk off.

In the kitchen, I catch Tom and suggest that he spill some wine on my favorite couple. He says he'll see what he can do. Then I hover over Larry. I prepare Miriam's plate myself, returning to her table with the unsatisfactory quail. I notice with joy in my heart that the dangers have vacated the premises. I'll have to do something very nice for Tom.

I set her plate in front of her and pour her some more wine. She looks up at me. "Do you have a minute? Can you sit with me?"

Her eyes catch mine again. I feel like I'm under some spell. I take a chair next to hers.

"I'm tired tonight," she says. "Long day." Then she cuts a bite of quail. "This is delicious. Try some."

I lean forward, our eyes meeting again. I think I might slide off my chair. "Gamy," I say. "I don't usually eat the small murdered animals. Only the big murdered ones."

"Do you ever stop with the jokes?"

I smile. "I'm better behaved when I'm not working."

She retrieves a wineglass from the table beside her, setting it down in front of me. She pours a little.

"Is this allowed?" she asks.

"Well, I'm the boss. I get to make the rules."

We're both quiet, looking over the bay.

"Is it hard to be so famous?" I say. God, her eyes are going to kill me.

"Yes. But there are benefits. I wouldn't have you for a waitress otherwise. Am I right?"

I think I blush. I'm searching for something more to say when Tom arrives, telling me Larry's having a fit in back.

"Sorry," I say, and leave.

Then we have a picky guy who doesn't like the Margaux he ordered and wants us to open several for him to taste. Then one of the waiters really does get sick and we have to shift around, pulling Tom off the wine, with me taking his place. By the time I get free, she's gone.

Josh hands me her ticket. On it she's written: "You were right. Quail was gamy. See you sometime."

I see Violet walking through Central Park, the wind catching her dress. She brushes her hair back from her face and watches the wind sway the branches of the lindens.

This is how it should be. That the two of us are here, free. That I can watch her walking, turning from the wind, pulling back her hair. Simple movements empty of moment, but filling the eye.

I wonder if in death, this is what we see, all these motions flagged in air, denied, now made into dream.

Tonight, cool air drains from Rivertown down to the water. The river whispers so that I lean forward, listening. It is winter, but spring is near. I can tell because of the hush and how the trees have gone still.

Even the dead have fallen quiet for a time, as though holding their breath, waiting for the flush of new growth and the sudden surge of the river.

I lie back, dreaming of Violet.

At home later, I sit and stare at nothing. I throw Miriam's CDs in the trash. Then I write a letter to Burt, saying that I have to leave because of an illness in my family. So long. Bye-bye.

I tear it up. But I never go to bed. I take my Uzi and sit in front of my one view of the street, staring until the sun comes up, wondering what worse thing can happen to me.

The next few days, I slide downhill steady and strong. By the time Monday rolls around, my day off, I bring home a bottle of Southern Comfort, my old friend, and make a day of it. I dress as Becker, drunk as a skunk, and stumble around the campus whistling at girls, passing out for awhile in the middle of a shrub.

It's a low point.

Two days later, I find Tom up in my apartment after I get back from jogging. I'd forgotten he had a key to the place, and I pull my Walther on him, scaring us both.

"What the hell are you doing in here?" I say. But I notice that he's holding the picture of Mama and me. Tom looks me straight in the eye. He searches my face, then turns and places the picture back on top of the dresser.

"Who is this?" he asks.

"A friend."

"Is this you?" he says, pointing to the little girl with Mama.

Now I see that a copy of the second edition of my book is lying on the kitchen table. Beneath it is that damned *Globe* article with the faked-up picture of me.

He watches me. "You're her, aren't you?" he says. "You're Clarisse Broder. You're not dead."

"Don't ask me that, Tom." I look away.

He twists his mouth around. "So were you a prostitute? Is that why you're running? Are the police after you?"

Standing with someone who knows who I am brings it all back to me. I feel myself going white and starting to shake. "God, no. The police aren't after me. I'm their star witness. I saw a murder. But I can't remember anything, so I'm not such a great witness, am I?"

"But you're Clarisse. And Beth. And Terri. You lied to me. To all of us."

"Tom, I didn't lie to you and your family because I thought it was a joke. I had to become Becca because my pimp is after me.

He doesn't play nice, which is why you have to forget about this."

I step closer to him. I want him to sense me as something living, easily damaged. "You haven't said anything to anyone, have you?"

He shakes his head no. "But the lie, Becca. Everybody thinks you died on a bridge. And other girls jumped off. God, you're not Becca at all. It's freaking me out." He turns away.

"Tom," I take his arm. He won't look at me. I pull up my T-shirt and stand in front of him.

"Look, Tom." He keeps his eyes away from me.

"No. Here. Look at these. They're whip marks, Tom. Listen to me." I grab his arm. "You know this scar, Tom. I was stabbed." I wait while he stares at my side.

"I could tell you stories that would make you sick to death, Tom. I was a runaway. The guy, Ben, got his hands on me. It's ugly. I had to jump off that bridge. I was hoping to die, but I didn't."

I wait for all this to sink in. "You can't tell anyone, Tom." I let my hand slide down his arm. "He'll come and he'll find me, and he won't kill me. He'll take me back for more of the same. He'll beat me. He'll whip me. He'll do things to me you can't even imagine. Do you want that on your conscience?"

Tom shakes me off and sits on the couch with his head in his hands. "It's just so weird, Becca. I thought I knew who you were. But I don't. It screws my head up."

I settle down beside him. "Tom, if this is the worst thing you've known to screw your head up, then you should feel lucky. There's so much that can go wrong in a life, so much damage that can be done. And for what it's worth, knowing you and your family, and then the life you helped me start here, have been the best things for me. You're a good man. And I need for you to keep this to yourself."

I reach over and take his hand, squeezing it.

He sits silent, looking down. "Okay," he says.

I hug him, turning his face to me. "You're not going to tell a soul, right? Promise?"

He nods and stands. "I have to go."

I see him out the door and lean against it after he's gone, my mind racing, wondering if I should pack now and get out of town before work, or should I wait and leave tonight?

John meets Brett and me as we're going down the stairs, then they each take an arm and lead me to one of Ben's favorite rooms. I hear a beat booming from behind the door. Brett checks his watch, then opens the door. Inside, the music is so loud and driving that it shakes me. And the lights are dimmed, casting a red glow, giving a deep flush to everything within.

This room is spare. The only piece of hardware is a large wrought-iron gate attached to one wall. It has iron leaves, petals, and birds worked between the bars. The gate had to be cut down to fit along the wall.

Ben liked it because he could tie a person of any shape or size flat against it in any position. "Versatile" was the word he used.

This night, I see a tall man sitting in a large, heavy chair on the other side of the room. The chair has carvings of lions' heads on the arms and the top of the chairback. It looks like a throne.

The man's face is turned toward me. He's wearing a dust mask, which isn't uncommon. The clean freaks that like to do some really kinky stuff wear dust masks.

So I think, he's afraid of germs. He's a clean freak. And my next thought is, what happened to Slim?

I look at the guy again. He's wearing sunglasses, and his long brown hair is gathered into a ponytail in back. On his head is a wide brim hat, and he has a full-length cashmere coat wrapped around him as though he's cold. He's wearing black gym shoes and on his hands are leather gloves.

He motions to Brett, who leans close to me. He has to shout in my ear so I can hear him over the music.

"He wants you to undress for him. Very slow."

Where did Ben find this guy? I look at the little video eye in the upper corner of the room. I'm glad that he's watching tonight. Something about this one is creeping me out.

John and Brett shove me toward the guy. I wait for a moment, then turn so he can see my back. I begin to sway to the music, letting it pound in my body. I reach behind and draw the zipper down slow, allowing my back to be revealed, feeling how frail, how ephemeral my flesh, my spine. I sense his gaze with the skin of my shoulders, as though I can see him, and in this manner of seeing, know not his shape, but his will.

He frightens me.

The gown drops as a hush to the floor, lost in the powerful drive of the bass, making me near blind. I step out of the gown, swaying, running my hands down the outside of my thighs, then turn to face him as I stroke myself upward.

I drop my slip and kneel, arching back, cupping my breasts in my palms, my fingers lingering upon my nipples. And gazing at him through narrowed eyes, I search him, desperate for clues. Because I'm certain of his danger to me now.

I stand, running my hands up again and kick off my heels, then undo the garters at the tops of my stockings. I allow the rhythm to turn me. He gets a good view of my ass as I drop my stockings in a flutter to the floor.

Just as I'm straightening, my eyes closed, near to my own revery, my nipples erect, my thighs aching for Violet, Brett and John grab my arms and drag me, fighting, over to the gate. They tie me onto it spread out, but not just at the ankles and wrists. They tie me several times along each leg and arm. They attach my waist and neck. I can't move other than to turn my head. Brett forces a gag in my mouth, then rips off my garter belt, throwing it on the floor.

The man waves them out of the room, then he sits without moving, watching me.

I think long and hard after Tom leaves. I can't just take off and not say a word to anybody. Burt or Josh would call the police.

I'm going to have to set it up. Death in the family. Whatever. I've gotten too settled and made friends like an idiot.

I dress for work and call a cab. The dangers buzz me. Now that Tom's figured me out, I think everybody knows. And the thought of dealing with Tutti gets the ghosts whispering in my head. So I make a quick decision and have the cab driver drop me at a big outdoor equipment store nearby, thinking I'll stock up on some items I might need. I'll hit the liquor store later for my favorite camping item. Whiskey.

After locating a pay phone, I call Burt, telling him I'll be late. I make up some lame excuse about having a flashback. Burt's all understanding and falling over himself, telling me to take as much time as I need.

Then I go shopping, checking out the gear.

As I'm happily testing different colors of sleeping bags against my skin to see which looks better on me, a voice comes from behind. "I wouldn't have taken you to be the outdoors type."

I turn and look, seeing Miriam Dubois standing with her arms crossed, smiling at me. My first thought is, uh-oh, not synchronicity. Maybe it wasn't Jeremy's problem after all.

But in the light of day, I find her eyes even deeper, cradling the ache in darkness where the undercurrents roam.

"I was trying out the colors. Isn't that the most important feature of a sleeping bag? By the way, what color are your eyes?"

She walks over and takes the bag that I'm looking at out of my hands. "This bag looks better on you," she says, setting one next to my arm.

I keep my eyes on her face, waiting for her to look back at me. "I'd say pale green, but I see streaks of blue and amber."

We're standing not a foot from one another as we hold each other's eyes. I break away first, feeling the dangers again.

I have to get out of town, I think. Tom knows.

Her voice is softer now, like she's in a room with a person who's sick. "This is a better bag anyway."

I look at the bag, but I see Violet's eyes. I remember her face the way it was the last time I saw her.

"Could I have your autograph?" Some guy in a four-hundred-dollar expedition jacket jams his face in between us.

She smiles and turns. I feel my chest press in. And for some reason I'm riveted in place.

When she's done, she turns back to me. "Would you like to have lunch?" she says.

"You want to have lunch with me?"

"Is that a bad thing? Are you dangerous?"

I stand silent, strangely tongue-tied. But I smell the river, and I see how my desire for her might surge out suddenly and over-reach the banks.

Miriam draws me along beside her. "There's a little place close to here," she says. "Students go there. It's not a Tutti." We wind our way through people staring at her and saying hello.

"By the way," she says as we get in the car waiting for her, "I don't know your name."

"Becca," I say, catching her eyes once more. "And have I said that you have beautiful eyes?"

She laughs at me.

We end up at a hole-in-the-wall café that might seat ten people on a good day. The waitress comes to our table chewing gum like a machine punching out sheet metal. She looks like she could be a sister to Cinda.

"Do you have a menu?" I ask.

She points up, keeping her eyes on her pad.

I look up. Sure enough, the menu is painted on the ceiling. It's in the middle of a mural that appears to have been conceived after a lot of hits on a bong.

"What if you ever change your mind about a sandwich or something? A little extreme, don't you think?" The waitress shrugs and keeps chewing.

I see that Miriam's watching me. She smiles when I look at her. I smile back and roll my eyes. She keeps back a laugh.

"I need a minute," I say. "I'm going to have to lie down on something so I can read the damn thing."

"We only have two sandwiches today anyway."

"Two total, or two in general?"

Miriam breaks in. "We'll both have the veggie special and two bottles of Evian." The waitress scribbles, blows a bubble and sucks it back in her mouth after bits of saliva have been thrown out. She leaves without a word.

"If you don't order the first time she comes around, you'll be sitting here for hours," she says.

"Great atmosphere," I say, taking in all the Becker look-alikes starting to wander in.

"Sorry."

"No. I'm sorry. I'm out of sorts today. I'm having a rough week."

The waitress returns and dumps two plates with sandwiches down on the table. She pulls our Evians out of her pockets, plops them in front of us, and trots off.

I watch Miriam as she drags her plate over and eats a bite of her sandwich. She's so much like Violet, but a Violet like she should have been. Her lips never learned the lessons of Ben's basement. Her skin never tasted his whip.

How could we ever know one another?

"You're not eating. You don't like vegetarian?" she says, catching me looking at her.

"I've been off my feed." But I smell the river again and the fulsome smell of the laybacks. I hear Mama's laughter, far off, as she's wobbling down the lane with her groceries.

I find myself staring at Miriam's lips. I look away.

"What were you thinking just now?" she says.

I swallow, my mouth dry. "I was just remembering."

She keeps looking at me, waiting.

"I guess I'm wondering what the hell I'm doing with my life."

"What do you mean?" She stops chewing and swallows.

"I don't know. I build my life around running away. It doesn't appear to work out well." I shift and feel my cheeks go red.

Her voice is soft again. "My boyfriend says that's what I do. He says I won't face anything."

I deflate. Argh. A boyfriend.

Her eyes are fixed on me. So I poke my sandwich with my finger, lifting the top to see what's inside. It reminds me of Mama's Dumpster. I smile.

"You look wonderful when you smile," she says.

Gazing back at her, I get caught in her eyes like the river has just reached up and grabbed me.

"When I was a kid," I say, "we tried for years to get a raft to float on this river we lived beside. You know, one time we did it. We floated."

Now something shifts in her, deepens. We sit silent, each watching the other.

"Shit," she says. She looks at her watch. "I'm sorry. I've got to split. I was supposed to meet with Peter five minutes ago. I forgot."

Her boyfriend, I gather.

She stands and throws money down on the table. I don't move.

"It was great having lunch with you. I liked the story." She smiles at me. "Becca." She has to worm her way through admirers to get out the door.

I sit and stare, feeling like shit.

By the time I hit work, I'm in a foul mood, bitching about whatever strikes my fancy. The ghosts are all over me, whispering and twitching me. Memories flash.

For some reason, Burt sequesters me right during the rush, wanting to know how I'm doing.

"Shitty," I say.

He nods. "It gets worse for awhile. But then it gets better."

"I don't understand the concept. Better."

We sit quiet for a minute. Then I remember Tom. My lunch fiasco with Miriam just adds fuel to the it's-time-to-leave-town

fire. "By the way, Burt, something's come up. My sister has cancer. I need some time off."

Burt winces. "We'll work it out. How soon?"

"I'm thinking this weekend."

"Can you wait until Sunday?"

I shake my head.

Afterward, I hit the john, puking. When I step out of the
bathroom, Josh catches my arm. "She's back," he says.

"What?" I can't get the taste of vomit out of my mouth.

"M.D. She asked for you. She's bayside again."

I escape back into the john and cringe in one of the stalls for
a bit. Some weird God is jerking me around for fun. I go to the
makeup mirror and decide there's not a thing I can do to give myself the appearance of being alive.

I weave my way over to Miriam's table, waiting while she finishes her conversation with the couple next to her. She stands up
when she sees me and smiles.

"Can you sit with me?" she says, gesturing to the chair next
to hers.

I nod and sit. Tonight she's dressed in a different tight sweater
that shows her nipples quite well. I drag my eyes away from them.

"I'm sorry about lunch," she says. "I felt like a jerk leaving
like that." When I don't say anything, she asks, "What do you
recommend tonight?"

"The seared tuna. Larry's best dish."

"Can you have dinner with me? I messed up lunch. Maybe I
can make it up to you."

I'm screwed. "I'm sure I'd be interrupted. Besides, I appear to
need *my* stomach pumped out tonight."

Tom arrives with her wine. I ask him to bring me a glass of
milk. My hands are shaking so badly that I hide them in the
pockets of my skirt.

We sit quietly. Cinda comes with my milk and whips out her
pad, taking Miriam's order. She looks at me. "Josh needs to talk,"
she says, turning to leave.

"Cinda dear," I say.

She looks back.

"Could you have Larry whip me up a bowl of mashed pota-toes?" I smile what I sense is a Ben kind of smile.

Cinda gets twitchy. "Whatever. Larry will yell about it. He won't do anything extra for me."

I try to decide whether she likes living dangerously or if she's actually this stupid. "Tell him it's for the wicked witch," I say. "And bring me ketchup to go with it."

She looks at me with disgust and scurries off.

"God, she's white," Miriam says.

"Can't stay off the sushi," I say.

Josh arrives and takes me away. He's got two reservations for the same table. After I get that worked out, I sit and eat a few bites with Miriam. Tonight, even the mashed potatoes aren't working.

"So tell me about the raft again," Miriam says as I push the bowl away from me.

I allow my head to fall to the side and close my eyes, bringing Mama to mind. "And the cool," I say, drawing it out like Mama did. "The cool, cool stream."

She's so still, trying to hear me over Mozart playing in the background.

"The lily leaves floating," I say and pause. "It's what Mama used to say if I was upset."

She's about to say something when Burt appears beside me. "We've got a problem, Becca." He pulls me away again. As a mat-ter of fact, I make up reasons to stay away from her table. But she keeps sitting there even after her table's been cleared.

"Go and talk to her," Josh says. "And cheer up."

"She's got a boyfriend," I say, sneering.

"Who cares? You have two boyfriends."

That makes me smile. I kiss him on the cheek and work my way bayside again.

"Would you like to go somewhere and talk?" she says. "I can see that's not going to happen here."

God. Life is kicking me in the gut. I look at her face, her eyes. So much like Violet. And seeing how her lips are tight, but only in the center, I feel the ache strong in her. I can't decide whether or not I'd like to end up like Grady.

Tom knows, I say to myself again. I have to leave, get out of town. This whole thing is a big mistake.

"Yes," I say, my mouth always betraying me. "I can have someone else close tonight."

We go to a bar nearby where a trio plays a type of loud jazz that makes my neck hurt. And people keep coming over, telling Miriam how much they love her music.

I yell in her ear so she can hear me. "I live close. You want to go to my place?" I try to remember if I put all my guns away.

"Yeah," she screams. "I need some peace and quiet."

By the time we climb to the fourth floor, she's out of breath. "I guess this will keep you in shape." She leans against the wall as I slide my key in the lock.

I take the opportunity to head in the door first, kicking the Uzi under the sofa. And as I'm scanning the room, making sure nothing else incriminating is showing, she walks to the dresser and takes in the doll's head and the toupee.

She picks up the toupee as though it's something that's been dead a long time, which I guess you could say it has. "How old is this thing?" She laughs.

"I use it when I go to church. You know. That cover-the-head thing." I run my hand through my short hair, thinking that I'm glad I stashed Mama's picture in the drawer.

"I wouldn't let that thing anywhere near my head." She drops it like it's alive and might crawl off.

"I don't have much to offer," I say. "Some O.J., milk, bottled water. I usually graze at the restaurant."

She plops down in the armchair, pulling up her knees and

checking the place out. "I'm done with drinking anyway. Maybe just some water."

I slip off my heels and open the fridge, retrieving two bottles of water.

"A little Spartan, isn't it?"

"I haven't been here long. Most of this stuff belongs to Tom, the wine steward. I don't know. I wasn't sure I was going to stay."

"Where were you before?"

Ack. Not that again. "Out east, in the great lands beyond the big water."

"But near a river," she says.

I'm amazed at how she does that, softening all of a sudden. I curl up on the couch across from her.

We sit silent.

"So," I say. "Tell me about the ache."

"Huh?"

"In your music," I say. "It's always there. A yearning. An undercurrent."

She gets almost shy, but her eyes take on a look I recognize. Maybe her mama burned up, I think. Maybe she knew her own Betty and Dave. Maybe she had a fake appendectomy.

"The ache," she says. "It's always been there. It's why I started singing, like I could make it go away. But it just gets deeper." Such sadness in those rainbow eyes. "Every day. Every year. Deeper. Can it go on that way?"

I lean forward. "I don't know," I say, my voice stripped down. I think of Mama's picture in my dresser drawer and me beside her. Sitting next to her at that moment, I must have been happy. I can't imagine it now.

She watches me so close it reminds me of how Kat watched me from across a room.

Those lips. Her skin. I look away, afraid she'll read me, see how Mama stands there, and me so breakable then, so unaware of how things spook you clean out of your skin.

"The ache is written all over you," she says.

I spill my water down the front of my dress.

Jumping up, I grab the towel off the sink and try to soak some of it up. While I'm messing with it, she comes up behind me. I feel her hands on either side of my waist, and then they slide around me. She presses her body against my back, and I rest my head on her shoulder, closing my eyes.

"Is this okay?" she says.

"Oh yes." You're going to kill me. You're going to murder me this way. "What about your boyfriend?" I make the last word sound like it's something unclean.

Now she moves one hand along my neck, sliding it up into my hair. "I just said that to see how you'd react. I'm sorry. It wasn't fair. So many people try to get next to me, wanting to be my friend. I throw out junk like that every now and then."

She pulls me closer. Stops. "What's in the middle of your back?"

I clutch. "My pistol."

"You carry a gun? Isn't that illegal?" She begins to edge away.

I hold her arms in place with one hand and reach behind, unclipping the holster from my skirt and tossing gun and holster onto the table.

"It's gone."

Now I take her wrists and pull her arms tighter. She kisses my neck.

I turn, reach behind her head and lie my lips along hers, thinking now of nothing but the touch of her lips and the press of her tongue. And as I sink, and as I grow ever so still, I slip beneath the surface, my eyes wide. It's Violet I see. Violet and her dark, dangerous eyes.

Miriam takes me in full, pressing forward. She kisses again, stronger, hungry, and I feel her hands moving over me. She reaches behind and unbuttons my blouse, still kissing, caught as I am caught in a river so strong that you have to let go. All you can do is let it grab you up and spit you out, hoping to hit the eddy at Fowler, where you can rise up drenched and shaken all the way through to the heart.

I run my hands beneath her sweater and up along her sides. She folds my blouse down from my shoulders, revealing my chest and the lace bra beneath. She runs both hands over my breasts, then back behind.

I find the soft, rounded flesh of her breasts, then curve my palms around, cupping, grasping her nipples, already erect. She presses me to her hard now, and we kiss blind, drowning.

Miriam and I make love like that river, settled down in the heat and aching beneath, the warmth and promise of her body and skin embracing me full.

I wake up crying in the middle of the night. She curls along my back and holds me.

10

Love

When I wake in the morning, I'm lying on my side. Miriam's standing sideways to me, naked, looking through my CDs. Her body is slim, her breasts small but round. Her skin is flushed, yet in a way translucent.

As if aware of my eyes on her, she looks over, and for a moment I see the ache in her eyes and then, like water, pouring through the remainder of her body.

Miriam smiles, taking me in. She walks to the bed and sits beside me, lying an arm over my back. Then she leans forward, kissing me. "Good morning," she says.

"God, you're beautiful," I say, running my hand over her thigh.

She sits back and peels the sheet off me.

"Let me see you," she says. "I wanted to in that freaky café yesterday. I wanted to jump all over you."

I brace, afraid, sensing how the river's run up close to the door, and how the current is stronger than I've ever known, but silent, and deadly where it undercuts the bank.

She presses me onto my back and gazes, moving her hands over me.

"What is this?" she says, touching the you-know-what scar. "And these?" A few of my other marks. I don't say anything. The appendectomy remark doesn't seem to work anymore.

She turns me over, running her hands along my sides, over my ass. "These?" she asks again. I can imagine what she's seeing.

"Not now," I say. I try to turn, but she holds me in place, her hands gentle, still stroking, learning the shape of my back. She kisses along my spine as Violet would have done. I want her again.

She stretches out beside me and we wrap together, making love, still caught by the water.

Afterward, we lie with her cupping one of my breasts in her hand, her leg thrown over. I feel I must have fallen into someone else's dream.

"I have to leave soon," she says. "I'm doing some work in the studio. It's why I had to leave yesterday."

I turn and kiss her again, tasting her, wanting to keep her in place, perfect this way.

"Can I see you tonight?" she asks as I draw back.

"Really?"

"Why not?"

"I thought maybe it was just for a night. I didn't know." I look away.

"Is that what you want?" She touches my face, turning me back to her.

What I want is a fucking gun to my head.

I lie my cheek against her chest and close my eyes, listening to her heartbeat. "I want to see you again. And maybe again. And then again. I think it might kill me."

"So you're not such a smart-ass," she says, kissing me. "And I still want to know about the scars."

I later learn that nosiness is her worst vice. I have to admit it's fairly benign when you think about my guns and Southern Comfort.

"When do you get done at Tutti tonight?"

"Late. Around one."

"I've rented a place for while I'm here doing some recording. It looks over the bay. I'll give you the phone number and the address. Can you come there? It's bigger than this apartment from Sparta."

"Yes," I say, my head reeling.

"And do you have to wear that gun? It makes me nervous."

"Have to," I say, running my hand beneath her breasts. "You should see my other guns."

We kiss long and soft. Then she leaves the bed and finds her clothes, strewn about the apartment. I watch her dress. When she's done, she sits beside me and kisses me once more, fondling me.

"I want you again," I say, whispering.

"Tonight." She stands and walks out the door.

Leaving early for work, I take another cab to yet another phone booth at the edge of the city. I ring up Bates.

"It's me again."

"Beth. I was wondering about you."

"I've got some information, but I think you're going to be disappointed."

"Go ahead."

"I had a memory of him sitting in front of me. He was wearing a dust mask, something the clean freaks do, and a pair of dark sunglasses. He had his long brown hair pulled back in a ponytail and wore a hat. He looked to be tall, but I don't remember him standing. He had on a heavy coat and gym shoes."

"A big guy. As big as Ben?"

"Yeah." I shudder at the sound of his name. "Very similar."

"Have you checked out the pictures again? Maybe somebody strikes you now?"

"No. I'll do that today."

"We're getting more evidence off the latest body. It just narrows things down, doesn't finger anyone in particular."

I wait a minute. "Bates?"

"Yes?"

"Have you been tracing my calls? Do you know where I am?"

He hesitates. "No."

"Would you lie to me?"

He laughs. "I might. Beth, you have to trust me. You're my best witness. I want to keep you safe."

"Did you see the article in the *Globe*?"

"Yes."

"One of my friends has figured me out. It's making me nervous."

"Hang on, Beth. I'm working on the Ben thing, too. I'd love to see him put away for awhile. Stay put if you can. Whatever you're doing to help you remember seems to be working."

I'm silent, unwilling to hang up. Talking to him makes my weird life more real.

"Stay in touch, Beth."

"You too."

I hang up and have the cabby take me to Tutti.

I remember Mama when she wasn't so fat. I remember the willows overhead and me looking up, listening. And Mama was nearby with Vin, holding both his hands as he learned to walk between her legs.

There are brightnesses that come and go swiftly, so that if you are not paying attention, they pass unknown. What I remember of the willows then was the striking of the sun and the shading down.

In the days that I live now, these knowings crowd the banks, having risen from a deeper place. As I ride the length of my river, they are all that remain. That and the whisper of the water through grass, sedge, and rushes, and the hiss of the coachwhip, a slender god gliding through the bushes.

At Tutti, Josh takes one look at me. "You're a goner now, Becca. Big bite."

Tom wants to take me aside and quiz me about Clarisse. He's started calling me Beth as though it's funny.

Around eight, Miriam shows up for dinner again. I think I might stop breathing. Tom waits on her since we're still down a

waiter. I pour her wine. Her scent, with which I am now familiar, makes me heady. Her clothing seems stripped back, revealing
warm, living skin.

"Sorry I can't sit with you. It's a mess tonight," I say, magne-
tized, remembering how I bent myself in just this way first toward
Kat and then Violet.

She looks in my face, her eyes full of something I've missed for
so long that I'd forgotten such a thing could exist. "I wanted to
be in the same building with you, that's all. I can't stop thinking
about you."

Maybe someone should shake me good and hard.

Tonight, she sits in the corner table next to the bay, her back
to the wall, affording her a good view of the water and the room.
Through the evening, I sense her eyes following me as I work the
restaurant.

And I watch her on the sly, seeing how she lifts her wine to
her lips and waits for just a breath, stretching desire. Her face
softens as her eyes drift toward the water.

As she's leaving, she stops me near Josh's desk, touching my
shoulder and letting her hand fall along my back. "See you soon?"

I shake my head, watching her walk out the door, as though
Violet has kissed me on the cheek and now disappears. Josh
raises his eyebrows at me and smirks. "Tragic," he says.

Once we close and everybody's cleaning up, I slip into Burt's
office with my envelope from Bates, taking out every picture and
staring. I try to imagine dust masks and sunglasses. Long hair. I
don't get a thing.

Tutti is deserted by the time I leave. I'm drawn out to the
loading dock. Taking a chair with me, I set it beside the Dumpster and stand on it, raking through garbage with my hands, feeling how my heart opens and fills with love. I want to jump in and
bury myself. That way when Mama comes, she'll find me.

After hosing off my hands, I call a cab. He drops me at
Miriam's address. Across the way I can hear the bay tapping the
seawall. Gulls sit on the rooftops, their heads tucked in. I have

the gym bag from the Dave and Betty fiasco. In it I packed extra clothes, the Uzi and the S&W, my notebook, and the envelope from Bates.

I ring the bell. Miriam lets me in and closes the door, pressing me against it. Her mouth covers mine, her hands slip under my clothes. I'm overcome with her scent, her talented lips and tongue, and the strength of her desire. I drop my bag with a clang. She doesn't notice.

She takes my hand and leads me up the stairs.

Her bedroom is lit by moonlight streaming in the bank of windows facing the bay. And so near now, I sense in my chest the blocky low growl of the water. I smell the weeds of the river, rank and swishing the banks along the Narrows. The mud gnats buzz, crawling my eyes like love.

Suddenly, I remember dropping from the bridge, the wind roaring. And here I am again, falling. Gazing at Miriam, I want her so badly I think I might rather be dragged into the river. How could I ever survive another Violet?

Miriam pushes me on the bed and starts stripping me fast, fevered. I run my hands through her hair, astonished by her.

"Jesus," she says, leaning over me, kissing above my breasts. She turns me and unzips my skirt, tearing it off. "You're killing me," she whispers, taking in my ass, the back of my corset and my stockings. Her hands course the sides of my ass, separating the cheeks, fingers probing, sliding between my legs, stroking wetly upward. I try to rise, but she holds me in place, removing the rest of my clothing.

Miriam makes love to me still dressed, pushing my hands away each time I reach for her. I come in a fury, clutching her against me, unable to wrap myself tight enough to beat back those other memories that I work so hard to forget.

She showers me with kisses while I sink down gentle and dreamy. As I lie floating, my head still socked in with pleasure, she leaves the bed and undresses, allowing me to take in her layer of lace, her skin, and the veil of her ache, all lit by the moon.

I slip off the bed and walk behind, brushing her with my fingers, then my lips.

"Waiting for you today was like torture," she says, closing her eyes as I run my hands down her sides.

"Waiting is good for you," I say, teasing her.

"If it's one thing I'm not good at, it's waiting," she says.

Hmm.

I stay behind her, grasping her breasts hard, tugging her nipples. She lies her head back on my shoulder. I allow one hand to glide down her stomach, then between her legs, sliding into her and grasping her that way, then slipping out.

"You smell like the air beneath the live oak," I say. "In the afternoon, when the shade gets thick and hot." I stroke her light, teasing, slipping in and out of her while my other hand slides down her back. I wet my fingers and find her other opening, entering gently. Miriam moans and her legs begin to tremble, so I lie her on the bed.

And watching her this way, as she's lost in pleasure, the moon striking her skin, I fall deeper. But I'm not fighting anymore. I want to hit the water so hard that I impale upon the ache.

She's gorgeous when she comes, head thrown back, her body arching.

We lie embraced, talking quietly afterward. From her bed, we have a clear view of the bay, the setting moon hanging over the water, and the gleam along the ripples.

Miriam tells me about her family in Maine. She goes through a list of lovers she's had and what went wrong, saying how the last breakup nearly killed her. She hasn't seen anyone seriously in a year.

"What about you?" she says.

"What?"

"Family? Where are you from in the land on the far side of the big river?"

"Ohio," I say. Why change now?

"Just Ohio?"

I run my fingers through her hair, trying to divert her. "I don't think about it anymore."

"Your family? Your entire childhood? You don't think about it?"

I'm catching the beginning scent of her nosiness thing. "Let sleeping dogs lie, Miriam."

She turns her irresistible eyes on mine. "But you do think about it. You lived by a river. And what was it? The cool stream?"

I'm quiet, wishing for the zillionth time that I knew how to keep my trap shut. "Please don't push me on this. Give me time."

"So you won't tell me about yourself? Same as with the scars?"

"Actually, I do think about all that. I just don't like to. And I really hate talking about it."

Miriam pulls back, turning from me.

"Soon." I catch her. "It's not you, Miriam. I just can't." I swallow, remembering my hands tied above and the rail hitting me right at the middle of my ass so that I was leaning back with my legs chained out. It was near the end, when Ben kept me separate from the others after the plays to gain power over Violet.

My head goes dark and I don't remember much after that except that Ben brought me back to our rooms afterward. There were marks on my body, and I was trembling all over. He laid me down and kissed me so tender about my breasts. Then he covered me and cooked up a spoonful of smack.

"Don't forget," he whispered right before he shot it in my arm. "You belong to me."

I notice Miriam watching me. I shake my head because my eyes are acting funny.

"Please give me some time." I take her chin, kissing her strong. She becomes fluid. I run my hand along her back, feeling her warmth. Reaching up to her bedpost, I remove the blindfold hanging there. It's for keeping out the streetlights at night.

"I want to put this on you," I say.

"Kind of a metaphor, don't you think?" She kisses me, opening my mouth with her tongue.

I pull back. "You're too smart," I say as I fit it over her eyes. I kiss her again, Miriam leaning forward now, searching for me. I hold her head still with both my hands, kissing her cheeks, her neck. I move down her body, kiss her breasts, then spread her legs and kneel between, holding her wrists by her sides, still kissing, now teasing first one nipple, then the other. Her body stretches. I see the gleam between her legs.

Leaving the bed, I find my skirt thrown over a chair.

"Where are you?" She's breathing heavy, turning her head in my direction.

I don't answer. Instead, I slide the belt out of the loops and return.

"How are you?" I say.

"God, I want you." She reaches for me. I lie the belt across her stomach and take hold of her wrists.

"I want to tie these together," I say. "Can I?"

Her breathing deepens. "It's scaring me a little."

"Then I won't do it."

"No. It's okay."

"Have you ever done this before?"

"No."

"Have you ever wanted to?"

She chews her lip, stretches toward me with her hips. "Yes."

"I'll be careful. I won't do it tight. You'll be able to get free if you want."

She nods.

I turn her on her stomach and tie her wrists together in back. She tests the strap, this new tension redefining the lines of her shoulders and back.

I separate her legs and kneel between them, not touching her, taking her in. I wait. She moves like waves are coursing through her. I reach with one hand and follow along her back.

She gasps.

I lean forward, whispering in her ear. "Do you want it?"

"Yes."

"Are you sure?"

She licks her lips, her breath coming in short gasps. "Please."

I lie myself against her. "Your body is mine now," I whisper. "For me to use."

Her breathing goes up a notch.

Turning her, I guide her mouth to first one breast, then the other as I circle her waist with my thighs. Miriam's body is rapt, thrusting slightly. I slide back against the headboard and grasp her head, lying her mouth against me. She takes me in so gentle, so careful. When I come, I almost start crying.

"Are you okay?" She's lifted her head, as though she can see me.

I lie my finger on her lips, shoving back the darkness, the ache, and that drop into the river. "Shh."

Miriam shudders, resting her cheek along my thigh.

I take her by her arms. "Sit up." I lift her and push her to the edge of the bed so her feet dangle over the side. And I sit behind, straddling her, spreading her legs.

"Lean back against me."

She does as I say. So obedient.

I reach around to her nipples. She moans, arches again and lets her head fall on my shoulder.

"Good," I say, still fondling. I slide my hand between her legs, push her closer to the edge of the bed, and hook my feet over her knees, stretching her legs wide. My fingers go inside of her.

"Touch me," she says. "I'm so turned on. You have to touch me."

"Not yet. Wait," I whisper. "You can wait a little."

"I hate to wait," she says between breaths.

"It's good for you," I say, pulling her knees farther apart. "Can you feel it in your whole body? The desire. Is it all over your skin? Is it pouring out inside?"

"Yes," she gasps. She chews her lip again. I feel her pull against the belt holding her wrists. I wait a little longer.

"Please?" I say.

"Please."

Now I stroke her, feeling how swollen and wet she is. She

comes so strong that I have to hold her up with the hand I have inside of her so that she doesn't fall on the floor.

I lie her back then and rest beside her, leaving her tied and blindfolded. I run my fingers down her side. "Did you like it this way?"

She turns her face to me. I lean forward and we kiss.

"Yes," she says, whispering. "You've done this before?"

God, what's a person to say? "Yes."

"Do you like it done to you?"

"Yes."

"The waiting thing killed me."

I run my hand over her breast. "It's good for you to wait. It flushes you good. Makes your skin sing."

She turns her face to me. "So, are you going to let me go?"

"You're gorgeous like this," I say. "I could come just looking at you." I stay as I am, touching her, letting her scent and her shape fill my eyes. Then I turn her on her side and let loose her hands. I remove the blindfold. When she turns back, her eyes seize on me, and I recognize that desperate look. She curls against me, and I hold her tight.

She's mine now. I trapped her good.

For a minute, I forget that it's me that's trapped. I'm in way too deep.

I can't move except for my head, and the beat is shaking the floor. The man in the dust mask paces back and forth along the far wall. Even in the red glow, I can see that he's getting a hard-on. He sits again suddenly, then unzips his fly, his prick poking straight up. He watches me look at him.

The door flies open. In come the boys with Violet. Her wrists are cuffed behind. She looks at me with miserable eyes, and I don't know what it means. I stare back toward the man. His attention is full on Violet, but something in his manner, a thing I can't pin down, gives me a shiver. Maybe he's thinking of germs, I think. I glance at the video eye again. Nothing seems right.

The man stands. He's breathing hard, fixed on Violet as though wooden, as though not a living thing.

I can't move. I can't scream.

The music beats.

"Hey. Wake up. Becca. It's okay." When I open my eyes, it's Miriam's face that I see. Sunlight is pouring over the blue water of the bay. She's staring at me, trying to read me. "You were having a bad dream."

"What time is it?" I sit up. "I've got an appointment today."

"A little after nine."

Jumping out of bed, I roam the house, finding my bag where I dropped it at the front door. I haul it up to her bedroom. "The appointment's at ten."

She watches as I pull on underwear and jeans.

"You know," she says. "There's something about you that's familiar. Like I've seen you before."

"Clarisse Broder," I say, throwing a T-shirt over my head. "Everybody says I'm a dead ringer, pardon the pun, for the famously drowned Ms. Broder. Josh and Greg want me to make appearances dressed as her. They're like little boys about this." I put on socks and gym shoes.

"You're right! Clarisse Broder. God, did you read that book?" She pauses and leans back.

I shrug and head for the john like a coward.

While I'm happily peeing, I hear, "What the hell is this?"

I crack the door. She's holding the Uzi like it's a less than adequate filet mignon. She glares at me.

As for myself, I'm beginning to get a clear picture of her nosiness problem.

"I don't believe you'd bring a thing like this here. I hate guns." She looks like she's going to pitch it across the room.

"God. Be careful," I say, throwing myself out the door, my jeans at my knees. "The thing's loaded." I take it out of her hands, pointing it away.

"You can't bring shit like that here."

"Look," I say, sounding like Burt, like I picked up my speech patterns during some nasty war. "If I come, the Uzi comes."

We stand glaring at one another. Packing the Uzi in my bag and then zipping up my jeans, I drop onto the bed, sitting with my head in my hands. My brain is screaming for me to leave. Get out.

But I can't.

"What's the matter with you?" she says, still glaring at me with her arms crossed. "Are you some kind of nut?"

I rock back and forth like an imbecile. Maybe I should cock my arm over my head. But in my mind I see shot after shot, stills of that night trapped in murder. And more than that. I see Vin, his eyes having gone dead. I see the ash heap. Love disappears without warning, without a whisper.

"Okay," I say, looking up. "You want to know about the scar? I was stabbed."

Her face goes blank. She stares at me in shock.

"I was stabbed by a really weird guy. And you want me to tell you about my last lover?" I'll make her pay. The snoop. "Well, that breakup really did kill her. He fucking cut her neck . . . her neck," but I can't finish. I start bawling like some kind of idiot.

"She was so . . . She was so . . ." I start to rise from the bed, looking for one more in a long series of escapes.

But she pushes me back and drags me full on the bed, holding me like I'm an imbecile all right. I see her beaten face. So much like Violet, but not. Violet is at Tutti, I remember. Some night I'll find her.

"Jesus," Miriam keeps saying. "Oh God."

I can't stop sobbing.

"Are you seeing anyone about this?"

I nod. "That's my appointment this morning."

"You saw it? He killed her in front of you?"

"It's why I need the guns," I say. I glance at the clock. "I've got to go." I break out of her embrace and stand. She looks lost, beaten back.

"Miriam," I say. "You don't know how much I want you with me. How much I crave you. I feel like I'm going to die. I haven't had a lover since that happened. I've had sex, but not like this. Not how I feel with you. Maybe we shouldn't see each other."

"No." She jumps up and takes me in her arms, kissing me so tender that it wounds me. I pick up the gym bag filled with its unwanted objects.

"Leave it," she says. "I want you back tonight."

All I can do is nod. I turn and run down the stairs as though something is chasing behind.

Once I get to my therapist's, she takes one look at me and starts talking about a psychiatrist again.

"I'm in love," I say. "It's like a gun to the head, like jumping off a bridge, like taking a bottle of Valium." I notice what I'm saying and stop.

She tries to get me to calm down, breathing slow and even. Breathing appears to be one of my grosser failures.

I hit Tutti with whiskey on the brain. Josh sidles up to me. "A picture of Miriam Dubois with Clarisse Broder would bring in a pile of money," he suggests. I think I'm having an imminent headache.

Tom has the *Time* article with all the Betty and Dave pictures. He wants to talk about it, but leaves off when I start shaking.

Miriam shows up for dinner again. It's all I can do not to start crying.

When I get to her place after closing Tutti and having another encounter with the Dumpster, her eyes are even deeper, like she can see all the way into me. I see that she's taken out Bates' envelope and has the pictures arranged on her kitchen table. I look the other way.

God, I'm going to have to train her out of her little snoopy thing.

She leads me up to her bed again and lies me down, holding me.

"What was her name?"

"Violet. You look like her, by the way."

She's quiet, staring out at the water and sky.

"Did you have to testify at the trial?"

I look away. "There was no trial. They never caught him."

"Oh my God."

"He smashed her face. They found her in a Dumpster. A fucking Dumpster. Like sushi, like veal, like . . ." Her eyes look terrified.

"Sorry," I say.

"Here? In Berkeley?"

"No. No. Far away. Those pictures on your table, the detective
sent them for me to look at."

"And the other scars. He did that too?"

God, why doesn't she stop? "No. That's something else. I really can't talk about that."

She holds me tighter, stroking my head. I look at her face
again, like Violet, but not. A new thing. She kisses me a long
time, then runs her lips along my cheek. After a few minutes she
holds my head still so I can't look away. "Tell me more about
Violet."

"Not tonight. I know I keep putting you off. I can't remember all of it, and what I do remember, I want to forget." I swallow
and close my eyes. "And I can't get the pictures out of my head.
The ones the police showed me. Can you imagine? A bunch of
stupid cops with cameras, shooting picture after picture of her
like that. It makes me sick."

She stops with the questions then and we lie together, watching moonlight play the sea. I fall asleep, unsure in my mind
which thoughts are of Violet and which are of Miriam.

In the middle of the night, we both wake, kissing with vio-
lence, as though the dangers have taken us over. Biting and
scratching, we push each other toward some edge over which we

both tumble, making love like it's a vicious thing, like we can save ourselves by hurting. I end up crying again, and she holds me, talking to me low in the darkness.

The next few weeks are like floating down that river, the heat making us drowsy, dulling my edge with love. The only time I go to my apartment is to pick up more of my clothes.

One morning I show up at her place dressed as Becker. I slouch around for her amusement. Miriam decides that she wants to be Becker. I dress her up.

So for fun, Miriam and I begin gallivanting around the bay area, one or both of us dressed as Becker or Marty, as she dubs her new persona. She especially likes to be Marty with me as Becca.

For her enjoyment, I wear a very short, tight skirt on these occasions. She pinches me on the ass as we sit in the park. "Now I'm a nobody just like everybody else," she says, running a hand up my thigh.

"Stop it." I slap her hand.

She takes to buying cigarettes, God forbid, pretending to smoke. She rolls the pack in her sleeve. I can't believe I'm hanging out with someone like Marty.

"You don't have the right edge," I say, pushing her hand off my thigh for the millionth time. A young married couple with two small children are staring. "You weren't beaten enough as a child."

She puts her hand back. "Is that a clue, a Freudian slip?" She's always egging me into giving her tidbits to feed her infinite curiosity about my past.

I ignore her. "If you die of some terrible, disfiguring cancer from those things, I won't come to your funeral."

The cigarette hangs from her lips. "Kiss me, babe."

At night we lie in darkness, letting the starlight or the moon flood the rooms. She's had a baby grand brought in. As she sings, I lie on the couch, drenched by the river. It reminds me of Mama.

"What?" Miriam says, running her hands over me. "Talk to me. What makes you so sad? It's Violet, isn't it?"

I pull her close and lay my ear to her chest. Her heartbeat is full and strong. But I worry. My God-awful past. Where does a person even start? I have to admit, I'm feeling guilty about all that I'm keeping from her, but not guilty enough to start talking.

Greg, Josh, Miriam, and I begin to hit the bars after closing Tutti, but it gets to be tiresome with so many people coming up to Miriam. She starts dressing as Marty, which Greg and Josh think is great fun. They convince Miriam to join them in coaxing me to dress up as Clarisse Broder.

"Just once," Josh begs as we're all shopping together one evening. We've stopped for a bite to eat at a small place where the price for a cup of cappuccino should be considered a felony. "Climb out on the edge of the Golden Gate, Becca. You'll give everybody heart attacks." He waves his arms.

"We'll whisk you away before the police can arrest you," Miriam adds as though it's an afterthought.

"Gee, thanks," I say, finishing off my latte. "Why don't we just drop this?" I leave the table.

Later that night, Miriam won't let it be.

"What's the big deal?" she says. "Why are you so angry about this?"

"I'm not angry," I yell. "I'm tired of it."

"Why is it different from being Becker or Marty?"

"Because she was real. And those kids jumped off and got killed. I don't think it's funny."

She takes her stance with her arms crossed.

"Why won't you talk to me about your past?"

"Why can't you just drop it?" I scream. "Just leave me the fuck alone."

That's when I leave, thinking I'm going to my apartment. But I'm overwhelmed with the push behind, the thing that chases. Because now I know. It's Violet that races behind me. But I don't want to see anymore. I don't think I'll survive it.

I don't go home. Instead, I roam around in the dark, ending up back at Miriam's. She's already conked out in bed. Before I know it, I find myself in the extra bedroom curling up on the floor of the closet. I keep the door cracked, but throw a blanket over myself, leaving enough space for me to look out into the room. The Walther is in my hand.

"Where are you?"

I lie still and close my eyes. She opens the closet door. "Jesus, Becca." She kneels beside me and draws the blanket off my head. She kisses me.

"Talk to me."

"I think I might do better alone right now."

She's silent. "No. I'm not leaving you alone like this." She lies down with her head in front of me. "Was it our fight? I didn't mean to scare you. I won't push you like that again." She touches me. I cringe. She pulls back. "I'm sorry."

"I know."

"Maybe you should see your therapist more. You should listen to her. A psychiatrist might help."

"I'll be fine tomorrow." I pull the blanket back over my head. Miriam lifts the side of the blanket and fits her body into mine. I put my arm around her and cling to her warmth, clutching the Walther in my other hand. I'm so worried about the gym shoes. I don't want them to discover Miriam.

The next day, I convince Tom to go on another shooting spree, practicing on the moving targets. The whole thing disgusts Miriam, but she holds her tongue. I can see that our night in the closet worried her.

Now if I have a day off, she drags me along to the studio with her. I'm amazed by the operation that surrounds her, musicians, sound engineers, marketing and image specialists, and so on, all geared toward taking one woman and a few songs, and turning it into wads of money. It has the flavor of a political machine.

Johnson, her manager and producer, comes and goes, keeping

an eye on the recording, but also setting up future tour dates, interviews, publicity events, you name it.

"Johnson doesn't like me," I say.

"He doesn't like anybody. Real friendship just gets in his way. Think of him as a politician. The marketing, the interviews. It's all just spin to him."

"Doesn't that bother you?"

"I wouldn't be where I am today without him."

"Which is where, exactly?" I find myself poking her on this point.

She rolls her eyes at me. "I wouldn't have met you if I wasn't famous," she says, scoring on me there, I have to admit.

"Never know," I say. "We might have met grazing the same Dumpster."

She doesn't laugh. "Is that another one of your Freudian slips or are you jealous?" she says.

"Yeah. I'm sure it's jealousy." I curse myself for having brought up Dumpsters again.

But she gets quiet then. "Johnson's worried about the gay thing."

"What gay thing?"

"You and me, Dumbo."

"Oh. I never think of it that way. I just love you."

"Well, he's worried that it will get around, slow down sales, interfere with my chances at a Grammy."

"I told you he didn't like me."

"Oh, just forget it," she says.

"Are you worried?"

"A little. I've always wanted a Grammy."

"God, what for? It's just a weird costume ball and marketing ploy. Everybody sits around and admires each other."

"You know, you have a shitty attitude sometimes."

I bite my tongue. "If that's what you want, Miriam, then I'll help you."

She kisses me. "We have to start keeping a low profile."

"I'm good at that."

She looks at me suspiciously.

As the weeks go by, the memories haunt. They come so quick that I don't always know what's happening. Some are of Violet, but others are of the basement, the rail, days spent in the box. I catch Burt watching me at work. And Miriam's getting used to me "going away," as she calls it.

"You're seeing Violet again, aren't you?"

Why does she have to be so smart? I nod my head, unable to speak.

"Becca, you know I love you. I wouldn't do anything to hurt you, so why won't you talk to me?"

I lie my head down. Sometimes I cry. She wraps her arms around me and I rest in her scent, making sure she's breathing.

Thanksgiving flies by. We spend it with Josh and Greg. Miriam whips up a great Indian meal. No puffed-up turkey in sight. No cameras.

I fall deeper in. The river presses close. Her eyes, her lips, the scent of her skin drags me, pushing me down, holding me under.

11

Johnson

In December, as the rains begin to set up and the fog settles in, Miriam finishes recording. She wants to get out of town for a couple of days while she has a break in her schedule. She decides that we should go hiking.

She hears about a redwood preserve somewhere in the Santa Cruz Mountains that has some great trails. She says, "Seclusion." She says, "Great views." She says, "Not far from the city." The last sounds the best to me. I've never been on a vacation in my life, not that I remember anyway. It sounds exhausting.

But then I find out about the gear. I learn about Gore-Tex and gaiters. Miriam gets me all set up.

That's when Johnson informs her that he's arranged a photo shoot for promos. It's the day we're supposed to leave.

"Shit," I say when she informs me. "I told you he hates me."

"This doesn't have a thing to do with you. And it's in the city. So I do the shoot and then we leave for our hotel. You'll come with me to the shoot."

"No. I don't think I'd like it."

"I want you there. It's hellish. If I can see you sitting nearby it will be better for me."

How can I say no?

A day before we're supposed to leave, I see a message from Beefy in the *Times*. It says, please call.

I have a hard time getting away from Miriam. She's become somewhat possessive of me. If she'd been Jeremy, I would have told her to sit. Stay. The problem with loving someone as smart as yourself is that you're forced into too much honesty.

I finally hit a nice abandoned area with a burned-out car and a phone booth that has seen better days.

"Bates here."

"Hi, again."

"This connection is bad. Are you on the North Pole?"

"As far as you're concerned I am."

He doesn't laugh.

"I want you to come here and do a lineup."

"Wrong. Bzzz. You lose."

"Beth, this isn't a game. We've narrowed it down here. Try to help us finger the guy. Think of all the kids he's killed."

I don't say anything.

"All you have to do is run into the city and run out. We'll bring you into the station under a blanket or something. It'll be just you and me on the other side of the mirror. I promise you, no other cops. You take a look at our candidates and out you go, back into oblivion where you like it so much."

I'm thinking Southern Comfort. I'm thinking Uzi.

"When?"

He lets out a breath. "So you'll do it?"

"I'm not saying yes or no. I have to think about it. When do you want to do it?"

"Any time, but we need two or three days notice to round up our suspects."

I chew my lip. I think I picked that up from Miriam. "I'm going away for a few days. I'll make up my mind by the time I get back. That's five days."

"I want to do it sooner than that."

"Tough," I say. "You've waited five and a half years. You can wait five days."

"Fine. Just peachy. You want me to send you the pictures of Matt? Isn't that how you knew him? Or the ones of Violet?"

I hang up on him.

At Tutti, I bitch around again. Miriam doesn't show up tonight. She's packing the Taurus since we have to leave early in the morning.

Miriam is pleased with the car.

"What else don't I know about you?"

"The Taurus is hardly me."

"In other words, a lot. Right?"

"If you're going to answer your own questions, why bother me with them?"

"Maryland?" she says, looking at the plates. "I thought you were from Ohio," she says.

"I don't tend to think of myself as being from any place in particular."

"Maryland?" she says again.

After I close at Tutti, I check the Dumpster, this time taking extra care to search all the corners. Then I go to my place, feeling like a stranger there. I take out the picture of Mama and look at her for awhile, tears in my eyes. In the corner of the frame, I've stuck the school picture of Vin.

Before I go to Miriam's, I pack the shotgun and some extra rounds of ammo in my duffel bag. She can't believe I own yet another gun. I pull the switchblade out of my purse, flipping it open. "Look at this," I say.

She rolls her eyes. "I feel like I'm going on vacation with Rambo."

"Who's that?" I say.

We drag out of bed about four in the morning, clean up, and eat a quick breakfast. Before we leave, I show her where I keep all my guns and ammo, just in case we need to blast our way out of somewhere. It doesn't appear to help her feel safe in any way.

We buzz into the city.

I should have gotten the hint that it was going to be a bad day when I pull up at the photography studio and several photographers and reporters are waiting for Miriam. They start toward us. I jam the Taurus in gear and get the hell out of there.

"What are you doing?" Miriam says. "That's the place."

"Fine. I don't want my face or my car getting splashed up in some magazine. I'll drop you nearby and you can walk in."

She stares at me. "What's the matter with a few pictures?"

"You're the one that said Johnson wanted to keep the gay thing quiet."

"You'll have to do better than that."

I stew. "I just don't want my picture taken."

"Or a picture of this car."

I don't say anything.

"Okay. Drop me here. I'll walk back. You can slip in later. But we're talking about this tonight."

I nod.

She leaves the car with her bag and I hide the Taurus in a parking garage, freaked about the reporters. By the time I get back, the coast is clear.

A pert, smartly dressed young woman named Suzy leads me back to where they're working on Miriam. I instantly hate what they've done to her face. Her ache is squashed, covered up by foundation. The lines of her face that show her depth and maturity have been erased. She's looking more and more like a sex kitten.

I don't say a thing. It's not my business.

By eleven, after a lot of fussing, they start looking at the wardrobe, with Miriam asking my advice. I try to let her and Stewart, the main promo guy, decide, putting in my two cents only if it's something I hate. By one, they're ready for pictures.

I'm exhausted.

"Are you hungry?" I ask her as we head for the place where the cameras wait.

"It will screw up the makeup," she says.

Good idea.

So I sit in a corner and watch, swearing I'll never do one of these with her again. That's when Johnson shows up. He and Stewart huddle. Then he watches as they adjust lighting. When they're in full swing, Johnson ambles over to me. He smiles, a strange thing to watch on his face. I don't think his cheeks know how to act.

"This is boring as hell," he says. "You hungry?"

I'm so famished my stomach hurts, but I sense that lunch with Johnson might be somewhat like dropping into a nest of water moccasins.

"Not really," I say.

"Come on," he says. "I know a good place nearby."

I don't move, weighing out the worst that could happen. I decide the worst would be if I shoot him, which wouldn't be bad for me.

Once we're settled in a quiet, tasteful café and have ordered our meals, Johnson looks at me, fidgeting with his Rolex.

"Just spit it out," I say. "Why'd you bring me here?"

He attempts a smile again, but he's quite bad at it. Somebody should tell him not to try.

"Miriam's such a good kid," he starts. I feel myself bristle. "She's very trusting, always thinking the best about people."

I wait, staring at his weak chin. Johnson is just a wee bit shorter than I am, narrow in the face, partially bald, and looking squeezed-in.

"So," he continues, "when she gets involved with someone, I try to make sure they're not just using her. You know."

Our food comes now. I don't respond until the waiter has left. Then I say, "No, I don't know."

He doesn't try to smile anymore, which is a relief. "She's worth a lot of money, Rebecca. Not just to herself, but to all of us that work with her. She's at the top of her game and going higher. We think she's in line for a Grammy this spring."

"Good for her," I say. "She'd like that."

"So you can see how important it is that we make sure there's nothing that could get in the way."

"Don't worry about the gay thing, Johnson. I hate publicity. I go out of my way to stay a perfectly happy nobody." I'm thinking about my jump from the bridge. That was a hell of a diversionary tactic.

"Ah," he says, eating a bite of his halibut. "I'm thinking about the problem with your birth certificate."

I sit stunned. The little creep has been investigating me. Fuck. Fuck. Fuck.

"What problem?" I keep my eyes steady.

"Well, we found out nothing about Rebecca Cross, you see, no credit history, no schooling, nothing but a birth certificate saying you were born in Philadelphia."

Oh my lovely Asian family. I want to kiss them all. They filed that birth certificate for me.

"So what's the problem?"

He looks at my plate. "You're not eating," he says. "The chef here is quite good."

"I'm sure." I don't make a move.

He lays down his fork and wipes his mouth, acting too much like Ben. "I don't understand these computer things, but my investigator thinks your birth certificate is fake." He says the last word, picks up that fork, and takes a hearty swipe off his potato, stuffing it in his weasel-like mouth.

A long line of overfilled Dumpsters enters my mind, holding all the leftovers Johnson is trailing behind.

"Does Miriam know you do this? Investigate her lovers."

His eyes, narrowed down, rise to mine. I'd been around Violet long enough to know that look.

"Yes," he says, and goes back to his plate.

I get the sense that Johnson views life as a string of events in which one either wins or loses. Johnson is determined to win.

"And if I don't check out?"

He shrugs. "I can't make Miriam stop seeing you. And Rebecca, I don't want to."

As I stare at his lips, compressed, I wonder if he ever makes one statement that's not shot as full of lies as a slash pine full of borers. Of course, I'm not one to talk about lying.

But I'm picking up the scent of Rivertown. I weigh my options.

"I witnessed a murder," I say. "I'm supposed to lie low and keep quiet. No one's supposed to know I'm still alive."

He takes that in. "Miriam told me about the murder."

I grind my teeth.

He reaches inside his suit to the inner pocket and takes out a memo recorder. "If you give me the name of the investigating officer and where he's located, I'm sure we can clear this right up."

If he had been Ben, I would have collapsed right away. Johnson has no idea that he doesn't hold a candle to my old pimp in the scare market.

"Oh, no, Johnson. When I say nobody, I mean nobody. That cop would get real pissed if he knew I said one word to anyone. If you want to screw up Miriam and me, you go ahead and try. You might find that you can't. It's a chance I'm willing to take, because if she dumps me because of something you tell her, then I guess it isn't as good a thing as I think it is."

He sits frozen, his hand still clutching his nifty memo recorder. I wouldn't have thought it possible, but his eyes narrow even further, and as I watch, they appear not to see me at all. A chill runs up my back.

He finishes his meal in silence. I don't touch mine. As we're leaving, I turn to him and say, "I'll walk back. It's not far."

He nods.

"Oh, and by the way, Johnson. I think the Grammy would be great. But it's not the end of the world if she doesn't get it. And I think Miriam would agree with me."

He twists his mouth and leaves, not looking back.

I walk to the studio where Miriam is dressed by others, where her face is created to be a thing that it is not, and where Johnson sets up the plays and the players. I think I might not know Miriam at all, and the cold starts working its way in like I wonder sometimes how death would feel.

When I hit the studio again, I'm in a state. I find myself thinking about the tip of my whip and Johnson's baby white ass. I think of him as an anesthesiologist.

But in quick moments, I find that it's Miriam I'd rather have crouching before me like the fawn, baring her back to me. I wonder what other things Miriam has done behind my back.

That Johnson's a tricky one. A lot like Violet. Only she had good reasons for what she did. He's doing it for money.

When I walk in, I see that Miriam is looking bad. They're taking a short break to move the lights and adjust the set while she fidgets up on her platform. I walk up to her, trying to look like nothing happened.

"You look tired," I say.

"Where did you go? You're supposed to be here for me, remember?"

"I'm sorry. I got overwhelmed. I had to leave."

Her eyes are red. I think she might start crying.

"I won't leave again. You want me to do anything for you? How about I get a bottle of whiskey and sneak you a shot every now and then?" I take her hand and hold it in mine.

"We're ready," the little pipsqueak Stewart says to Miriam. She squeezes my hand.

"How much longer?" I say to her.

She shrugs her shoulders.

"You look worn out. Why don't you call it quits?"

"I can't do that."

"This might be a stupid question, but aren't you the boss here?"

"Jesus, Becca. For being so bright, you can be really dumb sometimes."

"Do you always do what Johnson says?"

She rolls her eyes. "I don't even want to start this with you."

I pull her down toward me and whisper in her ear. "What's your favorite liquor?"

She kisses me light on the cheek and says, "I hate liquor."

"Cognac?"

"Yuck."

"Wine."

"Ummmm."

"I'll see what I can do."

After picking up a bottle of cabernet, I dump part of it in a McDonald's cup. When I get back to the studio, they're working Miriam hard. She's looking so tired that I don't know why they're staying at it. During a short break, I slip up and hand her the cup.

She lifts the top, smelling it first. Then she takes a hit off it, closing her eyes in happiness. She smiles at me. I go and sit in my corner, wishing I had an imbecile to watch. He would be a lot more interesting.

It's ten in the evening before Miriam's ready to leave. I retrieve the Taurus.

"You hungry?" I say as I shovel her into the passenger seat.

"I'm too tired to eat."

I drive us to our hotel, having to wake her when we get there. At least she's too sleepy to ask me about the photographer fiasco. I put her to bed and order some appetizers to be brought up. She's asleep by the time they arrive, so I turn off the lights and look out our big windows to see the Santa Cruz Mountains rising up dark against a deeper darkness.

I eat by myself and finish the bottle of cabernet, worrying about Johnson, trying to let that thing he birthed in me pass as light as a breeze. It won't go. I watch Miriam sleep, feeling my distrust widen and spread like the arms of the live oak, shading the stacks at Rivertown.

*   *   *

Miriam doesn't wake until nine the next morning. I've been lying in bed, trying to decide if I should bring up my conversation with Johnson or not. I feel her stir. She turns over and looks at me, her face still coated with some of that icky makeup.

"Hi," she says.

I lean over and kiss her. "We don't have to hike today," I say. "You can rest if you need to."

"I'd rather get out into the air. I felt like I was smothering yesterday."

"It was nasty."

She narrows her eyes. "How would you know? You weren't there for most of it."

I purse my lips. "I'll order us up some breakfast."

She nods.

An hour later, I'm in my new gear, ready to hit the trails. Miriam seems to have regained her enthusiasm, so we head to the first trail, a short one since we're getting to the trailhead late. Midmorning is late by hiking standards, I discover.

Surprisingly, I quite enjoy myself. But about halfway through, I get a nasty jolt. Miriam pulls out a camera. A Polaroid.

How perfect for the person who hates to wait.

"I loathe those things," I say.

"Get over it." She aims it at me.

I stick out my tongue. She ruins a whole wad of film on me.

As we lie in bed later that night, Miriam falling off fast and looking so peaceful in her sleep, I turn her body to me and hold her, feeling my chest fill with a thing better than desire. I want to protect her from all that can go wrong in a life. I'm thinking of Kat and Violet, of how they were lost in the surge that races downstream. And I'm thinking of Johnson and his plague, how I'm carrying it inside like a deadly infection.

The second day we nearly kill ourselves hiking from dawn to dusk. By the time we get back, I'm exhausted and irritable. Bates is on my mind. Johnson aggravates like a handful of fleas.

I start out dinner with a double whiskey neat. Southern Comfort, of course. I get snotty as dinner progresses. I try to solve the problem by drinking more.

"We need to talk," Miriam says about midway through dinner.

"It's not a good time."

"With you, it's never a good time."

I wait, still sober enough to hold my tongue.

"What happened yesterday morning?"

I've been ready for this. I have ammunition. "I think a better question might be why you would tell Johnson about Violet's murder. You had no right to tell anyone, much less that ass of a human being."

For once, Miriam is speechless.

"He took me out to lunch yesterday and informed me about an investigation he's been doing on my background, saying that you knew about it. Is that true?"

She looks down. "Yes."

"Thanks a lot. Thanks for the vote of confidence. I don't know why I'd want to tell you anything about me and my shitty past." Her head jerks up on that comment.

The waiter sets my third double in front of me.

Her head goes into her hands. I think she might start crying. She raises her head, her eyes red.

"I'm sorry. I'd be mad as hell if I were you. Johnson always makes things sound so logical. He told me he wanted to do a background check, and since you wouldn't tell me anything about yourself, well, my curiosity took over."

I pick up the glass of whiskey, still full, and down it in one swallow. "What do you want to know? Do you want to know that he slashed Violet's neck so hard and deep that her head was almost cut off?"

She looks horrified. I should stop, but I don't.

"And did I tell you he sliced her stomach, too? Her intestines were spilled out. Like sausage," I say. "Maybe I didn't tell you how she was the eighth that he's killed. There's been a ninth since. Is that what you want to know?"

"Stop it, Becca. You're making me sick. And you're using it to hurt me because you're hurt. I want to know about your past because I love you, goddamnit. It's not a game for me. And you never even explain *why* you won't talk about it. That would help. And why you don't want your picture taken, or a picture of your car. If you don't tell me anything, I start to fill in the answers myself. I begin to lose trust in you."

I motion the waiter to bring me another double.

"You've had enough," Miriam says.

"I'll decide that."

We sit and glare at one another. "What do you know about real life anyway? You're babied, pampered. You have all the money you'd ever want. Everybody thinks you're so swell because you sing up on a stage. I don't think you could ever understand my life. We're as different as night and day."

"How are we different? Because you work at Tutti? What's so bad about that? I don't get what you're so secretive about. And what do you mean, shitty past?"

"Oh fuck off."

She stands up. "I hate it when you drink." Miriam stalks out.

I sit, thinking what a stupid shit I am. And everybody around is giving me looks like I've done a terrible thing making the lovely Miriam Dubois angry. I move to the lounge, brooding over Bates' request and my memory of Violet's battered face.

And because I can't stand the thought of Miriam being angry with me, I go up to our room. When I open the door, I see her sitting in the dark, looking out to the mountains like I did the night before. I walk up behind her and bend over, lying my head on her shoulder, smelling her neck, kissing her. I act a little too much like Jeremy, nuzzling close, letting my adoration show.

She ignores me for awhile. Neither of us says a word. Then she stands and takes me by the arm, sitting me on the bed and stripping me, still angry. She pushes me onto the bed and lies me in the center. That's when I see she's already attached straps to the corners. Miriam straps me spread out and jams a gag in my mouth.

"Drinking is a vice," she says as she's getting off the bed. "Whiskey is bad for you."

Miriam goes and turns on the TV. I moan.

"And I'm not spoiled. And I'm not pampered. You saw what it was like for me at that damn photo shoot, so you should know better."

She starts flipping through the channels, leaving me like that for an hour while she watches some stupid movie on TV.

"Patience is a virtue," she keeps reminding me. "Drinking is a vice," she repeats. "Especially for you."

When she turns the TV off and comes over to me, she strips and slips on a harness, inserting the dildo. I shake my head no.

The dangers. You know.

I struggle against the straps and shake my head with vehemence.

She mounts me. "What's the matter? You can shovel it out, but can't take it?" Miriam positions herself and plunges in hard. God, it hurts. I try not to let it show, but tears come into my eyes, not so much from the pain, but from the whole thing.

She sees my eyes. That's when she stops. It's like her face disintegrates, and she collapses on top of me crying. All I can do is lie there, still penetrated by that damn thing. She pulls out slow and takes the gag out of my mouth.

"Miriam," I say, "I don't want this. I'll tell you anything you want to know. I'll tell you everything. Just let me go and let's never end up like this again."

She's still crying as she undoes the cuffs. I take her in my arms and hold her so tight I think I might squeeze the life out of her.

When she stops crying, she turns and we stare into one another's faces for a long while.

"I mean it," I say. "What do you want to know?"

She touches my cheek and kisses me. "Nothing. Not like this. When you're ready, you tell me. I hurt you, didn't I? I'm sorry. I wanted to hurt you. I've never done anything like that before."

I think she's going to start crying again. "Shh. Miriam. Don't cry."

"It's everything," she says. "I hate that stuff where I'm made into something I'm not. It gets me all turned around. And when you were gone for so long, I thought you didn't care about me. But it was Johnson, wasn't it? He took you away."

"Yes. He wants me gone, Miriam. That's why he let me know you told him about Violet. I felt like I couldn't trust you."

I take her head in both my hands and make her look at me. "I love you, Miriam. I love you hard and violent. I love you willow, willow wand, redfly and blubberbee. I love you way beyond Rivertown."

Her face looks like it might disintegrate again. "Even after what I just did to you?"

"God, Miriam, on my scale of reference for damage, that didn't register a bleep. The worst was that it was you that did it to me. And that you'd go behind my back like that with someone like Johnson. Let's forget about it. Let's start someplace new."

She cries some more and lies her head on my shoulder, kissing my cheek soft.

"What did all that mean? Blubberbee? Rivertown?"

I smile at her. "You said you'd wait until I was ready."

"Okay. You're right."

I kiss the top of her head, smelling her hair. "You remember about the river, right?" She nods, keeping her head against my chest. "I'll tell you about Rivertown."

So I say, press of the heat beneath the live oak. I say, rustling leaves. And little stone houses. I say, laid out on shelves like dolls flat on their backs, the rich man's stacks.

Stacking in Rivertown.

Watching the tooms.

Cottonwood tremble. Shush of the river and mud of the river.

Whisper willow willow wind.

Miriam falls asleep in my arms.

*   *   *

I wake feeling Miriam kissing me. Opening my eyes, I see sunlight. Miriam stops kissing me long enough to whisper, "Stacking in Rivertown."

I think of Mandy squishing in the mudflats, and I laugh for the first time in a long time. Then we make love so tender. I promise myself that I'm going to start talking to Miriam about everything.

We cut down our hike to half a day since we're both exhausted and bruised from our tangle last night. After we're done hiking, we fall into the Taurus and explore some of the back roads, trying out gravel and dirt drives, diving into the woodland, sometimes ending up nowhere.

As we come out into a grassland that slopes away toward the distant sea, we see an abandoned cabin with the roof still intact. We park and walk over.

It looks a lot like that old two-room down by the river. I keep walking around it, peering in the windows, like I might see Mama in her rocker or Daddy taking a swig of white lightning.

Miriam comes behind me as I stare into the cabin. "It reminds you of something, doesn't it?"

I shake my head yes. "It reminds me of Mama."

She's listening.

"Mama would sing in the evenings sometimes. We lived in a place no bigger than this. It was right on that river." I close my eyes and breathe in.

"What is it?" she says.

"Can't you smell it? The mud of the river. The yaupon crowding the bank. I can hear the bugs in the weeds, the slither of the coachwhip, and the screech owl screaming. That would scare you right up off the floor." Then I remember the smoke over me. I feel tears coming, but I don't want her to see.

And that memory of Mama and the smoke brings me back to that place I know so well. "This would be a good place to commit suicide," I say. I don't look at her, afraid I'll see Violet painted all over.

"Don't say that ever again," she says.

I gaze over the sea, which is picking up the sun, gleaming. "Okay."

And while I'm looking that way, she takes a picture of me with that shitty camera. I turn to yell at her, but the look in her face stops me.

"You're so beautiful," she says. "And now, if I can't see you while I'm on tour, I can still remember how you look."

After we leave, I write down how we got there, just in case I'd ever want to go back. Then we drive to the hotel and have a gorgeous bottle of Margaux with a meal that would have made Larry so jealous, he would have wrecked the kitchen.

The next morning, we drive to Berkeley, with Miriam in some kind of latent vacation bliss. Every now and then she rouses herself as if she's dreaming and talking in her sleep. She looks over at me to get my attention and says, "Watching the tooms," or, "Laid out flat on their backs." She reaches over and takes my hand, then looks off again.

I'm driving, haunted by Violet, knowing what I should do about Bates, but too scared to think about it.

I remember them bringing Violet into the room. I remember her misery. Her hands were cuffed behind, and the man presented his dick to her, not helping. The music boomed crazy in my body.

Violet took it in her mouth, eyes closed, her face looking to me now like she was already dying. I saw how she'd been going slow since the day we brought her out of the basement, how Ben and his plays were sucking the life out of her.

She worked him, but he didn't moan, didn't tremble or shake. He stared down at her face. I felt the dangers like they were crawling my skin, like they were tunneling into my eyes. I began to berserk, trying to scream at the video eye. Nothing happened.

Then came the first slap. He knocked her head to the side. Another. He took hold of her neck with a black-gloved hand so big that his fingers almost touched in back. And with his other fist, he beat her back and forth, back and forth on the face. Then he stopped. She slumped, being held in place by his hand on her throat. Then with the other hand, he grabbed her hair.

I don't think I saw the knife in his hand. It was like a magical thing, how suddenly Violet came apart, like a seam ripped, as though something from within had to leap out. And my first thought was, yes, this is how Violet is best, her wounds the truer wounds of a life shed years ago.

In that moment, I thought her face the most beautiful ever, for as his hand swept along her neck, she opened her eyes. They were empty of everything but surprise. A kind surprise, as though all was forgiven, forgotten, and let go.

And then she went to sleep, her blood squirting in my face and over my breasts until her heart weakened, sighed, reducing its flow to a silent, feeble bubble.

I wailed. I cried. But the gag kept me muffled. The man swept his magic hand along her stomach. Out poured pieces of Violet.

I watched her disappear. I waited as all signs of what she had been melted down into the red pool widening its reach to my feet.

Only then did I remember that he was there. I noticed the gym shoes on his feet, surrounded by red. I recognized the pattern of red across his coat, which Violet had painted there. His dust mask was spotted in a streak.

Behind his sunglasses, between the red drops, I knew he was letting me know and see everything.

Now that Violet had gone to sleep, he was thinking of me.

12

New York

We get back to Miriam's place around noon and unpack the Taurus. I leave her there, telling her I'm going to bring a few things to my place, park the Taurus in the garage, and return later.

I buzz into Oakland and dial Bates.

I'm shaking. "Okay," I say.

He lets out a sigh.

"When do you want me there?"

"Monday should give us time to get set."

"What time?"

"Come in early afternoon. We should be done by seven or eight."

"I thought this was just a lineup. That shouldn't take more than an hour."

"I want to talk to you face to face first. Go through everything you remember."

I'm trembling head to foot. "This is scaring me."

"I know. I'll be there with you the whole time."

"Somehow, that doesn't work for me."

"Where do you want me to pick you up?"

"I don't know yet. I'll phone you after I get travel arrangements figured."

We hang up.

I drop some guns at my place and park the Taurus. Then I catch a cab to Miriam's.

"You all right?" Miriam says when I get to her place.

"I've got to talk to you about something."

"Yeah," she says. "I've got to talk to you, too."

We stare at each other.

"I'll go first," she says. "Let's sit down."

We sit at the table in the kitchen.

"Johnson called. I'm wrapping up here." She says, "In a week or so, I'll go home to Seattle. Things will get wild after that. I haven't said anything to you before, but there's a long tour planned. And of course all the promos, interviews, a lot of media."

She takes my hand in hers. I can feel the blood draining out of my face.

"I want you to move to Seattle with me," she says. "There are plenty of restaurants in Seattle where you could work. We can get you an apartment, but I'd like to talk about you moving in with me. What I'd really like is if you don't get a job at all, but just go around with me. Interviews and touring are hell."

"So," I say. "You'd keep me?"

"Don't put it like that. What would be so bad about it? We'd keep you away from the cameras, which seems to suit you fine. We've got time to talk it out."

This is looking to be a tequila day.

"Now, what do you want to talk to me about?"

I wet my lips. "I got a letter from my sister. I have to go see her for a day. Next Monday. I'll leave in the morning and come back late, maybe not until two or three in the morning."

"What's going on?"

"She's sick." I need to brush up on my lying.

She turns my face to her and looks in my eyes. "You're lying to me."

Why does she have to be so smart? I pull my hand away and lie my head on the table for a minute. Then I look at her again.

"The detective wants me to see a lineup to try and finger the guy that stabbed me."

"I'm going with you."

"No." I hit the table with my hand when I say it and stand up, pacing. "It's too dangerous. I don't want you involved. If you got hurt, it would kill me."

"Why would I get hurt? What aren't you telling me? God, you look terrible. Will you come back here?"

"No," I say and start pacing with a vengeance. I glance at her. The look in her face hurts me.

"This is the shitty past part, isn't it?"

I take a deep breath. "When I was there, in New York, I was a prostitute." I watch her face go pretty damn white. "The pimp got me when I was sixteen. I was a runaway." I open the fridge and grab a beer, twisting off the top and drinking half the thing in one long swig.

"You wanted to know about the other scars," I say. "They were from him. He whipped me. I was with him ten years." I chug the rest of the beer.

"Those are whip marks? Jesus, Becca. Why didn't you tell me?"

"I don't know. I was afraid you'd leave. And I hate to remember about all of it. There were things that happened, things he did to me." I find myself edging back. I hit the refrigerator. "Things that happened," I try again. Miriam stands like she's going to come over. "No," I say. "Let me finish."

She sinks back down.

I force myself to walk to the table and sit down in front of her. I take both of her hands. "He let me go for five years, but then he made me start working for him again in June this year. He beat me the last time, and then gave me eight hours to get my stuff and come back to him so he could reacquire me. The fucker's in love with me." I see Miriam's eyes shut.

"So I ran away. That's how I came to Berkeley. I was getting ready to take off again when I met you. That's what I was doing in that camping store the day we ran into each other again."

I bow my head, then look back. "If that pimp finds me, I'll never see the light of day again. And if he knew that there was someone that I loved, he'd hurt you just to get me." I don't know if I've ever seen so much panic in anyone's face. I reach up and touch her cheek.

"I've thought at times that I should leave you so that you'd be safe, but I love you so much, I can't do it. So you have to stay here. I'm just flying in and back out. I'll cover my trail the best I can."

She's quiet. "Rebecca's not your real name."

"No."

"What is it?"

"That's anyone's best guess."

"You don't remember?"

"I've had so many names, I get confused."

"What if you don't come back?"

I wait a moment. "Do you want me to come back now that you know I was a prostitute?"

She shakes her head. "I don't care about that. Don't you know that I love you?"

I sigh, trying not to cry. She touches my face. "Then I'll be back," I say. "I'm getting good at this kind of thing. But I'll give you the name and number of the detective. Call him only if I don't show up by, I don't know, noon the next day."

"He calls you?"

"No. That's why I read the *Times* every day. He puts an ad in the personals for me. To Tut from Beefy."

She laughs. "Beefy?" Then she starts crying.

I walk behind her and hold her.

"That's how you got stabbed," she says. "As a prostitute." Her voice is hoarse.

"Yes. We were working a play."

"A play?"

"That's what he calls it. Ben is his name. It's like theater for the rich and famous. God, could I tell you stories about some famous people. We were prisoners there. Most of the time, it didn't seem too bad. But sometimes, for punishment, he did terrible things." I close my eyes. Lights are shooting off all over the room. "Violet was one of his, too. We were in the same room working the play, but I was tied. I couldn't move. I saw it all."

"And the guy stabbed you."

"I don't remember that part. For a long time I didn't remember anything. I thought I had an appendectomy."

She turns and clings to me, crying again. Then she stands and drags me upstairs onto the bed. We lie together.

"I'll come back. I promise."

"How did you get through all that? Ten years? I think I would have curled up and died."

"I didn't have any other choice. He beat the shit out of us. He whipped. He fed us drugs. He had this box just big enough to fold a person up in. He'd lock you up in that for awhile. You just make yourself get through it somehow." I'm seeing the ghosts now. They're all over the room.

She's quiet, but leaning over me, her fingers playing in my hair.

"I've got to make a phone call to get the plane flight worked out."

She lies down while I sit on the edge of the bed and pick up the phone. I dial Jill's number, feeling nostalgic about those days in Monongahela. They seem so set apart now, as though they were easy. But then the trout began to rise.

Jill answers the phone.

"Jill," I say.

"Becca. How are you? Did you get the package Daddy sent?"

"It was perfect. Tell him he has my thanks, but I could use another favor."

She waits.

"Do you think I look like Rob?"

Silence. "Is this a trick question?"

I smile. "No. I mean it. I think we're close enough. The ticket people at airlines never look you in the face anyway, right? I could say I'd had a face-lift since the ID was made."

She laughs. "Now that you mention it, I think you could slip by, maybe, if they're not paying attention. You should buy a trout vest."

"Don't tempt me."

"So where are you planning on flying using Rob's face?"

"I'm coming in to New York to look at a lineup. Could you make the reservations under your name? I'll wire you money."

She doesn't hesitate. "What do you need?"

"This Monday. A flight from San Francisco to arrive in Philly in time for me to catch a train into Penn Station. I need to arrive in New York by one. Return train from New York to Baltimore, leaving around nine. Then a plane back to San Francisco."

"No problem, Becca. How's the weather there?"

"Mild."

"I envy you."

"It's been damp and foggy as hell. Is Rob still getting the trout to rise?"

"Yes. And you?"

"Oh, they're rising. It's enough to bring a person to suicide."

"I wouldn't joke about that, Clarisse."

"Good one. So send the tickets with the ID same day mail to the address I gave you before."

"You're doing the right thing, Becca. And by the way, Merry Christmas."

"Ack," I say. "Bah humbug."

We hang up.

Miriam pulls me down to her. "I want her name, phone, and address, too."

"Okay."

"And if I ever hear you say the word 'suicide' again, I'm going to hire someone to watch you twenty-four hours a day."

I can see her point. And she doesn't even know my history on that subject. "Sorry," I say.

We lie silent for awhile. When she turns to me, at first touching me gentle, we kiss. But panic takes us over and we make love like it's despair, like it's misery made flesh, her body the device I use to bring myself sorrow.

Kat was gone for near a year and a half before Violet showed up. During that time I grew listless, and then so thin when my appetite dried up.

But when Violet came, I got a boost in the futures market. Ben watched. And I was aware of him watching. It wasn't long after that Ben prepared us our first round of speedball.

Ben gave everybody a blow that night, but when I look back on it now, I know he was doing it for me, tethering me tighter.

One taste is the love of the devil. Two tastes and the devil is your lover.

I was a straight addict by the time I ended up in that hospital where synchronicity got me in its cheery little paws. But Violet, she was a needle freak. She got off on the sight of her blood drawn up into the syringe and mixing with the smack. She said she loved it as soon as she saw it. I think her eyes had ahold of her heart.

That first night, Ben shot the others up. Then he led me out. I looked back before the door closed, seeing how everybody was blown out already. Ben brought me to a play room and stripped me to the waist, then had me sit in the only item in the room, a wooden chair. He tied me to it, but with my wrists tied in front to my knees.

"So you don't fall down and hurt yourself," he said.

He was right about the falling down part, but that's not why he tied me to the chair. Ben wrapped on the tourniquet and got a vein standing up. I watched as blood pushed into the syringe. Violet liked the blood. For me, it was death in a needle. My wish come true.

As soon as he dropped it in, Ben stood back, watching me. Then he smoked some coke, and I watched as all sorts of lines, shapes, and colors crept the world new. Ben's face came into view. His lips and eyes poured me like the river. His magical fingers circled my breasts, now strange to me, but beautiful.

Beside the river in autumn, the cottonwoods go gold. Slash oak gets a cast of crimson and the berries of the yaupon glow bright as blood.

And in the middle of the night, when the river's low and when the moon is near to full, you can wake and know the purest kind of still. It's something about the white of the moon and how the tupelo stand quiet, like they're waiting, and how not a leaf of the cottonwood turns.

Oh, morphine. She wakes me with breath blown against my eyes. She dresses in purest silk, and dies like air against my lips. I'm broad as the sky is deep. I'm soft as the night is soft of sound, and dripped like amber drowned in flies.

At night, the goatsuckers swoop and dive, singing, pity-pity-pit-pit. Pity the sleeper as the dawn begins to break. Pray for the devil, that his slender neck will break.

Sunday morning, Miriam and I drive to Hayward so I can call Bates. She stands with me in the phone booth.

"Hi again," I say.

"So what's the deal?"

"I'll call you on your cell phone when I hit the city around one. I'll tell you where to pick me up."

"Okay. And calm down, Beth. Everything will be fine."

"I'll believe that when I'm safely back here."

We hang up.

On the way to Miriam's, we stop at a thriftshop. I buy a hunting jacket and some torn-up gloves.

That afternoon at work, I corner Tom. "I need to talk to you."

"Hello, Beth," he says.

Why do I put up with this shit? "I'm flying to New York to try and finger the guy that stabbed me," I say.

"God, Becca. Want me to come along? I'm a great shot."

"No." I lead him back into the wine closet. "If I don't make it back—now shut up—if I don't make it back, you tell Miriam everything. I'll leave a note for her at my place, but I'd like it if you talked to her."

"Becca. It can't be that bad."

"You're right. Chances are I'll be back Tuesday morning just as planned. This is only the big 'what if?'"

"Okay," he says.

Sunday evening after I close, I go to my apartment. I look over all my old IDs and lie them out on the table, placing them beside my picture of Mama with Vin stuck in the corner. Next to that, I set out the two notebooks of stories I've been working on. Then I write a note to Miriam, telling her about Terri, Beth, Clarisse, and how Becca got to Berkeley. I tell her how much I love her.

I seal this in an envelope and put her name on it. Then I pack all my guns in my duffel with some clothes and my bag of money, which has grown since I've been working at Tutti. I take a cab to the Taurus and put the duffel in, but stick the Smith and Wesson in my jeans.

Once I'm at Miriam's, I pull out the pistol.

"I don't want this."

"I'll feel better if I know you have it."

"I refuse to shoot a gun. I don't care what's happening."

"Leave it here for me then."

She nods.

We get about two hours sleep. I dress as Becker, not wearing a gun for the first time in months. It's going to be hell.

She rides with me to the airport. I'll never forget watching her stand, leaning forward, wanting to go with me. I pass through the door to the plane. Her eyes, those eyes I have wanted to see me for so long, see nothing but me as I walk out.

The flight is tedious. I hit Philly, catching the scent of the East Coast as soon as I leave the terminal. I pull my hunting jacket close. A cold drizzle is falling. As I ride to the train terminal, I wonder how the Asian family is doing. I'm feeling a lot of goodwill toward them. I wonder what Bates threatened them with to get them to tell him about Rebecca Cross.

I catch the train up to Penn Station, paranoid as hell. The subway drops me in SoHo. I call Bates, telling him where to find me, and I wait in a gallery, watching the street. Sure enough, up pulls that good old Chevy Caprice. I slide in the back. He takes one look at me and whistles.

"Good disguise, Beth."

"Thanks," I say as I lie down on the seat.

We hit the station, him leading me in a back door, and me with a blanket thrown over. It's too reminiscent of Ben. We go into an interview room.

I sit down on one side of the table. He adjusts a mike and starts a recorder. He asks me what I remember about the night Violet died.

I talk, but this doesn't last long.

"Tell me about Ben," he says.

I shake my head no. He punches the machine off.

"That wasn't part of the deal," I say.

"Beth, you more than anyone have a vested interest in seeing him put away. Just tell it to me. Then I can get the same info out of the ones he has now. What you say to me stops here."

"That's why you brought me here. It's about Ben."

"No. There's a lineup later. But while I have you here, I'm going after as many birds as I can."

Bates punches the machine on. I force myself to start talking. I talk about the apartment where Kat and Ben got me. I tell him about the basement, Bates bringing me back again and again to the details, wanting me to remember more.

The harder he pushes me, the worse the ghosts come on. The room winks in and out, and I curl up in my chair. Bates' face takes on a glow, as if a red light has been flipped on, and the ghosts crowd close. They're so loud, I have to close my ears so I can talk.

"You're lucky you made it out alive," he says to me, his eyes having sunk back in, as though all his briefcases full of pictures have finally fleshed out, and here I sit, the walking dead, soaking the room in red.

I stare off, hearing voices in my head as I'm bound, gagged, and blind on that mattress. Even whiskey won't touch this.

We wait. He leaves for awhile, locking the door behind him. I curl up in the corner.

When Bates returns, he helps me up. "You'll do fine," he says. Throwing the blanket over me, he leads me down the hall. The blanket comes off. I look through the windows at an empty room with height markers like slashes under the fluorescents.

Six men file in. Each is wearing a heavy overcoat, a wide-brimmed hat, a dust mask, and sunglasses. I walk the length of the room trying my damnedest. I see lights roving. I hear voices.

He has them turn to the side so I can see the profile. One catches my eye. I stand in front of him, concentrating. I walk down the line, but keep coming back to him. There's something, but I can't place it.

Suddenly, I know. I turn on Bates, jumping him like hounds jump a coon.

"How could you? You fucker!" I'm trying to get to his face. "You goddamn mother-fucking shithead! You're just as bad! You're signing my death warrant. You think he won't figure it out?"

I run for the door, but Bates grabs me by the shirt and throws me against the wall.

"It's him, isn't it?" he says.

I look at the man again. It's Ben.

"Why would Ben murder Violet? He'd say that's a waste of his training. Why would he stab me? He says he loves me!" I squirm, going for his face again. "Let me the fuck out of here. I've got to get away from him!"

He throws me toward the door, then opens it, pushing me across the hall into an interview room. He slips in behind me, locking the door. I beat against it, pulling on the handle. Then

I turn and slide down. I notice that I wet my pants. I start screaming.

Bates goes white as he watches me.

Something happens inside me. It's like someone flips an "off" switch. I fall silent. He waits, mopping his head with his crumpled handkerchief.

"It's got to be Ben that did it, Beth. That's why the dust mask, the sunglasses, even the gloves on his hands. He didn't want you to recognize him. I don't know why he stabbed you. Maybe to teach you a lesson, but then he went too deep. You bled too much. Maybe that's why he let you marry Jeremy. Maybe he scared himself."

"No," I say. "You just want to get Ben so bad that you've screwed your mind around. I know Ben. He's a fucker, but not this. Not all those kids."

"What about Matt? Matt was one of his. I figure the others are the ones who didn't measure up in his basement. They were the failures."

The thought of Matt brings back that crack when his arm broke. I begin dry-heaving and crawl into the corner, burying my head. My feet and hands go numb. I can't see a thing but a dull gray with a dim light off-center. The ghosts come, this time screaming, like how Violet described them to me.

In time they fade. I feel the blanket that Bates tucked around me. My body begins to quake.

"Beth?"

"Yeah?"

"Finger him. I can get him locked up."

I sit in a stupor. "You're wrong about Ben, Bates. And if you think there's a judge in this town that will lock him up, you're stupider than I thought. He'll blackmail the judge, and if that doesn't work, he'll go higher."

My head wanders off again. I have to work hard to think straight.

"What time is it?"

"Quarter till eight."

"My train. I can't miss my train."

I feel his hands on my shoulders, lifting me up. Then he throws the blanket over me and opens the door. He has to help me walk. Then I'm curled in the back of his Chevy beneath the blanket.

"Don't let anyone follow," I say over and over. I have him drop me at Penn Station.

"You can still finger him," Bates says. "Just call me. Tell me he's the one."

"Then what? You want me to sit in a court in front of him and tell everybody what he's done? You don't have a clue, do you? If you'd been in that basement, you'd understand that nothing would ever make me lift a finger against that man. You've got the wrong whore."

I slide out and blend with the people moving in and out of the station. By now the drizzle has turned to a freezing rain. Still shaking and trying to work more feeling back into my hands, I load into a train car and let the train speed me into Baltimore. From there I take the plane to a layover in Memphis, screeching over the frozen rivers and fields.

I can't shake the sight of Ben standing in front of me wearing the dust mask and the sunglasses. I'm way past the dangers now, into some new territory so awful that I can't bear to know a thing.

Merry Christmas to me.

The man with the dust mask and sunglasses stared at me. He took a step in my direction, then appeared to hesitate. He forced himself toward me and towered above. I stopped fighting the straps. I stopped screaming into the gag. All that was going to occur in the next few minutes became known to me. I could do nothing to stop him. My brain exploded.

He hit my face hard with the back of his hand. Again. I went with it, easing the strike. I don't know why I bothered. Habit, I guess.

After a couple more punches, he stopped and looked down. I followed his eyes, gazing down also, for the first time seeing the switchblade pointing at my belly. From my ass to the top of my head, a fire passed through, and I felt a happiness, a white calm. I saw the knife slip into me, felt a sting, and heard a click against a rib. His hand jerked to the side. It reminded me of when Grady cleaned rabbits after he'd taken them out of his traps. My blood streamed over his hand, running between my legs, down my thigh, now breaking into rivulets, and winding downward along my leg.

I smelled his breath and said to myself, this is as it should be. We are the perfect lovers, having loved now complete. And I am looking for Mama. I am singing for Kat.

It doesn't make sense, but I think I see Violet standing behind him, looking around his side, her eyes following the course of my blood running in thick streams.

In the river, the water pours, disappears into the sea, evaporates, returns as rain, pours again. This is how it seemed to me as I sagged down, my head sinking to the side. The air swam with a glory of gnats and bees.

I heard sounds, saw someone grab him from behind, and had a sense of a struggle, of his hand spewing blood. Then I was on the floor, having been untied, lying in a bath of blood.

And I saw Kat looking older, and behind her was Violet again, both caring for me. I remember thinking how glad I felt that Violet wasn't dead after all. Someone wrapped me in a blanket and lifted me. Then I was in the backseat of a car. Lights went by and by. I was placed on a stretcher. I watched Kat recede as I was drawn in under lights. Glass doors closed behind me.

In Memphis, I change to another flight.

Ben's behind me. I'm sure of it. And Miriam's waiting. He mustn't see her.

I fly into San Carlos instead of Hayward and take a cab to Berkeley. The cab driver drops me a few blocks from the garage where the Taurus is parked. I hide in an alley for a long time, waiting for Ben to walk by.

No one comes.

Now I slink along the street, letting myself into the garage. My vision keeps going in and out, leaving me blind for minutes at a time. When I can see again, the red cast remains.

I sit in the Taurus. Every cell in my body is screaming for me to get out. To run. To blow town. But Miriam's eyes follow me. I think I hear her crying, but then I realize it's me as I lean against the steering wheel. Going to the back of the car, I yank out the Uzi and the Walther, then sink down, leaning against the side of the Taurus. I fall asleep.

I wake myself up talking, saying something to Ben like he's there. My vision goes out again. I wait until it comes back. Then I peek outside the garage. It's still dark. I slide on my holster and Walther and creep out, jogging, looking for a phone. I call Miriam. Her answering machine picks up.

"It's Beth, Miriam, I mean Becca," I say. "I'm okay. I can't come home right now. I'll call again."

Then I call Tom. He's groggy.

"Tom. It's Becca."

"Jesus. What time is it?"

"I'm not coming back for awhile. I left a message with Miriam. She's not answering. Can you go over and see if she's okay? I'm worried about her."

"You sound bad."

"I'm fine. Just go check on her." My vision wavers.

"Where are you?"

"It's better if you don't know."

"Come home, Becca. We can help you."

"Tell Miriam I'll be in touch."

I have no idea what I'm doing. Get out, I keep telling myself, but this time I can't get out. It was a snap to leave Jeremy. Love never figured in that equation for me. But now, I'm caught as good as a muskrat in a snap trap.

You're being crazy, I keep telling myself. How could Ben find me? Nobody followed me. Nobody knows I'm in Berkeley, not even Bates. Only Jill, and there's no way he can trace her.

I jog off again, heading back to the garage. I'm worried that Miriam might come looking for me there. So I put the Uzi in the duffel, sling the big bag over my shoulder, close up the car, hit the street, and start walking. The sky brightens. Cars buzz back and forth. I feel myself drawn to Miriam's, but I fight it.

After wandering all morning, I remember that I'm due at Tutti by noon. I call. Cinda answers.

"Tutti."

"Cinda, it's Beth, I mean, Becca." I've got to get my name right.

"Oh my God. Just a minute."

"Becca?" It's Burt.

"I'm sick, Burt. I won't make it today."

"We're worried about you, Becca. Miriam is a mess. You've got to come back."

Shit.

"Tell her I need some time, Burt. I'm fine."

"You don't sound fine." This is what I get for making friends. "Tell me where you are. I'll come and get you."

"I'll keep in touch," I say and hang up.

Now I think I might start bawling again, or maybe throw up. I escape the phone booth and walk hard. I think I'm just going nowhere, not caring, but before I know it, I'm on the street in front of my apartment.

I'll hole up for a couple days, I think. They won't check here. But I'm afraid to go inside. Ben could be waiting there. He's smarter than me. And he always wins.

I walk to the nearest liquor store and buy two bottles of whiskey. As night falls, I hide myself behind a Dumpster in an alley. I have a good view of the door to the apartment building.

That's where I stay all night, sipping my bottle, watching the door. I don't see Ben. I watch my neighbors go in and out.

By morning, I decide to take a chance. I dart across the street and slip through the door. Then I pull out my pistol and mount the steps slow, fitting my key in the lock and pushing the door open. I check everything. My IDs are just like I left them.

Getting out the bag I've kept them in since Cumberland, I slide in everything, the IDs, Mama's picture, the letter I wrote to Miriam. I throw it in my duffel, taking out all the guns and ammo.

Something cracks in me then. I start slamming things around. I pull the dresser drawers out, spilling my clothes. I rip dresses and skirts off hangers. I break my CDs. I throw what few plates I have against the floor, watching them shatter.

I hate Bates with a white heat.

Then I start on my second bottle of whiskey. I make a barricade by moving the dresser and the armchair to form a triangle with the wall. I bring in all my guns with extra rounds and throw my notebooks on the floor next to them. I sit drinking, pistol in one hand, watching the door.

I wake up to the sound of someone knocking. I peek at the clock. It's four in the afternoon.

"Becca, are you in there?"

It's Miriam.

"If you're in there please answer the door."

She keeps knocking and calling. God, it's killing me.

"Go away," I whisper. "Please go away."

Everything goes quiet. I begin drinking in earnest now, clobbering myself with liquor. I don't know how much time passes, but the room is dark. The whiskey is in my eyes, and my vision keeps blinking in and out.

I hear a sound at the door. The doorknob turns. I raise my pistol, my arms and hands shaking badly. Releasing the safety, I press my finger next to the trigger. I've practiced hour after hour for this.

The door swings open, the hall light streaming into the room. Three figures stand there. The one in the center is very tall.

"Get back," I say. "I'll kill you, Ben. Don't fuck with me."

"Becca." I know that voice. I shake my head, but the room's spinning.

"Give me the gun, Becca. It's Miriam."

A figure starts edging toward me.

I point at the heart. "I'll kill you, Ben."

The other two are edging in.

"It's me. It's Miriam."

I feel the gun wavering, my whole body quaking from the poison I've been dumping in.

She crawls over the chair and kneels beside me. One hand circles my wrist while the other pulls the gun free. She gives it to Tom, who flips on the safety and drops out the clip. I feel her arms around me, her cheek against my head. Josh kneels down on my other side. He hands my guns and ammo to Tom, who empties all the bullets and pockets them. He turns on a light and closes the door. They move the furniture back.

I'm too drunk to move, and I see that I've pissed again. They lie me back and remove my wet clothes. Tom and Josh carry me to bed. Miriam lies on one side, Josh on the other, both holding me. Tom loads the Walther again and sits in the armchair, guarding the door.

13

Old Friends

When I wake, I see Miriam sitting and reading my notebook in the armchair. Tom's conked out next to me. I smell like I've been rolling in whiskey and piss.

I guess I have.

I lie still, watching Miriam, thinking that for this moment, it's all worth it, all the beatings from Ben, the basement, all the death and the running away.

She looks up, catching me watching her. Her cheeks and lips are ragged, her eyes rimmed in red. I try to rise, but I slip and fall over the side of the bed. Miriam helps me sit on the floor, leaning back.

"Why did you do this? Why didn't you come home?" she says, tears streaming out her eyes.

Home. The word in her voice like that makes me wish I could weep. I've wanted to come home for so long. But there aren't any good directions, no maps, no travel brochures.

"I need some water," I say.

She pours a glassful and helps me to hold it to my mouth since my hands are shaking so much.

"He screwed me," I say. "That fucking detective is as bad as Ben." She kneels beside me, her touch bringing me back to her, away from Ben and Bates and all the memories that are eating me up.

"He put Ben in the lineup. God. I was so scared Ben would follow me and find you. I was afraid he'd hurt you." I start crying, and then I get the heaves again. The water I just drank comes spewing out.

Now I smell like whiskey, piss, and vomit. And I feel like somebody just dragged me out of Ben's box, like I've been screaming but nobody would undo the lock.

"He made me tell him about everything Ben did. He made me talk about the basement." Now my vision goes again, and I start quaking hard.

"What do you mean, the basement? Becca? Jesus. Becca, can you see me?"

"It'll come back in a minute. It's because of that fucking basement." As my sight comes back slow, I see Miriam waving her hand in front of my eyes.

"I'm taking you to a doctor," Miriam says.

"I can't go out. Don't make me. He's out there."

"It's all in your head, Becca. You're safe here. He doesn't know where you are. God, we know where you live, and it took us days to figure it out."

She runs her fingers through my hair. "After I get you to a doctor, I'm taking you to a psychiatrist."

I don't say anything. I want her to stay forever. I think at this moment, I would do anything for her. I'd jump off a fucking bridge.

"Gatorade," I say. "It's what Ben always gave us after, well, you know. I can keep that down."

There's a knock at the door. I twist away from her and crawl off, trying to hide. Miriam stares at me, looking sick to death. She goes to the door, checking first. When she opens it, Greg ducks in.

He makes a face. "Josh is right. It stinks in here."

Miriam sends him down for Gatorade. She helps me stand and

takes me to the bathroom. After undressing me, she gets me in the shower. Then I put on fresh clothes and make my way unsteady and near blind to the couch, lying down.

Miriam picks up my notebook and lies my head in her lap.

She continues to read.

The next few days, I don't move much except to hit the john. I suck down Gatorade and Seven Up. I refuse to see a doctor. By Saturday, I'm eating soft food again. Miriam stays except when she's meeting with Johnson. Tom, Greg, and Josh split shifts so that there are always at least two people with me. I think they're more worried that I'll go off the deep end again than they are about Ben.

Miriam starts making plans to leave for Seattle just after the New Year, which is a week from Sunday. Imagine, it's Christmas Eve. I'm feeling so jolly. She decides that I'm going with her, packing up what few clothes I have left in the apartment. Before I know it, she dumps out my duffel bag.

"My God," I hear her say.

I look over. She's checking out my bag of money.

"How much do you have in here?"

"I don't know, thirteen or fourteen thousand."

"You know, most people keep money in banks."

"I lived off it when I was running from Ben. I've kept it out in case I need to leave again."

"You won't need to keep running, Becca. He's not going to find you."

"You don't know that. You don't know Ben."

"So is this ever going to end? Because I can't live with the idea that you might just disappear someday. Promise me you won't do that."

I stare at her lips, so innocent of someone like Ben. She wouldn't survive a minute with him. "I tried to leave you. God, I tried. To protect you." I stare down at my hands, useless really. "I couldn't make myself do it."

Miriam squeezes my arm. Then she sits counting the pile of

money. "How does a prostitute come up with this kind of cash? Rob a bank?"

"Very funny."

"I'm waiting for your answer."

"I'm just a little pack rat. I saved every penny."

"There's more you haven't told me, isn't there?"

"Think of it as a continuing saga. You have to wait until next week for the final chapter."

"I hate to wait."

"Just as I thought."

"Beth," she says.

We stare at one another.

"That's what you said on my answering machine."

I look away. "You don't miss much."

"Not where you're concerned. And I think it's so smart of me, because from where I'm sitting, it looks like you need somebody to pay attention. Now tell me about Beth."

She does that thing again, softening all of a sudden.

"That's what my name was when I was with Ben," I say. "Bates knows me by that name."

"Beth what?"

"Elizabeth Boone."

She sits back on her heels, taking it in. But her attention turns to my zippered bag. She picks it up.

"No," I say. "Leave that."

She looks at me, calculating.

"Pandora's box?" she says.

"In a way. When we get to Seattle, I'll give it to you."

There's a knock at the door. Miriam hesitates. When she answers the door, I grab the bag and hide it behind me. Burt comes in. He takes one look at me and shakes his head.

"I freaked out one time," he says. "It was about a year after my tour was over. I holed myself up in the woods somewhere upstate with about five guns. I thought I was in the jungle again, looking for Charley."

"Did you point one of those guns at someone you love?"

"Leave it, Becca. Nobody got hurt, thank God. Miriam's right. You should see a psychiatrist to help you get through this. And take as much time as you need before you come back," he says. "Wouldn't want you pulling a thirty-eight because someone orders a baked potato." He smiles.

I look down at the floor. "I'm not coming back, Burt. I'm moving to Seattle with Miriam."

He drops himself into the stuffed chair and sits quiet for awhile. "I expected as much," he says.

"You could promote Mark into kitchen manager," I say. "As for the buying, you might have to pick that up yourself." I sit and think. "I can come in Monday afternoon, then work half days until Thursday to get Mark started."

After that we talk about some of the suppliers that Burt doesn't know that well. I begin to wear out, and I see Miriam give Burt a look.

"I've got to get back," he says. But when he's almost out the door, he turns to me and says, "Are we still on for tomorrow?"

I'd forgotten. Miriam and I are supposed to celebrate Christmas with Burt and his wife at Tutti. Larry and his girlfriend are coming, and so are Josh and Greg. I get into a sweat thinking about leaving the apartment and going out on the street.

Christmas Day arrives. Thank God my stomach is almost back to normal. The only problem I still have is that my vision keeps going in and out. I try to keep it from Miriam.

"You can't see again, can you?"

"No. But it will come back."

"What did Ben do to you?"

I feel my arms and hands go numb. "Please don't ask me to talk about it, Miriam. It's why I freaked so bad."

She lies my head in her lap again. I bury my face in her.

"I haven't forgotten about the psychiatrist," she says. "It's non-negotiable as far as I'm concerned. Once we get to Seattle, we'll find you one. And a therapist. And no more goddamn whiskey."

I sigh. How can I argue with her?

She calls a cab and holds my arm as we walk down the four flights to the street. I start shaking. During the ride over, she cradles my hand in hers. I keep checking behind to see if anyone's following.

"I'll get over this," I say.

She's looking out her window, worn out by my paranoia.

Larry outdoes himself on our behalf. After our meal, Burt's wife, Loretta, hands out fruitcake so full of rum, we get drunk just holding it in our fingers.

Later on, I give Josh the watch I bought for him, and for Greg I have an opal earring. The two of them give me a year's subscription to *Playboy* (gee, thanks a lot), a Clarisse Broder wig (they're really striking out), and an incredible bouclé sweater.

Miriam gives me a computer with the works and loaded with memory. But I can't see it until I get to Seattle since she had it installed at her place.

I ask her if the loads of memory thing is some kind of a metaphor.

"I just want to know what's in that bag," she says.

"Patience is a virtue," I remind her.

"I've always hated that. I think some weird martyr made it up."

I give her a heavy bracelet of worked silver, studded with rubies. She loves it. I picked it up on one of my pawnshop junkets in the city while looking for more firepower.

At some point, I get so overwrought from everything that's happened that I burst into tears, wrecking everybody's spirits.

Happy holidays.

Kat got sick and disappeared a week before Christmas that year. I'd picked out her gift a couple weeks earlier. It was a bracelet of gold with a single large opal surrounded by small rubies.

When I got back from shopping that day, Kat and I were alone upstairs. Kat unbuttoned my blouse and started making love to me.

I can see her so clear as she kneeled over me, her eyes round, and her hair, some of which had gotten loose, falling along her cheeks.

At that moment, something happened in me, like the morning glories that crawled up along the door of our old burnt-down two-room. They opened like sky come down to kiss you, Mandy said, like the bend of the river when the dead air chokes down the water, turning it to glass.

Kat folded me in her arms. I stared at her, amazed by her rapture of me. That's when Kat went flying through the air. She rolled onto her side, curling to protect her head.

"What did I tell you about this, Kat?" Ben stepped over me to go after her.

I grabbed his leg. "Leave her alone! It's my fault."

Ben turned on me. But the mask of his face had slipped and I could see into him, like when a 'gator yawns, and you see all those teeth in rows, but you also see how pink and soft it is on the inside. It wasn't the teeth that terrified me, it was that unnatural color of pink.

Ben yanked out his belt in one movement and started using it on me. I curled up.

He moved on to Kat. "You'll listen to me, goddamnit."

Then Ben grabbed her long braid. "Come on, Kat. Crawl for me." He dragged her to the door, but had to stop to get out his keys.

"So," Kat said between breaths. "Is it my turn now?"

Ben slapped her so hard she hit the floor. Kat raised on one elbow, wiping the blood off her mouth.

"I know what you've done, Benjamin. It will never be enough. Never." She said this soft, like it was a dream in my head.

Ben stood frozen for a moment. I panicked. But then he busted out laughing. "You think you're so smart, Kat, coming from your fancy background and going to your fancy-ass school. Look at you now. When I tell you to fuck, you fuck. And when I tell you to suck a man's cock, that's what you do."

He hit her across the back with the belt. "You're a fucking worm, Kat. Show Beth how you crawl. Come on. Out the door." He whacked her on the ass.

I cringed with each hit, edging back from the two of them. And Kat looked up at Ben as she started to crawl out the door. Her eyes were narrowed, but black all through. Ben shoved her out with his foot on her ass. She looked back at me. Her lips formed a kiss.

She wasn't at the plays that night. I dragged into bed naked, crying myself to sleep. When Kat showed up the next day, she sat so still in a chair, looking out over the city. There weren't any marks on her face, but Ben rarely hit her there.

She tried to keep it from me the next few days, but I saw the burns around her waist, the odd-looking bruises and punctures on her inner thighs and breasts. She was silent for the next two weeks. Then she started throwing up blood.

When Ben carried her out, his eyes never left her face, and his lips had gone slack.

For a long time I couldn't touch the bracelet I'd bought for her. Then one day I dropped it in the box of an amputee sitting near Penn Station. I hoped it would bring him better luck than it brought to me.

Tom arrives Monday and rides with me in the cab over to Tutti. He holds my hand like Miriam did the day before. I feel like maybe I'm about two years old.

As I'm getting ready to leave work around eight, Miriam shows up, beaming.

"Come see what I bought," she says.

Out on the street is a very shiny new Rav Four with all the cool extras. It's forest green. The tires are too clean.

"Isn't it cute?" Miriam says.

I roll my eyes.

We tool around in the new machine, taking it out on eight eighty for a spin. She hits the Oakland Bridge. I sink down in my seat, still a bit vertigoed on bridges.

"I've got the Taurus," I say. "What do you need this for?"

"For all our camping gear. Once we're in Seattle and we're hiking like crazy." She takes a turn too fast and squeals the tires. "We need both cars to get our combined stuff up to Seattle. We'll sell the Taurus once we get there. Then we can buy something a little less family."

I start thinking about what color of Porsche would look best on me. And I notice this "we" thing creeping into her vocabulary.

"Should 'we' buy some rings?" I say, teasing her. "Should 'we' register our names at Bloomingdale's? Which of us gets to wear the wedding gown?"

She rolls her eyes, but it gets me thinking of Jeremy Arf, Arf again. I'm trying to figure out how I'm going to break that tidbit of news to her.

On Tuesday, I ride into Tutti myself. I'm a big girl again. And I'm beginning to feel good about leaving Berkeley. I've left too much of a trail here. Too many phone calls to New York. And the thought of living with Miriam makes me float in a way that I like.

It's Tuesday about noon when I'm checking the *Times,* even though I'm still pissed at the crumpled Detective Bates. There's a message for Tut from Beefy.

"I'm in your town," it says. "Need to talk. Meet me in front of University Art Museum at four on Tuesday."

The creep. The little snake. I want to iron his face.

I arrange with Burt to leave work for a couple of hours, then have a cab drop me off in front of the museum.

Too bad. Bates won't have that stupid Chevy Caprice. I'm working myself up to give Detective Bates a big piece of my mind.

That's when I notice her. She steps out of a black Benz with dark windows and stands beside it on the curb. She's dressed in blue, which is what attracts my eye, a blue I would have chosen. And as I keep looking at her, I go weak. She's wearing my blue skirt and blouse. The clothes I left at Ben's that last weekend there. I begin to back up, but someone puts an arm around me from behind, poking something into my side.

"Be careful, Beth," a man says. I look up into his face, all smiles. "Let's walk over to the car."

Another man takes my other arm. They lead me toward the Benz. As we approach, I can't believe what I'm seeing. She's standing there perfect as you please, alive and well and wearing my clothes.

It's Kat.

She opens the rear car door and they usher me in. The door slams. I see there aren't any door handles in the back. Kat sits in the other side of the backseat with me and one of the guys sits in front, turning around to keep his gun pointed at me.

I stare at Kat, trying to clear my head. Her eyes are tired, but her lips are flushed, the color of roses. Her long hair is braided and wound up on top. It seems impossible, but the lines of her neck and chest have grown more lovely through the years.

Kat leans over and kisses me strong, just as I would have wished a thousand days since she's been gone. Then she settles back, turning to face me. She taps the driver on the shoulder, and he pulls away from the curb.

Kat holds out her hand, each finger flawless, as though she could not be alive, rather the idea of beauty created by an artist. "We know you're carrying a gun. Give it to me."

I reach behind and take out my precious Walther. I hand it to her. She gives it to the nice man in the front seat.

"You were there that night," I say. "I thought I was delirious. The night I was stabbed."

Her face goes gray. "That was a terrible night. I thought we were going to lose you. It would have been like losing a child."

"Where was everybody? Why didn't someone come in sooner? Where was Ben?"

She looks down, arranges the skirt over her knee. "We made mistakes that night. We've never made those mistakes again."

I sit in silence. "So you were there all the time, watching the plays." Bitterness creeps into my voice.

"I helped him run things. I still do. The business was getting too big for Ben, and he never liked messing with the money. I take care of the money and scheduling for him. And now you'll help, too."

It hits me then, and I almost lose my piss again.

They're taking me to Ben.

I lie my head down in my hands, resting on my knees. "Why did he let me marry Jeremy if he wanted me so much?"

Her hand runs along my back. "He had his eye on you the whole time, Beth. The night Violet was killed shook him up. He was worried about you. But he was ready to get you back."

I turn my head, taking her in, feeling how my love for her never faded. I put it away for a time, that was all.

Kat acts like she's going to say something, but stops. She looks away instead. "I'm sorry, Beth. I've tried to talk him into leaving you alone. He won't hear of it. You should have seen his face the night you jumped off the bridge."

"You were there." I lift my head, leaning toward her. "You were in the room when Ben was beating Jeremy. I heard your voice, but I couldn't place it. How could I? I thought you were dead." My body feels a hundred miles away somewhere. "And you were in the van. You saw me go over the side of the bridge."

"I thought I'd lost you, Beth. It was terrible." She reaches toward me, but I push her hand away.

"He brought you that night because he knew how I loved you. He was using you like bait."

"Yes."

"And that's why you're here now." I watch the buildings go by, then turn back to her.

"Don't you ever feel a little bad about all of it, Kat? Don't the dangers ever start fucking with your mind? God. You've helped him do so much damage."

Her eyes flash. I think she might slap me. But then she goes blank.

"I don't know how to get out, Beth. I tried once. I applaud

you. Jumping off that bridge was pure genius. And if you hadn't called Bates, Ben might have never found you out."

"Bates," I say.

"He's been after Ben for years, so we kept an eye on him. It became obvious he had some big card he was working with. Ben got one of his connections in the force to tap Bates' phone. We listened in on your last two calls. Ben went nuts when he heard your voice.

"We traced your second call to the bay area. Ben sent out a couple professionals to find you. It didn't take long. Rebecca Cross was receiving paychecks from Tutti. We knew about Rebecca Cross because we got a good look at Bates' files."

I sit in shock, knowing I won't last. I'll find a way to kill myself. And I gaze down at the floor, feeling like a totally screwed sixteen-year-old, a prisoner in a warehouse somewhere in New York and out of my head with terror, not letting Kat get more than five feet from me.

"Why didn't you come back? My heart broke. I thought you were dead."

She's quiet, but reaches over and takes my hand. I stare at her fingers, and I touch her lightly, remembering. "I wanted to, Beth. He was jealous. Ben wanted you to himself. My heart broke, too. And after I recovered"—now she hesitates, looks away—"it hurt me to stand behind the mirror and watch you."

"What was it, Kat? What happened?" I feel a "shiver," as Mandy would have said. "Why did you get so sick?"

Kat won't look at me. She moves a strand of hair back from her cheek. "I took some rat poison."

I think I make a sound. And a pain starts in my heart and spreads through my chest. I clutch her hand tight.

She turns back to me. "I thought I'd eaten enough." She shrugs.

"Ben kept me locked up in a play room. He hired a couple of Ekker's girls to nurse me back to health. After I recovered from the poison, they kept me in a straitjacket. I'm surprised you didn't hear me screaming. When Ben visited me in my psycho ward, I begged him to kill me. After awhile, I got better. I guess a person can get used to anything." Her eyes drift away.

We drive for a long while, both of us silent.

Kat closes her eyes and takes a breath. "As for the business at hand, we talked a lot about how to take you. Ben wanted to grab you and be done with it. I'm always the more reflective one of us two."

I'm not listening very close. I'm thinking about the stacks, the allowances that have to be made, the shifting around of corpses. I'm hoping that someone thought to save a space for me.

She continues. "Goddamn Bates got the FBI interested in Ben, but Ben never crossed that line. He's strictly a local problem. However, if we kidnap you, they can jump in with both feet. And it seems you've been associating with someone that is very visible and could make a lot of trouble."

Miriam! She's talking about Miriam.

Kat's face becomes a mask. She leans forward and reaches to the front seat. "Give me the bag, Jim."

He hands her a small black zippered shoulder bag, just like the kind Ben uses to carry around his devices. She places it on my lap.

"Open it, Beth."

I pull the zipper, looking in. I know what it contains.

"Take out each piece. I want you to do it slow. Really look at these things."

I reach in, taking out the first item. It's a hood.

"Slow, Beth."

The next thing is a gag.

I begin to shake. I can't do this again.

Under that are two pairs of double cuffs, one for wrists and one for ankles.

The basement. They're going to put me in the basement again. And when I gaze at her, I see a stranger beside me, the one that looks like Kat, but isn't.

"Why make me look at them, Kat? Just put them on me. I can't stop you. Is this some new foreplay for you? Are you getting off?"

She smiles a Ben kind of smile. "Keep looking."

I take out the last thing in the bag. It's a whip. But it isn't my whip, not the one that says BETH on the handle. It's not as thick and long. It's meant for someone with thinner skin.

"Read the name on the handle."

I look. It says MIRIAM.

Now I start crying. Without knowing what I'm doing, I leap on the guy in the front seat, grabbing his gun, trying to aim it at myself and push his finger on the trigger. He gets the gun free and hits me with it on the side of my face. I crumple.

Kat draws me down, putting my head in her lap. She smells of lilac and of a breeze come off the sweetbush. And I pick up that other scent I'd forgotten, of melon and ripe cheese. "What we need you to do, Beth, is break it off with Miriam clean. Make everyone believe you've left town of your own free will. Fake a suicide again, I don't care. We don't want any reports to the police from your friends about your disappearance. Do you understand?"

They're going to let me go. Again. Are they stupid?

"If Miriam makes a problem about this, we can get to her. You don't want that. And this time, we'll be watching you, and we'll be watching Miriam. If there's any sign that you're skipping out, we'll grab Miriam." She leans closer. "You don't want Ben to get his hands on Miriam, Beth. You don't know what he can do. What you've seen is just scratching the surface."

Her fingers tremble as they run along my cheek.

"You've got until tomorrow to make the break. Call this number before five. We'll tell you where to go." She hands me one of Ben's fabulous cards.

"Also, Beth, I wouldn't try to call Bates. He's in ICU with tubes coming out of him every which way. He had a car accident. Hit and run. These things happen."

She holds me there, still caressing me, and she leans down, kissing my cheek and neck. "I like your hair like this, Beth. I'll be glad to have you back. I've missed you."

Kat removes her scarf and ties it around my eyes, keeping my head in her lap. And she moves her fingers over my body, all the while whispering verse, Shelley and Dickinson. Then she whispers to me again of one clover and one bee and I am transported.

"I read your book, *The River,* several times, Beth. I was so proud of you."

She kisses me long and knowing, then sits me up, untying the scarf from around my eyes. We're back at the museum. The guy in the front seat jumps out, opening the door for me.

"Beth," says Kat.

I turn around, catching her scent one more time.

"See you tomorrow."

I remember the last time I saw Vin. He was smoking cigarettes with some friends, standing on the corner of Vine and Main. I'd just come off the Dumpster behind Betty's Café. Then he saw me. I'll never forget the look on his face.

I'd like to have just a minute with this God they all talk about. I'd ramble on about the river first of all, since there's something about the river that I think God would understand.

But I really want to talk to God about Vin.

Don't make him feel the ache, I'd say to God. Don't let him feel the dangers and the snakes. Keep Vin high in a tree. And when Vin falls, let him fall slow and green, passing through that film I see. Let him slip through easy.

Because I'm thinking of Vin's face when he turned to me. I saw Mama's death written all over his eyes. I saw the night our two-room went up in flame. I wanted to wipe it away.

Dear God. Keep the ones that I love safe.

I have twenty-four hours.

I take a cab to my apartment. A car follows. Once inside, I lie down on the floor in the center of the apartment and stare up. I can't cry anymore. And I can't think at all.

I call Tutti, telling Josh that I'm feeling sick again. I won't be back today. He wants to send Greg over, but I talk him out of it.

That night the minutes pass slow. I go through everything in my head, and I can't get things to come out right for me. But I'm determined that this will be the end. I've had enough. And when it's all over, I want Miriam to be safe and free like Violet never was. I will write this play. Not Ben.

I call Miriam around eleven. "I need to spend time in my apartment doing some cleaning. I'll see you in the morning."

"I'll help you do it tomorrow," she says. "I want to see you tonight. You don't sound good."

"I'm fine. I need some space." I pause. "Miriam."

"What?"

"I love you. Remember that."

"I know." She sounds peeved.

I lie down again, trying to get myself strong. I work and work my play, wanting to keep it simple. If it's simple, there's less chance anything can go wrong.

About five, I get up and lay out my most important things. The picture of Mama, the doll's head, my glued-together cup of the dragon and the lady with a parasol, and the notebooks of my writing. I stack up all my IDs, including Rebecca Cross, and I find again the folded sheets that had been in Ben's shoebox for so long. They were my first stories.

I remember how I hid them beneath my mattress, but Kat found them. Kat encouraged me. She and I went over them together, honing, sharpening. We read them out loud together.

As I sit in my apartment, the scent of Kat comes over me again. I pick up my picture of Vin and stare at it for a long time. Then I add it to the pile of my stuff. I throw in all my Clarisse Broder articles since I'd jumped off the bridge.

Then I write Miriam a letter.

Dear Miriam,

I hope you receive this letter. If it gets lost somehow, then you won't ever understand why I acted the way I did in the next few hours.

Ben has found me again. I'm supposed to make a break with you and all my friends so no one will know where I am. He has threatened to hurt you. I can't let that happen. Even if I do as he says, he will always be able to hold you over my head.

By this time tomorrow, I'll either be dead, or with Ben, in which case I'll kill myself as soon as I get the chance.

I want you to know how much I love you. You've brought happiness back into my life. I regret never telling you about Clarisse Broder. I intended to tell you when we got to Seattle.

These things with this letter are my most prized possessions. Do what you want with them.

Please don't forget I love you,

Terri	Becca
Beth	Becker
Clarisse	

Then I get out my long-suffering zippered bag and somehow stuff everything inside of it. On the outside of the bag, I stick on a Post-it. I write on it: "Tom. Please give this to Miriam sometime after Wednesday evening. Thanks for everything. Becca."

I take out my duffel bag and pack in what few clothes I have left in the apartment, thinking I might want them if I do end up at Ben's. In goes my bundle of money. I throw in all my ammo and guns, missing my Walther a lot. On top of that I put in the bag with its note to Miriam.

After calling a cab, I look around. Of all the places I've ever lived, this was the best.

I close the door behind me.

14

The Play

It's a little after seven in the morning when my cab pulls up. I open the door and toss in my duffel bag, waving at the two guys sitting in the car parked nearby.

I can't stop myself.

My first stop is Tutti. I want to be there before anyone else. Once inside, I take out the bag for Miriam. In the wine closet, I move some bottles and push in the bag. Tom won't be in until three today. By that time, my play will either be in progress, or safely over.

Now I sit in the kitchen, remembering how good it felt to be here.

I call another cab and leave by the front door, waving to the boys again. I have the cabby drop me at the Taurus. Once in the garage, I spread my guns around in their regular places. I stack the ammo with the Uzi.

I wait again until nine. Opening the garage, I drive the Taurus to Tutti, looking for Burt. He takes one look at the black eye I have from being pistol-whipped and has a fit.

"That's why I called in yesterday, Burt, because I was dizzy. Then I went home, took a shower and bang, slipped and hit my face. It's a nice look, don't you think?"

"What's going on? You're not dressed for work."

I look him in the eye. "I've decided to leave town today. I'm jumpy and paranoid. I'll calm down if I get on the road. In a few days, I'll meet up with Miriam in Seattle." I watch him close, hoping he's buying it. "I loved working for you, Burt. I'm going to miss everybody here. Tell Tom and Josh I'm sorry I didn't say good-bye. I'll write."

He smiles and hugs me. I hold on to him tight. I'm afraid I might start to lose it, so I take Burt's arm and we walk to the door. I kiss him on the cheek, then turn and walk away.

On my way out, I notice that one of the nice gentlemen in the car behind the Taurus is talking on a cell phone. When he sees me, he hangs up.

I drive to Miriam's.

I breathe deep.

After stopping behind the gleaming Rav Four, I knock on Miriam's door, my hand shaking. A block away, and parked in the manner of Bates, is a second car of Ben's thugs watching Miriam's place. I shudder, but the sight of that car bolsters me, tells me I'm doing the right thing.

Miriam opens the door.

"It's about time you showed up—" She takes a look at my face. "My God. What happened?"

I push in past her. Once she's shut the door, I turn back, crossing my arms. "You really cared about me, didn't you? I got you so good."

She was walking toward me, but now she stops, confused.

"You didn't have a clue, did you? You thought we were going to waltz up to Seattle like a happy little couple." I laugh. "You're such an ass."

Now I pace. "You bought it all, the story about my knifing, the whip marks. Ben. I knew that the way to really hook you was by being pathetic in some way."

Her eyes are narrowed, her face more like Violet's than I've ever seen. "What are you saying, Becca? What's going on here?"

"You snotty, rich star. You all think you're better than everybody else, dancing around up onstage, everybody going ga-ga over you. I caught you big, getting you to fall in love. In love." I laugh, close to hysteria. "You're a fucking fool."

"You're lying. I can tell when you lie. Something's going on."

"Fuck you, Miriam. I've been laughing at you behind your back and you didn't even know. It was a bet. Believe that? I bet a friend I could find you and suck you in." I smile a Ben smile. "I got you good."

Tears are dropping down her cheeks, but I keep that picture of Violet's face in front of my eyes, of it being bruised almost beyond recognition. I remind myself that I'm doing this for Miriam's own good.

I waltz through the apartment, picking up a few of my things. "I just came back to get some of my stuff," I say. "You can keep the straps and the dildo. In memory."

She catches me by the arm and stares in my eyes. "Tell me you don't love me. Look in my eyes and say it."

I laugh, the berserks near. "I don't love you. You stupid rich fucking bitch."

She slaps me. I'm panicked, and almost start crying.

I shove her onto the bed, pinning her arms with my knees. I slap her across the face I don't know how many times.

"Get out!" she screams. "Get the fuck out of here!"

I jump off her, but she stays on the bed crying. I end up on the street, not sure how I got there. In that moment I hate Ben a whole lot.

I speed off in the Taurus, crying. At a phone booth, I take out Ben's card and dial the number.

"Hello?" It's Ben.

"It's Beth, Ben."

"Tell me you're coming in, Beth."

I force back the tears. "I'm coming, Ben, but only to you. I don't want any of your fucking thugs. I know a place up in the mountains. I'm going there. If you want me, you meet me there. Nobody else. Just you and me. No Kat, either. After I hang up, you call off your thugs. If you don't, this time I really will kill my-self. I'm near the Oakland Bridge. I swear I'll drive off the thing."

I hear him breathing. "Don't fuck with me, Beth. You know I hate that."

"Believe me, Ben, the last thing I'd do is fuck with you. I just don't trust you is all. You meet me there. I'll come with you qui-etly."

I wait. "What have you got to lose? You've still got your boys watching Miriam."

I wait again, chewing my lip.

This isn't going to work.

"Okay, Beth. You're one crazy bitch."

I give him the directions. "Meet me there at three," I say to him. "If I see anybody else, that's it. I'm history. And don't for-get to call off your boys after I hang up."

"Don't you forget about that whip with Miriam's name on it. I'd really dig whipping the shit out of that skinny piece of meat with you tied up and watching."

I hang up, trying not to puke. We're the perfect lovers, threat-ening one another into being true.

On my way to the cabin that Miriam and I found that last day of our vacation, I begin to prepare myself. This time I'm not run-ning away, like I've done ever since I was sixteen and maybe be-fore. Now I'm going forward, my intentions clear. Only my heart is weak.

So I remember Violet. Violet and her whispery voice. And the night she was to be free, instead cut down, bled dry, and fed piecemeal to the waiting city. As I break free into the mountains, I gaze into her eyes, not sure if I'm seeing Violet at all. My mem-ories of Miriam are so strong in me. But when I breathe, I smell Violet's hair, remembering how it held the scent of bread baking. I recall how she loved to have her fingers rubbed.

I drive out of the woods and over the grasses, parking behind the cabin. Then I grab the Uzi and a box of extra clips, which I hope I won't need. Opening my duffel, I take out the cup, the candle, and the matches.

It's two thirty.

Walking to the front of the cabin, I look out, seeing how the slopes sweep down in a series of diminishing humps, and how clear it is today. I can make out, far away, the sun glimmering off the sea. How incredible that in the midst of the threats, the arrival of Ben, and the need to damage myself beyond repair, the earth can be so radiant and plain.

Then I sit in the center of the cabin, facing the door. Kneeling, I lie the Uzi and its ammo next to me. Lighting the candle, I blow it out three times, letting my love for Miriam fill me.

I turn over the cup.

Now I wait. I breathe one to five and back again. Last night, I first decided that I needed to kill Ben. But I have no confidence once I'm standing face to face with him that I can do it. Somehow in the basement, he bound me to him through terror and love. They've always been mixed up in me.

And I know that when it comes down to it, I don't have that kind of thing in me. It's why I never attained mastery with the whip.

So I sit waiting. It isn't very long until I hear a car coming down the road. It stops. Then a car door slams. I pick up my lovely and much-to-be-desired Uzi and point it at my chest, waiting.

He has to see it with his own eyes. I want to make him so sick that he'll forget Miriam altogether. Maybe my suicide will work itself into that place I saw briefly that day so long ago. I want to break it loose.

I hear his footsteps coming near, swishing in the grasses. I force my eyes forward. I want to look him dead in the face.

Then she stands there. Miriam, with a look on her face I can't describe. She falls to her knees and crawls to me careful and slow.

"Give me the gun, Becca. You don't have to do this."

My brain explodes. All my plans, my mastery, my trying to keep her safe. All a big waste.

I drop the gun at my side and grab her shoulders, shaking her. "You shit! Do you know what you've done? You've got to get out of here! Now!"

With the Uzi in one hand, I jerk her up by the arm with my other hand. I nearly carry her out the door.

"Let me go!" She fights me, breaking free. I run after her and get her wrist, dragging her forward around the side of the cabin, yanking her in front.

That's when I see him. He'd parked his van alongside the Taurus. The Rav Four is a little off by itself. In his hand is a roll of duct tape. In his belt is a pistol.

I stop dead and point the Uzi at him. Miriam stops fighting me all of a sudden, I guess seeing Ben for the first time.

"You said nobody else, Beth." He moves his hand toward the gun.

"Don't do it, Ben. Touch that gun and I'll fill you full of bullets."

He stops. His face works itself. "Now you've done it," he says. "You broke your own rule. I'm going to have to hurt you both."

A sound comes out of Miriam. I keep my eyes on Ben.

"She's leaving, Ben. You're going to let her go. Then I'm yours. You let her leave, I'm yours. It's simple . . . Don't." He's reaching for the gun again.

I make a circle around him, keeping Miriam behind my back, pointing the Uzi at his chest.

I get to the Rav and drop Miriam's wrist, opening the driver's door. I look at her face. She's lost in shock. I shove her in the car, trying to keep my eyes on Ben.

Now she sits at the wheel, her arms at her sides. I lean in and slap her. She looks at me, eyes blank.

"Get the fuck out of here," I say. "Get out and keep driving. Don't go home. Don't go to your place in Seattle. Hire bodyguards." I can't tell if she knows what I'm saying. "For me, Miriam. Keep yourself safe."

Ben's grinning now. It makes me sick.

I reach in and turn the key. She leans forward and puts it into drive. I step back and slam the door.

"Get out," I say again.

She drives away, disappearing into the woods.

Ben and I stand facing each other. I wait, wanting to give her a good lead. He steps toward me.

"Drop the gun, Beth."

God, I want to kill him. If only I could have learned to pull the fucking trigger, I would have saved myself a lot of trouble from that very first day of "my year."

I turn and pitch the Uzi back toward the cabin. It disappears in the grass. He smiles. Then he walks up to me, caressing my cheek. I stand and wait, just like I did for Daddy. I know what's coming next. Ben doesn't disappoint me.

He slugs me good on the mouth. I take it full, falling to the ground. He drops the tape and lifts me, grabbing me by the neck with his big left hand wrapped near around my throat and punches my face back and forth with the other fist. I fall to my knees, remembering.

That's the final chit. It took me awhile, because like I've said before, I can be a real imbecile.

He just beat me like the man with the dust mask had done Violet before he killed her. Bates was right. It had been Ben after all.

I moan, not from the pain, but from my stupidity. If only I would have believed Bates that night in New York.

"You killed her," I say. "You murdered Violet."

Ben laughs. "Sometimes you're such a stupid bitch, Beth. I hated Violet. And I was starting to hate you. She was poison, that girl. She wanted to take you away. I couldn't have that."

Blood is streaming from my nose and lips. "And you stabbed me. Were you going to murder me, too?"

He reaches down and caresses my head. "No, Beth. But I had to teach you a lesson, didn't I? The only problem was that you forgot everything. I never saw anything like that. So I left you with wag-the-tail Jeremy. You were never out of my sight. My players never leave me, Beth, unless they're dead. And you're the one I want most. You belong to me."

He stands me up and punches me hard in the ribs. I hear a crack and fall to the ground one more time. Now he gives me a good sharp kick. He rolls me onto my stomach and tapes my hands back.

True love in its finest moment.

"Up on your knees," he says to me. "Crouch."

He has to help me. When he grabs my sides, I think I might faint from the pain.

"I have to teach you things over and over, Beth. You have such a thick skin." He's got my arms and he's lifting them high. He's pushing up hard on my right arm. I remember Matt, how he did the same to Matt. Up my arm goes, he twists, and I hear a crack like it's coming out of the center of my head. The pain is white light. I hear myself screaming.

He lifts me and starts dragging me to the van. "You made me do it, Beth. If you'd only come back to me the way I told you, none of this would have happened." He slides open the side door and throws me in so that I land on my shoulder. Piercing lights shatter my head. He rolls me onto my other side and tapes my ankles. Then he tapes my mouth and eyes.

But now Ben kneels next to me. He sounds like he's crying. Ben lifts my body and leans me back against him, holding and rocking me. His tears drop on my cheek. Then I think that I pass out.

What I remember next is that he's quiet, and he lies me down gentle, stroking my head, saying, "I'll get you fixed up again, Beth. You'll be good as new."

Not one thing is making any sense to me.

Ben steps out of the van and slams the side door shut. I hear him walking behind the van, coming around to the driver's door.

That's when the first explosion goes off. Something hits the van, rocking it. Another explosion. There's a sliding sound. One more explosion.

Silence. I wait.

The side door slides open.

"Becca. Oh, Becca." It's Miriam. She's sobbing like crazy as she rips the tape off my eyes. Then the tape at my mouth. All I can do is moan and drool. She's choking and screaming, trying to get the tape off my ankles. Then she moves to my wrists, having calmed some.

For me, lights are flashing all over the place.

"Where's Ben?" I say. It comes out garbled.

She's weeping quieter now. "I shot him," she says.

I shake my head, afraid of passing out again.

"You shot him? Is he dead?"

"I think so. He looked dead."

"Help me up."

"No. I'm taking you to a hospital. I'll drive this van into town."

I grab the driver's seat with my good hand and pull myself up so that I'm sitting. "Miriam, listen. We've got to think this through."

The thinking part is coming a little hard for me. She's staring at my face like she's seeing a ghost or something. "Becca. He hurt you so badly. I have to get you to a doctor."

"Miriam, you don't want this on your hands. No. Stop it. Listen to me. There's things about myself I never told you. When this story hits the airwaves, all hell will break loose. They won't let you have a moment's rest. It could ruin everything for you."

"Becca. You're off your head. Lie down." She takes my arm and tries to force me back onto the floor.

"No. Listen to me." I shake her off. "We'll make it look like I killed him. As far as everyone else is concerned, you were never here. I'll bet there's a cell phone around in this van somewhere. I'll call the police and tell them I did it. No one will question me. I have every reason in the world to shoot the son of a bitch. I'll get off. Look at me. It's obviously self-defense."

She's quiet now, but blank, and blue around the lips. "I'm not leaving you like this. I don't care about my career."

"They'll send an ambulance. It'll be here sooner than you could drive me to a hospital. I won't be alone very long. Help me up."

She takes my good arm and I slide out of the van. I press my bad arm close to my side to keep it still, but it's screaming into my brain and my eyes.

"How did you know?" I say, as we take it a few inches at a time. "How did you find me here?"

"After you left, I couldn't get any of it to fit. I thought you'd cracked from the stress. I remembered how you said this cabin would be a good place to commit suicide. For some reason, I knew for sure that you were coming here. I didn't have a clue about Ben."

"They got me into a car yesterday. They threatened to hurt you, telling me to make you think I was leaving so you wouldn't call the police."

By now, we've made it to the back of the van. I sink to my knees, my head swimming.

"Ben's thugs," I say to Miriam. "The guys watching your place. Did they follow you?"

She kneels beside me, her arms holding me up.

"Oh God. They were from Ben? Oh fuck. I thought they were stalkers or crazy fans. I lost them in town. Over the last couple years, I've gotten good at that kind of thing."

"Help me up. I can't do it myself."

She puts one hand under my bad shoulder. I scream and almost faint.

"Becca. This is crazy." I feel her shaking now, and I wonder if the two of us can pull this off.

I grab her arm and hoist myself up with her help.

Now we edge around the van to where Ben's body lies. There are blood steaks along the side of the van where he slid down. His chest is a mess. She got him three times close to the heart.

"My dad taught me to shoot," she says. "When I was a kid. I guess you never lose something like that."

"Where's the gun?" I say. I lean against the van as she goes back to the Taurus, picking up the Smith and Wesson from where she dropped it on the ground.

"Wipe it off and give it to me," I say. Then I take it in my left hand, which is shaking so hard I don't know if I can aim the gun. I fire it into Ben's chest two more times.

"That will put traces of powder on me," I say.

I look at her. "You have to go. Don't go home. Get into a hotel or something. Take a shower right away and get rid of the clothes you have on. Make sure no one will ever find them. I'm serious about the bodyguard. I don't think anyone will try to hurt you now that Ben's dead, but we can't be sure."

"I still don't get why we're doing this. What can be so bad? What haven't you told me?"

"I'm a dead ringer for Clarisse Broder," I say, "because I am Clarisse Broder."

She stares at me now in a way that scares me. "Oh Becca," she says. "Why didn't you tell me?" She covers her face with both hands and starts crying hard.

I reach to her, trying to calm her. "I'm sorry I never told you. I wanted to. I just didn't want Ben to find out I was still alive. And if you confess to shooting him and get drawn into all this stuff about me being a hooker for Ben, and then my jump from the bridge . . . I don't know. I think it could screw everything up for you."

I start to slide down to the ground. "Go in the van and find the cell phone. Pick it up with your shirt or something so you don't put any prints on it. Bring it to me. And don't leave your prints on anything else."

She does as I say. I gaze at her as she stoops and hands me the phone. I search her eyes but don't see myself in them anymore. They're glazed over, empty.

I reach out and lay my hand along her cheek. She leans against it. "Wait for things to blow over before you try to contact me," I say. "Send me messages through Josh or Tom while the police are doing the investigation." Now I close my eyes, hating that she's going to leave. "I love you so much, Miriam. I'm going to miss you while this is getting cleared up. I tried to keep you out of it. I'm sorry. It's all my fault."

She reaches out and touches my neck, my chest. She looks pretty gone in the head. She doesn't kiss me, I guess because of all the blood on my face.

"Tom has a package for you," I say. "Now go. I'll give you five or ten minutes head start before I call."

I watch her walk away. She turns and keeps her eyes on me as she backs toward the woods where she left the Rav. She disappears into the trees. I hear the motor start. Then I see the Rav barrel back in. Miriam stops beside me.

"I don't have a good feeling about this," she says. "I want you to get in with me. I'm taking you to a hospital."

"No," I say. "Miriam. You've got to let me do this for you. We'll see each other in a week or two."

She starts crying again, leaning her head on the steering wheel. Then she jams it in gear and drives away. Watching her go just about finishes me.

I wait. Then I call 911.

"I've killed a man," I say. "I'm badly injured, send an ambulance." I give them directions.

By the time they arrive, I've got the ghosts. When they lift me onto the stretcher, I pass out, happy to be leaving the pain behind.

When I think of Ben now, I see him with five holes in his chest, three for his sins and two for forgiveness.

And when I dream of Miriam, she has a gun in her hand. I see her onstage with a spotlight showing a face I love so much that I yearn for her as strong as the undercurrent runs in that river.

Longing is in my heart like the head of the green snake, its tail poking out my mouth. The green snake is so beautiful, you think it might be a long, wet jewel. Then, before you know it, you have it in your mouth and it's worked its way to your heart.

But in the river, longing falls away. And the air roves free, and the light fades down so the moon can carry the sky. And I'm lying beside Vin again, his sleep swishing like weeds in a stream.

So once more, I find myself standing on the rise that we called Rivertown, watching the river go by and by. Many of us linger here beneath the live oaks and the tremble of leaves. It pleases us to do so.

15

Wish You the Best

I wake in a hospital room. At first, I'm groggy, but soon, I sense a thing I didn't expect. The room is stark, barren of anything but my bed. The door is thick, with a heavy lock and a small rectangular window.

I think I'm in a prison.

My second thought is how I feel like maybe an elephant is tromping on me. My upper arm and body are in a cast. My ribs are wrapped. The pain in my head is of such an intense quality that I'm hard put to see where it begins and ends.

The door is unlocked and a nurse enters. She checks my IV.

"Hello," I croak.

She smiles a dippy nurse smile. "The police want to talk to you," she says. She heads toward the door.

While I'm waiting, I try to move. It appears to be a bad thing to do. One side of my nose is swollen shut. The other is blocked by a tube. My lips feel like they're made of confetti.

Two detectives arrive. One is skinny with a crooked face that makes me think I'm going cross-eyed. The other is a real looker. He seems aware of that. The looker does all the talking.

He does the Miranda thing, calling me Mrs. Broder. The pain is socking my head in so much that it's not making sense, but I'm beginning to get a bad feeling like the dangers didn't go away with Ben, that there's something more persistent at work here.

The looker asks me several questions about shooting Ben. The way he says "five times in the chest" bothers me. I'm beginning to not like what he does with his hair.

The ceiling above me twists a little. I close my eyes to make it stop.

"Five bullets," the detective says again. "A little much, don't you think, Mrs. Broder? He was dead by the second shot. And the last two. Were they necessary, or just malice?"

"I wanted to make sure."

Then he starts going off about my cache of illegal weapons and the large amount of ammo stashed in the Taurus.

"Who made the arrangements to meet at such a remote location?" he says suddenly, catching me off guard.

I'm thinking that a lawyer might be an excellent move. But the elephants are tromping pretty heavy. And you know me. The imbecile.

"Me."

"So you lured him there, and you had a carful of weapons."

"I didn't lure him. The fucker was kidnapping me. What in the hell was I supposed to do?"

He gloats. I'm sure he's wearing a hairpiece now. It's not seated quite right.

"I am here to inform you, Mrs. Clarisse Broder, that the state of California charges you with murder in the first degree, which in the state of California can be punishable by death."

I think the elephants must now be trying to lie down on me. I am, believe it or not, speechless.

"Did you look at my arm, shithead? Look at my face. How about my rib cage? And you want to charge me with murder? What ever happened to the right to self-defense? Do you know anything at all about this guy's profession? Do you know what he did to me and others like me?"

He smiles a real Ben smile.

I shut up then, realizing I had just strengthened his case. "I want a lawyer," I say. "And I want my phone call. I do get a phone call in the state of California, right? Do I get it before or after you put me on the rack?"

The two of them stand. "We'll have you wheeled out to a phone," says the looker.

Before he leaves, I have to get in a shot. "There's better foundations to hide the puffiness around your eyes," I say to the looker, the vain little creep. "I could give you some makeup tips."

Crooked Face stares at him in surprise, angling to get a view of his partner's eyes.

They leave, locking the door behind them. I lie in my bed of pain, too astounded for any of what just happened to sink in. Eventually, two orderlies creak open my dungeon door and lift me onto a wheelchair. Out in the hall, police are posted everywhere. They stare at me. I'm wheeled to a battered pay phone and given change.

"What time is it?" I say to one of the orderlies, who happens to be of a size similar to Ben, but with even bigger hands. "What day?"

"It's four in the afternoon. Friday."

I phone Burt at Tutti.

"Becca," he says. "We've been worried sick about you. All we know is what we read in the papers. And Miriam's disappeared. She came with a man yesterday evening. Tom gave her something, then bang. Gone."

I breathe a big sigh.

"Ben beat the shit out of me, Burt. He broke my shoulder. But the worst is, get this. They're charging me with murder. Murder! Is there something I'm missing here? Do other people get to live their lives without being kicked in the head every time they turn around?"

"Murder? Shit."

"I need a lawyer, Burt. I need an ace. I need somebody that doesn't like to lose."

"Well, I think any lawyer would jump at your case. What

publicity. You're in all the *Enquirer*s and such. The talk shows are buzzing with you."

"Gee, thanks. I needed to know that. Oh, and Burt, have the cops talked to any of you yet?"

"No."

"If they do, I'd like it if you didn't mention Miriam. I want to keep her out of this mess."

He's quiet. "I can't ask them to lie."

"I know. Do what you can."

As it turns out, I don't get to my arraignment until Tuesday, because of the holiday. You know, "Should auld acquaintance be forgot?" and all that.

By then, Burt has called some woman lawyer and badgered her into taking a look at my case. Apparently, she's well known in the bay area for winning most of the time. She'd gotten one of Burt's buddies off of some assault with a deadly weapon charge even though he really did it. I'm hoping that bodes well for me.

By the time Tuesday rolls around, I've had six hours sleep, total. For my trip to court, they sit me in a wheelchair and manacle my ankles and left wrist to it. I don't know what they think I'm going to do. The whole thing reminds me a lot of Ben.

Outside that door it's like walking into a human-size beehive. Cameramen swarm in and a wall of reporters surges forward, shouting questions to Clarisse. Cameras flash bright and fast. At the courthouse, we worm through another batch of reporters and cameramen who could certainly have better things to do with their time.

By the time I get inside, I only get a five-minute consult with the lawyer Burt found for me, Cynthia White, a polite, exquisitely intelligent black woman that knows how to dress. I feel pretty ugly in my hospital gown and slippers. I can only imagine what my face looks like.

"I didn't go there to kill him," I say.

"We'll discuss that later. For now, you're pleading not guilty to the murder by reason of lawful defense. And you're pleading guilty to the weapons charges. Correct?"

"You got it."

Once I'm in front of the judge, he refuses me bail. I have too famous a reputation for leaving bad situations and disappearing. The media circus only adds to his decision.

As they wheel me out, I wave at Josh and Tom as much as the handcuffs will let me. Looking at my face and cast, they both go Scranton white, if that's possible for Josh.

The two detectives, Cynthia, and I all arrive back at my pleasantly appointed hospital room at about the same time.

Cynthia wades right in. "Any statements made by my client in your interview Friday when she was barely conscious are not admissible in court."

The looker sniffs once. "We have more questions."

During this interrogation, I learn about all the holes in my not-so-carefully laid plans. They found tire tracks from the Rav Four in two different places. Not only that but a second set of fingerprints was found on the door of the Taurus, the van, and in my apartment. This information makes me sweat.

I suggest that they belong to one of Ben's thugs.

The crooked face guy is watching me without blinking, just like a 'gator. I'm thinking he's really the brains of these two. I stare back at him.

They go on punching holes in my version of the story, bringing me back over and over to Ben beating me. I keep feeling how his fists made my ears block up. Soon, I can't really hear the detectives. And the sound of my shoulder breaking reverberates.

Cynthia cuts in, looking at me in a strange way. "My client is showing too much strain. We'll take a break. She's badly injured."

The two of them hesitate. Then the looker stands. "We'll resume our interview tomorrow morning," he says.

After they leave, I look at Cynthia. Ben's fists are still banging away at my face. I wish somebody would make him stop. I don't think I can take this kind of thing anymore.

Cynthia shifts her chair so that it's facing me and removes a DAT from her purse. Setting the microphone up near my face, she looks me straight in the eye.

"Now let's have the truth."

One day I got sent home from school for beating up some stupid kid during recess. I dawdled my way home, then searched the bank for a suitable fishing pole. Daddy caught me on my way into the house to raid me and Vin's stash of fishing line. I don't know, maybe he hadn't had enough to drink yet. By the time Vin got home, I was barely conscious, lying on the front-room floor. Daddy'd left a long ways back, drunk by then, I guess.

In the winter, we had days and days of rain. We grew tired of the sound of drops falling from leaves, of trickling leaks, of buckets set beneath to prevent damage.

But each day, hour after hour, the river drew close, edging up the grass.

"Someday," Mama said every now and then. "Someday this old river's gonna wash our two-room right away." And she'd shrug.

When Vin came home and found me that day that I thought Daddy was going to kill me, he got me on my feet and hid with me all night in a thicket by the river.

What I remember about that night was how bright the moon fell, lighting up like it was day, like we were fuller, deeper, wider than what we looked most other times. The trees, more like magic, drooped over the river. And the black water ran slow beneath our white covering night.

Cynthia sits in silence writing down notes. I think I drowse for a bit. Then lunch arrives and I'm presented with some packets of stale crackers and a bowl of liquid that looks like sewer water. I push it away.

All of a sudden, Cynthia comes alive.

"So you went there," she says, the end of her pen pressed

against her full lips, "intending to kill yourself." She looks up. "But you couldn't. Instead, you let him beat the crap out of you."

I nod my head.

She sits back, staring at me. "Sorry, but I'm not buying it. You're going to have to come up with something better than that because I don't think the police are buying a damn thing you're telling them. With the tiremarks and the fingerprints, they're probably thinking accomplice. A carefully planned murder in the middle of nowhere. You leave and nobody knows the difference."

"Then why did I call the police?"

She sits and thinks. "Why indeed?" Her eyes go wide. "You're covering for somebody. You had help getting out of the tape. Where did you keep the Smith and Wesson?"

I don't answer.

"Beneath the front seat? That's where most people keep concealed pistols in their cars. That and the glove box. That's why the fingerprints on the driver's door." Her eyes narrow now. "And the last two shots close up." She looks me straight in the eye. "So you would have traces of the shots. You didn't kill him. You were taped up in the back of the van."

She should get the Perry Mason snot nose award.

"Look," I say, like I'd been around Burt too long, "Ben was my problem, my responsibility. If anyone should pay a price for his death, it should be me. If I'd gone back with Ben sooner, none of this would have ever happened."

"That's the stupidest thing I've heard in a long time." She looks me straight in the eye. "This is serious, Becca. The way your case stands now, I'd say you've got a fifty-fifty chance of winning in court. I don't like those odds. And your history as a hooker won't endear you to any jury. They'll think a beating by a pimp might be what you deserved. And since you didn't try to call the police and get help, they'll say you took the law into your own hands."

"So I'll cop a plea."

"If you'd tell me who shot him, you wouldn't have to do that."

I pretend I'm overcome with pain and let out a small moan. She ignores me.

"You had a lover, didn't you? The word at the restaurant is that you were having an affair with Miriam Dubois." She waits after dropping this bombshell.

I lie my head back. All my assorted pains get worse as if somebody cranks up the dial. I moan again, this time for real. And thinking about Miriam, my longing for her hurts so deep that I decide I'd much rather feel the elephants tromping on me.

"Let's just assume for a minute that it was Miriam up there," Cynthia says. "Everybody I talk to says she's a gentle, good person. Not the kind to go out and just shoot somebody. So," she eyes me, "her case is clearer than yours. You were in imminent danger of great bodily injury, as the law states in the statute for lawful defense. If I'm guessing right, she came upon the scene having no prior knowledge that Ben was there, meaning that her shooting of him couldn't be premeditated.

"And she had no time to call the police in order to protect you from him. On top of that, she's a well-respected figure without the history you have that makes you easier to convict."

"I don't want her dragged into my muck."

"And if it came down to life in prison, you'd accept that?"

That's a kicker. "I want to say yes, but I might get cowardly as this goes on."

"What would she do if it looked that bad for you?"

I stare at her, blank, because I remember Miriam's eyes when she drove off in the Rav. How they were dead, empty. I realize that I'm not sure what Miriam would do.

"Okay," Cynthia says, checking her list. "I want you to give me a good description of this Kat person that got you into the car near the museum. I need any information as to where you think we might find her. And I'll get in touch with Detective Bates in New York, or the men on his team, to get his notes on the murder investigation."

Now she writes something on her pad. "All right. Is there anything personal you want me to check on?"

"Jeremy," I say. "We are still married, after all." I look away. I don't want to start crying in front of Cynthia.

Her voice is softer now. "I'll take care of it," she says, gathering her things together as she stands to leave.

"Thanks for helping me," I say.

"My pleasure," she says, smiling. "And don't talk about any of this to anyone."

I salute her with my good arm and out she goes, leaving me deflated and sinking into darkness.

The next few days are hazy, interrupted now and then by interrogations with Beauty and the Beast, as I've begun to think of my two detectives. Cynthia tells me she's gotten in touch with Johnson, who is refusing to give out information about Miriam's whereabouts. He even threatened her with a lawsuit.

"What a great guy," I say, lumping Johnson, the looker, and Ben all together in my mind.

They move me at the end of the week. It's a new facility for prisoners who pose a high-security risk. When I get to my new home away from home, I'm put in a cell with a large black woman whose shape is reminiscent of Mama (which endears her to me), and who apparently has a fondness for stealing credit cards and amassing lots of stuff. She doesn't like messing with the cash that she gets out of women's purses.

"Small potatoes," she says.

I find that, for the most part, my fellow women prisoners think rather highly of me because the word is out that while a prostitute in New York, I screwed some pretty important men. Even the president, the rumor goes.

Not this president.

As the days go by, I let my hair grow again, looking more like the old Clarisse. I even begin to feel like the old Clarisse, seeing how the dangers are everywhere. I dream of the days when gun stores were a dime a dozen, when all I had to do was turn the key in that Porsche and put my foot on the accelerator.

I nag my roommate, whose talents with acquiring stuff have landed her in a position of supply inside the prison. I want her to get me a weapon.

"You don't want to mess with no tools now, Becca-Clarry." That's what she's gotten to calling me. "You just get yourself in a pot of trouble."

Eventually she comes up with a piece of a knife, the tip chipped and most of the handle busted off. I get that special feeling again.

Finally, I'm cleared to have visitors.

The first time they tell me someone's waiting to see me, I'm on cloud nine. My depression has been dropping me off tall cliffs faster than I can count.

I walk in the room and sit down in my booth.

It's Jeremy.

He looks like he's aged ten years since I saw him last, and maybe has taken a hit in the cheerful department. I think he's run a little short on bright sunny days.

"Clarisse?" he says like he's not sure it's me.

"Jeremy?" I say. My humor is always lost on him.

"I didn't believe it was you at all for awhile," he says. "I'd gotten used to the idea that you were dead."

"You can hold on to that if you need," I say.

"So when are you coming home?" he asks, looking gray.

"Well, I'm not going anywhere until the trial."

"Oh yeah."

Had he forgotten about that? "I don't think I'm coming home, Jeremy. I think it's over between us."

The lines beneath his eyes ease.

"Who've you been seeing?" I ask.

His cheeks go red. "Just somebody I met at the hospital. You know, from the night you left. The night Ben came over?"

The night Ben came over? He says it like Ben was his guest.

"I felt bad about that, Jeremy. About him beating you up."

Then Jeremy looks around as though to make sure no one is listening. "Was it really you that weekend? You know. At Ben's."

" 'I don't like a hood,' " I say, repeating his remarks. " 'I like to admire their markings.' "

He swallows and his face goes the color of a fine variety of beet.

"I could have saved you a lot of money, Jeremy."

He leans forward. "Maybe after you get out, we could visit every now and then?"

Oh God. Why me? "I don't think that's best."

He sits back. "Oh."

"I want a divorce, Jeremy. We can split everything down the middle, even my book earnings. I'm assuming it's been a fairly big lump."

"Oh yeah." Then he races into a long spiel about how he's invested in this market, that set of stocks, foreign currencies, futures (my personal favorite), etc., etc. He's made a killing (killing might be the only thing he and I have in common at the present moment) and is looking for an even bigger house. Not only that but he's had an incredible offer from some magazine to tell the true story about Clarisse Broder.

"Leave out the part about our afternoon date at Ben's," I suggest.

After he's gone, my longing for Miriam surges up inside of me. She hasn't written or sent a message through Tom or Josh. No one has seen or heard from her.

The news of her tour is all good. Miriam is selling CDs like hotcakes, and the rumors are that she's in line for a Grammy. I've gotten to the point where thinking about her hurts so much that I try to pretend she was a dream I made up in my head.

Beauty and the Beast heard about her through Cinda, I gather. They forced a short interview, but it must not have come to much. Cynthia got a brief report about their conversation. The police tried to get a set of fingerprints, but Miriam's lawyers went ballistic. The police would have to come up with a subpoena. In which case, they threatened to sue the state for loss of revenues.

My agent makes an appearance, overjoyed with my celebrity, as though I'd planned it all along, and she talks about the book I'll write about my jump from the bridge and my time on the lam. Huge publishing houses are vying for the rights to it, offering her "large six-figure advances," as she's fond of saying.

It takes me awhile to figure out what that means, and when I do, it disgusts me. It gets me to longing for those days by the river with Mama and her groceries.

Things go along for awhile, and as the weeks pass, Tom, Josh, Greg, and Burt take turns visiting, trying to keep me cheerful, my most ingrained failing.

I keep harping on Cynthia about copping a plea, but she wants more leverage.

"Why are the prosecutors hanging on to this?" I say.

"It's an election year," Cynthia says. But then she starts in on that thing I won't talk about. "You don't have to shoulder this, Becca. Where's Miriam?"

I shrug and leave the room.

But at night, I wake up reaching for Miriam, searching for her body and its warmth. Sometimes I wake myself up talking to her, telling her the things she always wanted to know, the things I kept from her.

I lie in my cot empty and filled with guilt. No wonder I haven't heard from her. I almost got her killed. And I led her to believe I was someone that I wasn't. I was a fake, a lie.

There's an especially bad day at the beginning of February when I'm lying in my cell. I think I hear her voice. I sit up, following the sound into the lounge, and there on MTV is Miriam being interviewed about the CD and another new video just released.

She looks so good. So beautiful. Tears start in my eyes. I sit mesmerized, hurting like I don't think any beating or whipping from Ben could have ever done. I search her arms for the bracelet I gave to her. She's not wearing it. I look for anything at all that connected the two of us. There's nothing. Even her clothes are new. She's let her hair grow too, but it's been lightened and cut to make her look younger.

I watch her new video all the way through and go back to my cell, lying still, too terrified to move.

A few weeks later, they come to get me. I have a visitor. When I sit in my booth, I don't recognize her at first. She's wearing a wig and a sun hat.

It's Kat.

"Beth," she says. "It's Katherine. You remember me."

"Yeah, Kathy. How's the kids?"

"Gone to the four winds."

I search her face and stare into her eyes. I follow the shape of her lips. Her voice fills me like the first time I heard it. I want to wrap her in my arms, desperate for touch. But she's so thin. So drawn.

Her clothing is something Kat would have never worn before. Two red scratches run the length of her neck, and inside one arm I see tracks, some fresh, some purple.

"I was the first he ever took to the basement," Kat says. "He had a small place in Brooklyn then. I met him at Columbia my second year at school. I didn't have much of a family, just like you. He was always looking for that. But he got me to come to his place one night. I didn't see the light of day for six months.

"By that time, I was his. I've seen it work so many times. To survive, I learned to help him. And now, I don't know what to do. I don't know where to go. I never imagined that Ben would be gone."

And looking at Kat, to remember her skin, her arms, I ache so sudden. And in my head it's as if I see Miriam disappearing, turning her back to me as she walks away. I know I never deserved Miriam's love. Yet before me sits Kat, my first love, anyone's heart's desire.

But her eyes. God, her eyes are like Violet's in Bates' photos, having been drained of life, having siphoned down into the

Dumpster. I notice for the first time how the human face is not a whole thing but an assembly of parts, easy to unmake.

"I came because I wanted to see you so badly," she says. "And to tell you I'm sorry for everything I did to you."

"No," I say, interrupting.

"Shh, Beth. Let me finish." Now her head falls to the side. "I'm most sorry about that last day in the car. I just wanted you back safe. I didn't want Ben to hurt you."

I think of her naked then, and how her skin was like milk, creamy and cool.

"I'm going to talk to your lawyer. But I had to see you first." Her eyes intensify. "I love you so, Beth."

I'm trying hard not to cry. "Don't, Kat. I don't care if I'm in prison. Wait for me. I want you to be free."

She smiles, but it's a terrible thing, a face behind a face, having been kept secret within.

"I want to make things right, Beth. From that first night I drugged you, I regretted everything. But then having you with me in our prison brought me such happiness. So I want to help you now."

My tears are running down my face. And the scent of her comes over me.

"It wasn't all bad, Kat. You taught me how to be a person. You taught me about the best things in life. I would have never written that book if it hadn't been for you."

For one moment, I see that I've gotten through, that I've touched something inside of her. "I'm rich now, Kat. When I get out, I'll take care of you."

She looks at me with the eyes that spent six months in Ben's basement, those eyes that brought powerful men near to tears. She doesn't say anything.

A guard tells me time is up. Kat stands. I keep looking back.

I remember her hands, how she pressed them together in front of her chest.

Kat is arrested on her way out of the prison. There are also outstanding warrants for her arrest from New York in connection with Ben's murders. Kat is sucked into the California system of so-called justice, disappearing from my view.

"I've got to see her," I keep harping at Cynthia. "She's sick. I know how to help her."

She stares at me. "Becca, have you talked to the psychiatrist yet? I told you to do that weeks ago."

"She needs me," I say again.

Kat, arrested and indicted under her birth name, Alissa Moulin, gives evidence that verifies my story about the threats made against me.

Cynthia is on cloud nine.

Then Bates is taken off the critical list. He learns about Ben's shooting, and how I'm being charged with murder. From what I hear, he blows a tube, of which he still has a few poking out.

Now Cynthia's ready to negotiate.

They offer me second-degree murder and the baseline sentence of fifteen to twenty.

Cynthia laughs.

She begins to talk like we should go to trial, saying that the chance of me walking is now in my favor. I balk. I worry. The dangers get me.

I'm certain that if I go to trial, I'll lose. It's been one thing after another, starting with Mandy's appendicitis and ending with Miriam's desertion.

At this point, there's nothing else it could be. She'll write, I keep thinking. She'll call Josh. But she never does.

So I refuse to go to trial and order Cynthia to get me the best deal she can wrangle. "I spent ten years with Ben," I say. "Prison is a walk in the park."

She stares into my eyes, but I look away. I don't tell her that I'm terrified, that the great Clarisse Broder, who jumped from the Brooklyn Bridge, is scared shitless to be walking around free with only a memory of Miriam in her head.

But I can't stop myself from searching out news of Miriam. I watch while her CD goes up the charts and her sold-out concerts are given great reviews. As the weeks progress, she's lauded, praised, and called a shoo-in for a Grammy.

The cliff I'm dropping off gets a lot more treacherous. I stop seeing visitors. I don't read my mail. I have periods when I can't move at all, even if I try. I somehow manage to keep this a secret.

Now I'm one of the ghosts flicking through, haunting the cells, where all my lovers lay, stacked, put away, like dolls flat on their backs, sleeping in Rivertown.

Beloved lover.

Then the final bargain comes through.

Cynthia arrives and they usher me into the lawyer room. "Manslaughter," she says, not smiling. "Three years including time already served, possibility of parole as soon as fifteen months."

"Yes," I say.

Cynthia paces. "As your lawyer, it's my responsibility to do my best for you. I think the bargain is decent, but my advice is to go to trial."

I get my mouth open, but she interrupts, pounding the table.

"You can beat this thing, Becca. With Kat and Bates on your side, I can shred their case. Everybody wants you to go to trial, Becca. Burt, Josh, Greg. They're upset that you'd accept this plea."

I lie my head on the table.

"I know you don't want to hear this, but I'm going to say it one time. Give evidence on Miriam. All you have to do is confirm she was up there that day. Then the police can force a fingerprint check."

Cynthia stops in front of me, one hand leaning on the table. "Why keep up the charade, Becca? She hasn't done a goddamn thing for you."

I raise my head, my eyes burning, feeling for the first time that if I had a gun in my hand right now, I'd pull the trigger. Cynthia takes a step away from me.

I lie my head back down.

"Okay," she says. I hear her packing up her stuff. "I'll come back tomorrow. But I'm sending the prison psychiatrist over to see you this afternoon."

"The last thing I need is a fucking shrink," I say.

"I don't think you're in any state to know what you need."

I jerk my head up. "So who the fuck does? There isn't anybody. Zilch. Zero. I'm sure the state would like to step in. That would be grand."

"Stop it, Becca. Stop it right now." She glares at me. "You're impossible." She picks up her briefcase and folds her raincoat over her arm. "I'm sending the psychiatrist today. I'll see you tomorrow."

That afternoon, they take me from my cell and drag me to see the shrink.

Just a nervous breakdown. Women have them all the time.

When Cynthia comes back the next day, we argue again. This time it's me pounding the table. "Do I have to fucking spell it out for you? I don't want to get out. I want to stay right here."

Cynthia's face goes blank. She stops her pacing and sits, staring at me for a long time.

"Okay," she says at last. "We'll take the plea."

Before she leaves, she steps behind me and puts both of her hands on my shoulders. "Things will get better, Becca. You'll see. You've got friends who care about you."

I nod and put my head down. She leaves.

The bargain goes through. A week later, I stand before the judge. I'm charged. I plead guilty. I'm sentenced.

Three years. Fifteen months if I can keep my shit together. My thoughts now are fixed on Kat. In my mind, I tell her to hang on, that I'll help her. Just fifteen months, I promise.

Three days later, Cynthia shows up. Her face is splotchy. She sits and searches me with her round, brown eyes.

"Becca, look at me."

I allow my eyes to drift to hers. But in my head, I hear the willows beating the air. I smell the heat off the mudflats. At times, I can forget I'm in a cell and locked up. I have moments where Miriam disappears altogether.

"Becca. It's about Kat. They were going to transfer her to New York tomorrow. She was facing nine counts of accomplice to murder." She stops.

I look straight through her.

"She's dead," I say.

Cynthia looks away. "Hung herself off her bedframe."

It's strange how the river becomes so plain, like I'm standing in the grass again. The night presses close. The mists grow heavy. The frogs sing.

I remember that one year I heard Daddy saying something to Mama about how a sudden surge of the river had swept off a whole herd of cows, and that parts of them ended up in people's houses along with the muck. Daddy laughed. That was my first inkling that our houses were a lot like Dumpsters.

But in this moment of Kat and the world of our secret suffering, I see how what I am is nothing more than a Dumpster, a receptacle for that which no one else finds valuable. I see how Kat is broken, like Violet, and perched upon garbage, her blanket drawn back. Strangers stare at her beautiful body. That body that I loved.

I don't cry. I stand and walk away, turning at the door. Cynthia hasn't moved. She's staring down at her hands resting on the table.

"Claim her body for me. I'll take care of her burial."

Cynthia closes her eyes and nods.

I leave and lie on my cot, not making noise or bother. I think about the times when Kat and I used to act out *Romeo and Juliet*.

> I will kiss thy lips,
> Haply some poison yet doth hang on them,
> To make me die with a restorative.
> Thy lips are warm!

Kat would be lying still upon her mattress, having died of poison. I'd kneel beside, clutching the bread knife we used.

. . . then I'll be brief. O happy dagger!
This is thy sheath.

I have no more room. My quotient of loss is filled too full.
When weight has gathered beyond its limit, something must be
removed.

But will the soul do? Is it lighter than a feather? Would I find
the film and slip through easy?

The next day I wake, unable to remember some important
things. When our cell door is unlocked, I sit on the edge of my
bed, staring. The large black woman who was sleeping where
Vin should have been is halfway out the door when she looks
back.

"Come on, honey," she says, taking me by the hand.

Things begin to blur out. The next thing I remember is that
I'm sitting in front of the TV. I hear a voice that I remember. She's
a lovely woman. Oprah is smiling at her and acts like they've
been chums for years. I keep staring at her face, trying out
names, thinking that I know her.

Oprah lays her hand on this woman's arm. She's thin, thinner
than she should be, I think I remember. And for a moment, I
catch a slight tremble in her hand. She hides it beneath her leg.

"My guest today, as I'm sure everyone knows, is Miriam
Dubois, whom all the experts say might walk out with an arm-
load of Grammies tonight."

Miriam. That was her name. I knew a Miriam once. I loved
her. And now I feel her hand along my back. Her fingers run
through my hair.

Oprah turns. "So let's pick up where we left off before the
break. I'm sure everyone wants to know the answer to this question."

The young woman's eyes sparkle with a thing that I think I
misplaced somewhere. When she smiles, the corners of her eyes
are so tender.

I want to touch just there, where the tenderness has come

alive. And then perhaps to sit. Not near, but close enough to watch, to sense her presence in a room with me. I think I should die for that.

Oprah leans close, like girls telling secrets. "So tell me, Miriam, there were rumors months ago that you'd found someone special in your life. I'd love to be the first to know."

Miriam laughs. My head tilts. I feel a thrill run through me.

"Come on, girlfriend. You can tell me."

Miriam smiles. She shakes her head. "No."

I'm so attentive now, all of me hanging on her words. And I catch in the camera close-up of her face, the gleam of those eyes. "No," she says again. "There's no one."

I find that I'd leaned forward, and now I sit back as her words settle. Maybe they're just sheets of paper, so thin you'd never know the weight of them. Weight is a tricky thing anyway.

No. There's no one.

I can see why she'd say that. I understand. Yet I keep searching that face, those lips, looking for a slight sign. A giveaway. That she's lying.

But she's so smooth. Her delivery so sure and unbroken.

No. There's no one.

I know that. I know how she's right. There is no one. No one at all. There's no one.

By nine, we're locked in our cells. By nine thirty, my credit card–loving roommate is snoring up a storm.

I rise from my bed and take out a piece of stationery that Josh brought me. I think I remember, like some long-ago dream, that I wrote a note like this once before. Only it was different then. At that time, I was only pretending.

I write:

> Lovely Miriam,
>   A Grammy would be nice for you.
>   Someone asked me today whether, just in case I died,

there was anyone I'd like to name as my beneficiary. I had to think. Then I said, No. There's no one.

　　I wish you the best.

　　　　　　　　Becca

I kneel and slip my knife from its hiding place. It's so good to keep a weapon nearby. Just in case.

I lie on my bed and read my note again, then let it drop on my chest. The knife isn't easy to work. In order to get to the arteries in my wrists, I have to do some hefty slashing.

And as I'm drifting, keeping my eyes fixed on the willow leaves trembling, I float with Vin and Mandy again, watching the banks ease by, hoping for a little rest.

The night Vin and me sat by watching our house go to ashes, he wrapped his arms around me. Neither of us ever cried.

I always wondered why we never even tried to get help. I think we'd already given up hope about something that should have been as natural as air.

So by the time I'd gotten to the real meat of my wrist and exposed a bit of bone, it wasn't Miriam I was thinking of anymore. I found that in the center of my body, lying silent and red along my skeleton, I'd kept that last memory of Mama, fresh as the day she died, and promising her over and over, I will be true. I will be true. And beside her apparition and below, was that prevenient groan, whose nature can be known only by its shadow.

It is our lovers who cast us this shadow. How could we ever turn away?

So it is Ben that I cling to now. Ben and his multiple wounds divine and bathed in radiance. I desire no other. Having seen the shadow plain, having guessed at its unseen nature, I shrink back, beaten down at last by that which I have carried secret and blind in my own broken body.

PART III

Rebirth

16

Stacking in Rivertown

I wake in a big room. It's stuffy. I hear a TV.

I try to move but can only turn my head. One of the prison guards is talking to a man in a white coat. Now a nurse looks in my face, turns, and says something. The man in the white coat approaches and leans over, staring at me. Above my head is a bag of red fluid. I follow the red tube that comes out of it, seeing it go down into my hand. A wad of bandages circles my wrist.

The doctor and nurse disappear from view. I try to shift, but sense how I'm strapped in place. My head lolls to the side. I see beds lined up in a long row. The women in them are staring blank-eyed at the television that's bolted up in the corner.

The nurse reappears and squirts water from a bottle into my mouth.

"That's good," she coos.

I hold it on my tongue.

Then I get a picture in my mind of Ben slumped on the ground with five holes in him. I see Kat, her neck stretched, her face bright red. Then something floats in.

No. There's no one. Nobody. No.

I spit the water in the nurse's face.

She doesn't move. I can see she wants to slap me. But everyone in the room is silent, watching. She walks off, wiping her face.

I lie still. I don't struggle. I've had a lot of training for this kind of thing. I can feel how they couldn't strap my wrists. Too much damage. Instead, they have me bound mid-arm. I press my forearms back, slipping the straps toward my elbows. I reach wrist to wrist, working through the bandages and gouging the stitches out. I rip off the IV and blood feed.

So this is happiness, I think, feeling my body go light. And I find that I'm smiling. Funny how happiness isn't all that hard when you know what you really want.

My blank-eyed neighbor screams. They come. I try to fight them. The blood makes my arms slippery. The doctor pulls the blanket and sheet off one side, yanks up my gown, and spears my thigh with a needle.

Now I'm floating again, seeing Ben. I want to tell him how much I love him and how everything that happened is forgotten now. It doesn't matter anymore.

When I wake once more, my hands are enclosed in mitts and I have a tube taped in my mouth. I swing my head side to side to get it out. I try biting, but they have something rubber between my teeth. I scream and thrash. The doctor and nurse consult. I get another shot, but it doesn't put me out, just keeps me groggy. The nurse comes in with Cynthia. Her eyes are red. She sits by the bed.

I look away.

"Becca," she says. "Josh is a wreck. Burt broke down and cried in my office. You've got to stop this."

Because of the stuff in my throat and mouth, I can't explain to her about the little house I built. It's made of white stone and sits on a rise above a river. In this house, the dead are stacked deep.

On the bottom is Mama, still fat and wedged into her slot. Then Mandy. Beloved friend.

Ben is stacked but still breathing. He'll always sleep half-awake.

Then my lovers lie in slumber. Dear Violet, in a light sleep, tossing and turning. And Kat, my fairest love, trembling from her dreams. Above Kat is Miriam, murdered by her vicious lover as she slept.

In the top slot is the freshest body of all, laid out like a doll flat on her back. Across her stomach on the left side is the scar she mistook for an appendectomy. I smile, remembering her confusion. I find myself reluctant to leave her side because I miss her so deeply. She is the one I loved best.

Her skin is white now, bleached but pliable. Her lips I find to be soft as I touch mine to hers. They are dead, though. No mistaking that.

I glare at Cynthia. I throw my head side to side. She cries some. In time, she stands, squeezes my arm, and leaves.

The next few days are bleak. They drug me up, feeding me through the fucking tube. Eventually they wear me down. Eventually I begin to let them feed me. Ben's basement again. I expect them to give me a new name and teach me to give pleasure to men.

But in my head I go for long dreams, floating down the river. Listening to the sound of wind and leaves.

They keep interrupting. The orderlies unstrap me for short periods while in the custody of some hefty guard watching me like I'm a criminal or something, like I'm a prostitute gone bad. I try one more time when I'm peeing by myself in the john. I wreck my wrists, opening the wounds that have just knit together. I can't get in deep enough. And I wedge myself as tight as I can beside the toilet.

I think of the statue of the sad woman that Mandy and me adorned with a hat years ago. Her face was turned to the side. And she was turned at the waist also, as though having thought to move in that direction, but maybe had decided not. Perhaps she knew that no direction would satisfy, and that all her suffering had come to nothing.

I curve my arm around, rocking and drooling, clutching my

legs up tight beneath. That's when my guard opens the door and his face goes red like he's angry, not sad at the sight of me in such a sorry condition.

The guard grabs me by my ankles and drags me out. We roll around on the floor in a red embrace until they hit me with another syringe.

And so I dream and drift once more to sleep. I walk to the edge of the river. I unbutton my dress and let it drop. When I step forward, the water is cool. I let the current take me.

On the far bank now, the shadows have lengthened. The night-jars have come out, swooping and diving, and the sun has bleached the cypress golden. Someone has propped me on a willow branch, swaying as the willow sways, and high in the upper limbs, the peewee calls, *pee-a-wee*.

"All right, Clarisse. Wake up." A hand is gripping my chin, shaking my head. "You've got company."

My eyes open a slit. The blood drip hangs above me again. The tube has returned to my mouth. I jerk my head out of the nurse's hand. When she steps back, I see Cynthia.

A nurse walks by with a tray of food for the woman in the bed next to mine.

That's when I notice him. He's sitting quiet beside Cynthia. He's wearing a Chicago Bulls cap and sunglasses that are familiar to me. Then I remember. That's Becker's hat. It's Becker's sunglasses.

The fucker. Nobody gave them to him. Tears are running out from beneath his sunglasses. I glare at him.

Cynthia leans forward, lying her hand on my leg. "Your brother's here to see you, Becca. You remember Vin."

I shake my head no. It's a trick. Vin was bigger-boned. He had darker skin. And he'd be older now. Do they think I'm stupid?

Now the fake Vin stands and sits beside me on my bed. I turn my head away.

"Look at me, Becca."

I know that voice. It's not Vin.

"Becca." He takes hold of my head and forces me to turn toward him, his hands trembling. He takes off his sunglasses, and I stare at him, remembering. It's Violet. After all these years, she's come to get me. I see that her neck isn't separated from her head. Bates lied to me.

"I didn't mean what I said in that interview. I've been sick to death with wanting you, to see you, to talk to you. I've been such a coward. I'm so ashamed. I made a terrible mistake."

I stare at her, seeing how pale her skin, the dark lines beneath her eyes.

"Do you know me, Becca? Do you know who I am?"

I keep trying to remember, thinking about flames and how they shoot higher and higher as the two-room burns, how I worry for the willows that they'll catch fire, and how Vin and me have to keep moving back because of the heat.

She starts crying and lies her forehead against mine, whispering. "Please stop hurting yourself."

I sense her hands rubbing my head.

Now Violet sits back and turns to Cynthia. "Get the nurse." She stares at me. "You're going to eat now."

When the nurse comes, Violet says, "Please take out the tube. She'll let me feed her."

"I'll have to ask the doctor. He's not here."

"What have you got to lose?" Violet says, not mean but soft, like someone might be dying nearby.

The nurse leaves and I see her pick up a phone. Then she's talking on it, gesturing.

Violet leans close to my ear, talking low. "I should never have listened to you that day. I'm such a stupid shit. Nothing could be worse than this."

The nurse returns with a tray. She sets it down and leans forward, releasing the strap behind my head, peeling away the tape. As she separates my teeth, she steadily pulls the tube out. I start gagging.

Violet waits, then lies a bottle against my lips. "I want you to drink."

I lie still, staring into her eyes, remembering pictures that someone showed me a long time ago of a woman in a Dumpster, another piece of trash thrown out. How did she awaken from her silent death? Did the Dumpster prove fertile for the quickening of limbs? I throw buttercups upon her gentle grave. And I lie her beneath the willows. I wet her eyes with the river.

Violet squirts liquid in my mouth. I hold it there, trying to remember how to swallow.

"You can do it."

I choke on it, but get it down. A burn starts in my stomach.

"More," she says.

I swallow another mouthful.

She hands Cynthia the bottle and takes a bowl and spoon. "You're going to eat some soup."

Cynthia props up my head with a pillow. Violet offers me a spoonful. I shake my head no.

"Just a little."

We wait.

"Just a little," she repeats.

I open my mouth and I swallow, following its course to the fire that is my stomach.

"Again."

She keeps feeding me until I shake my head no.

"Okay. That's good for starters. But now you have to do it on your own. I can't come every time. You can do it for me. Remember that I want you to eat and to drink. And I want you to leave your wrists alone. Let them heal."

Violet hands Cynthia the spoon and the bowl and holds my head in her hands again.

"They're going to make me leave soon."

I shake my head, but she holds me still.

"Shh, Becca. I'll be back. But you have to eat and get better before I can come back."

She leans forward, hesitating, then touches her lips to mine.

Her scent comes over me and she lies her forehead against my cheek, crying. Then she sits up. "Before I go, I want you to talk. I know that you can say my name."

I stare, trying to memorize her again, because I sense I've forgotten something.

"Say Miriam, Becca."

Vin sleeps by the river, but I'm awake. And the moon lights the mists silver. The live oak rustles, high on the rise and lit from behind.

"Miriam, Becca. Say it."

The river of a sudden flows heavy, having broken loose from some northern freeze, carrying its Dumpsters full of bodies. And I hear my voice whispering, full of mud, full of wormtree.

"You say, 'One clover. One bee. And revery, revery.'"

And now it's like when you're in the box and first you're whispering. Not long after that, you're screaming, but you don't know why.

It's the fire having leapt into the willows, spreading to the tupelos. The nurse and the doctor scurry like rats on a log. I see another needle. Cynthia gets between them and me, gesturing.

The 'gators climb out of the river and drag me in.

Violet's laid her body over me.

Kat loved for me to plait her braid. I'd lean her back in a chair, still naked from the play, still scared some, and always like she was, a little sad. Sigh no more, I'd say in her ear. I'd recite it for her as her hair fell free.

> Sigh no more, ladies, sigh no more,
>   Men were deceivers ever;
> One foot in sea, and one on shore,
> To one thing constant never.
>   Then, sigh not so
> But let them go,

> And be you blithe and bonny,
> Converting all your sounds of woe
> Into Hey nonny, nonny.

And all the time I brushed her hair over my fingers. With each turn of the plait, I loved her more. With each wind about, I kissed her neck. She smelled of scented lotions and semen. Of roses and sweat.

Mama smelled of river-washed cotton. Her breath was heavy with milk, and her fingers were shaped like sausages, but smelled of rain.

So when it rains, I think of Mama. How she loved thunder and wind. We'd sit on the porch watching the storms come in. She'd take off her stretched-out shoes and her knee-highs, already fallen down to her ankles. We'd run out and get drenched. I'd stomp puddles. Vin would slide along the grass, buck naked, showing off his white ass.

Our bodies and minds are made from a thing so fresh, so fine. But we regress to that which wilts, folds down, and disappears.

So I live inside the river now. If you want to find me, you look for me here. Above me, I see cottonwoods atremble. I see trap-jaws dropping off logs. I see the willows draped over.

How they sway. How they sway.

A guard comes and gets me from my cell, leading me to the visitor's room.

It's Miriam.

I stare. Cynthia told me that she was going to come, but I didn't believe her. She told me that Miriam had seen me in the hospital, but I didn't believe that either.

I gaze at Miriam, trying to remember that feeling I used to get whenever I saw her. That something in my heart. But I'm not all the way alive just yet. I'm still carrying around the body of a dead woman.

Neither of us says a thing for a long time, and I feel myself floating, like on that raft. I put my hand on the glass separating us. She takes off her sunglasses and I see her eyes.

I have to admit, she looks pretty damn bad.

"You've got to eat more. I told you about that," she says, tears starting to run down her cheeks.

I don't say anything. I hang up in the air, knowing how close she is to me, and that she isn't some dream I use to bring myself suffering.

Miriam swallows and looks down. "I fucked you over bad, Becca. I owe you an apology."

"No, Miriam. Let's not waste these few minutes on that."

She nods, wiping her cheeks with her hands.

"I want to tell you a story. You've always wanted me to tell you things. I want to tell you about Mama."

She's looking up at me now, crying.

"Well, as you can see from the picture, she was fat. Mama couldn't read a word, and we were poor, but she gave Vin and me something that was better than all that. You know, everybody thinks it was your interview with Oprah that did me in, and I have to admit, it was pretty bad. But you didn't start it."

Now she puts her head down for a minute and sobs good and hard. I wait until she's looking at me again.

"I don't know when it started, but I do know that it was the fire that night that's gotten into me so deep. That and Ben's basement."

I brush my hair out of my eyes and look down.

"Anyway, Vin woke me up. There was so much smoke. We all slept in one room on a big mattress next to one another. Vin and me shook Mama. We hit her and kicked her, trying to get her to wake up. She wouldn't wake up!"

I pause for a moment, wiping my eyes. "Because of the smoke, I guess. We each took an arm, pulling hard. She was too heavy. Vin and me couldn't budge her."

Now I start crying. "I lay down on top of her like I was going to keep the fire off, and I could hear her heart still beating so strong and hard. I wrapped my arms around her neck and told her I would never leave her. But Vin, he was bigger than me. Vin dragged me off her. I fought him. I tried to break his face. He wouldn't let go, just pulled me out of there." I have to stop for a bit.

"I always blamed myself for her death. And Vin, of course. We weren't strong enough. It was my fault."

She leans forward and places her hand on the glass, looking like she's going to say something.

"No. Let me finish." I try to blow my nose, but it's impossible. Ben broke it so bad that no air can get through.

"The real kicker is that nobody came. We were just the rats that lived down by the river, eating out of their Dumpsters. Vin and me sat and watched the whole thing burn down to nothing."

I wait for a bit, trying to compose myself. "But that's what I want to tell you. I've spent my whole life doing crazy things like jumping off of bridges because when it came right down to it, I knew nobody would come.

"So you can apologize all you want, and I do think you fucked me over some. But we can talk about that some other time. I want to thank you for coming."

We both sit very still, like the people in Rivertown. I don't know how much time goes by.

"Becca," Miriam says breaking the silence. To hear her say my name again hurts me. But I close my eyes because I sense how glad I am that she's here.

"I've talked to Cynthia," she says. "I'm going to turn myself in. She thinks the most they'll charge me with is withholding evidence."

I nod, staring down at my hands.

"That means they'll have to release you," she says.

I don't look up. "Maybe," I say. "Maybe it would be better if you didn't do anything. I don't think I can go out there right now. I wouldn't know what to do."

She's silent for a long time. "Please look at me, Becca."

STACKING IN RIVERTOWN   299

She waits until we're staring at one another.

"I know I haven't given you any reason to trust me," she says, "and that you might not want to do this, but I want you to come home with me. I know you're not right yet. But I can help you."

She's quiet then. I don't know what to say to her. Home. What a strange word. I never have been able to understand what it means.

That's when the guard comes to let us know that time is up. I stand.

"Cynthia and I are going to the judge this afternoon," she says before I leave.

I nod, looking down at the floor. But as the guard leads me off, I turn, walking backward so I can keep her inside my eyes.

She doesn't waver. Her eyes never stray. I am all that she sees.

Home

This is my morning ritual. I wake and lie still, listening to Miriam's breathing. I feel her heart against my back, and how she trembles with each breath. Her body, naked, is wrapped around mine.

I move just a bit, and she wakes, pressing herself closer. Then she props herself on an elbow and stares into my eyes. She runs her hand along my side. We kiss and kiss, long and soft, not making love, just touching each other like we've been murdered and now wake up damaged but kinder.

Her warmth brings Mama to mind, and Mama's voice those nights so long ago when the river swept by, when the stars at night were so clear and white they made your heart ache just to think about the day and how it begins fine as silk in a corner of the sky.

"Everything's fine now," Miriam says, whispering in my ear. "It's all over."

I close my eyes, feeling her breath against my cheek. I don't say a thing, because I know she's wrong. It will never be over. It plays and plays in me. I repeat to myself that I must learn to wait. I must gain the moment of the ache and pass it through so that it goes from one end of me to the other.

Over time, I hope to learn to make more space. So far, I've managed to avoid slipping through the film, to ride the length of the undercurrent, and to surface somewhere near Rivertown.

Miriam sits on the edge of the bed. I mold my body to hers, kissing her back. She lies against me and takes one of my hands, running her fingers over mine.

We dress and eat breakfast, then get in the Taurus that we rented at the airport. Coming in from downstream, we hit Fowler first. I step out of the Taurus and take a long look at the eddy. It's still collecting junk. Some things don't change.

We cruise the little town with Dew Street, with the Beauty Box still in business, and Mama's favorite Dumpster in place, only it's bigger now. As we drive down that dirt road where Mama walked a thousand times with her grocery bags in her hands, Miriam's eyes take in the shacks. The yards are full of scrawny dogs with tits dragging the ground, and piles of broken stuff nobody else wants.

Miriam starts going pale. "When I read your stories, in my mind it doesn't look like this," she says. "Your stories are so full and rich."

"We were rich," I say. "And Mama would sing."

I park the Taurus and stroll through the grass, making my way to where the two-room stood. I can see the outline of the house because the weeds grow taller there. Beside it the butter-cups still bloom. And now a mimosa has taken root, arched over like a vase.

"This is Mama's grave," I say to Miriam. I kneel down, lying my head where Vin and Mama and me slept so many nights. And I feel the heat that is trapped in this place.

A fire that hot never burns off. It smolders and waits within. And someday, my fire will be as wild and hot as Mama's fire. Those that watch me burn will have to keep moving back, worrying for the willows.

I take Miriam by the hand, pretending I'm fine, and we walk to the river. It's low in the banks. The mudflats are full of footprints and gnats. Miriam sits along the water's edge and I sit behind her, holding her, watching the river, brown and glassy with swarms of bugs and damselflies. A single leatherback rises out on the mud and slips back.

My eyes take in the far banks, a sky hazed over with heat, and the secret moving of the river.

By evening we're in Rivertown. The sun is lighting it up like alabaster and pearl. I talk to all my people, thanking them for watching the tooms. I drape buttercup necklaces over the statue of the beloved daughter.

Then I kneel beside the box that I've kept safe these few months, and I open it with a knife. Inside is a plastic bag. Inside the plastic bag is ash.

Beloved Kat.

Be you blithe and bonny.

I start to cry. Miriam takes the bag from me until I'm done. Then I lead her to the rise, where you can look out over the river, seeing how it winds and turns about. Nearby, the big old live oak waits and watches.

"This is where Mandy and I used to sit," I tell Miriam. "We'd watch the river, seeing how it looked like a solid thing. But we knew better, even back then."

Miriam hands the bag to me. I take a handful and throw it over the edge, watching it sift the air onto the water. I throw out another and another.

She is carried away, all her caresses, her hands, her lovely body. And her voice, the voice that awakened me. She is gone like a breath is gone.

Sleep water and sleep fire, beautiful Kat. Sleep without shivers, without the long hiss of trouble and love. Sleep like grass, like sheen of the August moon, gentle as a leaf, stroking the mad river into solace while the willows hold still, trapped in memory.

Silly me. Memory is myth, shortness of breath. Love us for what we are not. Then leave us with a kiss.

About the Author

Barbara Bell, a poet, songwriter, and professional gardener, lives in the Indianapolis area. This is her first book.

9 780743 242547